ID1003396

I dedicate my first ever book to my three favorite men:
Nick, Cole, and Cody.
You are my world. I love you more.

Chapter 1

Quinn

Orphan.

I stared blankly at the documents in front of me. They had just arrived via courier. I had known about them for nearly three months already, but receiving the hard evidence rushed my emotions back like the first day I got the news that my parents had perished.

Despite being an independent and somewhat successful twenty-six-year-old, I simply wanted to curl into a ball and whimper like the little girl I felt like. Instead I took a shaky breath and skimmed through the stack of papers enclosed in the envelope that left all my parents' earthly possessions to the sole heir of their estate.

I had always ached for a sibling to share life's transgressions with—a sister to whisper secrets under the covers with past bedtime or a larger-than-life brother who would always protect me from other playground bullies. But my parents had waited a little later in life to have me and assumed they would still have time. When I was born, there were some complications, and just like that, I was destined to be the one and only. And now I had never felt more alone in my life.

I stood up and walked to the window of my small apartment

in the outskirts of Chicago and watched the snow falling. Despite the warm sweater I wore, I could still feel the chill coming from the windows. When my parents announced they were both retiring and moving to Hawaii, I had been somewhat taken aback, but I'd also been incredibly happy for them. It was our favorite family vacation destination, so I shouldn't have been surprised, but I hadn't really expected it either, at least not yet. They had barely reached retirement age, but they were probably tired of waiting for me to produce some grandchildren for them and decided to enjoy themselves while they could.

I remember the day they confessed their plan to me like it was yesterday, but the cruel irony of it all was it was a year ago to the day. A stubborn tear slid from my cheek, and I angrily pushed it away. I was so over crying and felt like there had to be a maximum allotment of tears.

I was quickly learning there wasn't.

Chapter 2

One year ago

So, we wanted to talk to you about something," my mom said, beaming at me.

It was sometimes freaky to look at her because the older I got, the more it felt like I was looking in the mirror, just fast-forwarded a few years. We both had the same slender face and slightly rounded nose and a pair of matching dimples. Our sleek dark hair reached below our shoulders in the same exact style.

When I turned eighteen, I was determined to not look like my mother's twin, so I hastily chopped it off into a stylish bob that I grew tired of within twenty-four hours. I accepted my fate at that point and always politely smiled when strangers commented that we could be sisters and not mother and daughter.

"Nora..." my father warned. He tried to look stern but couldn't help but grin as he looked at my mother, still completely in love with her after thirty-four years. They were sitting closely together in the booth across from me, and their enthusiasm was contagious, but all the same, I felt slightly nervous at what their declaration could be.

"Go ahead, Quinten," she said, nudging him with her elbow.

They both took a deep breath and looked at me.

"Quinn, we are going to retire and move to Hawaii," my father said calmly, though they both looked ready to burst.

"But, honey," my mom jumped in, "we don't want you to feel abandoned. If you need us to stay in Chicago, we won't think twice about it."

"What about the diner?" I asked. It was the first question that formed in my scrambled brain as I looked around at their only pride and joy other than me.

"Well, we already have an interested buyer," my father explained, "but that's only if you don't want it."

I fought back a snort because I didn't want to sound rude or ungrateful. My parents had owned the diner since shortly after they got married, and though I had a lot of good memories there, I had no desire to pursue a career in the food industry. I had paid my dues waiting tables all through high school and quickly realized people didn't mess around when it came to their food.

My parents had always supported my career aspirations to be a web designer. The diner was small and nothing fancy, but it was the cozy environment that kept people coming back. And for over thirty years, my parents made it home for a lot of people. I quickly cleared my throat and reminded myself to smile. It wasn't that I wasn't happy for them, and I suppose that I would be lying if I said I didn't feel a *tiny* bit abandoned, but who was I to stop their happiness? And Hawaii? Sign me up!

"This is so great!" I exclaimed and let out an excited giggle as I clapped my hands.

They proceeded to share with me the details of their plan, which was more in motion than I think they wanted to admit, for the sake of my feelings. Once they laid out all the details, we began to discuss what I could do to help them. They had decided to buy a vehicle when they got there rather than shipping theirs over. And since they were going to be retired, they didn't see the sense of needing two. So if it didn't fit in a suitcase, they weren't going to take it with them. Our family had never been extremely passionate over possessions—we preferred to have memories—which was where our vacations to Hawaii came into play.

"Do you think Aaron would be willing to come with you to help us get settled?" my mom asked, referring to my long-term boyfriend.

"Right," I said sarcastically. "Like anyone would turn down an opportunity to go to Hawaii!"

Despite being together for over two years, Aaron and I hadn't made the last trip to Hawaii with Mom and Dad. In fact, I hadn't been there since I graduated high school.

"As long as we can both get time off at the office, we should be good to go."

Now that they had broken the news to me, my parents could move forward with their plans, complete the sale of the diner, and start their happily ever after.

Chapter 3

Five years ago

My happily ever after started the day I met Aaron Keller, when I walked into Franklin Marx Advertising halfway through my senior year to start a six-month internship to graduate with my web design degree.

He was an ad executive, so our paths shouldn't have crossed all that often based on our careers, but I still seemed to see him on the 5th floor more often than seemed reasonable. As an intern, I was determined to advance my career—one that hadn't even officially started—the correct way. So I avoided him as much as I could, but that didn't mean I didn't notice how that one tie brought out the green flecks in his eyes or how he always ran his hand over the side of his sandy blonde hair while he was chatting with colleagues. Oh, I noticed.

Once I graduated, I was offered a full-time position within the company, and since we weren't technically in the same department, there were no restrictions prohibiting us from dating. Not like that could have stopped us—like *that* rule hasn't been broken before in corporate America.

Even so, Aaron took his time in asking me out—so long that I had convinced myself that the stolen looks and flirtatious smiles were all imagined in my creative brain. We still saw each other nearly every day, even if it was the all-too-brief elevator ride in the morning or the mandatory weekly staff meetings. This was enough to keep my interest focused on him.

Not only was he attractive with his tall, fit build and his contagious laugh, but he knew how to be very charming and make you feel like you were the only person in the room when he was talking to you, even if it was only the briefest of hellos. I'd had a few boyfriends in high school and college, but nothing stuck. Aaron, on the other hand, was a legitimate, mature, successful man who, low and behold, had his gaze fixed on me.

Despite this, he took nearly eight months from my hire date to properly ask me out. Not that I was keeping track or anything. All it took was a casual Friday dinner and a walk along Navy Pier, and I fell in love with him and everything about him. A week later, on my twenty-third birthday, he officially asked to be my boyfriend.

Most of my college friends had taken jobs scattered around the country, so I didn't have any close friends nearby. I enjoyed most of the people I worked with at Franklin Marx, but there was no one I really considered a good friend, no one I could call up for a mani-pedi on the weekend. I quickly became interwoven with Aaron's family, and by default became best friends with his twin sister, Ashley, and even his younger brother, Adam.

His parents, Mark and Gina, instantly welcomed me into the family as well, and his dad liked to joke that it took Aaron long enough to secure me before some other lucky bastard beat him to it. I had always appreciated the closeness I felt with my parents and how they granted me space to grow and be my own independent person but at the same time always made me feel loved and wanted. However, I didn't fully realize the family dynamic I had been missing out on my entire life until I was included in Sunday family dinners.

It was like an episode of *Blue Bloods*. We quickly became "Aaron and Quinn," and I forgot who I was without him, but in the best way possible. My parents loved him, and though my friends hadn't personally met him yet, they saw enough gushingly sick Facebook posts to know how happy we were together.

One night, about six months after we began dating, I curiously asked him why he'd waited those eight torturous months before asking me out. Sure, I could've been a confident, go-get-'em female, since it is the twenty-first century and all, but that's just not really my style. If I didn't think it was possible to love him any more, his response sealed the deal.

"Well, I knew you had a lot on your plate with graduating and beginning your career. I wasn't going to jeopardize anything and had to remind myself to be patient every single day, because I knew once I had you that I was never going to let you go."

I knew in that moment that I had found my forever. That night, he asked me to move into his condo with him, and his bachelor pad naturally transformed into our home sweet home together. We spent a lot of time together in comparison to most couples, but we functioned better that way. We carpooled together, ate lunch together nearly every day, and of course went home together.

It wasn't like we spent every waking moment together, though. We did our own things, like Aaron's pick-up basketball games with his brother and some of their childhood friends or my girly movie nights or yoga with Ashley.

Three years passed at an alarming speed, but we were busy and fulfilled with our lives together. I was well respected at Franklin Marx, and our families were happy and healthy. I began fielding questions a few years in on why there wasn't a ring on my finger, and I usually shrugged it off. I never doubted Aaron's commitment to me, and I sensed he was just taking his time in the same manner as he did asking me out the first time. I didn't need a piece of paper to convince me of his love for me.

But if I had to be honest with myself, I admit as time went on that I was getting a little impatient and starting to wonder if he was ever going to ask. Ashley and I spoke of it often, even though she would say that the official piece of paper I was hoping for wasn't going to make a bit of difference to her because she already considered me her sister.

By the time we were preparing for our trip to Hawaii to help Mom and Dad with the move, I had convinced myself he was planning on proposing to me there. What better place for a romantic proposal than paradise? I didn't need a flash mob or some insanely orchestrated master plan to ask for my hand in marriage, but I began envisioning gorgeous sunsets watched from a white sandy beach. Aaron would drop to one knee with a ring picked especially for me.

Or better yet, maybe he would get creative and pop the question while exploring the endless blue depths, snorkeling among sea turtles and rainbow fish. The possibilities were creeping into my conscious, and I knew I shouldn't get ahead of myself, but it just made sense. Aaron was always so sweet and made me feel so loved, and I had no doubt that the proposal would make me feel like the luckiest girl in the world.

Our trip to Hawaii was approaching quickly, and soon I was too engrossed with helping my mom hammer out all the details, so I tucked away images of diamond rings and Hawaiian seascapes in the back of my mind. I knew the trip would be tiresome and not all fun and games with helping Mom and Dad get settled, but we had also allowed for some extra time to sightsee, since this was Aaron's first time to Hawaii.

When we got there, we spent a day touring Pearl Harbor and Waikiki and every spare moment meant time at the beach, soaking up the sunshine or snorkeling. I found myself curiously staring at Aaron during the two weeks we spent in Hawaii, waiting for him to stop acting so calm and relaxed and looking for signs of the proposal.

But it never came. Our last morning there, my mom and I took a walk along the beach nearest to their house. Reality had sunken in, and I was feeling melancholy. I was going to be returning to Chicago without my parents and a bare ring finger. I was so thrilled for my parents and could already see how happy they were going to be with their retirement, but not having my mom so close was going to be difficult.

"He never said anything?" my mom quietly asked, sneaking a peek at me as we walked.

"Who?" I asked, confused.

"Aaron. You thought he was going to propose, right?"

I debated denying it, but my mom knew me too well. I never could lie to her, not that I tried often. My mom had always been my biggest confidant, and all it took was a simple "hello" from her, and whatever was troubling me at the time would come pouring out.

"I thought we were ready," I said, fighting the tears.

"Oh, honey," she said, reaching out and pulling me into a hug.

We stopped walking, and I just let my mom hold me as the tears flowed. I hadn't realized how much I was expecting the proposal until it didn't happen.

"We've been together for nearly three years. Three years! What is he waiting for?" I pulled back and started angrily pacing in the sand.

"Have you talked to him about it?" she asked me.

"Not recently. But we've had plenty of conversations about our future and how many kids we want and where we were going to live. We're both doing well in our jobs, we love our condo, but I'm not getting any younger!"

"Maybe you need to talk about it again," she suggested.

"I was going to, but I didn't want to ruin the surprise." My face crumbled as more tears came. "Why am I crying?" I said, frustrated. "It's not like he doesn't love me. I just want to be his wife."

"It's okay to be disappointed. I honestly expected him to propose by now, too. I think it's time to talk to him," she said gently.

"Thanks, Mom," I said, hugging her again. "I'm sorry that I ruined our last morning."

"Oh, stop. You didn't ruin anything. I couldn't have made it through these last few months without your help, and I'm so glad you guys got to come get us settled. Now, if we could only convince you and Aaron to move here!"

"That would be amazing," I said. I could picture us living in Hawaii. Aaron seemed to like it, and I considered bringing it up to him.

Despite being a self-sufficient adult, I was a mess when it came time to leave for the airport. I had lived within thirty minutes of my parents my entire life, and now I was going to be 4,246 miles away. I'd googled it. I could tell my mom was feeling guilty and second-guessing their decision to move. I couldn't leave with her doubting herself.

"Mom," I whispered in her ear as we hugged, "you have raised me and done an excellent job at being my mom. It's time for you to enjoy your life!"

"Okay," she said, her voice wobbling. "I just don't know if this is the right—"

"No," I cut her off and looked her in the eye. "It is. I want you and Dad to live your retirement to the fullest. And we will visit every chance we can. Right?" I asked, turning toward Aaron.

"Of course." He nodded and reached out to rub my shoulder sympathetically. After one last hug from my parents, we finally left for the airport.

The distance was difficult but not unmanageable. With all the technology options, we could email, text, talk, or Facetime anytime we wanted. The time difference provided a challenge, but we worked around it. I became accustomed to the distance, and seeing how happy my parents were made it worthwhile. My mom would give me weekly FaceTime tours of the house to show me her latest accomplishments. Dad even started taking the phone so he could show me what he had done with the yard.

They talked about their sweet neighbor, Adrienne, who I had the pleasure of meeting while I was there. They loved the church they had gotten involved with and a few charities they volunteered for. Mom said their favorite thing was walking the beach every single morning. They had loved the diner, but it was stressful running a business. Their move to Hawaii had somehow made them seem younger and carefree.

Aaron and I kept busy with our lives, which helped fill the void of my parents' absence. His family was always happy to have me around, and we kept busy with them and our friends.

Marriage was still in the back of my mind, but every time I considered bringing it up, I would lose my nerve. Plus, Aaron had been working a ton on a new ad campaign, and that was stressing him out enough. I just wanted to do what I could to support him. On the nights he worked late, I would typically hang out with Ashley or go the gym. I finally voiced my frustration about all of Aaron's late nights to Ashley one evening.

"I know he's so busy with work right now, but I barely see him!" I vented over a glass of wine.

"Yeah, I've barely talked to him, either," she said. "Mom said all he does is work."

"I keep telling myself this campaign is temporary, but it feels like it's taking forever. We haven't even had lunch together in the past month, and that was our daily routine."

"Well, at least you know it's temporary," she said, trying to comfort me.

"Yeah," I said quietly. "I was hoping we would get married in the near future, but I'm afraid to even bring it up now."

"I really thought he would propose in Hawaii," she said.

In the three months since our trip to Hawaii, I had seen no signs that he intended to ask me to marry him. I still wanted to talk to him about it, but then he got involved with this ad campaign, and it wasn't a topic I wanted to bring up at the wrong time. With all the hours he was working and the intensity of the campaign, he had been on edge.

We had been sitting there quietly for a few minutes when Ashley sat up straight. "Think about it, though! Your three-year anniversary is next week. And your birthday! Maybe he's planning something!"

Her excitement was contagious as I considered the impending occasion. We had dinner plans with his family at my favorite restaurant. Three years together. My twenty-sixth birthday party would be a pretty sweet setting for the perfect wedding proposal.

Chapter 4

Aaron had flowers sent to my desk on my birthday, and I texted a picture to my mom. I had confided in her my suspicions of his proposal, so she knew how anxious I was for dinner that evening. Aaron had a late meeting, so we had driven separately to work, and he was going to meet me at home before we headed to dinner around six. After I got home, I raided my closet to try and pick out an outfit. I FaceTimed my mom, and she helped me narrow down my dress choices until I finally settled on a royal blue one with black lace accents.

"You better call me if he does!" my mom said.

"Of course. But I don't know if he is going to," I said, though my heart was so full of hope at that point. I didn't know if I could handle another disappointment.

"Happy birthday, sweetheart," she said as we hung up. I was ready by 5:45, but Aaron still wasn't home. I texted him to see if he had left the office yet, but no response. Just before six, Ashley called me.

"Aaron got stuck in a meeting, so he wanted me to come pick you up, and he'll meet us at the restaurant," she said.

I was disappointed he wasn't the one taking me, but I also wondered if Ashley was in on the proposal and this was part of the plan. I convinced myself that was something she would do to keep me in the dark.

We arrived at the restaurant, and Mark and Gina greeted me with hugs as well as Adam and his girlfriend, Maddie. Soon after, my anxiety started to outweigh my excitement. Aaron showed up thirty minutes late with a hurried apology about his meeting. The stress all over his face was enough to convince me that my birthday celebration was just inconveniencing him. There was no surprise proposal.

I avoided eye contact with Ashley as I forced a tight smile and received Aaron's hasty kiss to my lips. We ordered too much food, and I drank too much wine to drown out my disappointment. Mark and Gina surprised me with a beautiful bracelet, and Ashley and Adam had put together a gift basket with my favorite perfume, lotions, and bath salts.

"Ashley picked it all out; I just supplied some money," Adam admitted with a sheepish grin.

"Babe, I want you to book a spa day," Aaron said, leaning over to kiss my forehead. "Whenever you want."

"Okay," I replied brightly, but inside I knew this just meant he hadn't taken the time to get me a gift. Not only that, but he never mentioned anything about it being our three-year anniversary. I tried to focus on the chatter around the table and enjoy the company of his family rather than focus on Aaron's lack of attention. I wanted to linger after dessert, but Aaron's repeated yawns were clear.

"Well, I better get this guy home to bed," I joked, patting his arm.

"Oh, we don't need to hear about that!" Adam quipped.

Though I wanted to celebrate with the man I loved, there was no love-making that night. We drove home in near silence, but then he gave me a long hug and wished me happy birthday once we were back at our condo. I closed myself in the bathroom to freshen up and put on some new lingerie I had purchased for the occasion, but when I opened the door, I found Aaron fast asleep in bed already. I climbed into bed and turned my back to him, and the tears quietly fell.

He was already up the next morning when I woke up. I quickly got in the shower because I sensed he needed to get to work early, so I wanted to be ready. I walked out with the towel wrapped around me, but he was already grabbing his bag to head out the door.

"Aaron?" I asked, confused.

"Sorry, Quinn, I have an early meeting."

I crinkled my face at him. He never called me by my name.

"All you do anymore is go to meetings," I grumbled.

He sighed, visibly annoyed.

"I'm sorry I've been busy," he said, though he obviously wasn't sorry.

I didn't want to start our day off fighting, so I offered a hug to him. Normally he would've used that as an excuse to drop my towel and have a quick make-out session before he went out the door. Instead he only offered an awkward half hug.

"Have a good day," I said, stepping back.

"Thanks, you too," he said, opening the door. It slammed shut before I could even say "I love you."

Now I was starting to worry. The way he forgot our anniversary and barely acknowledged my birthday was unlike him. The last few months had been tough on him, but I was trying to support him and give him the space he needed to do his job. I saw the other ad executives at work, and their jobs could be very demanding. I wasn't going to be that nagging girlfriend, but I also felt like it might be time for us to talk. As I dressed for my day, I decided that we would talk tonight. This couldn't keep going on. Yes, he was busy, but I also didn't deserve to be ignored.

Fortunately, I had an extremely busy day at work, so I didn't have time to dwell on it. I never even saw Aaron, and I slipped out of the office for lunch and a chance to call my mom. She had figured my birthday didn't go as I had hoped when she didn't hear from me.

"I'm sorry, sweetie," she said, "but don't you think it's time to talk?"

"Yes, I'm gonna talk to him tonight. I need to know that we're on the same page for our future," I said. We talked a few more minutes about my birthday, and then I asked her what they had going on for the week.

"Oh! We got invited on a plane ride to tour the island tonight!" she said excitedly. One of the other couples they met through church had their own plane and often did sunset tours around the island.

"I bet Dad is really excited," I said. Dad loved everything about airplanes.

"Like a little boy on Christmas morning," she said with a laugh.

"You better take lots of pictures," I said. "I'm so jealous!"

"Maybe we can take you and Aaron when you come for Christmas?" she said. "I'm sure they wouldn't mind."

"That would be so much fun," I said. Hopefully Aaron and I would be in a better place by the time Christmas rolled around.

By then I had picked up some soup at a nearby deli and was almost back at the office.

"I need to get back to work, but have fun today!" I told her, hovering outside the lobby door.

"We will!" she said. "If you get a chance after you and Aaron talk tonight, let me know, okay?"

"I'll try, but if anything, I'll make sure to call you tomorrow," I said.

"Okay, sweetie. Well, keep your chin up. Everything will work out. It always does."

I smiled at my mom's encouragement. That was always her motto in life. Every time I did poorly on a test in school or when

I got into a fight with a girlfriend: Everything will work out.

"Tell Dad I love him," I said. I heard Mom relay the message to my dad. I should've figured he was nearby. They were never far from each other. "Love you, Mom."

"Love you too, Quinn," she said.

I was smiling after we hung up. Talking to my mom always made me feel better.

I left work promptly at five, hoping to make it home and cook a nice dinner to soften the mood for my talk with Aaron. I felt the tension in my shoulders as I opened the front door, trying to convince myself that this talk was essential to our relationship.

"Oh!" I said, startled when I realized Aaron was already home. I hadn't heard from him all day, not even a text. I could've just as easily sent a quick text, but I knew I was being stubborn at this point. He should've been the one reaching out to me.

Aaron was sitting on the couch with his tie loosened around his neck and his shirt untucked. He looked tired, and I immediately wondered whether he was going to be in the right mindset for this conversation. I swallowed hard and reminded myself we were in this position because I had allowed myself to be pushed to the back burner for the past four months.

"Aaron," I started, setting my purse down on the floor.

He stood up, and the look on his face stopped me cold.

Chapter 5

"I got a promotion," he said.

That wasn't what I had expected to hear. This was also going to hugely impact my determination to talk to him about our relationship.

"Oh, wow!" I said, reminding myself to be excited for him. This was huge for him, and he had worked so hard for it. I reached out to hug him but stopped when I saw how reserved he was.

What the hell?

"It's in New York."

My jaw dropped at his revelation, but I was still stuck on how hesitant he was to touch me. Did he think I would be mad? I wondered if they would allow me to do my job from the New York offices. My parents were in Hawaii now, so there wasn't really any logical reason I couldn't move to New York. My mind started racing as I studied Aaron's face. For the first time in our relationship, I couldn't read it.

I eyed him suspiciously. "What else?" He was acting too weird. This wasn't the Aaron I knew and loved. He seemed so cold.

"Sit down." He gestured toward the couch. I almost didn't,

just for the fact that he told me to. I wanted to demand he give me answers. Instead I sat as instructed and waited for the other shoe to drop. "I'm going to take it."

"Well, obviously," I said. He would be stupid to turn down the position.

"I'm going alone," he said firmly with no emotion.

"Excuse me?" I started at him. I must have heard him wrong. "What do you mean you're going alone?"

He sighed. "Quinn."

"Stop calling me by my name," I said, raising my voice.

"Quinn," he said, ignoring my request and looking down. He couldn't even look me in the eye. I knew what was coming, and the asshole couldn't even look at me. "I think it's time we go our separate ways."

"What the hell are you talking about?" I said, raising my voice even higher this time. "I thought we were going to get married!"

"I know you've been expecting it," he said. He finally looked up at me for a moment, but then his eyes went back down to his feet. "But I just don't think I can spend the rest of my life with you."

In that single moment, my heart shattered.

"Why?" I whispered, trying to swallow the enormous lump that had formed in my throat.

He shrugged.

"You owe me an explanation," I said through gritted teeth. "We have been together for three years. *Three* years! Doesn't that mean anything to you?"

"Of course it does," he said, but he had to be lying. The lack of emotion on his face betrayed him. He was more uncomfortable trying to get rid of me than he was concerned for my feelings. "I just don't feel like we're headed in the same direction with our lives."

"What kind of bullshit excuse is that?"

"Our careers are at different levels, and you're ready to settle down, but I need to focus on my job." He trailed off, clearly struggling to come up with excuses.

"Is there someone else?" I asked, not truly wanting to know the answer.

"No," he said, grimacing. "Like I have time for that. I can't even keep *you* happy." The annoyance on his face felt like he was stomping on my already-broken heart.

"I'm so sorry wanting you around is so horrible," I said bitterly.

He stared at me blankly.

"Just tell me why. For real." He owed me an explanation.

"My job—"

"Aaron." I was not going to settle until I got the truth.

"I just have a lot going on right now, and this promotion is going to take precedence."

"Tell me," I said, my anger was starting to drown out the hurt. Did he think I was stupid? He wasn't going to dump me after three years and not tell me why.

"Fine!" he erupted and stood up. "I don't want to be with you anymore! I'm bored!"

There it was. I recoiled like he had slapped me. He had promised me he was never letting go. What happened to forever? I pushed down the tears threatening to bubble over. I was not going to let him see how much I was hurting right now.

"Okay," I said, my voice betraying me as I attempted to sound indifferent. I looked down at the floor, wishing it would swallow me up. I wasn't sure what my next move was. I wanted to retreat to my bedroom, but it was our bedroom. My mind was foggy as I struggled to react. My world had just been turned upside down, and I didn't know what to do. I wanted my mom, but she was too far away. My next thought was Ashley, but I tossed that idea aside since she was his sister. What was I supposed to do?

Aaron spoke up first. "Shit, Quinn." He paced the room. "I can give you a few days to pack your stuff up and find a place. I'll get a hotel."

"Wait, what?" I shook my head and looked up at him. "*I* have to leave?"

"Well, yeah," he said, looking at me like I was stupid. "It's my condo."

It had been our home for so long that I didn't even think about being the one who had to leave. I was so screwed.

"Fine," I said abruptly. "Give me through the weekend and I'll be out."

My mind ached at trying to figure out how I was going to do it in three days, by myself, but I would figure it out. Maybe my mom would be able to catch a flight and help me. I could ask Ashley, but again, she was his sister, his *twin* sister, and this was surely going to affect our friendship. And yet, we had been best friends for almost the entire three years, so there was no way she would abandon me.

Aaron disappeared into our bedroom for a bit and walked back out with a bag. He had been home long enough to gather what he wanted. He hesitated in the living room and looked at me.

"I didn't want to hurt you, Quinn," he said quietly, sounding remorseful.

"I'm sure you didn't," I said, glaring at him. My heart was closed off.

He took a step closer and laid a hand on my shoulder. I angrily shrugged it off and turned away from him. I just needed him to leave so I could fall apart. He stood there, like he'd suddenly had a change of heart and hadn't turned into the complete asshole who had just told me I meant nothing to him.

"Get out. You said you'd leave, so leave." I stood up and walked to the opposite end of the room. I didn't give two shits if it was his condo or not. He looked at me with a combination of guilt and defiance, probably at the fact that I had the gall to order him out of his own condo.

"Get the fuck out!" I screamed at him and threw a throw pillow at his head. He glared at me, stunned by my childish outburst. Then he turned and walked out the door, slamming it shut.

I fell face down on the couch and sobbed into the remaining throw pillow. I couldn't believe it. I'd thought I was going to spend the rest of my life with him, but he wasn't interested. I wasn't enough. I was too boring. I cried for a few minutes, then I abruptly sat up and angrily wiped the tears away. I had work to do.

I walked out the front door and angrily slammed it behind me.

I bet our neighbors love us tonight. I went to my car and drove to the nearest office supply store and threw boxes, packing tape, and other miscellaneous moving supplies into a cart. I didn't need three days. Tomorrow was Friday, so I was calling in sick to work. I would sort and pack all night if I had to, but I would be out of this place within twenty-four hours. What had once been my home, my haven, was now polluted.

I contemplated calling my mom, but I knew they were going on their sunset flight, and I didn't want to bring her down. I would talk to her tomorrow when I was calmer. I assembled boxes and began filling them. Some of the items were things we had already owned but we had bought a lot in the past two to three years. I quickly realized there wasn't a lot of our life that I wanted to keep. It would only serve as a reminder of three years of my life that I had wasted with a douche bag.

I suffered through waves of anger, and then I would sit and cry as I sifted through photos and mementos of the life Aaron and I had built.

There's no way he was bored the whole time, I thought as I glanced at pictures of us with his family and our friends. I finally threw the pictures in the trash and moved to the kitchen. I pulled open the cupboard to grab my favorite coffee mug when his favorite mug tumbled out and shattered on the floor. I stared at it for a minute and then decided that it was fine there on the floor. We both had a favorite spatula that we liked to cook with, and I defiantly threw it in a box. I knew I was being childish, but I didn't care. I moved through the kitchen and helped myself to all the small utensils I knew he liked.

I was probably going to regret not taking more when I had to restock my new place, wherever that was going to be, but I didn't want to take any remnants of our life together. My clothes took up the most space, but I chose not to pack the blue dress from my birthday dinner. That was ruined.

I stacked the boxes at the door. How pitiful was my life that it could be contained in five boxes and two suitcases? When I'd moved in with Aaron, his furniture was nicer than mine, so we'd donated all of mine. I was regretting that decision now. I could probably take some of his, but I didn't want it.

By two a.m., I was beyond weary. I had almost everything packed, and there wasn't much left I could do. I had cried more than I thought possible and broke a fair share of dishes and picture frames. The final straw was when I was ready to crash. There was no way I was sleeping in that bed. I stared at it from the doorway like it was the enemy. I recalled Sunday mornings cuddling beneath the covers after a passion-fueled Saturday night, always crawling into bed at the end of the day and snuggling until we both got too hot and rolled to our assigned sides. I hated that bed.

I turned and walked into the kitchen and hastily grabbed the vase with my birthday flowers, the ones he had sent me. I chucked the entire vase at the bed and watched it bounce and settle onto his side. The water spilled and soaked through the blankets, and the roses scattered across the comforter. I prayed he would get a thorn stuck in his ass.

I grabbed a blanket and retreated to the couch, where I curled up in a ball and cried the last unimaginable tears until I feel asleep.

Chapter 6

I awoke to the shrill ring of my cell phone, buried in my purse, still sitting by the kitchen table. I sat up, dazed. I could tell it was still night by how dark the living room was, but my mind was too groggy between the tears and trauma to my heart. The ringing stopped before I could untangle myself from the blanket.

It was only silent for a moment before it started ringing again. I stumbled in the darkness and fumbled for my purse. I glanced at the clock on the stove and saw that it was 4:12 in the morning. Was Aaron having remorse? Had he told Ashley and she was worried about me? I finally located my phone and pulled it out to see who was calling, but I didn't recognize the number. My fuzzy brain finally registered the 808 area code as being Hawaii when it started to ring again. What the hell was going on?

"Hello?" My throat was thick and my voice hoarse, and I struggled to clear it and say hello more clearly. At first all I got was silence, and I thought maybe it was a wrong number. Then I heard someone also clearing their throat on the other end of the line.

"Yes?" I needed to know who was calling me. It better be

important to be waking me up on tonight of all nights.

"Quinn?" The voice was unfamiliar and sounded timid.

"Yes?" I said, confused and exhausted.

"This is Adrienne. I live next to your parents." Her voice broke at the end, and I suddenly became awake and alert.

"What's wrong?" I asked, feeling panicked.

She sniffled before continuing. "There's been an accident. A plane crash."

I sank slowly into the kitchen chair. *No, no, no.*

"Are there survivors?" I whispered.

"No," Adrienne barely whispered back.

"Oh my God," I said, dropping the phone to the floor with a clatter. I had to be dreaming. This was a nightmare. All of it. I ran to the bedroom and flipped on the light switch. I saw the roses scattered on the bed and turned back toward the kitchen. The light from the bedroom spilled on the stack of boxes by the front door. I looked back at my phone laying on the floor and I could hear my name being called faintly from it.

"No!" I cried. I took painful steps back to the phone and dropped to my knees to pick it back up.

"Are you sure?" I asked.

"Yes," she cried. "I'm so, so sorry."

I sat in stunned silence as she said words like "engine failure" and "ocean" and "Coast Guard" and finally, "no survivors." Everything else she said barely registered, and my mind threatened to shut down completely.

"What do I do?" I asked to no one in particular. "I don't know what to do."

"Is there anyone I can call?" she asked me.

There was family to call. My mom's sister, Nancy, was going to be devastated. She lived in Indiana and was recently widowed. My dad had a brother, Carl, but they hadn't spoken in years. With me being the only child, that was about it. And now after losing Aaron, I felt like I had lost everyone.

I knew I needed to call my boss. Calling in on Friday was suddenly so much more complicated.

"Um, I don't think so. Not yet," I said.

"I'd recommend notifying your relatives before the news releases any names," she said quietly. "And please do not hesitate to call me for anything. I know the distance can make things even more difficult in these situations, and I'll do whatever I can."

Her kindness meant so much to me, even if I couldn't voice it right then. She had only known my parents for a few months and met me once, yet she was willing to help me.

"Thank you," I said, closing my eyes and willing away the heartache starting to overcome me. "I'll be in touch."

When I was the most upset over anything in my life, the first person I called was my mom. Who was I going to I call about this? I couldn't even comprehend what needed to be done. Instead, I sank to the hardwood floors and sobbed. I'd thought my tears were dried up from the night before, but there was a never-ending well in me now.

I dozed on and off for the next two hours as I was swallowed by my grief. I had no one. I felt like the world was crashing down on me, and I was drowning. I finally sat up and took a shaky breath. My hair was matted to my face from the tears, and my throat and eyes burned. I stumbled to the coffee maker and went through the motions of brewing coffee. I knew that it was the middle of the night in Indiana, but I had to call Aunt Nancy.

"Hello? Quinn?" she answered as if I hadn't woken her in the dead of night, but I could hear the concern in her voice.

"Aunt Nancy." I couldn't even say her name without breaking down. "There was a plane crash. Mom and Dad.... They're gone." I choked on the last words, having to say them aloud.

"No!" she cried out in shock. "Are you sure? Who told you?"

I explained the phone call, and I could hear her fumbling for the remote and turning on the news. "There isn't anything on the news!"

I hadn't even thought to check the news, though the story would unlikely be covered nationally. I found my laptop and typed "plane crash Oahu" in the search engine. Immediately, a local Hawaii news website came up.

PLANE CRASHES INTO OCEAN OFF WEST COAST OF WAIANAE. FIVE FEARED DEAD.

I skimmed quickly through the article and relayed the information to Nancy.

"Sweetie, it's going to be okay," she said. She sounded so much like my mother when she said it that I felt the next wave of tears crash over me. We cried on the phone together until she told me she would pack a bag and start driving my way.

"I can get a hotel if you would prefer," she said. That just made me cry more.

"Aaron and I broke up," I struggled to get out. "Last night."

"Oh, dear," she said.

There was nothing else to be said. We hung up so she could get ready to make the drive to Chicago. I stood in Aaron's condo and looked around, trying to decide on my next steps. I should shower, but I didn't want to spend another second longer than I had to in his place. I made the trek up and down the elevator multiple times until my car was packed to the max.

I drove to a hotel near my parents' old neighborhood, wanting to be as far away from Aaron as possible. I checked into the hotel, also booking a room for Nancy. Around nine a.m., my phone rang, and I glanced down at the screen, knowing that nothing else could be done to hurt me further. It was my boss, Kate. I had never called in.

"Kate," I said, my voice nearly a whisper from all the crying.

"Hi, Quinn," she said sympathetically. How did she know already? I hadn't told anyone besides Nancy.

"Kate, I'm so sorry I forgot to call you this morning," I said. The last thing I needed was to lose my job along with everything else.

"I talked to Aaron when I realized you hadn't shown up," she said. "He explained you were no longer together and that I probably shouldn't expect you today."

That bastard. How dare he reveal details of my personal life to my boss. And the nerve he had to assume that I wouldn't be able to function well enough from his betrayal to do my job.

"It's not that," I said. "My parents were killed in a plane crash last night."

"Oh my God," she said, clearly stunned. "I'm so, so sorry, Quinn. Is there anything I can do?"

"No. Just that I don't know when I will be back in the office," I said.

"Of course. Take all the time you need," she said. "Please let us know if you need anything at all, Quinn."

I appreciated her sincerity, but my relationship with her was purely professional, and I wasn't about to lean on her in my time of sorrow.

I spent the next few hours on the phone. Once Nancy arrived midafternoon, she took over with the phone calls so my voice could rest. I was so grateful for her presence and needed a real adult to take over. She seemed to know exactly what to do and spoke with authorities in Hawaii as well as a funeral home in Chicago. Though they had started their new lives in Hawaii, we felt doing the funeral services in Chicago was more appropriate.

Nancy finally insisted I go to my room and take a nap, since I was barely functioning. I fell into a deep sleep in my exhausted state and woke once darkness had claimed the day again. I realized my phone was ringing, and the screen was casting shadows across the unfamiliar hotel room. I reached for it and squinted at the screen and groaned when I realized it was Aaron calling. I nearly threw my phone against the wall but opted to answer it instead.

"What?" I wasn't about to grace him with kindness.

"Quinn, where are you?" he asked, sounding panicked.

"That's none of your concern," I said stubbornly.

"I came straight to the condo from work when I heard the news, but you weren't here."

"No, I'm not, and as I stated before, that's none of your concern anymore. You made it clear that you don't want me anymore."

He sighed and spoke like he was talking to a child. "You shouldn't be alone right now."

"I'm not," I said. "Aunt Nancy is here. Besides, you're the last person I want to see right now."

"Babe, maybe I was too hasty with my decision," he said. Was he serious? He was acting like the fate of our relationship was something as simple as choosing where to eat lunch.

"It's fine, Aaron," I said. "And don't ever call me 'babe' again. It's clear our relationship wasn't headed in the direction I thought it was, and the sooner we cut all ties, the better. I have a lot of things to deal with right now, and you are not one of those things." I felt proud for stating my piece, especially since I couldn't even process our breakup when it was happening.

"Quinn, please," he said, sounding dangerously close to begging. "You need me right now."

"Like hell I do," I said. "I will be just fine, and that's no thanks to you. Now leave me alone, and don't call again."

I ended the call and tossed the phone on my bed. Now I just felt irritated and even more tired than before. Five minutes later, my phone rang again. I let out a frustrated groan and grabbed it, ready to give Aaron an earful this time. I was not in the mood for this shit. I quickly calmed down when I realized it was Ashley calling. I really could use my best friend right now.

"Ashley," I answered, my voice breaking and tears welling up in my eyes once again.

"Oh, Quinn, I can't believe it!" she said. "I'm so sorry. What do you need me to do?"

"I could really use a hug," I said, breaking down.

"Well, where are you at?" she asked. "Aaron said you weren't at the condo."

"So, you know what he did?" I asked, curious as to what he had told her.

"Yes, and he knows he made a mistake," she said. "Please just hear him out."

"You're kidding me," I said, stunned. Yeah, he was her brother, but I hadn't expected her to fully take his side after what he did to me.

"He really screwed up, and he knows it, and he wants to be there for you now. Just tell me where you are, and we'll come pick you up," she said.

Ugh, she was with him. I knew it.

"No," I said firmly. "Ashley, your brother is a selfish prick. He broke my heart and said some really cruel things to me. Why does my parents dying change any of that?"

"He didn't mean it, he was just really stressed with all the job stuff," she said.

I couldn't believe she was covering for him.

"So, that's it?" I asked.

"What?" she asked, confused.

"You're on his side," I stated.

"There aren't sides, Quinn. You guys are meant to be together!"

"No, it's all very clear to me now," I said. "And I thought my best friend would at least be sympathetic to what he put me through, but I guess you're just like him." I knew I was being mean, but I didn't care. If I had any time to be selfish, this was it.

"What are you saying?" She sounded like I'd hit her.

"I think my boyfriend and my best friend are a package deal," I said.

"Well, no," she said, but she said nothing else to back that statement up.

"I get it," I said. The reality of losing everyone near and dear to me was sinking in.

"He's my brother, Quinn," Ashley whispered.

"Family is family," I agreed. "And you aren't mine anymore."

With that, I hung up and sat in silence. Not even the tears would come. I was all alone.

Chapter 7

On top of planning a funeral service, I had to go apartment hunting that weekend. Aunt Nancy was a godsend and helped me make most of the decisions concerning the funeral. Apparently she and my mom had had in-depth conversations regarding their wishes, which made the process a little easier. The service was scheduled for the following Thursday, a week after their deaths.

It was only a matter of time before my social media accounts were flooded with condolences from friends and distant relatives. My college roommate, Amber, called me right away, but unfortunately she couldn't come to the funeral because she was due any day with her first child. I appreciated her call, but honestly, I was so numb at that point that I really didn't want anyone around.

Nancy respected my privacy and gave me room to grieve. I stayed in contact with Adrienne, and she agreed to keep an eye on my parents' house until I decided to make the trip to settle the estate. I pushed that thought to the back of my mind because I couldn't even begin to know how that was going to be handled.

In the meantime, I was able to secure an apartment near

the hotel. It wasn't much farther from work than the condo had been, but it was in the opposite direction. And it was tiny. Still, I didn't care what it looked like as long as it was clean, and at least I had a place to rest my head at night. I made a trip to Ikea to purchase the bare essentials and called it good.

On a whim, I elected to only sign a monthly lease because I wasn't sure if I wanted to stay in Chicago. I didn't really know what my other options were, but everything in my life had changed over the course of twenty-four hours. I stared at the sparse walls in my new apartment, and I could almost swear I heard my mother's voice.

"Everything will work out."

Nancy and I decided to only do a small visitation before the funeral service. Both of us were hurting, but we didn't see the sense in dragging it out for days. The day of the funeral, I chose a dress my mom had helped me pick out during one of our many shopping trips before they moved to Hawaii. It was pale yellow with a delicate floral pattern. I was leery of it when she had initially pulled it from the rack, but once I zipped it up, I loved how the tight bodice complemented my curves and the skirt flared out, making me feel girly. I knew my mom would approve of me wearing this versus standard black.

Adrienne had mailed me my parents' personal affects after they were released from the coroner. I took their wedding rings and put them on a long gold chain so that they were close to my heart. The hardest part was receiving their cell phones and finding pictures on it prior to taking off on their flight. They looked so happy and excited, and I tried to convince myself that I would remember them this way. I missed my mom's calming voice and our daily phone calls, but what I wouldn't give for one of my dad's big bear hugs right now. He wasn't a man of many words, but for as long as I could remember, I could always count on his hugs.

Once I arrived at the funeral home, I walked into the room

the service was going to be held in. The funeral director nodded at me with kind eyes, then slipped from the room quietly to give me privacy. I sat at the front of the room and stared. The urns containing their remains were on a table, and rather than selecting individual pictures, Nancy and I had chosen to have a large one of the two of them together, embracing, happy and still in love after so many years. I took comfort in the fact that they were at least together when they died.

I was startled when I felt a hand on my shoulder and turned, surprised to see Mark and Gina. They had sent a beautiful arrangement of flowers, and I sheepishly glanced at where I had crammed them in the corner of the room, where you could barely see them. Though it was hard to see them again, I quickly reminded myself that they were not to blame for their son's actions. It was hard to believe it was just over a week ago that we were all sitting at my birthday dinner.

My shoulders slumped. With everything that had happened, it hadn't even occurred to me that I was losing them as well. It was almost like losing both sets of parents in the same week. I stood to greet them and fell into Gina's embrace. Mark circled both of us with his large arms, and I allowed them to comfort me. We stood there for a long time, and they cried with me, and I knew we weren't just mourning my parents.

"We love you, girl," Mark said hoarsely.

"You will always be welcome in our home," Gina whispered in my ear. "Always."

"Please don't hesitate to ask us for anything," Mark said, his watery eyes meeting mine.

I nodded with appreciation, though I knew I would never ask for a thing. I loved these people as if they were my own parents, but I didn't think I would see them again after this.

They walked to the back of room to look at the pictures we had posted on boards, and I turned my attention to the steady flow of visitors coming to pay their respects. Though we didn't have much for family, my parents had a lot of friends, many of them regular patrons from the diner. I knew my parents would be pleased at the outpouring of love I experienced that day.

The service was difficult, but I gripped Nancy's hand as we wept together. The preacher spoke kindly about my parents. He spoke of my mom's passion for feeding anyone in her presence. It didn't matter whether it was someone at the diner or a friend stopping by the house, everyone was always offered food. My dad was remembered for his dry sense of humor, his immaculate lawn that everyone teased him about, and his unconditional love for my mother. I laughed nearly as much as I cried, and I was grateful for the closure. My grieving was only beginning, but this was a good first step.

At the end of the service, I glanced around the room, noting all the familiar faces in attendance. I froze when my eyes met Aaron's and stiffened when I realized Ashley was at his side. I braced myself for drama, but I found I just didn't have it in me. Aaron looked at me with eyes full of sympathy, regret, and a lingering hint of love and settled for a simple nod. Ashley was clutching a tissue and looked at me with tears streaming down her face.

I felt the pull toward them, but I shook it off, gave them a small smile, and stood firmly in place. The damage was done, and that part of my life was over. I would never be able to look at Aaron again and feel the same. I would forever associate him with my parents' deaths, always questioning if I was good enough for him and always preparing for disappointment on my birthday. And my best friend? She was the collateral damage. I turned away from them before I could change my mind and walked over to my parents' picture one last time.

"I love you. So much." I choked back a sob and pressed a kiss to my fingertips and then to the picture. My fingers were met with the cool glass, but I closed my eyes and pretended I could hear my mom's chiming laughter and feel my dad's bear hug. I had lost everything close to me, but nothing could take away my memories.

Chapter 8

In the months that followed, I struggled to find a new normal. Fortunately, by the time I returned to work, Aaron was already in New York. I felt like I was the new kid, walking the halls of high school, with all the stares and whispers as I made my way to my desk. I had seen Kate and a few of my coworkers at the visitation, but as I stood staring blankly at my desk, everything felt so foreign.

I worked throughout the day and spoke only when necessary. I had nothing to say to anyone. I would leave at the end of the day and go to my tiny apartment, which I still felt indifferent about. I'd convinced myself it was just temporary, so I lived out of boxes and made no effort to make it feel like home. I didn't realize how much weight I had lost until Nancy came up for a visit and was shocked at my appearance.

"Quinn, you are skin and bones!" she said. She insisted on taking me out for a burger to "fatten me up," but I had little appetite.

"I'm just not hungry," I said. Anyone who knew me knew this was unusual. I worked out hard at the gym to counteract my love affair with food. I had also inherited my mom's sweet tooth, but I could barely look at a Twix without crying.

"You know," Nancy said cautiously, "your mom would be very unhappy if she could see you right now."

I just stared at her, daring her to say more. Which she did. Aunts are like that.

"You have a lot to offer this world. How can you let one person affect your view of yourself?"

Apparently we were well enough into the grieving process that she felt it was time for some tough love, because she wasn't backing down. "Have you considered what you want to do with your life? You don't have to stay in Chicago, you know. You could start over, move down to Indiana with me."

I loved Nancy, and I appreciated her offer, but it didn't feel like the right move. I wasn't sure what was.

"I don't know," I mumbled.

"Have you considered moving to Hawaii?" she asked.

I snapped my head up and gawked at her.

"Why would I do that?" I asked.

"Everything is there, as your parents left it. Talk about a chance to start over! A new place to live, a new environment, new people. You're still young, Quinn."

Her words resonated with me as I mulled them over. I hadn't even considered it. I had been avoiding the inevitable trip to Hawaii to settle everything. I knew it was all being left to me, but I hadn't been able to progress enough in my grieving process to consider what I was going to do with it all. It felt incredibly wrong to benefit from their deaths.

"It's what your parents would want," Nancy said, reading my mind. "Your mom would've been mortified at the stunt Aaron pulled. She would've encouraged you to be brave and try something else. And your dad would have done whatever it took to care for you. If starting over is what you need, then do it!"

A week later, I stood holding the legal paperwork in my hands. I sensed Nancy had known it would be settled soon and that I just needed a push. I paced my living room as I considered my options. Chicago had nothing left to offer me. Nancy was right. There was no reason for me to stay anymore.

My job didn't provide the same satisfaction for me that it once had. Though Aaron wasn't at the office anymore, his name was still frequently mentioned, and just seeing it on office memos annoyed me. I had to find a new gym in my quest to avoid Ashley and our regular yoga class. I tried going to the diner once, but I barely made it through the door before I turned around. It was too much. The city had the imprints of my childhood and of love lost. It was too painful. I kept expecting it to get better, but after three months, it felt hopeless, and I was numb. I was simply going through the motions, but I wasn't living my life.

I opened my laptop and began searching for flights to Hawaii. Typically, I would've spent months debating a decision like this. I liked to research and have all the facts and think and think about it some more before I would make a decision. But before I knew it, I was booking a one-way ticket to Oahu. I stared at the confirmation on my screen, unable to believe I had just made such a reckless decision. Was there still time to cancel my ticket?

But then I realized I felt something. Hope. Promise. I felt like I had a future again. I turned in my chair and looked around my apartment. It honestly wouldn't be that difficult to leave. I didn't have much. In two weeks, I could erase my life in Chicago. That settled it.

I submitted my two weeks' notice immediately. Kate was sorry to see me go, but she wasn't surprised. I half expected to hear from Aaron but was relieved when I didn't. No one asked me to stay, and the reality stung, but it also made ripping the Band-Aid off that much easier. I sold my car, donated my furniture, and packed a few suitcases. Nancy insisted on coming up and driving me to the airport, even though I tried telling her I could take a cab. She wouldn't have it, and I was secretly glad she was so insistent.

"I'm really proud of you, Quinn," she said as we stood outside the entrance to O'Hare Airport. "You will do great! I'm sure of it." We hugged and made promises for her to visit soon, and then I was off.

I finally made it to my seat toward the back of the plane, beyond irritated by the delays I'd already encountered, but getting on board had a sobering effect on me. It hadn't even remotely occurred to me to be excited about the enormous change I was making in my life. I had been too busy hashing out the details and planning how it should go and not reflecting on the fact that I was walking away from everything that I had ever known, all that was familiar, my home.

The weight of my decision was heavy on my shoulders as I struggled to fit my carry-on bag in the overhead compartment, which was already crowded. I finally squeezed it in and flopped into my window seat with a frustrated sigh and leaned my head against the side of the plane, closing my eyes. I prayed desperately that the seat next to me would remain vacant, because frankly, I had no patience for a nosy middle-aged housewife or a snoring businessman.

No sooner had the thought crossed my mind when I felt the seat next to me shift with the occupant claiming it. An irritated groan involuntarily escaped before I realized what was doing, and I sheepishly peeked one eye open at the stranger next to me. The clear blue eyes staring back at me looked amused, but he said nothing as he busied himself with settling in for the long flight.

He seemed to have picked up on my embarrassment, so I turned slightly away from him and pretended the entire exchange never happened. I grabbed the magazine I had stuffed into the seat pocket and tried to focus on mindless entertainment gossip to pass the time as the flight crew prepared for takeoff.

Not only had it not occurred to me to be excited about embarking on my new adventure, I hadn't given much thought to flying. I suddenly felt sweat beading on my forehead. My chest tightened as I was realized I was about to be in the sky. Flying had never scared me before, and I never understood people who had a fear of flying. But this was all before my parents boarded a plane and never came back.

It didn't matter to my panicking brain that they had crashed in a small private aircraft and I was currently strapped into an enormous flying machine. I struggled to take a deep breath and stare at a picture of Dwayne Johnson smiling back at me. The plane started to creep forward, and I reached over and slammed my window shut so I could pretend we weren't moving. I stared back at the magazine article and read the first sentence three times and still couldn't comprehend what it said. I silently apologized to Dwayne and placed the magazine back in the seat pocket at the same moment the plane sharply accelerated and went screaming down the runway.

Before I could mentally give myself a logical pep talk about how everything would be okay, I found my hand frantically grabbing for something. What, I don't know, but it did find a rather large tan hand setting on the armrest. Rather than rip his hand away from the hysterical woman next to him, the stranger grasped my hand tightly, and his thumb immediately ran smooth circles over my hand.

I chose to pretend this wasn't actually happening by closing my eyes again and leaning my head against the seat. I used my other hand to wipe away the solitary tear that leaked out of my stupid eye and attempted to breathe deeply as we ascended. The stranger continued to rub circles with his thumb, and I found it oddly calming. Aaron never did that when we held hands.

Why was I even comparing this stranger to Aaron? But then, considering I hadn't held another man's hand in years, maybe it wasn't so odd after all. We eventually reached our cruising altitude, and my heart chose to stay in my chest and returned to normal. I had gradually released my death grip on the stranger and fought to come up with some reasonable explanation but came up, empty-handed.

I finally settled for giving him a side eye and pathetic smile as a silent thank-you and then once again reached for the magazine as well as my phone and earphones. I thought maybe if I listened to music then he wouldn't feel obligated to make awkward small talk with me for the next nine hours. He returned my smile and reached for his tablet and began watching a movie, honoring my silent request to move past what had just happened.

I grew bored with the magazine after a short while and stole a glance at my unexpected savior. He didn't appear to be overly tall like Aaron, but his legs were long enough to make sitting in the cramped airplane seats look uncomfortable. I quickly did a double take at his calves, surprised to see how muscular they were, surmising that he must either be a runner or some sort of athlete. I was also amused to see he was wearing board shorts and not pants like every other person departing Chicago in the dead of winter.

I always get cold on airplanes, but he apparently wasn't concerned, since his top was just a T-shirt. His hair was light brown and hung down in his eyes slightly without looking sloppy. I also happened to notice, as he had his head propped up on his hand, that he was not wearing a wedding ring, and I was silently relieved that I hadn't just been holding hands with a married man.

My eyes were examining his strong jawline when I decided to sneak a look at his eyes again and found those clear blue eyes staring back at me. I quickly averted my gaze and scolded myself for making a fool of myself for the third time in less than an hour. I grabbed my tablet and started a movie before the crew demanded an emergency landing and forced the creepy stalker woman off the plane. I quickly engrossed myself in some classic *Pitch Perfect*, determined to watch something that was not going to make me cry. The music calmed my nerves, and I soon forgot about the handsome stranger next to me.

Chapter 9

*T*he sun glistened on the turquoise waters as Aaron and I
looked over the picturesque view. I snuggled up against
him as he wrapped his arm around me and pulled me close
while planting a gentle kiss on my forehead. He reached for
my other hand, and I gasped when I saw the diamond ring he
was holding between his fingers. This was the proposal I had
been waiting for...

Wait, what? I slowly opened my eyes and surprise washed
over me as I felt the rhythmic breathing coming from the
stranger next to me. Why could I feel his breathing? Well,
maybe because my head was on his shoulder and my body had
curled toward him as I slept. He was sleeping as well, and so I
moved ever so slowly away from him. My jaw dropped open at
the sight of a small wet spot on his shirt. Once again, I went with
the explanation in my head that none of this had happened.

I ran a hand through my hair and tried to recover from the
shock of waking up on a stranger. What was happening to me? I
was not this hot mess! I was the one that had my life together. I
didn't get sloppy drunk or show up at work late or go shopping
with my shirt inside out. I was polite and proper and just... *not
this*. Apparently all one had to do was put me on an airplane
and I was out of control.

I slid away from Mr. Board Shorts and sighed with immense relief that he hadn't woken yet. Hopefully my drool would dry, and he'd be none the wiser of my latest slip up. Despite the relief, I instantly missed the feel of his warm body and the comfort of another human being. Other than my parents' funeral, I hadn't had much physical contact in nearly four months, and that had left me feeling a huge hole in my heart.

I relocated where I left off in my movie and focused on the screen for the next hour. At one point, I felt the guy stir next to me but remained fixed on my movie to appear indifferent. It was hard, though. His presence was somewhat overwhelming.

As soon as my movie was over, I started another one, intent on keeping a space between us. Halfway through the movie, I felt a nudge. I glanced up at him, and he gestured toward a flight attendant with a plastic smile, waiting for my drink order. I requested a Diet Coke and the featured sandwich and quietly ate without another exchange with Board Shorts.

An hour later, I was cursing myself for chugging that Diet Coke because now I needed to use the dreaded airplane bathroom. I nudged the guy and mumbled that I needed to get by. He paused his movie and set it aside as he shifted his knees to the side to allow me room to pass. As I was struggling to squeeze between him and the seat in front of us, we hit a patch of turbulence, and I fell backward into his lap. Between my thin leggings and his board shorts, there wasn't much preventing me from feeling his crotch rubbing against me. I felt my cheeks flush as I bounced out of his lap and glanced back at him. He said nothing, giving me a slight nod with a hint of a smirk. I stretched my legs and did my business and returned to my seat, but he was gone, apparently using the bathroom himself.

Eventually I felt the plane make a slight change in altitude, and the pilot came on the overhead speakers to inform us that we were approaching sunny Honolulu and would arrive in approximately forty-five minutes. The time passed with no further embarrassing antics on my part, and we began our descent to the island.

I'd thought the plane taking off was scary, but the landing was even more terrifying. I tried to push images of my parents frightfully clinging to each other as their plane plummeted from the sky, but they kept coming, and I started breathing harder. I felt a nudge and could barely bring myself to look at the guy. He held up his hand, palm up, his eyes encouraging me to take his hand. I didn't need to be told twice, and I placed my seemingly small hand into his.

Once again, he started the smooth circles with his thumb, and I felt myself gradually calming down, focusing on the feel of his hand. As the landing gear creaked out, I gripped his hand a little tighter, and he covered our hands with his other hand, creating an even more calming effect. I let myself enjoy the feel of his skin and the warmth radiating from him until the plane jerked back as we touched ground.

Even though my fear dissipated after we touched down, he didn't move, and neither did I. I kept my eyes closed but felt the warmth on my cheeks, knowing I should be embarrassed. Finally, the plane stopped, and the seatbelt light dinged as everyone around us bolted to their feet, which was silly, since it wasn't like standing there would get them off the plane sooner. I opened my eyes and looked at Board Shorts, my hand still engulfed by his.

"I am so incredibly sorry, I..." I began before I was interrupted by his tender smile. There was no amusement in his eyes, only a gentle kindness.

"No worries," he said, breaking his silence for the first time in nine hours. "A lot of people have a fear of flying."

I opened my mouth to explain to him that this was a new fear and that I normally wasn't this way and then promptly closed it, thinking there was no point going into detail with this man who I would never see again. Instead I opted to be grateful. "Thank you...?"

"Luke," he told me with a full smile.

"Quinn," I said as we both laughed a little as he shook my hand with both of his. At this point, he let go, and I told myself not to pout. We focused on gathering our personal items and waited for our turn to stand and gather our carry-on bags from the overhead. I started to tug my bag out when I felt his hand on my shoulder.

"Let me help you," he said, and I stepped aside so he could pull it down, which he did with ease.

"Thank you," I said with a shy smile and began walking forward down the narrow aisle. I was aware of him behind me the entire time, but once we got off the plane, I beelined it for the nearest bathroom. I splashed water on my face and stared in the mirror, somewhat horrified at my appearance. My hair looked like it hadn't been brushed in six years, and my face was red and blotchy—probably from my near-death experience of dying of embarrassment.

I pulled a comb from my purse and attempted to make myself a little less repulsive and applied a little lip gloss, which did little to combat my tired appearance. I started walking through the airport toward baggage claim but only saw the man from a distance after that. He must not have checked any bags, because he disappeared out the doors and out of my life.

Chapter 10

Luke

I made it through the airport and crowds of people and burst out the doors, gulping the fresh Hawaiian air. I found that anytime I traveled away from the islands, one of the best parts of returning was the air. There was no logical way to describe why the air was better here, but it just was. It was hard to get me away from the islands, but my little sister just got engaged, and my family had met up in Chicago to celebrate her engagement to Derrick.

Derrick seemed like a decent guy, even though I hadn't had the opportunity to get to know him very well. Mia had moved to Chicago to go to college with her best friend, Sarah, and she met Derrick her freshmen year. He was dating someone else at the time, so they were only friends throughout college. They reconnected a few years after college and had been together ever since.

Mia and I grew up as military brats and became accustomed to moving around the country. When I was ten, my parents announced we were moving to Hawaii. We were living in California at the time, and I enjoyed the warmer climate more than the other places we had lived, so I was pretty excited about our move. The instant I stepped foot on Hawaiian soil, I just felt like I was home. We enrolled in a new school, and while I knew Hawaii was still part of the States, I felt like we were a world away. The other kids were nice, but I was suddenly aware of how white my skin was and how different they spoke. One day at lunch, one of the boys plopped down next to me like we had already met.

"You want a piece of nori?" he asked, holding out a green sheet of some foreign food to me.

I eyed it warily but was afraid to turn him down out of fear of being rejected. I took it and popped it in my mouth and gagged it down. *It must be an acquired taste,* I thought.

"I'm Cody!" the kid said with a toothy grin. His skin was dark, but not nearly as dark as some of the other kids. He had long black shiny hair, which I wasn't too sure about. I wasn't used to seeing boys with long hair, but it seemed to be normal here in Hawaii.

"I'm Luke," I said. "I'm new."

"I know," Cody said cheerily. "You're the latest haole!"

"Haole?" I asked.

"It means you not from here. And you a white boy. But it's cool. We're friends now." He said it so matter-of-factly that I chose to just believe him.

The next four years, we were inseparable. Cody taught me everything I needed to know about living on the North Shore of Oahu. I was always amazed at how differently the *keiki*, or children, lived here compared to the rest of the United States. Cody knew how to spear fish, surf, boogie board, shore break—that terrified my mother—and how to scale a coconut tree.

His family didn't live far from us, and it didn't take long to convince my parents that I could just ride my bike to Cody's house. Cody's family got so used to seeing me there that they usually just assumed I was staying for dinner every night.

Cody was the only boy out of four siblings, so I think his parents were happy he'd found another boy to play with since his three older sisters were busy with their own lives. I usually preferred to go to Cody's house because Mia wouldn't leave us alone when we played at my house.

Cody's dad, Steve, was white, but his mom, Noelani, was Hawaiian, born and raised in the islands. Most of our adventures consisted of surfing. Cody insisted on taking me out one day, and I was curious to learn, but I also wasn't sure if I could do it. I fell a lot and got a lot of salt water up my nose, but it wasn't long before I got really good at it.

"He's got natural talent," Noelani commented one day to my mom.

After that, my parents encouraged the surfing and bought me my first board. I became obsessed with the sport and surfed every day that I could. My young teenage body became toned and muscular from all the paddling, and my parents could barely afford to feed me. Eat. Surf. Sleep. Repeat. That was me.

I had to do well in school, though, because my parents threatened to take surfing away from me. I think they were just bluffing, but I wasn't about to find out. I had already entered a few competitions and done really well, and sponsors were beginning to whisper about the new grommet. Up until that point, I just surfed to surf, and because I loved it, but as a teenager I was starting to wonder if I had a shot at making it to the professional circuit.

Then a few days after my fourteenth birthday, my dad got his orders. We were moving to Missouri. I immediately grabbed my board and took off for the water. The swell was small, and there weren't very many waves, but I sat in the middle on my board and stared out at the open ocean. It didn't take long before I heard a splash and turned to see Cody paddling out to me.

"Your mom called," he said quietly as he sat up next to me.

"Yeah?"

"Yeah," he said.

There was nothing left to say, so we both sulked in the middle of the ocean.

Before I knew it, we were in Missouri, and I hated it. There was no salty fresh air, no ocean, no surfing, and no Cody. I was old enough to understand how the military worked, but I didn't like it. I tried to adapt at first, but then I decided I didn't care. I was doing poorly in school and walked around with a chip on my shoulder.

Within six months, I had been suspended twice for picking fights at school. I knew my parents were pissed, and I didn't blame them. After picking me up from the principal's office one day, my mom was seething. I didn't say a word on the car ride home because I swear you could see the smoke coming from her. I got home and threw my backpack on the floor and started up the stairs to my room.

"Not so fast, young man," my father said sternly from the dining room table. I hadn't realized Dad was home early and the look on his face instilled a little fear in me. My mom sat next to him and ordered me to sit in the chair across from them.

This is it, I thought, taking a seat. I wondered if they were going to send me to military school or to live with my grandparents or maybe something worse.

My father cleared his throat and glanced at my mom, who had quickly gone from pissed... to sad? Her eyes filled with tears until she looked away from me and down at her hands.

"Your behavior is unacceptable," my father started. "You cannot behave like this when things don't go your way."

I cringed a little as I hung my head in shame and waited for my punishment.

"This is not the man I'm raising you to be, and I refuse to have a bully living in my house!"

He was silent for a bit, and I heard my mom crying quietly, which made me even more ashamed. I was so caught up in what I didn't have anymore that I didn't think about how it was affecting my parents.

"That being said," my father continued, "we are sending you back to Hawaii, and you will be living with Cody's family."

My head snapped up so quickly I thought I was going to have whiplash. I didn't think there was any way I had heard them correctly.

I looked at my mom, who was still fighting tears, but now she was smiling at me. "Honey, we know this hasn't been easy for you. We don't want to reward you for your behavior, but we also know what you had to give up for this family, and we don't want to jeopardize your future."

Two weeks later, I hugged my dad as he dropped my mom and me off at the airport. I tried telling them I was old enough to fly by myself, but they wouldn't hear it.

"It's bad enough I have to give you up," my mom said. "I'm not giving up any more time than I have to."

Mia sat in the backseat pouting because she was mad that I got to move back to Hawaii and she didn't. I was surprised when she clung to me and cried because I didn't think she really cared that much. We fought all the time and didn't do that much together, so I figured she would benefit from being the center of attention for a while.

Moving in with Cody's family was pretty seamless, considering how much time I had spent there. Walking inside that plantation-style house and smelling freshly baked malasadas was like coming home. They had gotten bunk beds and shoved an additional dresser in the corner since Cody and I had to share a room. His two oldest sisters had already moved out, but there were still one, Zoe, living at home. After I got settled into my new room, I gave Cody's mom a big hug and kissed my mom on the cheek before racing Cody to the truck and throwing our boards in the back. Cody's dad drove us to the beach. We surfed until the sun went down that night. A week later, I was officially a sponsored surfer grom gearing up for a life in professional surfing.

Now, here I was, sitting outside of baggage claim and waiting for Cody to pick me up. It wasn't long before I spotted Cody's late model Ford pickup slowly cruising outside the baggage claim area. I waved him down. He pulled over, and I threw my bag into the bed of the truck, jumped in, and soon we were on the freeway in the middle of Honolulu rush-hour traffic.

"How was your trip?" Cody asked as he navigated around delivery trucks, commuters, and tourists.

"Cold!" I shivered just thinking of the frigid air in the Windy City.

"I still can't believe your baby sister is getting married," Cody said.

"Yep. Man, you missed your chance," I said wryly.

The only response I got was a snort. Cody would never admit it, but I always suspected he had a thing for my sister. He probably never acted on it because for one, she's my sister, but the five-year age gap didn't really work at the time. He hadn't seen her in quite awhile, and I doubted they interacted much other than a handful of likes on their social media accounts.

"How was your flight?" he asked, slyly changing the subject.

It was my turn to let out a little snort accompanied by a smile.

"What put that shit-eating grin on your face?" Cody asked curiously, clearly amused.

I started to tell him a little about the interesting girl who sat next to me on the flight.

"Oh, so one of those crazy chicks who thinks the plane going crash every five seconds?" he asked.

I shook my head slowly and tried to make sense of the situation before responding. "No, I don't think this was normal for her." I sighed when Cody gave me a skeptical sideways look. "I don't know how to explain it, but it's like she had something going on in her head." I was failing at finding the words, but I could tell Cody was enjoying the story.

"Was she at least hot?" he blurted out.

I smiled as I pictured her bent over her tablet, intently watching her screen and trying to ignore me. Her silky hair kept falling into her face, and I'd had to refrain from tucking it behind her ear on multiple occasions. Most of the flight she seemed stressed, but as she was watching her movie, she would chuckle or crack a smile often enough for me to catch a glimpse of those adorable dimples.

I was caught off guard when she first grabbed my hand as the plane was taking off, but she looked so terrified that I didn't have the heart to pull away from her. If a pretty girl needed to hold my hand to calm herself, then who was I to say no? I would've been okay if she wanted to hold my hand the entire flight, but unfortunately that didn't seem necessary once we were in the air.

It got even better when she dozed off while watching her movie. I had snuck enough glances at her to see the progression of being relaxed to eyes becoming heavy, and then her head began to nod. I hadn't really expected her to lean my way, but once sleep claimed her, she just naturally fell in my direction. At first it was just her dark hair brushing against my shoulder, and I might've smelled a hint of coconut shampoo.

Then her head finally bounced against my shoulder, and she settled on me. I was afraid to move out of fear of waking her, so I just relaxed and made sure she was comfortable. I had observed enough to figure out she was not having a good day, whether it was because of the flight itself or something else, but I felt a need to protect her. If letting her sleep on my shoulder for a bit and forgetting about her troubles helped, then great.

I thought I'd died and gone to heaven when she curled her

body closer to mine, and I desperately wished the armrest wasn't between us. Her body was so soft against mine, and the smell of coconut was damn near enough to drive me crazy. I slowly rested my head against hers and tried to fall asleep to stop myself from pulling her on top of me and kissing her like crazy and making her forget all her fears.

When I woke up over an hour later, she was about as far away from me as she could get within our four feet of space. Our interactions for the remainder of the flight were limited, though I rather enjoyed the moment she needed out to use the bathroom. I was already enjoying her perfect ass in my face as she tried to squeeze through, but then that patch of turbulence? Couldn't have come at a better time. Praise God for leggings! I scolded myself for being a pervert, but after the hand holding and sleeping next to each other, I would be lying if I didn't feel an attraction to her.

It was a foreign feeling to me, and I couldn't even recall the last time a woman had held my attention for more than a passing minute. Then there were several minutes of walking behind her on the way off the plane. I had considered asking her for coffee or something, or at the very least asking for her phone number, but she darted to the bathroom so quickly that I concluded that the attraction was not mutual and gave it up.

"Dude!" Cody snapped his fingers in front of my face to regain my attention. "That chick must've been pretty hot if you checked out that long! Damn, braddah!" He slapped his steering wheel as he laughed.

"Yes, she was very hot." I laughed, nodding. I didn't go into details about how I would consider her more of a classic beauty than hot, but whatever. We changed the subject then, so Cody could update me on the business.

We had a partnership in a surf school and gave lessons. We mostly catered to tourists but also mentored several kids who had the potential to go pro in the surfing circuit. We dreamed of having a brick and mortar business eventually, but the increasing property costs in Hawaii made that complicated.

For now, we would have to settle with our tent set up on the beach every day. Though I use the word "settle" loosely, because who would complain about having to sit on the beach every day for their job? This wasn't how I'd envisioned my life, but I loved my job. I relished the look on a kid's face when they nailed a new maneuver or the excitement from a tourist surfing for the first time because they could cross surfing off on their bucket list. We had to spend a fair amount of time building our reputation, but my name got us business we might not have otherwise.

It had been two years since we started our partnership, and it was awesome. Cody and I were like brothers, just minus the blood, and we worked well together. We had each other's backs and worked around our schedules as needed. Our biggest struggle was finding additional surf instructors during the busy seasons. The North Shore of Oahu was often a stepping stone for most people, and they were either surfers just passing through, military families, or whatever other transients we might get.

Some days we would be in the water giving lesson from seven a.m. until dark, but we had to take advantage of the winter surf whenever we could. During the summer season, or "flat season" as we usually called it, we did some lessons and excursions paddle boarding. We also did yardwork on the side.

I would do whatever it took to stay in Hawaii. This was my home.

Chapter 11

Quinn

I watched the carousel at baggage claim go around and around and finally admitted defeat. I slung my backpack over my shoulder and grabbed my sole suitcase and preceded to customer service. I tried to remind myself this was just a mild inconvenience and not a sign that I wasn't supposed to make this move.

I pulled my cell phone out of my purse and called Adrienne to let her know I would be a few minutes late. The customer service agent was pleasant and helpful and assured me that they would have the bag dropped off at my house within the next forty-eight hours. With nothing else to be done, I stepped outside and took a deep breath of that fresh Hawaiian air.

I waited on the curbside until a small blue SUV pulled up, Adrienne waving excitedly at me. She popped out of her car and bounced around and surprised me with a warm hug and placed a lei around my neck. The flowers smelled amazing, and I appreciated the aloha my parents' neighbor was gracing me with. Adrienne was beautiful, her long black hair in a side braid with a real hibiscus tucked behind her ear. Her eyes dark eyes shone with the aloha spirit, and I envied her complexion and her naturally tanned skin.

I hadn't expected Adrienne to be my biggest ally in my move. I had met her briefly when I helped my parents move and instantly liked her. She was sweet and easy to talk to, and I had spent a few hours chatting with her and her grandmother, sipping lemonade on her quaint lanai one afternoon. I considered myself fortunate to have a potential friend, especially one close to my age, for a neighbor.

I thanked her for picking me up and graciously accepted the can of juice she offered me. The guava flavor was refreshing, and I sipped it as she chatted on the drive back to the North Shore. Her voice was pleasant, and I was happy to listen to her rather than focus on what I was about to do.

I was actually disappointed when we turned onto the street, and I swallowed hard, fighting the anxiety creeping in. Adrienne looked over and smiled sympathetically as we pulled into my parents' driveway, or rather, my driveway. She parked the car but left it running and helped me get my luggage out. The house wasn't large, but it was perfect for my parents. The plantation-style home was a quaint, tropical-blue color surrounded by green foliage and exotic flowers begging you to stay awhile.

"I hope you don't mind, but I had a friend help me give it a good cleaning yesterday," Adrienne said as she unlocked the front door. "I also had pest control come in and spray for bugs, so you shouldn't have any issues for a while."

"I really appreciate everything you've done the past four months," I told her. Adrienne was there to help with so many of the details I couldn't bear to handle during my worst grief. In reality, I should've flown to Hawaii immediately to handle the house, car, and everything else, but I just couldn't.

"Don't even mention it," she said, silencing me with a hug. "You know I'm right next door if you need anything. I'll check in with you in the next day or two, but for now I'm going to give you some space."

"Thanks, Adrienne," I said with a sincere smile as she slipped out the door.

Then I was alone. I stood frozen momentarily, trying to gather the courage to continue. My mom's feminine touch was all over. I had enjoyed helping them move and get somewhat settled into the house, but so much of the decorating and soft, homey touches had been made in the following months.

The living room, small dining area, and kitchen were an open layout tastefully decorated in beach décor. I imagined them cuddled up on the small gray sectional couch, watching movies. Or Dad sitting at the table doing word searches while Mom baked in the kitchen. The wall in the dining room was covered in framed photographs, several with me in them, but a lot of them depicted the life they had built for themselves in the short amount of time they were able to live out their dream. I turned to the living room and glanced around at the random photographs placed around the room, and my eyes landed specifically on one.

"Oh, hell no," I said and briskly grabbed the photo of Aaron and me smiling in front of a waterfall and slammed it face down. That picture would be torn to shreds, but I wasn't dealing with it right now. "Bastard," I muttered to make myself feel better.

I walked back into the kitchen and opened the fridge. Of course, it was empty. I was grateful that Adrienne had thought to clean it out because I could only imagine how awful it would smell after all this time. I would need to make a trip to the grocery store soon. I ran my hand over the smooth granite countertops and started opening the white cabinets to take stock of supplies.

I stopped in my tracks when I saw the notepad sitting on the counter with my mother's delicate handwriting all over it. I choked back a sob as I realized it was a grocery list. My mom had no idea that she wasn't going to ever make it the grocery store, and that harsh reality was a lot to take in. This house was lived in, no evident signs that they expected to not come back.

I walked down the hallway to the guest room, or my room, since I was the main guest they expected to visit. The room was cozy, decorated in light blue with coral accents. My mom and I had picked out the pineapple quilt together at a cute shop in the town nearby. Mom and I had sanded the dresser we found at a thrift shop and painted it turquoise to match the pineapples on the quilt. The room was simple but would be sufficient for me because I couldn't even realistically consider staying in their room right now.

I left my luggage in there and wandered to the end of the hallway to the master bedroom. The room was spacious and decorated in shades of blue. The large window looked over the back of the fenced-in yard lined with palm trees. I'd nearly forgotten about the small cottage at the back end of the property. It was a selling point of the property, and my parents intended on keeping it rented out for extra income, but the tenant they had when they first moved in chose to move back to the Florida, and they hadn't gotten around to renting it back out.

I couldn't even comprehend that right now, so I turned back into the bedroom. The walk-in closet separated the bedroom and the master bathroom, and my senses were flooded the moment I opened that closet door, washed over with the smell of my mom's perfume and my dad's familiar masculine scent. I touched one of my mom's shirts and brought it to my nose and inhaled deeply.

"Oh, Mom." I shut my eyes tightly to keep the tears at bay. I quickly exited the room and shut the door. I was obviously not ready for that yet.

Despite not having eaten dinner yet, I was simply too exhausted to go in search of food. It was really too early for bed, but Chicago time said it was plenty late enough. I opened my suitcase and realized all my pajamas were in the lost luggage.

I shoved the suitcase off the bed, spilling clothes all over the floor but not giving one single damn. I had reached my capacity between the traveling and the emotions, and I was just done.

I peeled off my clothes that I imagined to be covered in a million germs from my endless day of travel and pulled a clean T-shirt over my head. I eyed the clean sheets and considered taking a shower but decided I didn't care enough. I crawled into bed and let the tears flow.

I momentarily forgot where I was when I woke the next morning. I had cried myself to sleep and slept like a rock. I was determined to start my day fresh and maybe even make it through the day without any tears. I had a renewed determination to accomplish anything that made Hawaii feel like home. But first, coffee.

I peeked out the window and saw that it was lightly misting, so I opted to throw on a pair of leggings and a tank top and grabbed my flip-flops. I checked my purse for the car keys that Adrienne had given me the night before. I had debated what to do with the car, and it seemed silly to move mine or buy a new one when my parents had left me a perfectly good Chevy Equinox. It felt like I was joyriding in my parents' car, but I reminded myself that it was my car now.

I recalled the coffee shop my mom and I had frequented when I visited before and headed that way. I was surprised at how busy the shop was at the early hour and got in line to place my order.

"Aloha!" said the cheerful blonde with "Molly" on her nametag when I stepped up to the counter. I placed my order and then joined the small group waiting for their morning fix. I glanced around, looking at the coffee shop customers immersed in conversation.

"Howzit?" the guy next to me said.

"Excuse me?" I asked, turning to see if he was talking to me.

"Howzit?" Then he laughed and leaned forward slightly. "How's it going?"

"Oh, good," I said. "You?"

"Living the life," he said. "Where you visiting from?"

I was kind of surprised he assumed I was just visiting, but then I remembered my mom talking about what a small community the North Shore was. This guy probably knew I wasn't a local. Or at least that I had been a local for a mere twelve hours.

"I actually just moved here from Chicago," I said, testing out the words.

"Right on! You surf?" he asked.

"Um, no. Like never," I said, laughing. "It sounds fun, though."

He reached into his pocket and handed me a business card. "Hit me up sometime. I give surf lessons."

"Oh, nice," I said, not really intending on taking him up on his offer. I was never overly athletic and couldn't envision myself as a surfer chick. I cracked a smile when I read the name of the business: Two Braddahs Surfing.

"How 'bout in the morning?" he suggested.

"Oh! You mean like *tomorrow*?" I said, eyes widening. I felt kind of put on the spot, but he seemed like a nice enough guy. He looked to be Hawaiian with his dark skin sprinkled with tattoos and his jet-black hair.

"You should totally do it!" Molly said, reaching over the counter to hand Surfer Dude two coffees. "Cody is a really good instructor!"

"Um..." I hesitated, not really sure what to do. Then it hit me. I was here to start a new life, to start over. I couldn't keep letting my prior life define who I was if I was looking for a change. "Sure," I agreed with a decided nod.

"Right on!" Cody said, raising his coffee cup like a toast. We officially exchanged names and planned to meet at eight the next morning, and he gave me directions to the beach park.

As soon as he left, it hit me that my swimsuits were also in the missing suitcase. I didn't want to rely on it being delivered before tomorrow morning, so I thought maybe I should do a little shopping.

"Here you go," Molly said with a smile as she handed me my coffee.

I asked her about the nearest bikini shop, and she recommended the big yellow one down the road, but they wouldn't be open for another hour. I decided to enjoy my coffee and walk down the street while peeking in the storefronts. It didn't seem like that long ago that I had done the same thing with my mom.

Before I knew it, the hour was up, and I realized I had enjoyed myself and thought of fond memories without crying. I made my way to the yellow shop and immediately felt overwhelmed at the assortment of swimwear. I took my time browsing and selected a few bikinis to try on. I really liked the hot pink one and thought it made the girls look amazing, but I also didn't think it would be very conducive to surfing.

Then I had one with a high neck top in royal blue that was still quite flattering while practical. I knew that logically I should get the blue one, but I longingly looked at the hot pink one. I quickly concluded that my new life also required new bikinis and grabbed both swimsuits and headed to the register. I felt a little spring in my step as I walked back to my car, marveling at the power of retail therapy.

Chapter 12

Luke

I plopped next to Cody in our beach chairs positioned in our surf school tent and handed him a cup of coffee.

"Mahalo," he said gratefully as he took a sip.

We were usually set up by 7:30, sometimes earlier if we had lessons. We tried to be diligent with our tent presence because a fair amount of our business came from people just walking up and making a spontaneous decision to surf. It wasn't difficult to convince tourists enjoying a vacation in Hawaii to take a surf lesson.

"What's on the schedule for today?" I asked, not bothering to crack open our schedule book.

"I've got one hot chick booked at eight," Cody said, cracking a smile.

"How'd you manage that?"

Cody booked the majority of his lessons by pure charm. It seemed that no girl could resist the good-looking Hawaiian.

"Met her getting coffee yesterday and convinced her to give it a shot," he said with a shrug.

I shook my head but smiled. I had a lesson booked for nine with a couple of middle-aged businessmen from Texas, so it was clear who the winner was.

"And there she is." Cody nodded his head in the direction of the parking lot as a silver Chevy Equinox pulled in.

No way.

"Shit!" I jumped up as my hot coffee spilled down my bare chest.

"Dude, how'd you manage that?" Cody asked, tossing me a towel to dry off.

"No, listen, man." I looked at Cody realizing I was on the verge of begging. "That's her!"

Cody just looked at me with a blank stare, questioning my sudden change from half asleep to off-the-charts intense.

I glanced over and saw Quinn pulling her hair back in a ponytail while standing outside of her car. She was still out of earshot, but I only had a few minutes to convince Cody to give her up.

"That's the girl from the plane!" I said with desperation creeping into my voice.

"No shit?" Cody asked in disbelief.

I could see the struggle on his face as he debated whether he was going to give up that easy. Finally, he groaned and tossed his arms up in the air. Then he pointed at me. "You owe me so bad. Like forever."

"Whatever you want," I said, biting the side of my cheek to keep from smiling.

"Um, good morning." She had snuck up behind us, and we both spun around at the same time.

"Good morning," I said with smile. I hadn't anticipated the look of sheer terror on her face when she recognized me.

"Oh my... No, not you," she stammered as her face turned an endearing shade of red. She couldn't even look me in the eye, and she pivoted like she was ready to bolt while mumbling something about this being a really bad idea.

"Hey," I said, gently grabbing her by the elbow. "Everything's cool."

She finally glanced up at me and bit her lip as her blue eyes met mine. Cody looked back and forth between us, clearly amused at our exchange.

"Hey, Quinn! Glad you could make it," he said, reaching out and giving her the customary Hawaiian kiss on the cheek. "Luke here is going to give you your lesson today."

"Wait, what?" she asked, eyes widening. "I thought you were!"

"Nope," I said. "Cody has a lesson scheduled with some gentlemen in about an hour. But he said he would be more than happy to snap some photos for you if you would like."

Cody gave me a look that stressed how badly I owed him. I looked back at Quinn with an encouraging smile. She still looked hesitant, but I could tell I was winning her over. And hot damn! If I thought leggings looked good on her, it was only because I hadn't seen her in a bikini. She was lean and curvy at the same time, with a feminine softness to her. I liked the way the morning sun was shining on her hair and making her face appear to be glowing.

"Well," Cody said, loudly clearing his throat to get my attention, "you should probably get started."

We already had the boards down on the beach, ready for the land lesson. I handed Quinn a reef shirt, disappointed to be asking her to cover up, but it was necessary if she didn't want a rash from the foam surfboard.

"I'm going to show you the steps you will follow once you are out on the water," I began explaining, trying to remain focused. I wanted her to get the most out of her lesson and enjoy herself and also reminded myself that being focused guaranteed her safety.

"We're gonna start by paddling like this." I lay on the board to show her and gestured for her to do the same. "Now, these movements are in slow motion on land, but out in the water, you're gonna want to try to do it as one fluid motion. I'm going to tell you to paddle, push up with your arms beneath you, bring your knee forward, and then stand like this."

I ran through all the steps as I instructed her. She listened intently and followed the motions as we ran through them a few times. She had a look of determination, and I had no doubt this was going to be my best lesson ever. I really owed Cody.

"Do you have any questions?" I asked her when I felt like we were ready to begin.

"I don't think so," she said quietly. "I'm just not sure if I'm going to be able to do it."

"You will be fine. I won't let anything happen to you." And I meant it. I walked over and grabbed the leash from her board and bent down to wrap it around her ankle. I had to refrain from running my hand along her leg to test if it was as smooth as it looked. I'd found Quinn attractive the moment I laid eyes on her on the airplane, but having the chance to see her again, I decided I'd never seen anyone more beautiful.

We laid the boards in the water, and I held hers steady so she could lay flat on it. I jumped on mine and stuck my foot on the nose of her board so I could tow her out and save her some of the paddling. We remained silent on the paddle out to the first surf break, and I moved her into position.

"Okay, I see a little something on the horizon," I said, peering out into the ocean. I quickly ran through the steps with her again and then geared up to give her a push into the first wave. I watched her paddle just the way I taught her, and I hollered for her to push up.

She made it to her knees, but then abruptly fell off the wave. She disappeared under the water for a few moments, but then resurfaced sputtering. I could see her frustration as she tried to get back on the large board and paddle back out.

"Hey, don't beat yourself up," I said once she got back to me. "It usually takes a few tries before you get it. Just relax and try to have fun."

Over the course of ten minutes, we had a couple more failed

attempts, but I could tell she was beginning to get the hang of it, as each time her motions were less automated.

"Come on, Quinn! You got this!" Cody hollered out from his position closer to shore, where he held our waterproof camera.

Finally, I saw a larger wave coming, and I looked Quinn in the eye.

"You can do this," I told her.

She gave me a confident nod and started paddling. I gave her a nudge and sent her board forward into the wave. This time she stood up with ease and rode the wave. I threw my arms up and cheered, ecstatic that she had done it. Cody's cheers echoed off the water as he had the camera raised, snapping multiple pictures.

When Quinn paddled back out to me, she was beaming. Her frustration had turned into pure elation. This was one of my favorite parts about giving lessons, and not just because it was her.

"I knew you could do it!" I stopped holding my hand out for a high wave. She leaned forward and gave me a wet smack with her hand.

"That was like the best thing ever!" she exclaimed, water dripping from her hair.

"Are you ready to do it again?" I asked.

This time she was prepared and started paddling before I gave her the go-ahead. I swam forward to catch up and gave her board a shove into the wave. She leaped to her feet and gave Cody a shaka and a big grin. I laughed at her enthusiasm and waited for her to paddle out, surprised that she hadn't grown tired yet. At that point, we reached a lull in the waves, so I encouraged her to take a few minutes to recover from the excitement.

Her disdain at seeing me this morning seemed to fade away as we floated on our boards and soaked up the sunshine.

"So, do you surf a lot?" she asked as she twirled her fingers around in the water.

I held back my laughter, though I was pleased that she didn't know who I was.

"Every chance I get," I told her.

"And you and Cody do this together?" she asked. "I like the name of your business, but, um, I'm assuming you aren't actually brothers?"

I laughed then, because Cody and I couldn't look more different. "Well, we like to say we are brothers, minus the blood. We've known each other since we were ten, and I even lived with his family for a while." I didn't elaborate, and she didn't pry, though she looked somewhat curious.

"So, what about you?" I asked, hoping to gather some intel on this beautiful woman. I wasn't big on fate or destiny, but it also seemed like more than a coincidence that our paths would cross again.

"I just moved here," she said, looking down at her board.

"Oh?" I asked inquisitively, hoping she would share more. "What brought you here?"

"Well," she started with a long exhale. "My parents retired here last year. They died in September in a plane crash." Suddenly the images of her terrified on the plane made sense.

"Oh man, I'm so sorry to hear that," I said. "I think I heard about that."

We sat silent for a moment before I decided to brave some more questions.

"What made you decide to move here, then?"

"I decided Chicago held nothing for me anymore. I went through a bad breakup, my parents are gone, and I just decided screw it. I'm starting over."

"Man," I said, shaking my head. "Sounds like a rough year." I wanted to bring the smile back to her face, so I went on. "It's a good thing you came to Oahu, then. It's proven to be the most powerful place for second chances." I smiled.

"Oh, is it, now?" she asked with a hint of a smile.

"Sure is," I said. "And more waves! Paddle!"

Chapter 13

Quinn

I had given up on trying to appear calm and cool and decided just to be happy and excited for the time being. Though I was absolutely horrified when Luke turned around, he had ended up giving me the best day I'd had in a long time. He gave me the confidence to not only give surfing a try but actually do well at it under his instruction.

We surfed for about an hour, until my arms felt like rubber and I was convinced they were going to fall off. Cody had disappeared after a while, and we later saw him out in the water with two rather large men. I wasn't really sure how they were going to balance on a surfboard, but I gave them credit for wanting to try. There was obviously something about this place that nudged people out of their comfort zones, myself included.

"Thank you so much for this," I told Luke as I paid him for my lesson. "It was way more fun than I ever imagined."

"Sure thing. I'm glad you enjoyed it," he said, stuffing the cash into a lockbox. "I believe Cody has your information, and we should have your pictures in the next day or two."

"I can't wait to see them." I smiled. We stood there

awkwardly for a moment, and then Luke nervously cleared his throat.

"Um, I can give you my number if you'd like," he said. The ultra confidence he projected earlier seemed to be missing. I didn't know how to answer.

On one hand, he was obviously a really cool guy. Between his chivalry on the airplane to getting me to let my hair down and have a good time this morning, I kind of wanted to get to know him more. On the other hand, my brain was overanalyzing the situation and how I was still in mourning over my parents' death, not to mention my relationship with Aaron. I didn't know that I was in the right mindset to start a new relationship.

"I don't think so," I said, instantly mentally kicking myself. "I mean, maybe. Just not right now."

His face fell but he quickly recovered. "No worries, Quinn. You can just stop by anytime if you want another lesson. We can give you a better rate if you're interested in doing a series of lessons or something."

"Okay, sweet," I said, gathering my things to leave. "I'll probably see you around?"

"See you around." He lifted his hand in a wave.

I walked back to my car, talking myself out of turning around. I was determined to start a new life here on the North Shore, but I also felt like I needed to be reasonable, and surf lessons and new bikinis were as far as I could go right now.

I still couldn't shake the high I felt from such an incredible morning as I went about my day. After I showered and washed away the salt water covering my skin, I decided today was the day I was going to restock the house. I started a list that quickly turned into two pages. I questioned whether I needed that much food for one person, but I also needed to start from scratch, as most of the condiments were outdated, and the spices were ruined from the moisture in the air.

I drove to one of the large chain stores and started my

shopping. I remembered Mom telling me how different some of the stores were compared to the mainland. Sometimes the shelves were bare, or you couldn't find the same brands. I vaguely recalled this from doing light grocery shopping while on vacation, but it was different this time trying to stock my own house.

Between the surfing and the drawn-out grocery shopping, I was beat by the time I loaded up the car. I stopped to grab a refreshing smoothie and made my way back home. I was in the process of juggling as many bags on my arm as I could to avoid multiple trips when Adrienne showed up.

"Goodness, Quinn." She rushed to grab the gallon of milk hanging precariously from my fingers. She grabbed a few more bags and helped me get them in the house.

"Once again, you're coming to my rescue." I smiled at Adrienne gratefully.

"Do you feel like you're getting settled in?" she asked cautiously.

I felt like Adrienne was one of the only people I knew who seemed to understand how I was feeling. Maybe because she knew my parents, I felt a bond with her or even the fact that she was one of the only ones who helped me through this, despite barely knowing me. Either way, I was quickly considering her a friend.

"I do," I said, finally believing it after three days. I was starting to adjust to the time change, which helped enormously with my mental state. Unpacking my bags and buying groceries cemented the normalcy that I needed.

"So, I was thinking," she said, pulling a box of Cinnamon Toast Crunch out of the bag with a raised eyebrow.

"I like kiddie cereal." I justified with a laugh.

"Anyway, I need to search for more shells and sea glass for my jewelry and wanted to know if you would go with me to the beach in the morning," she said.

Adrienne designed jewelry and art from recycled products, commonly using shells, sea glass, and driftwood. I hadn't seen much of her work, but I remembered my mom raving about it.

"Sure, that sounds great," I said, sincerely meaning it. I thought a healthy balance of making this island my home and slowly exploring it would help me in my healing process.

A knock at the door interrupted us, and I went to answer it, pleased to see my lost luggage had arrived. Adrienne and I made plans for the next morning, and she left me to put away my groceries.

After that, I went to the bedroom to unpack my suitcase. I was glad to have all my clothes now, but I quickly realized that I did not own enough island-life attire. I made a mental note to ask Adrienne to go shopping with me one day. I had donated most of my winter clothes and hadn't see the sense of packing heavy sweaters, scarves, or thick jeans for this place.

After I made myself dinner that evening, I decided to walk around the backyard and take a renewed look at the property. I grabbed the keys to the cottage, wanting to take a closer look at that as well. I loved the lanai on the side of the house, which gave me a nice view of the front yard as well as the backyard. Two large mango trees towered over the lot like protectors of my Hawaiian paradise. There was also a small grove of banana trees and one avocado tree.

I remembered how excited my dad was to have fruit trees and how Mom said he would spend hours in the yard. My mom had initially encouraged him to hire a yard service so he wouldn't have to maintain it, but he insisted on doing it himself. I think puttering around the yard was one of his favorite parts of retirement. I bent down to pick up an avocado that had fallen from the tree and started dreaming of the different recipes I could use it for.

I reached the cottage and pulled the keys from the pocket of my romper and let myself in. It was certainly a small space, but it was very well laid out and utilized the limited square footage. The door opened into a living room, and off to the left was a small efficient kitchen space.

The opposite side of the living room led into a bedroom with an attached bathroom. It was completely empty, and a fresh coat of paint wouldn't hurt, but otherwise it was in great condition. I stepped back outside to the small covered lanai and decided the cottage would go to the top of my priority list. Leaving my job had been a bit of a hasty decision, and my small savings plus the small inheritance my parents had left me wouldn't last long. My parents had put a lot of their retirement into buying the house, and they had lived a simple life to get by.

I was fortunate to be gifted a house and a car, but those things came with pricey maintenance costs, and I needed to be prepared for that. Plus, the completion of the cottage would be a welcome distraction.

I brought my laptop out on the lanai that evening, along with a glass of wine, to research how to maintain fruit trees. The bright porch light seemed to attract bugs, so I made a mental note to look for some cute outdoor lights. The lanai wasn't overly large but had two comfortable chairs and a coffee table as well as a bistro table set in the corner. I knew Mom and Dad had enjoyed their coffee in the mornings out here, but otherwise I wasn't sure how much they utilized it.

I decided in that moment that it was my favorite part of the house, and maybe that would be the first place I would personalize with my own touch. I couldn't live in the house like it was a shrine forever, but I really struggled with making it my own. I didn't dislike my mother's decorating touches, but that was just it—I felt like I was living in my mother's house.

After researching the fruit trees (who knew there was so much to learn?), I checked my email for anything pressing. I was pleased to see I had one from Cody with my surf pictures attached.

Aloha Quinn, please accept these photos as our gift to you. Welcome to the North Shore. We look forward to seeing you more.

It was signed by both Cody and Luke, but I noted the email address was Cody's. Not like it mattered or anything. I began clicking through the pictures, not sure what to expect between possibly unflattering angles in a swimsuit or just the look on my face, as I was so focused on catching waves.

Instead, I was pleasantly surprised at the quality of the photos and how much I actually loved them. There was one comical one of me launching over the side of the surfboard as I fell, but also a really good one of my first wave and the huge grin on my face once I registered I was actually standing. Even better was the look of triumph on Luke's face in the background as he cheered for me with arms raised.

I laughed out loud when I came across the one of me heading toward Cody, giving him a shaka. I stifled a smile as I came across several of Luke and I out in the water, in between sets, lying on our boards and chatting. I hadn't realized Cody took any at that point but was secretly happy to have them. I studied Luke's profile as well as the tattoos covering his chest that I hadn't allowed myself to focus on. The Polynesian ink around his shoulder went down his chest in an intricate pattern and ended with a sea turtle.

I stared at the pictures and felt my heartbeat quicken slightly as I looked at Luke's handsome face and smiling eyes and chastised myself for passing up the opportunity to get to know him better.

I promptly loaded the pictures up to a photo printing website and ordered prints. I selected the one of me giving the shaka to enlarge and knew just the frame I would use to display it. I also made an extra copy of the one of Luke and me holding up the large surfboard at the end of the lesson with broad smiles and wet hair. That one just might go on the refrigerator.

I went to bed that night feeling the slightest sense of belonging. It had only been a few days, and just the travel alone made for a huge adjustment. I had doubted my decision to leave everything behind and move across the country many times, but now I felt something different. Just a thought.

That maybe this wasn't such a crazy idea after all.

Chapter 14

Iawoke early the next morning feeling well rested and something resembling contentment. I took my coffee out to the lanai and settled into one of the comfy chairs. Sipping coffee and listening to birds was my new favorite hobby. I lingered long after the last drop of coffee was gone and finally peeled myself out of the chair and headed in to dress for my morning with Adrienne.

I chose my new pink bikini and threw a white coverup dress over it and grabbed a light sweater in case I got chilled. I was walking over into Adrienne's yard just as she walked out of the house.

"Good morning!" she said brightly.

"Good morning!" I replied, feeling equally as cheery.

We drove about fifteen minutes to the beach she had been telling me about. I was surprised when we pulled up alongside the road because there was no beach in sight.

"Where are we?" I asked, turning to her in confusion.

"It's kind of hidden," she said with a smile.

We walked down a dirt path that opened into a large pathway. I gasped when I saw the towering banyan tree.

"Isn't it something?" Adrienne asked, looking up at the intricate web of branches.

It sure was. You couldn't tell where one tree ended and the other began. I grabbed my phone out of my beach bag and snapped a few pictures.

"Here, let me take one of you." Adrienne held her hand out for my phone. I playfully posed, and she snapped a few shots. I grabbed it back and gestured to her for a selfie. I felt the warmth spread within as I realized something as insignificant as a selfie could be so fulfilling just because I might have found a friend to be silly with.

We lazily walked the beach and allowed the cool ocean water to lap at our toes. As my feet sank in the sand, I felt the strain in my calves and envisioned the toned leg muscles I would have if I did this every day.

Adrienne had a keen eye for shells, and within ten minutes she had a small bag full of shells and sea glass.

"How do you decide what's worth collecting?" I asked, examining a small sliver of a shell I had found.

"I look for the beauty in everything," she explained, holding up a half shell. "It doesn't have to be whole to be beautiful. Just like people."

I nodded thoughtfully, figuring she was directing that at me and my broken soul.

"You can take a hundred broken shells and make a beautiful scene on canvas or recycled wood. I prefer to use whole shells for my jewelry, but sometimes I don't know what I'm going to use it for until it hits me. Sometimes it's a missing fragment for a larger piece I'm working on."

I smiled, admiring the passion she exhibited while talking about her art.

"What about this one?" I asked, holding up a small white shell with black dots on it.

"If it catches your eye, then you should grab it," she said.

"It caught your eye for a reason, and you can always figure out what to use it for later."

I quickly learned how rapidly you had to grab the shells. You might spot one down by your feet, but the waves could sweep in and claim it as its own. I became engrossed in the process and even burrowed myself in a section of sand, sifting through the treasures. I squealed in excitement when I found my first piece of green sea glass and held it up, awaiting Adrienne's approval.

"You have a natural eye!" She beamed, sharing in my excitement.

We searched for over an hour before we had baggies bursting at the seams.

"So, this helps?" I asked, checking out our loot.

"Definitely," she said as we settled on our beach towels to relax for a bit. "I have a lot I can work with."

"How often do you do this?" I asked curiously.

"You can always find something, but the best time to come out is after a big swell or storm. That's when you get rewarded," she explained. "It's amazing what a good storm can blow in. I also try to pick up trash then too, because that tends to come in with the treasures."

"Thank for inviting me today," I said as I basked in the sunlight warming my face.

"Anytime, Quinn."

We lay in a comfortable silence and listened to the waves on that quiet weekday morning until our stomachs groaned in protest. We headed back to Adrienne's car and headed straight to a food truck she insisted had the world's best tacos. The oceanfront view wasn't all bad either, I thought as I ate half my body weight in tacos. I was going to have to walk the beach every morning if I kept eating like this.

I thanked Adrienne for a wonderful morning as we went our separate ways. I was tempted to take a catnap on the lanai but decided it would be a good opportunity to get my paint for the cottage. I headed out to the nearby hardware store and started analyzing paint samples.

I finally selected a bluish-gray color and went to the counter to order a few gallons. While I was waiting for the paint to mix, I grabbed a few paintbrushes, rollers, and other necessary supplies.

I was in the midst of debating between a plastic or metal paint tray when I heard a voice that made me freeze. I peeked around the rack and saw Luke checking out at the register. He started to glance up as he pulled his wallet from his back pocket, and I ducked back behind the rack. I considered saying a friendly hello but completely chickened out after fearing I wouldn't be able to keep it casual. What if he was insulted that I'd declined to exchange phone numbers the other day? Or worse, what if he didn't really care since he probably gets gorgeous girls' phone numbers daily?

Even so, I continued to hide behind the rack until I heard the front door ding at his departure. I retrieved my paint and paid and cautiously made my way back to my car, keeping an eye out for handsome surf instructors. I wasn't sure how successful I would be in avoiding Luke in this small community, but I was certainly going to try.

Chapter 15

Luke

My morning was busy with lessons, but I had a break midafternoon to run some errands. I had just left the hardware store and almost to my truck when I heard someone call out my name. I turned to see a couple of young guys approaching me.

"Sorry to bother you, man," one of them said, "but we thought that was you and couldn't pass up the chance to shake your hand."

I smiled and shook both of their hands, used to the interruptions.

"Super stoked," the other guy said, eagerly shaking my hand. "We come here every year from Florida to surf and watch the competitions. We've been watching you since we were groms."

"We were so bummed when you left the tour," the first one said. "That was such a gnarly wipeout!"

I smiled, appreciating their enthusiasm of meeting me, but I didn't need a reminder of my career-ending accident. My knee was more than happy to remind me on a regular basis. I agreed to snap a picture with them and then politely excused myself.

Moving back to Hawaii had been life changing for me. I qualified for the championship tour right before my eighteenth birthday, and back then, my life revolved around training, surfing, and traveling the world. I got to see places I had only dreamed of, I got to surf the most epic surf spots known to man.

My parents and Mia would fly to watch me compete whenever they could and even made it to Europe once. We didn't have a lot of time to sightsee on tour, but we would take advantage of any lay days we had to enjoy the locale. I started out as the local boy people were watching and ended up a household name in the surfing industry.

I quickly climbed the ranks and was known for my hard work and determination as well as my risky maneuvers, which earned me some decent sponsors. Though surfing was a competitive sport in nature, we were also a tight-knit group, and the guys were like my brothers. The traveling could be exhausting, but we had a lot of fun together too.

The hardest part was missing Cody, since he never qualified for the championship tour. He got so close on several occasions, but he never quite made it. Our paths would cross at some of the qualifying events, though, and of course the tour ended in Hawaii.

And then we got a few months off, so I enjoyed my down time and surfing my home surf during break. I used to worry that Cody would resent me for making it further than he did, but if he did, he never showed it. Instead he was one of my biggest supporters.

I didn't date much since the life of a traveling athlete made it challenging for anything substantial. I did casually date one of the female surfers, but we decided we made better friends than a couple and cordially called it off.

Twelve years flew by like it was nothing at all. Several of my peers came and went, but I remained steady at the top as well as a handful of the other guys. The year I turned thirty, I was in the final four gunning for the world champion title. I hadn't wanted anything so badly since I had returned to Hawaii. I had a lot of respect for the other three guys, but we were all competitive enough to fight for it.

Finally, we reached the last event of the season, and I had everything weighing on this competition. Even though I had a lot at stake, I didn't even feel nervous. I just let my training and instincts take the lead as I dominated heat after heat.

I made it to the semi-finals, and with two minutes remaining, I aggressively chased down a wave. It was a bomb. All it took was the slightest mistake, a late drop on a closeout wave. I went head first into the water, and my knee crashed into the reef. I remember the intense pain when my kneecap shattered, but the wave wasn't done with me yet. For twenty-two seconds, I was mercilessly tossed around in nature's washing machine, with no control and little hope.

I don't recall hitting my head on the reef. In fact, I don't remember anything else until I woke up in the hospital two days later, and even that is foggy, but I watched the TV footage over and over again. It was almost as bad as watching your own funeral. You see me fall and get lost in the closeout and hear the collective gasp from the crowd watching on the beach. You see the water patrol race over on their jet skis, scrambling to find me underwater as my surfboard bobs up and down on the surface. You see my dad rushing to grab Mia as she screams and races to the water's edge as they drag my lifeless body to shore.

Then several moments pass as the other competitors paddle in and the commentators somberly discuss the next steps in the competition. I was unconscious for two days with a steady flow of visitors, but only family was allowed in the room with me. The nurses were smart enough not to question my mom when she told them that Cody was my brother. The doctors said there was swelling on my brain, but they couldn't know how extensive the damage was until I woke up. Fortunately, because of the rapid actions of the water patrol and lifeguards, I wasn't underwater for too long.

When I woke up, it felt like concrete had been poured down my throat and my eyes had been sewn shut. Don't even get me started on the jackhammer being used on the side of my head. I squinted in pain and tried to focus on the bodies in the room.

Cody was sleeping on the couch in a rather uncomfortable upright position, with Mia passed out on his shoulder. I turned my head, instantly regretting it, and winced as my blurred vision focused on my parents huddled close and talking in quiet tones. My mom gasped and bolted from her chair the second she realized I was awake. Dad leaned out the door and called for a doctor immediately. Mia and Cody woke up with the commotion, and then I had four blurry faces leaning over me. The doctor and nurse came in, and slowly the blurry faces came into focus as the doctor questioned me on my name, what year it was, and how many fingers he was holding up. Mia poured me a cup of water and pushed the straw to my lips, and I drank like a man in the desert.

"Slowly," Dr. Sanders cautioned me.

That word became the bane of my existence for the next several excruciating months. I spent three more days in the hospital while they kept me under observation to rule out any lasting effects from my head injury. Forty-eight stitches left quite the mark on the side of my forehead, just below my hairline. The doctors weren't concerned that I couldn't remember the moment of impact, since rest of my memory was intact.

Rehab on my knee was long and brutal. Being isolated with crutches for eight weeks was a form of torture for an active guy like me. In reality, my body wasn't the thing that was the most battered in this whole experience. My mind ran over the incident repeatedly, and I wondered how I could've slipped up so badly. Any good surfer knows the risk, but it's easy to convince yourself that you're invincible when you remain fairly unscathed for that long.

My confidence took the biggest hit, and I told myself that I couldn't even get on a surfboard for eight weeks and that I would be fine by then. The eight weeks felt more like a deadline that I knew I couldn't meet. When I thought about paddling out into the big surf, my chest would tighten, and I would relive the moments underwater, when I thought I was a goner. I tried to shrug it off like it was no big deal, and I had plenty of opportunities to do so, since that was the question of the hour. Everyone wanted to know how Luke Cole's mental state was after an epic wipeout like that.

Reporters called constantly, wanting to know if I was done surfing. While I was terrified just thinking of surfing again, I was even more terrified of never competing professionally again. Professional surfing had quickly taken over my life and molded me into the person that I was. Without surfing, who was I? Most surfers are humble enough to know that their career has an expiration date. However, I hadn't considered mine to be so close. I was supposed to have time. I was supposed to win that world title.

My coach, my sponsors, and everyone involved were patient and sympathetic. But ultimately, I had to make a decision. Cody respected me and gave me the distance I needed during my rehabilitation. Mia, however, didn't honor the bullshit. She had made it her personal mission to heal my body and mind and flew out to Hawaii for a few weeks to take care of me. She knew when I was lying and practically rolled her eyes when I told people I was doing great and my recovery was moving right along.

One evening, we were walking along the beach. It was part of my recommended recovery, and Mia patiently walked at my painfully slow pace.

"What are you going to do, Luke?" she asked.

"Um, go get some dinner after our walk," I said, playing dumb.

"Whatever, smart ass," she said, giving me a wicked side glare as she kicked sand at me. "You know what I mean!"

I sighed as I struggled to find the words. I wasn't even sure what decision I had made until I said it aloud.

"I think I'm going to retire," I said, hanging my head in defeat.

"Really?" she asked, stopping to stare at me.

"I don't know. Yeah, I guess," I said. "I'm not getting any younger. I'm at the top of my game, but this setback is huge. Surfers have come back from worse injuries than this, but typically they were younger." I stared out at the water, waiting to feel peace accompanying my decision, but the ocean offered nothing.

"It's okay if you're scared, Luke." Mia reached out to touch my arm.

"I guess that's part of it. I almost died," I said, my voice barely a whisper.

"I know. I was there," she said. Mia had no idea how often I replayed that TV footage in my mind. Watching what my injury did to my family was a large factor in my decision. How was any sport worth putting them through that again?

"I don't like ending my surfing career on this note, but at this point I don't know if it's worth continuing it and risking another injury. I can still surf, just not professionally."

"Luke, I get it," she said. "I just want to make sure it's a decision you can live with."

"Honestly, I'm getting kind of tired of the lifestyle."

This was the first I had admitted this to anyone. Traveling most of the year grew tiresome after a while, and I had been doing it for twelve years straight. One thing I had learned from other veteran surfers was once your heart wasn't in it 100%, it was time to bow out. Surfing was dangerous enough without being distracted. I don't know if that had anything to do with the slipup that caused my injury, but I also didn't want it to lead to anything worse.

"Then let's make your announcement," Mia said, giving me a hug.

Though I was disappointed to be giving up, I also felt like a huge weight was lifted off my shoulders.

I hadn't considered the impact my leaving the tour would make, but it resulted in a brief press tour. Apparently my retirement was big news, and more people cared than I realized. I spent a week traveling and giving interviews, and then it was time to go home. Leaving the tour was the biggest decision I had to make, but along with that came a dozen more.

I needed to decide where to live, what to do for work, and what I was going to do with the rest of my life. I had an offer to work behind the scenes on the tour, but I felt like I needed to make a clean break, or I would be filled with regret. I went home to Cody's couch. I usually stayed with him during my off times or would go visit my parents, who had moved to California after my dad retired from the military. I traveled so often that I never felt the urge to buy a house and have the responsibility of maintenance or property taxes when the most important thing to me was the next big swell.

Cody was in the beginning stages of starting his own surf school while I was on my final tour. He had approached me early on and asked if I would be interested in being a silent partner. He needed investors to get started, and I had some money to spare. I wasn't rich by any means, but with the sponsors I had acquired and the prize money I earned from contests, I had a healthy savings. I wouldn't be where I was if it weren't for Cody teaching me how to surf in the first place, so I never had any qualms about helping him out.

By the time I retired, he had everything lined up. The night

I decided I was done, I walked back to the house and pulled him aside.

"I want in," I said. "All in."

And that's how Two Braddahs Surfing came about. Cody and I were used to being together all the time, since we practically grew up together. But after a few months of my new life, I started to pay more attention to the *For Sale* signs in front of houses. I scoured the listings online and gave some consideration to the type of house I would like. I felt like I was ready, but I wasn't sure how Cody would feel about it, and after everything he had done for me, the last thing I wanted to do was hurt him. He was my brother.

Unfortunately, I wasn't as stealthy in my home search as I had thought, and Cody figured it out on his own before I had a chance to talk to him about it.

"So when you moving out?" he asked me one afternoon as we fished along the shoreline.

"How did you know?" I asked, glancing at him and trying to read his mood.

"Every time a new For Sale sign pops up, you get whiplash," he said with a laugh. "Plus, I know you've been saving any money you didn't have to spend to travel and figured a house would be your next step."

"So, you're not mad?" I asked.

"No! Why would I be? Shit, dude, it's not like we're married."

"I know that, asshole!" The love was real. "But if you can be serious for one minute, I just want to make sure there's no hard feelings. You've done a lot for me."

"Nah," Cody said, shrugging it off. "It's cool." Emotions were never really his thing.

"Besides, I might have a lead on a better rental," he added.

"What's that?"

Turned out, one of our other mutual friends, Grant, had just found a beachfront rental but needed a roommate. He wanted to know if Cody knew of anyone.

"Well, you better call him right now before he finds someone else!"

Within a month, everything had changed again. I took over the lease on Cody's current rental while I looked for something of my own. He moved in with Grant, but I was over there just as much. We were hanging out, watching the waves one morning from their lanai, when I saw a Realtor putting up a For Sale sign on the house next door. I was out of my chair before the sign was fully upright.

"Hey, when can I look at it?" I asked the realtor. She was an older woman, and I recognized her face from flyers around town.

"Oh! Well, hello, Luke Cole," she said, blushing slightly.

"When can I see it?" I asked, resting my hand lightly on her arm.

"How about now?" she suggested. "It is vacant."

"Okay, yeah," I said. I turned back to Cody and Grant. "You wanna see it?"

"What? Look at that dump?" Cody asked comically.

I looked back at the house. It *could* use a facelift. The lanai was dilapidated and beyond repair. The paint was peeling, and the front door was a hideous shade of orange. On the plus side, it looked like the roof and the windows were fairly new. We entered through the front door, and I was surprised at how open the floorplan was. The living room was large with high ceilings and led into the kitchen to the left and a dining nook to the right. There was also a built-in desk off the side of the living room and a tiny half bathroom. A small hallway led to two bedrooms. The master bedroom with attached bath was large and had French doors that led out to the unusable lanai.

The view itself was priceless, and I could only imagine waking up to that every morning. I glanced down at the information sheet the realtor, Karen, had given me. The price was steep, being oceanfront and all. It would take nearly all my money to buy this place. I looked at the outdated wood paneling on the walls and the yellowed linoleum floors in the kitchen. It would take me some time to save up enough money again to do renovations. But that view.

"Let's take a peek upstairs," Karen said, leading us back to the stairs near the front door. We walked up the wide wooden staircase to a loft. If I thought the view downstairs was amazing, this one was even better. Though it was the same view, the floor-to-ceiling windows did the view justice. I looked at the sheet again. I could make it work.

"I'll take it," I said.

I could look beyond the work that needed to be done and see the potential of what the house could be. With a little TLC—okay, maybe a lot—it could be an awesome home. Don't even get me started on the location. Of course, being next door to Cody was a perk, but beachfront at my favorite surf break wasn't all that bad either.

Grant worked for his dad's construction company and was able to cut me a deal on fixing the lanai and restoring it to its former glory. That was the first thing that needed to be done, because having a lanai to sit on at the end of the day and watch the waves or Hawaiian sunsets was important to me. I was also able to paint the house blue and do a little landscaping so it didn't look like such a shithole.

The inside was incredibly outdated, but I made do with it in exchange for the location. Other than the money I put into our business and the exterior of the house, I saved every spare penny I had in hopes of renovating the inside. Now here I was two years later, and I felt like I was finally there.

I talked to Grant, who had become one of my best friends in that time and got a formal quote for renovations. We were installing hardwood bamboo floors throughout the house and a new kitchen. The hideous wall paneling would be ripped out and replaced with fresh drywall. The bathrooms would be completely remodeled as well. New light fixtures, paint, and everything would make it feel like an entirely new house. I had tolerated the outdated and slightly musty-smelling décor for the past two years, but it was time, and I had to admit I was excited.

"So, there is a slight catch," Grant told me hesitantly as we went over the final details and his estimated six-month timeline.

"What's that?" I was concerned because I was depleting my savings once again to complete this renovation.

"Honestly, I think you need to stay somewhere else while we do the work," Grant said.

"Oh, shit, I hadn't thought about that," I said, scrambling to think of where I could stay. I knew I would be welcome on Grant and Cody's couch, but I had become accustomed to having my own space. After all the years of traveling and staying in random hotels and such, you would think that wouldn't faze me. But I had become comfortable with having my own home and wasn't really ready to give that up. Temporary or not, six months was a long time to camp out on someone's couch and live out of a suitcase.

"Can you give me a week or two to find other accommodations?" I asked. This might become more complicated than I had anticipated. Winter on the North Shore brought in surfers from all over the world, on top of the high volume of tourists. Finding a place to stay wasn't going to be easy.

"I ran into Adrienne the other day, and she mentioned her neighbor might have a place," Grant spoke up.

"I bet you ran into her." I snorted. Grant and Adrienne had history, but Grant had screwed up big time and was still trying to get back in her good graces. "But for real?"

"Yeah, you know where Adrienne and her grandmother

live. It's the blue house next to it, I think. Maybe just stop by and check it out," he suggested.

"I better do it right away before it gets snatched up," I said, gathering my paperwork. "Thanks again, man. The plans look great. I'm really excited to see what you can do."

"Sure thing," Grant said, waving goodbye. "Later!"

Chapter 16

Quinn

Now that I was focused on completing the cottage and preparing it to rent, I poured blood, sweat, and a few tears into that little place. I started out with a fresh coat of paint, which did wonders and brightened it significantly. I also touched up all the window trim with white paint and scrubbed the tile floors until my fingers bled.

I remembered Mom telling me she had hired someone to clean it when they first moved in, but the months of neglect had caught up, and there were dead bugs, gecko droppings, and dust in every crevice. Despite it being tremendous work, I liked having a purpose. If I was working on the cottage, I wasn't focused on my loss quite so much. Or Aaron. I hated to admit I missed that prick, but I'd thought our life was good together. We had our issues and he had his downfalls, but I thought we were happy. What did that say about me if I could live three years thinking we were in a terrific relationship and headed for marriage while he was just looking for his first exit?

On top of missing Aaron, I missed Ashley. It was incredibly unfair that I lost my parents, my boyfriend, and my best friend all in the same night.

Finally, I stood up to take stock of my work. The cottage

was ready. Even though it was small, I thought it would make a nice home for someone. In fact, after all the work I put into it, I was almost ready to live there. I wasn't entirely sure what the next steps were, but Adrienne, of course, had an answer. She helped me snap some pictures and post an ad online. She made me promise not to show it without her knowledge, so she could be around.

"Safety in numbers," she insisted. I hadn't given that any thought until she said that, and now I was nervous. Not only did I need to show the cottage to prospective renters, but I also had to choose who would be living in the cottage in my backyard. Once we posted the ad, I was overwhelmed by the influx of inquiries, and I showed it five times in the first day. I struggled with reading between the lines of each person that came and what I could gather from first impressions.

The next morning, I was already ready for a break from the process. I wanted to go to the beach and forget about everything for a while. I hadn't been to the beach other than my surf lesson with Luke my first week or going shell searching with Adrienne, and wasn't that the point of living in Hawaii? I threw on my pink bikini and some shorts and grabbed some snacks, sunscreen, and a book to throw in my bag. I peeked out the window at the sunshine and bright blue skies as I ate some yogurt, eager to begin my beach day. I trotted out to the car and then immediately stopped.

"Son of a bitch!" I cursed when I saw the flat tire on my car. This was not part of my plan. I tossed my bag in the car and went to the hatch to retrieve the spare tire and tools I would need. I mentally ran through the steps my dad had taught me countless times but felt intimidated because I had never actually been required to change a flat tire. I loosened the first two lug nuts with ease.

While I was congratulating myself for my female proficiency, I began to struggle with the third lug nut. I strained to loosen it and looked around helplessly for something to do it for me. I wanted to be a strong, independent female, but in reality, I just needed help. My frustration was quickly turning into tears, and I tossed the tire iron aside and dropped my head down in defeat. Every time I felt like I was making progress with my newfound independence, I was quickly reminded that something insignificant could set me back. Who knew all it took was a flat tire to defeat me?

"Excuse me?" said a voice directly behind me, scaring the living daylights out of me. I hadn't heard the approaching footsteps and whirled around, barely registering the voice.

"Well, shit," I said before I could stop it.

Luke stood in front of me, silently shaking with laughter at my outburst. He glanced down at the tire iron and lug nuts scattered around the driveway.

"Do you need help?" he asked with concern.

"You would be here," I muttered under my breath.

"What's that?" he asked.

"Just surprised to see you." I plastered a polite smile on my face. "Small world."

"Small island." He smiled back.

"Why are you here?" My bluntness sounded so rude to my own ears, and I chastised myself. The guy must have thought I was nuts. Why he ever wanted my phone number was beyond me.

"Um, I heard you might have a rental available?"

I felt the blood drain from my face. There was *no way* I could have this beautiful specimen living fifty feet from my door and even remotely function in day-to-day life. I made a fool of myself every time I saw him!

"Uh, ya," I stammered, trying to find the words. On one hand, it would be incredibly rude to deny him the chance to even see the cottage. Plus, he was an acquaintance now, whether I liked it or not (I mostly liked it), and I would probably feel safer having him live next door rather than some of the people I had shown the rental to the day before.

I realized I was staring blankly at him and glanced back toward the cottage. "It's back there," I said, gesturing with my hand.

"How about I help you with this first?" He bent down to pick up the tire iron.

"Oh, that's not necessary," I said. This could not be happening. Maybe it was a small island, but what were the chances that I would forever be running into this man?

"I think it is," he said with a sympathetic smile and went to work. He popped the troublesome lug nut off with no effort at all.

"Good thing I loosened for you," I joked.

He burst out laughing as he got the remaining lug nuts off. He had the flat tire off and the spare on so quickly that I didn't even have an opportunity to make small talk.

"Thanks a lot," I said. "I do appreciate it."

"Not a problem at all." He stood up, dusting his hands off.

"Okay, so the rental is back here," I said, walking down the driveway. He followed me and looked around the yard.

"You have a lot of fruit trees," Luke commented.

"Yes, and it's very overwhelming for someone who lived in Chicago her whole life," I said.

"My sister lives there," he said.

"Is that why you were coming from there?" I asked.

"Yeah, she just got engaged, so I went for her celebration dinner," I said.

"Is that where you're from?" I asked. I hoped he wasn't bothered by my questions, but obviously we were going to keep crossing paths, so I might as well get to know him more.

"I'm from all over," he said. "But I've been here since I was ten, except for a short time when I lived in St. Louis with my family. Dad was Air Force," he explained. "I ended up moving back here and living with Cody's family."

"Oh, wow," I said, eyes wide. "You parents just let you move back here at such a young age?" Oh my God, where was my filter? "Not that I'm judging or anything," I stammered.

"No worries, I get it. Now that I'm older, I'm actually really surprised they ever agreed to it. But this place can just swallow you whole, and I wasn't the same after we moved back to the mainland."

I nodded thoughtfully. I had been here only a month, and I could understand what he was saying. The sway of the palm trees in the warm breeze, the smell of the ocean air and exotic chirping birds had me convinced. I didn't anticipate wanting to leave this island anytime soon. I wasn't sure if I would stay here forever, but for now, this was my home.

We reached the cottage, and I decided to stop interrogating him for the time being. I opened the door and stood aside so he could enter and take a look. He wasn't in there long before he came back out and said, "How much?"

I told him the number Adrienne suggested and saw his face fall.

"That's a bit out of my budget," he said, crestfallen. "But thanks for taking the time to show me."

"Wait a minute," I said. I was intending on returning to work eventually, and I still had some of my savings and inheritance. There wasn't a magic number that I was required to get from this rental. I looked at it more as a supplement to my income to help offset the high cost of living in Hawaii. "Maybe we can work something out."

I knew I shouldn't have, but I was just overcome with an urge to bring that smile back to his face. Even though I felt the need to avoid him for my own sanity, I couldn't let him leave.

"Yeah?" he asked, perking up again. "What did you have in mind?"

I instantly blushed as my mind traveled straight to the

gutter. I was hoping he didn't notice.

"Yardwork?" I blurted out, trying to think of something, *anything*, to make him take it.

"You mean trade services for a reduction in rent?" he asked hopefully.

"Sure, that sounds good," I said. "I need help with the yardwork. I just don't know what to do with it all, especially the fruit trees."

"There's one thing you should know, though," he said. "This is only temporary. I just need a place for about six months while my house is being renovated."

I felt slightly bummed knowing it would be temporary, but maybe that was for the best. It would help me get on my feet more with the yardwork and having that extra income. I felt myself warming up to the idea of him living there. Maybe it wouldn't be so bad after all. I struggled against my growing attraction and tried convincing myself that this was simply a business transaction.

Within two minutes, we settled on a price, and the arrangement was made.

"When will you be moving in?" I asked.

"Probably next week, but I'll let you know for sure what day."

"Okay," I said, nodding. There wasn't much more to be said, but I was stalling, wanting him to stick around. He was easy to talk to, and his smile was disarming, but he made me so nervous.

"So, do you think I can have your phone number now?" he asked with a sideways smile and teasing eyes. "Purely for business reasons."

I sensed a touch of sarcasm with that last part.

I bit back a smile and nodded as I recited my phone number, and he entered it in his phone. Immediately, my phone dinged with a text notification.

Hey landlord

I laughed aloud and shook my head at him.

"You know," he started, "since you're cutting me such a deal on rent, maybe we can throw in some more surf lessons. If you're interested, that is."

"Yes!" I exclaimed. So much for playing it cool. "I had so much fun, and I thought about maybe doing some more lessons, but I wasn't sure."

"All right," he said, starting to walk back up the driveway. He turned back with that charming smile accompanied by a wink. "I'll call you."

As soon as he turned away I gritted my teeth. That *wink*. It was killer. I watched him walk away before I headed back to my car and finally made my way to the beach. I spent an hour soaking up the sun and reliving my encounter with Luke. I still couldn't believe the way everything had unfolded, from the way he stepped in and changed my flat tire to making arrangements for him to live there. I thought leaving everything behind and moving to Hawaii was going to be the biggest challenge in front of me, but this charming surf instructor and now my tenant, was going to test that challenge.

In the end, I decided that while I might not have been in the right place for a relationship right then, it wouldn't hurt to have some eye candy in my life.

Chapter 17

Luke

I hadn't been to Adrienne's house in years, so I drove slowly down the block until I recognized the plantation-style house. I waved to Adrienne's grandmother, who was sitting on her porch swing and began looking for the blue house Grant had told me about. I was hoping it was okay to stop by since I hadn't had the opportunity to talk to Adrienne to get the facts. I was afraid I would miss out on this rental if I didn't jump on it immediately, but I hated going in with no information.

I walked down the driveway and saw a silver SUV in the driveway and hoped the owner was home. Then I saw a flash of hot pink and heard a loud clanging as a tire iron bounced off the ground. I sucked in a sharp breath when I saw the familiar floral tattoo. I had spent a lot of time staring at that tattoo on Quinn's lower back when I was instructing her on how to surf. I wasn't sure what I had done to deserve God smiling down on me, but I wasn't about to question it. This was going to be good.

"Excuse me?" I didn't want to scare her, but she apparently had not heard me approach, and I was glad she no longer held the offending tire iron.

"Well, shit," she said.

That wasn't really the reaction I was hoping for, but I had

also begun to enjoy Quinn's bluntness when she was caught off guard. I was quite amused, but I could tell by her flushed cheeks and wet eyes that she was on the verge of losing it.

I insisted on helping her, even though I was still a little fearful about her picking up that tire iron. I could tell it wasn't easy for her to accept my help, but I disregarded that and took charge, sensing she needed me to, even if she never would admit it.

I nearly forgot why I had even gone there until she bluntly demanded to know why I was standing on her driveway. Her feistiness was rather amusing, and with that pink bikini on, she was a sight to behold. She kept blushing, and I studied her curiously, wondering if she felt the same pull I was feeling. She seemed to be really uncomfortable around me, but you can't keep running into the same person as we continued to do and not feel some sort of a connection.

After I got the flat tire off, I looked over and completely caught her looking my body up and down. She quickly looked away, but I had already seen the look in her eyes. Yeah, she was definitely interested.

I finished up the job as she continued to thank me.

"Okay, so the rental is back here," she said, walking down the driveway. I followed her and relished watching the gentle sway of her hips. That tattoo was going to be the death of me, and the way that hot pink bikini fit in all the right places? Heaven.

I commented on all the fruit trees, attempting to make small talk as we walked. She mentioned growing up in Chicago, which I zeroed in on as a talking point, telling her about Mia living there.

"Is that why you were coming from there?" she asked.

"Yeah, she just got engaged, so I went for her celebration dinner," I said.

"Is that where you're from?" she asked.

I considered twenty questions a promising sign that she was interested in getting to know me more, so I freely told her about my military childhood. It never bothered me to talk to people about my life. I suppose I was used to it after the years I spent in the spotlight.

We reached the cottage, and she allowed me to go in and check it out on my own. It could've been a cardboard box and I would've taken it if it meant being near her. It was going to take a lot more than a polite refusal to get me to give up. However, I was actually pleased with the cottage. It was a lot smaller than my house, but it sure beat sleeping on someone's couch for six months. It looked freshly painted and had a quaint feel to it.

"How much?" I asked.

Her response deflated me like a balloon. There was no way I could afford it with the renovations. Maybe I could cut something out? My mind scrambled to find a solution, knowing there had to be a way to make this work.

"That's a bit out of my budget," I said. "But thanks for taking the time to show me." I thought I could go home and run over the numbers again and see if there was a way I could make it happen.

"Wait a minute," she said quickly. "Maybe we can work something out."

I couldn't read her in that moment, but I was instantly filled with hope. Why would she care if I could afford it when she was most likely fielding unlimited requests for a place like this? I liked that she blushed after suggesting it, and my mind instantly went into the gutter, wondering what she was thinking.

I nearly laughed when she suggested yardwork. She was making this too easy on me. Cody and I did enough yardwork in our off times that adding one more yard to our roster wouldn't even faze me. I'd clean her toilets if it meant living here.

I was, however, worried that only needing it short term was going to be a deal breaker for her, but she didn't seem to mind.

We quickly settled on a price, and the arrangement was made.

After we discussed when I would move in, I stood there awkwardly, wondering if she would reject my advances again. Other than that, I couldn't come up with a legitimate reason to stay.

"So, do you think I can have your phone number now?" I asked, not being able to resist teasing her a little. "Purely for business reasons."

The moment she bit her lip in an attempt not to smile, I knew. She liked me too. But she was obviously not going to admit it. Challenge accepted. She gave me her number, and I texted her immediately.

Hey landlord

She laughed hard, and I decided then and there that was my new favorite sound.

Another idea occurred to me, and I couldn't believe my luck when I convinced her to accept free surf lessons as an added bonus for her cutting me a deal on rent. She eagerly agreed and told me how much she enjoyed her first lesson. It was moments like these, when I caught that glimpse of excitement in her eye and she let her guard down, even if only for the briefest of moments. I was determined to knock that wall down even if I had to do it brick by brick.

I finally forced myself to walk back up the driveway, but I looked back one last time with a smile and a wink and promised to call her. The smile she returned nearly stopped me in my tracks.

Shit. I was smitten.

Chapter 18

Quinn

After Luke left, I raced next door to tell Adrienne that I had already found a tenant. I no longer felt the sense of dread that initially flooded my emotions when I first saw him. I was worried about my first, second, and now third impression I had made upon him, but I couldn't help but feel the mysterious connection with him either. I jogged up the steps and stopped short when I came to her grandmother, Malia, sitting on the porch swing.

"Hi, Auntie," I greeted her with a kiss on the cheek.

"Well, what brings that beautiful smile to your face this afternoon?" she asked me. Malia was so sweet, and I enjoyed living next door to her, even though I didn't see her nearly as often as Adrienne.

"I found a tenant for my cottage," I answered cheerfully.

"You did? Already?" Adrienne said as she stepped outside.

I laughed and nodded my head, still unable to comprehend how this had all unfolded from the first time I met him.

"It's Luke!" I exclaimed.

Adrienne's jaw dropped, and she started laughing.

"No way!"

I had confided in her after my surf lesson and told her all

about the airplane ride and then how I ran into him again. Adrienne kept joking that it was fate and that we were going to get married and have babies together, but I initially just shrugged her off.

However, this third meeting was just too much to ignore. Yes, I realized that it was a small island and the North Shore was an even smaller community, but still, that had to be some kind of sign of this being something more significant than a coincidence.

"Luke Cole?" Malia asked.

I nodded and bit my lip, trying to damper my enthusiasm in front of Adrienne's grandmother.

"Well, he's a very sweet young man," she said. "But I thought he bought a beach house with his all his prize money."

"Prize money?" I asked, confused.

Adrienne looked at me and smiled. All she had told me was that she knew Luke and had gone to high school with him and Cody, but they were older than her.

"Luke was a professional surfer," she explained.

"Not just any professional surfer," Malia huffed from her seat on the swing. "He was the best of the best. That boy was going places until that awful injury ended his career."

I was slightly amused at Malia's apparent interest in surfing, but that shouldn't have surprised me since we did live in the surf capital of the world. However, I was more interested in this new information.

"What happened?" I asked, suddenly very interested in professional surfing.

"He was on his way to win the world title, but in his final competition, he fell off a wave. It was a major closeout, and he almost died. It was terrible," Adrienne said.

"Just awful." Malia nodded in agreement. "We were there. Thought he was dead when they pulled him out of the water.

The beach was completely silent, despite all the people there. It was really eerie."

"But obviously he didn't die," I said, eager for more details. I couldn't wait to go back home and Google the shit out of this. There was a lot more to Luke Cole than I ever expected.

"No, and there was a lot of speculation about whether he was going to return to the circuit. He could've, but he was already thirty when it happened, and I think between that and his recovery, he just decided that he couldn't return," Adrienne said. "I don't really know the details because I don't know him really well, but it was the biggest gossip around town for quite a while. Everyone was sad to see him retire, but I don't think anyone blamed him after that. It was bad."

"Hmmm," I said thoughtfully.

"But doesn't he have a house?" Malia asked again, confused.

"Yeah, he is doing renovations on it," I said. "It's only for six months, but it's a good way to get me started with renting it out for now."

"Just long enough for you to fall in love," Adrienne said with a mischievous grin.

"No," I said quickly, feeling the blush on my cheeks.

"Ohhh," Malia said with a renewed interest. "It's amazing no one snatched him up. And not just cause he's famous. You should lock that down."

I bent over and laughed hard at Malia's unexpected remark. The woman was a riot to be around because you never knew what was going to come out of her mouth. We chatted for a bit longer, and I headed home with a lame excuse of needing to check my email when I actually just couldn't wait to Google Luke Cole.

The search results were endless, but near the top was an article from over two years ago with a headline about Luke Cole cheating death at Pipeline. I read the entire article even though I didn't understand some of the surf lingo about snaps, air reverses, and closeout waves, but I gasped when I reached the pictures.

There was one of him on the wave, and he looked untouchable. The next picture was when they pulled him out of the water, and I could see what Malia meant. He looked dead. I felt a chill run over me as I thought about him dying and never getting the chance to meet him.

There was a video link below and I clicked on that. I watched, horrified, for five minutes as he rode the wave and then disappeared, swallowed whole by the water. The commentators discussed how this could impact his chances at the world title, but they quickly became concerned as the jet skis raced over to his board floating on the surface. One of the lifeguards jumped off the jet ski and swam to his board and pulled on his leash until Luke resurfaced. The pictures were scary enough, but seeing the video made me tear up knowing the tragedy he experienced and how scary that must have been for everyone watching.

At the corner of the screen, you see a young woman running toward the water, and I wondered if that was a girlfriend, but then the commentators mentioned how difficult it must be for Luke's parents and sister to witness the events unfolding. The suspense was killing me just watching it, even knowing that Luke survived it.

They loaded him in the ambulance, and sirens screamed in the distance when the camera went back to the commentators' booth. They discussed the fact that Luke was breathing, though he wasn't conscious, and it appeared he had a head injury. The video ended, and I felt like it left me hanging. I clicked back to the search results and scoured all the articles and interviews I could find.

There was mention of his injuries and how badly his knee was destroyed, but fortunately the head injury only left him a nasty scar. I thought back to how his hair hung down a little lower on his forehead, and I wondered if he kept it at that length to cover his scar. Finally, I found a few interviews from after he announced his retirement. You could see a touch of sadness at the initial press conference, and I could only imagine how difficult it had to be for him to walk away from his surfing career. I also found a few of his social media accounts, but it didn't look like they were very personal and more of a professional level.

I didn't realize how long I had been hunched over my computer until my stomach began growling. I glanced up and realized it was dark outside and way past dinnertime. I heated up some soup as I contemplated all the information I had just learned. Luke seemed to be doing well, and I didn't see any obvious lingering effects of his injury or his general disposition. I was curious whether or not I would get to know him more with him living here and if we followed through with the additional surf lessons.

One thing I knew for sure was I was deeply intrigued by this man.

Chapter 19

Luke

I went home after looking at the cottage, still shaking my head at my luck. What were the chances the only available rental in town belonged to the blue-eyed beauty I had been so unsuccessful at getting out of my head? Instead of walking in my front door, I walked around back to find Cody and Grant lounging on the lanai. I sat down and accepted a beer Cody offered me from the mini fridge.

"You look like the cat that ate the bird," Grant said, eyeing me curiously.

"You guys aren't going to believe this," I began.

"Did you find the rental I was telling you about?" Grant asked.

"I found it all right," I said with a chuckle.

"What?" Grant and Cody asked impatiently in unison.

"It belongs to Quinn," I finally told them.

"Who the hell is Quinn?" Grant asked, confused.

"That's the chick he stole from me!" Cody said, reaching out to smack me with his hand.

"I had first dibs," I said, defending myself.

"Wait, this is the girl you met on the airplane?" Grant asked for clarification.

"Yes," I said, giving Cody a pointed stare. "I met her on the *plane*, and we hit it off."

"You cuddled with her and held her hand!" Cody practically shouted, slapping his leg as he laughed.

"That's not exactly how it happened, but anyway," I said, turning back to Grant. "Then Cody met her the coffee shop, not realizing I had already met her. He convinced her to do a surf lesson, and when she showed up and I saw her, Cody gave up his claim, since I met her first."

"So, let me get this straight," Grant said, leaning back in his chair. "You show up at her house today, wanting to rent her cottage, but having no idea that it was going to be her?"

"Bingo," I said, taking a big gulp of my beer.

"Man, you so owe him," Grant said, shaking his head.

"He already owes me so bad!" Cody exclaimed.

"I mean, what are the chances?" I asked no one in particular.

"He's already in love," Cody said in a low voice.

"Hey, not everybody wants to whore around!" I said to Cody.

"Don't hate the playa, hate the game." Cody couldn't even finish his statement with a straight face. I chucked my bottle cap at him and laughed.

"Five bucks says they're married this time next year," Cody said, looking at Grant.

"Fucking destiny," Grant said, shaking his head. I knew they were yanking my chain. "Well, wait a minute, is she even interested in you?" Grant asked.

I didn't answer right away. No one could deny there was a connection between us. But I also knew based on the scarce information I had on her that she had been through an awful lot. The guys and I could joke about her carrying my babies, but I had a sinking feeling convincing her to date me wasn't going to be easy.

"I don't really know," I said, serious for a moment. "But I'm hoping I can convince her." Then I looked back to Grant.

"She lives next door to Adrienne. Do you think they're friends? Maybe you can talk to Adrienne?"

"Are we in high school?" Cody cackled.

Grant snorted. "I can barely get Adrienne to say two words to me." He said it casually, but his face wore the regret. Adrienne and Grant had become friends in high school, but she was only a freshman when he graduated. They remained friends, but he worked a lot for his father's company, so they didn't see each other much. Once she graduated, she moved to Honolulu to attend the University of Manoa, and no one saw her much.

Then one weekend they both ended up at a party on the North Shore and reconnected. Grant wanted to date, but she wasn't interested at first, since she was busy with college and trying to get her business degree. I don't know exactly what happened, but he was on the verge of convincing her to give him a chance when she caught at a party in a hammock, fooling around with another girl. She'd barely spoken a word to him since.

"Cuz you couldn't keep it in your pants!" Cody said.

"Like you can talk," Grant shot back.

"I don't have anybody to answer to," Cody said defiantly.

He said it like it was a good thing, but Cody himself had been burned by love. He'd had a serious girlfriend, Carrie, and wanted to marry her after they graduated, but they had different expectations. She wasn't happy that he was pursuing surfing as a career rather than going with her to college in California. They did the long-distance thing for a year, and Cody was starting to get discouraged because he hadn't qualified for the championship tour yet.

He was participating in an event in California and drove down to her college to surprise her. Instead, he was the one surprised when he discovered she had an entirely different life than she had told him about, complete with a college boyfriend. Ever since then, he'd swore off love and had taken it upon himself to be the North Shore Playboy. He played it off like he loved the bachelor life, but I knew him well enough to know that Carrie completely broke his heart, and he didn't want to trust anyone with it ever again.

"Girls," I warned them sarcastically.

"We *sound* like a bunch of girls sitting around talking about Luke's love life," Grant muttered.

"Yeah," I agreed. "Hand me another beer."

We changed the subject slightly and discussed my house renovations. Grant said the sooner I moved out, the sooner he could get started. With me out of the way, he could start the demolition while he waited for the supply delivery. Cody was going to work for him whenever he could fit it in to earn the extra money. Cody had worked for Grant's dad on and off over the years between pursuing his surfing career, and then again when he was trying to come up with the money to start his surf school, or rather, our surf school. I felt good knowing these two were going to be at the helm of my home project.

But moving meant I had to figure out where I was going to store all my stuff. I could take some of it to the cottage, but not much was going to fit in there. Nothing like having to move, only to move back again. Cody and Grant offered up their garage, and we figured between the two places, I could make it work. I stayed until the sun set, but then I went home and eagerly started packing. I debated about calling Quinn but thought maybe she would feel less threatened by a text.

Hey landlord. Can I move in this weekend?

Her response was almost immediate.

Hey, sure. Stop by on Friday and I can give you the keys and have you sign the lease agreement.

I decided to go bold. *How about I give you another surf lesson on Friday and you can bring the keys with you then?*

Her response took forever, and I impatiently stared at my phone, waiting for her answer.

Okay. What time?

8?

Okay, see you then.

I wasn't going to get much out of her tonight like I was hoping. I didn't let that get me down, though, and instead sorted through my belongings to decide what I could live without for the next six months. I found myself smiling multiple times throughout the evening and anxiously looking forward to Friday.

The rest of my week went quickly as I continued packing and began moving boxes and furniture to Cody and Grant's garage. It was also a busy week for lessons, and I was exhausted by Friday. I momentarily forgot about Quinn's lesson when I woke up on Friday morning, still beat from the effects of my busy week. As soon as I remembered what I had that morning, I jumped out of bed with a burst of energy.

Cody and I walked out of our houses at the same time, and he waved.

"Morning, lover boy," he called out.

"What's up, douche bag?" I replied with nothing but love.

"How come you look so cheerful?" he asked.

"I have a lesson with Quinn," I replied with a smile.

"Of course you do. I swear, that's the only time I see that goofy grin on your face. How'd you manage that so fast?"

"She's going to bring me the keys so I can move in this weekend, and I convinced her to do a lesson."

He just shook his head in disbelief as he smiled at me. We both climbed in our trucks and headed to the beach. Some days we carpooled, but we generally ran different schedules, so it was easier to drive separately.

We had just finished setting up when Quinn pulled up. She looked nervous, but I smiled brightly at her, attempting to put her at ease. We paddled out and took a shot at the first wave, but she lost her balance right away and fell in. She was sputtering when she surfaced and looked annoyed.

"It's all right," I said reassuringly. "We'll just try again."

However, this continued for the next several waves. She just couldn't seem to stabilize herself, and she grew increasingly frustrated. She had done so well on her first lesson that I think her expectations were too high, and she was just being too hard on herself.

Finally, as we were sitting side by side, I reached out and patted her leg.

"Don't let it get you down," I said. "Some days are just like that. Just promise me that you'll keep trying." I looked her square in the eye as I said it, attempting to get the message across. I was really hoping she wasn't ready to throw in the towel on surfing because I really wanted to spend as much time with her as possible. Plus, I saw how much she enjoyed her first lesson, and I would have done anything to put that smile on her face again.

Fortunately, she ended up catching a few waves toward the end of our session, and that seemed to satisfy her. She looked exhausted as we began paddling in, so I towed her rest of the way to shore.

"How was it?" Cody asked, meeting us at the water to help bring in Quinn's board.

"Eh." She shrugged and let out a disgruntled sound.

"Hang in there," Cody said. "Everybody has bad sessions, even us." I was hoping Cody's encouragement would reach her. "Don't give up."

"Yeah, we'll try again, okay?" I said, hoping she wouldn't say forget it.

"Okay," she said with a small smile. We walked to her car, and she gave me the keys and I signed the six-month lease for the cottage. That seemed to perk her up, and I wondered if she was more excited about me moving in than she was letting on.

"So, I'll see you on Saturday?" I said. I couldn't wait to live that close to her and felt hopeful I could convince her to go on a date. This girl had gotten beneath my skin so quickly, and I knew the feelings weren't just going to fade away.

Chapter 20

Quinn

I lay awake on Saturday morning with nothing motivating me to get out of bed. I was somewhat anxious and excited about Luke moving in today, but I wasn't even sure if I would see him. Just because he was living on my property didn't mean I would see him all the time. My best bet to spend time with him was to continue with the surf lessons, but I seriously wanted to hide under a rock after my last one.

I was initially looking forward to it, but then I had a horrible night, tossing and turning and reliving my parents' death, my heartbreak from Aaron, and still feeling unsettled in my new home. Everybody told me time heals all wounds, but I felt like my memories were drowning me. One day I could nearly make it all day without thinking about it, but then the next day it would hit me like a tsunami, and I could hardly function.

I had been living in Hawaii for about six weeks, but I didn't really feel ready to call it home. Yet Chicago didn't feel like home anymore, either. I felt so displaced. My friendship with Adrienne had quickly blossomed, but besides talking to her and Grandma Malia, I didn't interact a whole lot with other human beings. I just felt so... lonely.

I'd had lived a busy, fulfilling life in Chicago, and suddenly not being surrounded by all those people I loved was nothing short of devastating. I considered therapy, but what was anyone going to say that I didn't already know? I was trying to give myself time to grieve, but maybe five months was long enough. Maybe I needed to pull up my freaking big-girl panties. I had to find something to keep myself busy.

I knew I should look for some sort of work, but I wasn't ready for that yet. I didn't feel like I could be the best version of myself and take pride in my work until I was in a better frame of mind. This was exactly why I'd rejected Luke's first request for my phone number. I was a mess, and once he got to know the real me, he would be running for the hills.

Would I ever experience being normal again, or was I letting grief redefine me? It certainly affected my surf lesson. I should've called and canceled that morning, but I thought seeing Luke would cheer me up as well as further my determination to stay busy.

However, being with him again made me nervous, and I was exhausted from my sleepless night and couldn't concentrate. I felt so embarrassed as I fell off wave after wave, especially now that I knew what an experienced surfer he was. And yet he was so sweet, he continued to encourage me, and that gave me enough confidence that I was finally able to catch a few waves and a little redemption.

Cody was just as kind when we got to shore. My gut told me that these two guys would be nothing but loyal, wonderful friends to have in my life and help with my healing. Except I wasn't entirely sure how I could just be friends with Luke. The chemistry between us was undeniable, and I could hardly handle being near him without wanting to jump his bones, but I constantly reminded myself that it was a bad idea. If Aaron was so quick to discard me, after all the time we spent together and the love I thought we shared, maybe I didn't have anything to offer. Especially now that I was so broken.

I finally sighed and rolled out of my bed of self-pity. That was going to get me nowhere fast.

I savored my morning coffee on the lanai, all the while trying to convince myself that I wasn't out there waiting for Luke to arrive, which was stupid, because I totally was. After an hour or so, I grew bored of waiting and went inside to half-heartedly clean.

In Chicago, I struggled to find the time to clean, even though our simple condo wasn't difficult to keep tidy. Here, I discovered that the dust would accumulate quicker, and the mud could be a challenge since it rained nearly every day. But with a serious lack of a social life, I had no problem keeping on top of it.

Every couple of minutes, I would find an excuse to walk by the window and peer down to the cottage. Luke had no reason to check in with me, but I was secretly hoping he would. Finally, around ten a.m., I saw his truck pull down the driveway, loaded with furniture and boxes. I considered going to offer my help, but he had Cody and some other guy with him. I decided I couldn't stand by the window all day, so I texted Adrienne to see if she wanted to do anything.

Almost as soon as my text went through, my phone rang.

"Hey, I'm helping my grandma with her church, so I'm not available until later this evening," she said.

"Oh, no problem," I said, trying to hide the disappointment in my voice. I really needed a distraction today.

"Of course, you're welcome to join us, but I doubt you want to spend your Saturday picking up trash on the beach," she said.

"Yes! Okay!" I said entirely too quickly, which made Adrienne laugh.

"Okay, well, great!" she said. "We were just ready to walk out the door, though. How soon can you be ready?" I glanced down at my tank top and jean shorts.

"I'm good to go! I'll meet you next door." I grabbed my wallet and water bottle and headed next door.

"Oh, Quinn, it's so sweet of you to help us," Malia said sincerely, wrapping me in her arms. Malia gave the best hugs, and I relished her touch.

"No problem. I don't mind helping out," I said, and I meant it.

It was saddening to see the amount of trash on the beach. Some was from tourists or beachgoers who were careless or didn't notice what they left behind, but there was also an alarming amount of plastic and fishing nets that washed up from sea. It was back-breaking work, and my legs burned from walking in the sand, but it was rewarding to see the bags full of trash we were accumulating. I was impressed at the number of people who chose to spend their Saturday giving back to the community. Even though we were technically working, it still felt rewarding to do it with the sun shining and the smell of the salty air.

What I hadn't realized was that Malia went to the same church as my parents. I was curious how I never knew this but also satisfied that my parents would be proud. After we loaded all the trash bags in a few pickup trucks, a woman approached me.

"Quinn?" she asked a bit hesitantly.

"Yes?" I said. We hadn't been introduced when we arrived, so I wasn't sure how she knew my name.

"I thought so," she said with a kind smile. "You are the splitting image of your mother."

I sucked in a sharp breath and fought the tears surfacing.

"I don't mean to upset you," she hurried to explain, "but I just wanted to tell you that in the short amount of time I knew your mother, she really made an impact on our community. I'm so terribly sorry for your loss."

"Thank you," I said sincerely with a wobbly smile. "That means a lot to me."

She patted my shoulder and then turned away. Adrienne had witnessed the exchange and walked over and slipped her arm around my waist. I gratefully accepted her gesture and leaned into her hug.

"Will it ever get easier?" I barely whispered.

"It will," she said, staring out at the ocean. "I promise."

We stood that way for a few minutes, and then she stepped away, and I slowly let out the breath I hadn't realized I was holding.

"You know what will make you feel better?" she asked.

"What?" I asked.

"Chocolate chip cookies," she said confidently.

I had to laugh at her suggestion. My mom always did the same thing to cheer me up. Maybe chocolate didn't heal, but it certainly wasn't going to hurt.

We grabbed sandwiches from one of the food trucks and headed home. Malia was ready for a nap after walking the beach, so Adrienne and I escaped to my house and began baking.

"So, Luke moved in today?" she asked, licking a spoonful of cookie dough.

"Maybe," I said innocently.

"Have you talked to him?" she asked.

"Nope," I said, shoving a spoonful of dough in my mouth to avoid saying anything else.

"It's okay if you like him, you know," Adrienne said. "And from what you've said, it sounds like he likes you too. Why wouldn't you give him your number again?"

I tried pointing at my unladylike mouthful as an excuse not to answer her, but she wasn't buying it. Instead she handed me a glass of milk and impatiently eyed me with her hand on her hip.

"It's just too soon," I said, feeling my excuse fall flat.

"I'm not buying that," she said. "Who cares if you were in a long relationship? Aaron doesn't deserve to hold this power over you even after you've split up."

I had confided in her over the phone shortly after my parents died when we were discussing some of the logistics. She didn't know everything, but she knew enough to know I had been burned.

"I'm not trying to give him power," I said defensively.

"Yes, you are," she argued. "I understand he hurt you, and you will always carry that with you. It may have felt like terrible timing, but maybe it was the best timing possible."

I eyed her suspiciously, trying to figure out where she was going with this.

"Think about it," she said. "If he had waited, then he wouldn't have wanted to break up with you while you were dealing with your parents. Or maybe he would have anyway, since he sounds like a first-class asshole," she said thoughtfully. "Anyway, what if he had stayed with you longer, but it was just delaying the inevitable and just wasting your time?"

"I never thought about it like that," I admitted.

"So, allow yourself some happiness!" she exclaimed. "You have been through enough. What if all this tragedy brings you something beautiful? What if you and Luke are soulmates?"

"Now you're just jumping the gun," I said sarcastically. "I barely even know him."

She gave me another pointed look.

"You can only run into the same guy so many times until you are forced to admit it's hopena."

"Say what?" I asked, confused.

"Hopena," she repeated. "Destiny."

I liked the way the Hawaiian word rolled off her tongue.

"I don't know," I said, still doubtful. "I can't jump into anything too fast. And what if he just wants a quick lay?"

"Girl, would that really be the worst thing in the world?" she asked, laughing.

I shrugged and smirked as I thought over her words. It really wouldn't be.

"You still have needs," she pointed out.

I felt my face heat at the thought of being intimate with Luke and the hundred different scenarios I could envision.

"Not while he's living in my cottage, though," I said quickly.

"Why not?" she asked, scrunching up her face like I was crazy.

I laughed. Adrienne always came across so sweet and innocent, so seeing the dirty side of her mind was rather amusing.

"Isn't that like a conflict of interest?" I asked.

"More like convenient," she corrected me.

I laughed again, and then she finally changed the subject, much to my relief. As she placed the cookies in containers, she stopped and looked at the large amount we had.

"You know we're never going to eat all these," she said, staring at the dozens laid out on the counter.

"Don't challenge me," I said, joking. Well, half joking.

"You know," she said, looking at me with a half-smile. "You should take some of these down to Luke and welcome him. Officially and all."

I shook my head, but I could tell she was serious.

"Really? You don't think that's too forward?"

"Not at all," she said. "And it's a great way to break up some of this sexual tension between you two."

"True," I said, not denying the sexual tension.

"Maybe you could eat them off his rock-hard body," she said, looking up at the ceiling dreamily.

I laughed hard and threw a cookie at her.

"Oh, stop!" I said. "If you like him so much maybe you should go for him!"

"Nah, he's not really my type," she said.

"Who is your type?" I wanted to know. "And why are you still single? I can't believe you are with how sweet and beautiful you are!"

"Oh, pfft," she said, giggling. "The North Shore is kind of like Never Never Land. There are a lot of guys, but most of them don't want to grow up. They want to play all day—surfing, fishing, or riding dirt bikes. They aren't looking to settle down and build a life. And they certainly can't commit." Her last sentence had a bitter edge to it.

"All right, who broke your heart?" I asked curiously.

"That's a story for a different day," she said, sealing up the containers and thrusting one at me. "Now go sweeten up that man!"

"You wanna go with me?" I asked hopefully.

"Nope, that's all you!" she said. "Besides, I need to get home to Grandma and make sure she took her evening meds."

I nodded, having momentarily forgotten how much Adrienne helped care for her grandma.

I walked down the driveway, clutching the container of cookies as I tried to work up my courage. I knocked on the door, which felt odd, since I had just spent so many hours in the quaint little cottage preparing it to be occupied.

Luke pulled open the door and seemed pleasantly surprised to see me.

"Hey!" he said. "Come in!"

I stepped in but was startled to see the cramped quarters filled with people. Cody was the only other one I recognized, and he stood up to give me a hug. I gave a friendly smile and wave to the two girls and another guy, who I had seen earlier when they arrived with the truckload.

"Um, I should've brought more cookies," I joked, holding up the container to Luke.

"Hey, awesome!" he said, immediately opening them. "No way! They're still warm!" he exclaimed, eyes wide.

"Give those to me!" Cody demanded, reaching out for it. He snatched one and then passed the container around.

"That was so sweet of you," Luke said.

He looked so good, even after a day of hauling around furniture and boxes. Pizza boxes were stacked on the table, and I glanced around, pleased to see his belongings there. I glanced back at the two girls, wondering who they were.

"I'm Quinn," I said, waving to them again.

"Oh, sorry!" Luke said around a mouthful of cookie. "This is Grant, Megan, and Elicia." He pointed to each of them, and they responded with a wave.

"Looks good in here," I said, glancing around again.

"It will after I get everything unpacked," he said, gesturing to the stack of boxes in the corner.

"You're on your own with that," Grant said. "You can play house. I was just here for the muscle. And free pizza and beer."

Grant was good looking as well, but in a more rugged way. He had dark-brown hair and a full beard. Gotta love a good beard on a man. Between all the eye candy in the room, I envied the girls. I just couldn't figure out who they were to these men.

"Well, I'll let you get back to it," I said, moving back toward the door.

Luke looked like he wanted to ask me to stay longer, but then Cody stood up.

"Yep, I'm gonna call it a day," he said. "I have an early morning, as do you," he said, pointing at Luke.

"And I get to start demo on your shithole house," Grant said, looking at Luke.

"Hey now, it's not a shithole," Luke said defensively.

"It won't be when I'm done with it," Grant said cockily.

"Okay, that's our cue," Megan said, and the girls stood up as well. I was secretly glad they weren't sticking around.

"Thanks for the help, everyone!" Luke called out as we all exited the cottage. Then he looked at me. "And you're welcome anytime, especially when you bring cookies." He winked at me before he shut the door.

I was glad it was beginning to darken outside and was hoping he couldn't see me blush. Our encounter was brief, but I was glad I'd listened to Adrienne. I considered her other suggestions but shook my head at the thought of approaching Luke so boldly for the sake of sex. I had zero experience when it came to that—not the sex, but the no-strings-attached method.

I was definitely behind the times.

Chapter 21

Luke

After everyone left, I considered chasing after Quinn. It sounded like a good idea, but I couldn't come up with any legitimate excuses besides she forgot a kiss. I was sure that wouldn't have gone over well. Things I did today: Moved in to my new place and tried making out with my landlord on the same day. Smooth.

No, I would only succeed in spooking her if I did that. My gut kept telling me that I needed to take this slow and be patient. You couldn't go through the world of hurt Quinn experienced and not come out unscathed. I felt like there was a glimmer of herself beneath all the pain, but I needed to slowly help chip that pain away. Very slowly. It seemed that God or fate or whatever was so determined we were going to be in the same place at the same time, not to mention the pull I felt to her.

I had never experienced an instant attraction so strongly before, and I struggled knowing how to deal with it. I didn't want to come on too strong, but I had to think she felt it too. I had this intense need to pull her close and protect her from everything else the world dared to throw out at her. But I had also seen enough to know that she was strong, and she would make it through this with or without me. I just hoped it would be with me.

My thoughts were interrupted by my phone alerting me to a FaceTime call. I was pleased to see it was Mia. I hadn't talked to her nearly enough since my trip to Chicago. I grabbed a couple more cookies and poured a glass of milk as I settled in for the call with my little sister.

"Hey, I want one!" she said when she saw my cookies.

"Nope, I'm not sharing!" I said, laughing with my mouth full. "They are amazing!"

"Where did you get them from?" she asked, knowing I couldn't bake anything.

"Quinn. My landlord." I hadn't told Mia much about my current living situation besides a few texts telling her I was going to start renovations and had to find a place to stay.

"And she brought you cookies? Must be some landlord!" she said.

"I kinda knew her before this," I admitted, knowing I was going to be opening a can of worms.

"Oh, so there's more to this story? What are you not telling me?" She leaned forward and peered into the phone as if willing me to spill my guts. I debated how much I wanted to tell her, but then I realized that was pretty stupid because Mia could read me like a book. Even with our age gap, we had always been close, especially these last few years. I don't think I would've ever gotten through the fallout of my injury without her support.

"Fine, I'll tell you," I said, dusting cookie crumbs from the corners of my mouth. I started from the beginning on the plane ride, the chance encounter for the surf lesson, and then the cottage.

Mia stared at me with her mouth gaping open. It wasn't very often my sister was rendered speechless.

"Marry her!" she demanded.

"Uh, I met her like six weeks ago," I said, stating the obvious.

"Luke, you can't make this shit up! You don't have chance encounters with a beautiful woman three damn times and not fall madly in love. It's like a freaking Hallmark movie!"

"It's not that easy," I said.

I didn't want to betray Quinn's privacy, and truthfully, I didn't really know that much about her situation besides her parents dying and going through a bad breakup like she said. But I could just sense the intense sadness that seemingly consumed her. I'll admit I felt like I was going into this blindly. I needed to know more about her before I knew how to make her fall in love with me.

"How so? You're *Luke Cole*. Women fall at your feet," Mia said. She loved to tease me about all the surf groupies I had accumulated over the years. It didn't hurt the ego, knowing all those women wanted to sleep with me, but rarely did I ever take advantage of it. I didn't want a woman throwing herself at me. I wanted someone I could be myself with. Just me, not Luke Cole, professional surfer.

"Ha-ha, you're so funny," I said dryly. "No, seriously, she's been through a lot. Her parents died in a plane crash and she went through a breakup, and that's how she ended up here. Her parents owned the house she's living in, and that's where the cottage is."

"Aww, so that's why she was so afraid to fly," Mia said sympathetically. She always had a kind heart and hated it when people were hurting, even if it was a stranger. "But Luke, it's like destiny. All those things happened to bring her to you."

"That's what I keep hearing," I muttered. "But get this, she moved here from Chicago."

"Oh my God, are you serious?" she exclaimed. "What's her whole name?"

"Quinn Olson," I said.

"Man, I know Chicago is a big city, but wouldn't it be funny if I had known her too? Then it would really be destiny!" Mia was so animated when she talked, and she was shaking her phone, nearly making me sick.

"Calm down there, killer," I said, laughing. "I literally just moved in today. I've only given her two surf lessons, but I'm hoping she'll continue doing them so I can spend more time getting to know her."

"You better keep me informed!" she said. "I can't believe you didn't tell me about her sooner."

"You sure are bossy for a little shit," I remarked.

"I'm little, but I'm loud!" Mia reminded me.

We talked for an hour, and it was nice to catch up. She filled me in on her wedding plans and how excited she was for her fall wedding. I described the renovations I was planning, though it was hard for her to envision since she hadn't seen my house in person. She hadn't been to Hawaii since my injury, and I was hoping she could visit soon, but I knew she was busy with the wedding and her job as a photographer. At least she would be able to see it once it was complete, since her and Derrick were planning on spending their honeymoon in Hawaii. I couldn't wait to see her. It had been nice to see her when I went to Chicago, but she was so busy that we didn't get any quality time like I had hoped.

"All right," she said finally, yawning.

"Yeah, you better get to bed. It's late there," I said, just now considering the time difference.

"Love you, Luke," she said. "Marry her."

I laughed and told her I loved her too, and we disconnected.

It felt odd having so many people in my life aware of this connection with Quinn when nothing concrete had even happened. Had she told anyone about me? Then it struck me that she didn't really have anybody left. It sounded like she knew Adrienne, so I hoped maybe she had a friend in her. Adrienne was cool, but I didn't know her that well. If they were actually talking about me, I sure would like to be a fly on that wall.

It felt weird waking up the next morning in a new place, especially knowing I was going to be there for six months. I had unpacked some of the essentials the night before, coffee maker included. I looked out the window longingly at the little lanai and wished I had time to lounge in the chair I brought from my house as I drank my coffee. However, my morning was jam-packed with surf lessons for the first round of spring breakers, and I spent so much time in the water that day I was convinced I had salt water running through my veins.

I was grateful for the healthy cash flow, but I was beat by the time I got in my truck at the end of the day. I nearly missed my turn to Quinn's since my body was on auto-pilot and headed home. I had received a text photo from Grant midday that showed the unrecognizable pile of rubble that once was my kitchen. I definitely didn't want to go there.

I pulled into the driveway and noticed immediately the lights illuminating her lanai. My heart did a little leap in my chest at the sight of her curled up in a large patio chair with a book, and I wished I could join her rather than go down to my empty cottage. Instead I simply raised my hand in a wave when she glanced up momentarily. I wondered if this was all I should expect with living there. I didn't know how to approach things. I wanted to get to know her, but I needed to go slow.

Everyone thought Luke Cole was confident and charming, but when it came down to it, I knew nothing about relationships. I wasn't even sure what I had to offer to Quinn. I was a washed up, has-been surfer. But damn, did I want her.

I walked in my door and looked for a few moments at the stack of boxes that I should deal with. Instead I headed straight to the shower and enjoyed the hot water washing over my achy body and getting salt off my skin.

After I dressed, I once again contemplated joining Quinn

on her lanai, but finally admitted I was too tired even for that. Maybe tomorrow, I thought as I fell face down on my bed.

Chapter 22

Quinn

The weekend flew by, despite my lack of social life. On Monday morning, I woke up with the determination to go on a hike. I had to do something to work off those chocolate chip cookies before they went straight to my ass and thighs. I huffed and puffed as I climbed to the top, reminding myself that I needed to do this more.

When I got to the top, I was surprised to see there weren't many people enjoying the view. I found a large rock to sit on and gazed out at the horizon. It was nice to take a few minutes to simplify things and only focus on the beauty surrounding me.

However, that proved to be too much for my over-thinking brain, and I began to think of what I could do to speed up my healing process. I needed something to take up some time and steal my focus from my self-pity. When I was busy, I could go for hours without dwelling on the destruction of my life.

Eventually I climbed off my rock and began my descent. I counted five dogs on my way down, amazed at all the pets who seemed eager to hike. An idea began to form in my mind, and by the time I pulled back in my driveway, I'd formulated a plan. A dog was the solution to my problems. I mean, who didn't love dogs? And what a great thing to focus on. Not only would it distract me, but having the companionship would be incredible.

I took a quick shower and opted to let my hair drip-dry. I grabbed the first pair of shorts and tank top I could get my hands on and raced to the door. I didn't know why I hadn't thought of it sooner. My parents loved dogs but never felt like they should own one with the hours they put in at the diner. My mom had talked about wanting to get one after they got settled into their retirement more.

And then there was the other reason: I had always loved dogs, but Aaron never wanted animals. He said we were gone all day, and then we would have to worry about them if we traveled, so he always shut me down when I brought it up. I eventually dropped the subject completely. The good thing about being alone was you didn't have anyone telling you what you couldn't do anymore.

The anticipation of picking out my new best friend had me racing out the door to my car, so I was startled when I saw Luke walking over to drop some trash in the bin. I still wasn't used to seeing someone walking around in my driveway. The way his face brightened up when he saw me didn't go unnoticed.

"You look happy," he commented.

I felt so excited about my new mission that I wanted to tell somebody.

"I'm going to get a dog!" I told him.

"Oh, really? What kind?" he asked.

I laughed, realizing how unprepared I was for this spontaneous idea. "I'm really not sure yet. I want to visit some of the shelters and see what I can find."

"Oh, that's cool," he said. "I love dogs. We always had them growing up, but I've never actually had one of my own."

"I've never had one," I admitted.

"Really? Never?" He seemed surprised.

"It can't be that hard, right?" I asked, starting to doubt my plan.

"I'm sure you'll pick out a great one," he said, smiling reassuringly.

Another crazy, spontaneous idea sprouted in my brain, and I spoke aloud before really thinking about it.

"Do you want to go with me?" I asked. "I mean, if you aren't too busy," I said quickly.

He hesitated for a moment, and I could tell I'd caught him off guard.

"Sure!" he answered. He seemed sincere, and I thought about rescinding my offer but couldn't bring myself to do it. "Can you just give me a quick minute?"

"No problem," I said. "I'll just wait in my car." I couldn't believe I asked him to go with me. But I was also glad to have someone with me since I really didn't know what I was doing.

The first few minutes of our drive was filled with an awkward silence, and I scrambled to find something interesting to talk about. I came up empty-handed, but he spoke up first.

"So, you don't know what breed you want to look for?" he asked.

"I really don't," I said. "I do know I don't really want a tiny dog. They're too yappy," I said, wrinkling my nose. "I want a dog I can take on hikes with me."

"Maybe a lab mix or pit bull?" he suggested. "They can be high energy, but if you want one you can take with you, that might be a good fit."

"I'm a little nervous," I admitted. "It's just too quiet in that house by myself." Why was I telling him that?

"You're telling me," he said. "I like my own space the older I get, but I'm really not used to being alone all that often."

"Um, I heard you used to be a pro surfer," I said cautiously, looking sideways at him. "Did that mean you had to travel a lot?" I hoped he wouldn't be mad at me for bringing it up.

"All the time," he said, seemingly unaffected by my question. "I was only home a few months out of the year and sometimes in between, so I always stayed with Cody."

"When did you get your house?" I asked.

"After I retired from surfing," he said. "I'm assuming you heard about my injury too?"

I blushed a little and felt embarrassed, like he knew I'd googled him, but I nodded.

"I never wanted to buy a house while I was on the tour because there was no point. But once I knew my career as a professional surfer was over, there really wasn't a reason not to. I had no plans of leaving Hawaii, so I figured I might as well try to settle down permanently."

"That's cool," I said. "This is the first house I've owned, and it still doesn't really feel like mine."

He nodded but didn't say anything.

We rode in silence a little longer, but I couldn't stand it.

"So, did you like traveling?" I asked.

"At first I did, but it did grow tiresome," he said. "I loved seeing different places and surfing all over the world. That was pretty sweet."

He talked about the different places he had visited over the years and friends he made. It sounded fascinating. I went with my parents to Paris once when I turned sixteen, but otherwise I never left the country.

Talking with him helped the time fly, and before I knew it, we were approaching the animal shelter I had looked up online.

I felt like a kid in a candy store as we entered the shelter. We were greeted at the front desk and then directed to a doorway. It wasn't difficult to figure out which way to go because the excessive barking was a pretty good indication. It was overwhelming when we walked through the doors and saw the dogs all clamoring for our attention. I wanted to save them all.

Well, except for the yappy furball that I was convinced would eat me in my sleep.

I walked slowly up and down the aisles and observed each and every dog. The shelter had treat buckets outside of each cage so you could interact directly with the dogs through the kennels. There were a lot of lab and pit mixed breeds, and I kept in mind what Luke had told me earlier. I turned to talk to Luke, but he was a few cages down, enamored by whatever was in that cage. I couldn't remember which dog that was, so I backtracked to where he was kneeling in front of the kennel. It was a beautiful blue pit bull with the most adorable doggy smile.

"Looks like you found a best friend," I said, smiling.

"He looks so happy, even though he's stuck in this cage," Luke commented. He finally stood up and looked around. "Have you found one yet?"

"I think I'm going to walk around again," I said. I didn't want to hastily pick out a pet, but it was hard to narrow it down from the outside of a kennel.

"Remember they said they would get any dogs out that you want," he said.

"I have to narrow it down first," I said, slowly walking and looking back and forth. My heart went out to each and every one of those dogs just looking for their forever home.

Suddenly, I stopped in my tracks and backed up to one of the cages. A black-and-white dog was curled up in the corner, not begging for my attention. I scanned the information sheet hanging from the front of the kennel. Pit mix, female, approximately two to three years old, found as a stray.

"Hi, Penny," I said softly as I crouched down in front of her, hoping to coax her from her corner. Her tail thumped a few times as she acknowledged my presence. Her eyes looked so sad. "Do you just need someone to love you?" I asked, feeling the lump building in my throat. I could relate. "Come here," I encouraged her, patting my leg. I looked up to see Luke handing me a treat to give to Penny.

Slowly, Penny stood up and cautiously made her way to the cage, wagging her tail the whole time. She gently took the treat from my fingers and gulped it down. I figured she wasn't offered many treats if she was too shy and kept to her little corner. Hell, I didn't even notice her my first time around the shelter because there were so many dogs vocally begging me to pick them.

"I want to see her," I said, standing up. Luke and I walked out to the front desk and asked to see Penny. They led us to a small room and asked us to wait while they retrieved her. We sat silently for a minute until they opened the door and brought her in. For a second, I thought it was a different dog. She danced around on her leash, and her tail was wagging so fast I thought it might fly off. Gone were the sad eyes and shyness as she bounded over to where I sat.

I looked at Luke and laughed, not able to believe the difference.

"I think you found your dog," Luke said, laughing.

Penny was so excited to be out of her cage and with me, there was no way I was leaving the shelter without that dog. Sometimes a girl just needed someone to see past the sad exterior and love them for who they were.

I glanced shyly at Luke, grateful that he couldn't read my thoughts. We were left alone to bond with Penny, even though my decision was made from the moment she walked in that little room. She calmed down after a few minutes and sat down and leaned against my legs as I pet her in long strokes.

"I think I'm in love," I said quietly. I was so glad I'd made this a decision, and I could see how beneficial getting a dog was going to be to me. Already, I felt calm and content simply sitting and petting her. It probably didn't hurt that I had a handsome man sitting beside me either.

I let the front desk know we were ready to proceed, and they said it would take a few minutes if we wanted to wander the floor in the meantime. Luke immediately went back to the cage with the blue pit bull. The dog got excited as soon as he saw Luke approaching.

"You should get him," I said, watching them bond through the cage.

"I don't know if my landlord allows pets." He looked up at me with a sideways smile.

I shrugged, not even registering that it was ultimately up to me.

"I don't think she would care," I said.

He stood up and looked me in the eye.

"I dunno. I'm not sure if it's a good idea," he said, instantly appearing disappointed. Diesel, as the sign read, wagged his tail excitedly and tried to regain Luke's attention. "I'm gone a lot, I'm living in your cottage, and will be for six months. Just... probably a bad idea."

"The best things usually are," I remarked. Where the hell did that come from?

He looked thoughtfully at Diesel and finally relented and tried petting him through the small openings of the kennel. The woman from the front desk came back out with the application I needed to fill out for Penny.

"Are you thinking of going home with two?" she asked hopefully. "Get one for each of you!" she exclaimed.

"Um, we're not together," I said, blushing. Luke looked at me but didn't say anything.

"Oh, well, Diesel is new to the shelter," the woman explained. "But he is a favorite of ours. He's very friendly, but I have to admit he seems very partial to you," she said, looking at Luke.

Diesel started wiggling his whole body and getting really excited. He knew we were talking about him.

"He's adorable, but I'm not sure if it's the best time for me to get a dog," Luke said doubtfully.

"Well, how about you take him into the room and think about it some more?" she pressed. Before we knew it, we were back in the tight quarters of the room, waiting on another dog.

"Are you sure you're okay with this?" Luke asked me.

"Sure." I shrugged. "If it means another dog finding a good home, I don't have a problem with it. Maybe Penny and Diesel could even play together sometimes."

Maybe their owners could play together too. I blushed again at my own thoughts.

The door opened, and Diesel burst through, a ball of energy. He could hardly control his body as the entire thing wiggled. Luke laughed and pet him, urging him to calm down. Diesel looked at me momentarily but seemed to sense that Luke was the one he needed to convince. He sat at Luke's feet and rested his head on Luke's knees and stared at him with the most pitiful eyes.

"Oh!" I laughed. Diesel knew exactly what he was doing. Who could say no to that?

Luke's resolve was quickly crumbling as he stared down at Diesel and pet him. He let out a groan and finally gave in to the losing battle.

"Okay, fine, you can come home with me," he said. Diesel raised his head and stuck his tongue out. I swear he was smiling.

We spent the next half hour filling out Luke's application for adoption and going over the necessary information. I'm sure we were a sight to be seen as we walked out the door with matching grins and happy dogs. Luke seemed to forget his hesitation as he opened the back door of the truck and patted the seat for Diesel to jump in. Diesel jumped in and never looked back. Penny was a little more timid about it, and Luke finally scooped her up in his arms and settled her in the seat next to Diesel. They had sniffed each other out inside the shelter and didn't seem to mind one another.

"I think we're going to need to make a pet store stop," Luke said as he started the truck.

I laughed and agreed. "Most definitely."

We went to the pet store and loaded up on dog food, treats, dog beds and the essentials to accommodate our new furry friends. On the way home, we chatted while the dogs finally calmed down and snoozed in the back. I'd enjoyed learning about Luke on the way to the shelter, so I asked him more about his life and his childhood. He told me about his father's Air Force career and what that meant for their family, traveling from state to state and changing schools. I asked him about his sister, and his face lit up when he talked about Mia and their close relationship.

We arrived home in no time, and I was all smiles. I wanted to know everything about him but didn't want to cross the line and ask too much. He had been respectful of me and didn't press for any details, even though I peppered him endlessly with questions. I knew I would have to open up to him eventually if I wanted to continue learning about him, but for now I was content letting Adrienne be the only one to breach my walls.

Luke helped me unload all the dog purchases as I led Penny around the yard and let her sniff things out. She was still a little skittish but seemed to warm up to me and kept returning to my side.

"Thanks for going with me," I told Luke before he got back in his truck.

"Of course. I guess it worked out pretty good for Diesel," he said, gesturing to the dog, who was currently licking the window of his truck.

"Yes, it did," I said. "Well, good luck tonight!"

"Same to you," he said.

I wasn't really sure what to do next since I had never had a dog before. I let Penny in the house and allowed her to explore.

The shelter said she seemed to be housebroken, so I shouldn't expect any issues with that. I found an empty corner in my bedroom and put her bed in there. The gentle presence of a pet already made my empty house feel livelier. I moved around the house the rest of the evening, going about my business as normal, but with a black-and-white dog attached to my hip.

Once I was ready for bed, I patted the dog bed and encouraged Penny to try out her new bed. She circled around it a few times but finally settled down, and I smiled at how cute she looked curled up in her bed. I went to the bathroom and brushed my teeth and walked back to my room, ready to crash. I stopped short when I reached the doorway. The dog bed was empty, and Penny was curled up on my bed.

"Oh, you think so, do you?" I tried to look at her sternly, but I was biting my lip to keep from smiling. She looked at me so innocently, and her tail thumped a few times.

"Well, at least make room," I said, flipping back the covers and squeezing in. She moved to allow room for me, but then inched over until her head lay on my stomach. I lay stroking her fur and closed my eyes with a smile on my face.

"My lucky Penny," I murmured.

Chapter 23

Luke

As Diesel bounded from room to room in my small cottage, I began to question my decision to adopt the rascal. He wanted to explore every corner of the cottage and all my belongings and even raised his leg to mark the couch before I stopped him.

By the time I was ready for bed, Diesel probably thought I'd changed his name to "No." I was exhausted from trying to keep him in line all evening, and I was ready to crash. Thankfully, Diesel seemed to understand it was time for bed, as he curled up in his dog bed. I turned off the lights and settled underneath the covers.

I was nearly asleep when I suddenly felt a cold nose press against my cheek, and I sat up, startled. I turned on my lamp to see my crazy dog smiling at me. He slowly lifted one paw up to the bed and stared at me, daring me to tell him no. When I didn't, he jumped on the bed in one fluid motion and settled down by my feet.

I thought about demanding he get down, but I kind of liked having him up there with me.

I was awakened early the next morning by that damn cold nose again. Apparently, his nose was how he communicated. He jumped off the bed and stood in the doorway, looking back at me like he was telling me to get my lazy ass out of bed.

"Do you need to go potty?" I asked him. Diesel obviously knew that word, as he darted out of the bedroom and to the front door and turned again to make sure I was following. I decided I'd better get up before he made a mess in my cottage. He quickly did his business, and I stood against the doorway and yawned, still not quite awake.

Suddenly, Diesel took off toward Quinn's house.

"Dammit," I said as I took off after him. I was afraid he was going to run off, but then I rounded the corner of Quinn's house and saw Quinn and Penny in the front yard.

Diesel and Penny were happily greeting each other and participating in the obligatory butt sniffing. I inhaled sharply when I saw Quinn standing there in booty shorts and a tight tank top. I might've noticed she wasn't wearing a bra either. She was laughing at the dogs, but then looked embarrassed when she saw me and quickly crossed her arms.

"I guess they missed each other!" she said, the laughter still shining in her eyes.

"Apparently," I said, fighting another yawn.

"Long night?" she asked raising her eyebrow. Her gaze lingered momentarily over my bare chest.

"He slept good, but before that he was into everything," I told her.

"I'm sure it will just take some time to get him acclimated," she said. She looked fresh and bright eyed as she cupped her coffee mug, forgetting to keep her arms crossed. I noticed it was a bit chilly.

"Was Penny getting into everything too?" I asked.

She smiled a bit before she answered, and I savored the look of her ruffled hair and pajamas.

"She did pretty awesome," she said. "But she slept with me instead of in her dog bed."

Lucky dog.

"So did Diesel," I said wryly. "I think he's going to keep me on my toes," I said.

"Just give him some time," she said again.

"I know. Just not sure what I'm going to come home to today," I told her nervously. "I have lessons booked all morning and won't be home until well after lunchtime."

"I'm going to take Penny on a hike and see how she does, but I can check on Diesel when I get back if you'd like," she offered.

"That would be awesome," I said, relieved. I would certainly feel better knowing he wouldn't be unsupervised that entire time. "I'll leave it unlocked. Can you just text me when you check on him, so I know he's good?" Shit, I felt like a father leaving his child for the first time.

"Of course," she said, giving me a warm smile. I wanted to stare at that beautiful smile all morning and then pull her in my arms and kiss her senseless, but I had to get going.

"Okay, Diesel, time go home!" I said.

He stared at me like I was stupid as he rolled around in the grass playing with Penny. I patted my leg, and he jumped up and followed me. At least he listened. I got dressed and made some toast and coffee while Diesel ate. He seemed to think he was following me out the door, and I felt bad leaving him alone on his first day with a new owner. This was exactly why I didn't think I should get a dog. Hopefully he would forgive me.

On my drive to the beach, I replayed my previous day with Quinn. She'd certainly caught me off guard when she asked me to go with her to the shelter, but I jumped at the chance to spend time with her. I had hoped to get some information out of her to know her more, but she seemed determined to learn as much about me as she could. It was frustrating how little I really knew about her, but I hoped the fact that she seemed to want to know more about me was a good sign. I never expected to leave the shelter with a dog of my own either, but my resolve wavered when I sensed she wanted me to get Diesel.

When I got to the beach park, Cody already had the tent set up. I didn't even feel like I was that late, but he didn't seem to mind when I arrived. That was one of the many things I loved about Cody. He could go with the flow of pretty much everything.

"What's up?" he asked as I sat in my chair. We both had lessons booked right at eight a.m., so we were expecting our customers to show up anytime.

"I got a dog," I told him.

"No shit?" he asked, surprised. "What brought that on? Does Quinn even allow dogs in her cottage?"

I had to laugh at his questions.

"Well, I got the dog *because* of Quinn," I stated.

Cody just stared at me in disbelief. I told him how I ran into her and how not only did she ask me to go to the shelter with her, but she convinced me to get Diesel too.

"I'm telling you, man, next step is picking out baby names," he said, shaking his head.

I snorted in response.

"When are you making your move?" he asked.

"Not right now," I said. "I hardly know anything about her, and she seems to want to keep it this way. I'm hoping over the next six months I can convince her to at least go on a date with me."

"That's a long time to wait, don't you think?" he asked, glancing at me.

"I'm hoping she's worth it," I admitted. "I'm learning to be patient, but I just have a feeling about her. I can't explain it."

Right then, our customers arrived, cutting our conversation off abruptly. The next two hours flew by, and I never even had a chance to worry about Diesel, let alone look at my phone. When I finally got a brief break in between lessons, I was relieved to have a text from Quinn. She also included a picture of Diesel and Penny, posing perfectly together.

"What are you smiling at?" Cody asked as he walked up, toweling off. I turned my phone to show him the picture. "Which one is yours?" he asked. I pointed out Diesel to him. "And this one is hers?" he asked, pointing at Penny.

"Yep," I replied as I texted Quinn back to thank her for the update. She had said that it didn't appear that Diesel got into anything, and he was chewing on one of his toys when she got there.

"So let me get this straight," he said, sitting down next to me. "She's even dog sitting for you today?"

"Yeah, she offered since he was going to be home all day alone," I said.

Cody snickered and shook his head again.

"I'm telling you, baby names."

The rest of the day flew by, and I spent the majority of my time in the water giving lessons. Spring break was always one of our busiest times, and we relied on the boost for our business. It was late in the afternoon by the time I made the trek home, and I hoped Diesel hadn't destroyed the cottage and forfeited my security deposit.

What I didn't expect was to pull into the driveway to find Quinn, Adrienne, and the dogs lounging in the yard. The dogs were panting, and a tennis ball lay on the ground between them. Quinn was wearing cut-off shorts and a cropped tank top that made my heart beat a little faster. I parked my truck and walked back up the driveway to where they sat. I could handle coming home to this every day.

"I hope you don't mind that I got Diesel out to play," Quinn said as I approached.

"Not at all," I said. "I appreciate you getting him out of the house for a while.

Howzit?" I said to Adrienne.

"I'm good, thanks," she said, smiling at me.

"Did he get into anything?" I asked Quinn.

"Nope, he was very well behaved from what I saw," she said.

"Good," I said, sighing with relief. "How did Penny do with her hike?"

"Great!" Quinn exclaimed, lighting up. "I swear this dog just needed someone to give her a chance. She's so well behaved, and she seemed to enjoy the hike and greeting everyone we came across."

"Maybe I need to hike with Diesel," I said. "He could stand to burn some energy."

"Just let me know whenever you're going to have long days, and I can try to help out with him," Quinn offered.

Maybe I could win her heart over with my dog.

"Thanks, that would be awesome," I said. "I'd like to take him to the beach with me and see how he behaves there, but it's too hard to do it when I'm this busy."

"You should take Diesel up there one day to see Luke," Adrienne suggested, looking at Quinn. Quinn blushed, and I eyed Adrienne, wondering if there was something more to her suggestion.

"Yeah, that'd be sweet," I said. I hesitated for a minute, considering joining them on the grass. Then I thought about the stacks of boxes that I still hadn't dealt with. I'd intended on doing it last night, but instead I got a dog. I wanted to get everything unpacked and put away before Diesel decided to shred the cardboard boxes.

"Well, thanks so much for your help," I said as I patted my leg for Diesel to follow. "Nice to see you, Adrienne," I said.

"See you, Luke," Quinn said, smiling.

"Bye," Adrienne said with a wave.

Diesel and I walked back down to the cottage, and he watched me unpack for the rest of the evening. Apparently Quinn had worn him out enough because he didn't get into anything and just watched me curiously as I walked back and forth to put things away.

I couldn't believe how nice Quinn had been to help me out with Diesel. That girl really was confusing. It felt like she was using one hand to push me away and one hand to pull me closer. I had to remind myself that I hadn't even lived there for a week, and even though I'd met her almost two months ago, my time with her had been very limited.

Within a few hours, I had everything put away and the boxes broken down. I was happy with my progress and felt more relaxed now that was done. I needed to start working on the yard since that was part of our deal, and I didn't want Quinn to think I wasn't holding up my end. I wasn't sure how I was going to do it all this week between the back-to-back surf lessons, taking on a new dog, and unpacking.

So instead of doing anything else productive, I took Diesel out to the lanai and cracked open a beer and thought about everything I had to do.

Chapter 24

Quinn

The remainder of the week flew by, and the only time I saw Luke was as he drove down the driveway after another long day. I felt bad for him and could only imagine how exhausted he was. We had discussed postponing my weekly surf lesson since he didn't have much time in his schedule, and although I understood, I was still disappointed.

I continued to let Diesel out during the day and let him play with Penny long enough to wear him out. In the meantime, I kept busy as best as I could, but that didn't stop me from missing Luke. I didn't want to admit it, but I really liked having him around. Even on the days where I merely saw him pulling in the driveway and waved from the lanai, it was still the best part of my day.

I was grateful to have Penny and wondered why getting a dog wasn't the first thing I did when I arrived on the island. I had often heard that animals could be linked directly to healing, but now I was living proof. My shy little dog had developed quite the personality and was always cheerful. How long would she have sat in the shelter if I hadn't decided to give her a home? In reality, it felt like she was the one who adopted me. She was so well behaved on our weekly hikes, and I was ready to introduce her to something else.

It was hard not knowing her history, but I was curious if she would like the beach or if she had ever been before. That Friday afternoon, I needed something to keep me distracted. Luke was gone, Adrienne was taking her grandma to a doctor's appointment, and I was looking for something to do. I quickly threw together a beach bag, and as soon as I grabbed the leash, Penny started her happy dance. She ran out to my car and waited for me to open the door. I had just let her in when Luke's truck pulled down the driveway. My heart raced a little, and I waved to him but was surprised when he stopped and rolled down his window.

"Hey, Quinn," he said. He looked tired but was smiling and seemed pleased to see me. "What are you girls up to?"

"I haven't taken Penny to the beach yet, so I wanted to try it out and see how she likes it," I told him. I tried not to stare at the five o'clock shadow on his face but was distracted with how sexy he looked.

"Do you want company?" he asked. His question surprised me, especially with how tired he looked.

"Um, yeah, sure," I said. "Where should we go?"

"Well, I'd like to check out the progress on my house. There's a long stretch of beach there that would be perfect to run the dogs," he suggested.

I loved the idea of seeing his house and where he lived.

"That sounds great," I said. "Do you need some time to change or eat or anything?"

"Just give me a few minutes. I can drive if you just want to follow me to the cottage," he said.

"Okay," I said. I retrieved Penny from the car and walked down the driveway to the cottage. Luke let me in and disappeared into the bedroom. I had been letting Diesel out so often that the cottage was familiar, but it felt a little different being in there with Luke.

He walked out in dry board shorts and a clean T-shirt, and I found myself struggling not to stare again. How was this guy single? He quickly threw together a sandwich as Diesel bounced back and forth between the two of us, seeking attention. It felt oddly domestic climbing in Luke's truck beside him with our dogs in the back seat.

"How have you been this week?" he asked.

Again I felt a warmth inside me that he seemed to care about me and wasn't simply making small talk.

"Good," I told him. I was trying to figure out something exciting to tell him, but my week had been so dull. So instead I told him about the dogs' antics that week. Even though I sounded like a crazy dog lady, Luke laughed at my stories and relaxed with his arm across the back of the truck seat. Every so often his hand would graze my shoulder and I felt a spark travel through my body. I glanced over at him and wondered if he felt it too, but his face was unreadable.

Right about the time we were close enough to smell the ocean air, we turned down a side street, and Luke drove slowly as kids skateboarded by or walked with surfboards tucked under their arms. It was a busy neighborhood with lots of activity, but I noticed how Luke would smile and wave at most everybody, and I assumed he knew them all. We reached a driveway, and my jaw dropped when I saw the ocean view.

"Are you friggin' kidding me?" I asked, gaping at him.

"What?" he asked with a nervous laugh.

"You live here?" I was stunned. I knew he lived by the beach, but I didn't realize his house looked over the ocean. It seemed to go forever with no land in sight, and with the sun shining high in the sky, the different shades of blue were unbelievable. If I lived here, I would never get anything done.

"Yes, I do," he replied proudly. "It took every last dime I

made surfing, but it's been well worth it. Once the renovations are done, it will be even better."

"It's a dream house," I said, still stunned. I had grown to love my house, but I still struggled with feeling like it wasn't really mine.

"Come check it out," he said, climbing out of the truck. I could hear hammers pounding and lots of banging coming from inside. "I'm lucky Cody and Grant are my closest neighbors, and they obviously aren't going to complain about the construction noise."

We walked around a large dumpster filled with debris and up the steps, and the dogs followed us like they owned the place. Once we were inside, I looked around in awe at the complete overhaul being done on the house. I wished I had seen it beforehand to completely understand the set up because it was hard to envision right now with no walls.

Everything was stripped down to the studs, and it was pretty much one large open room. You could see where the bathroom was and what I guessed were the bedrooms, but otherwise it was hard to tell. A few guys walked past us with dark wood paneling on the way to the dumpster and gave a chin-up hello to Luke. I saw Grant and Cody in the corner, ready to hang the first piece of drywall.

"Oh, you came just in time!" Cody said, then grunted as he held up the heavy drywall and Grant started screwing it in.

Grant glanced over before grabbing more screws.

"And he brought help!"

I laughed at their teasing and felt overwhelmed just taking it all in. I don't know how they even knew where to start because it was obvious so much work was being done. No wonder Luke couldn't live here during renovations.

"Everything looking good?" Luke asked.

"So far, so good," Grant said. "The framework is solid, and I don't see any signs of termite damage or anything like that."

"That's good, but man, what a mess," Luke said, shaking his head and looking around.

If I felt overwhelmed, I could only imagine how he felt since this was his home.

After the drywall piece was installed, Grant and Cody walked over to us, and they both gave me a quick hug and peck on the cheek.

"You're welcome to stay and work," Cody piped up.

"Nah," Luke said. "That's what I'm paying you guys for! Besides, Quinn and I are going to take the dogs to the beach."

Grant and Cody looked at each other and exchanged smiles. I glanced over at Luke curiously, but he was looking around the room. I could've sworn he was blushing too.

"You want to see the upstairs?" Luke asked me.

"We just finished tearing that apart, so watch your step," Grant warned.

We cautiously made our way up the stairs and sidestepped to avoid getting in the way of the crew.

"Oh my," I said, feeling speechless. The loft was beautiful, even being in the state of destruction it was. The entire front wall was windows, providing an unobstructed view of the Pacific. I was in awe and slightly jealous. "This would make an incredible office," I said.

"I considered making it my master bedroom," Luke admitted. "But there's no bathroom up here, and I just didn't have room in my budget to add one."

"What do you even use this room for?" I asked curiously.

"Kind of a catchall," he said, laughing. "I keep a bed in here for guests, but I have a guest bedroom downstairs too, so it's not really necessary."

"I would kill to design this room," I said, looking around at the clean slate.

"Knock yourself out," he said.

I let out a little snort. If only. I looked at him and realized he was serious.

"Are you for real?" I asked.

"Sure," he said with a shrug. "Decorating isn't really my thing, and once the renovations are done, I'd really like the whole place to look nice."

"I'm not exactly a decorating expert," I said.

"Can't be any worse than me," he quipped.

"Okay, well, we can talk about this in a few months when it's closer to being done," I said. I was excited about decorating the space but also told myself to keep my expectations low. I mean, how else would I ever see him once he moved back to his house?

"Um, where are the dogs?" Luke asked, glancing around. They had been following us around the house, but never made their way upstairs.

"Looking for the dogs?" Cody asked as we made our way back downstairs.

"Yeah, have you seen them?" I asked.

"Yep," he said, laughing and lifting his chin toward the lanai.

I walked over to the window and laughed. Diesel and Penny were curled up on the lanai, basking in the sunlight. The breeze coming from the ocean was ruffling their fur, and they looked content.

"Do you think we should still walk the beach?" I asked, not wanting to disturb them.

"Sure," Luke said. "They still need the exercise." He whistled, and both dogs jumped up. We hooked them to their leashes and headed down to the water. I was still in awe at the proximity to the water.

"I can't believe you live on the beach," I said.

"I do love it," he said. "This is my favorite place to surf, and the view never gets old."

"I don't see how you could not love it," I said, staring out at the ocean.

"The only downside is the wear and tear on your house and vehicles," he told me. "The salt water can wreak havoc."

"Hmm, I never thought of that," I said. I turned my attention back to the dogs, who seemed just as happy to be there as I was. The beach wasn't busy, so we decided to let them off their leashes. They raced alongside the water but didn't go in. The shore break was wicked this time of year, and this stretch of beach wasn't currently suitable for swimming.

"So, are you planning on staying in Hawaii long term?" he asked.

I didn't reply immediately because I wasn't sure how to answer that. When I'd made the decision to move here, I wasn't exactly thinking about long term. I just knew I needed to get out of Chicago.

"Honestly, I hadn't thought that far ahead," I answered. "Kind of focused on the right now. How about you?" I glanced at him.

"Yep," he replied easily. "It's home for me."

"Well, when you have a beach house like this, I can't blame you." I laughed.

"Yeah," he answered.

I felt like he wanted to say more, but he stayed silent. I wondered where his mind was at, but it didn't seem like it was my place to ask. Luke intrigued me, but I still couldn't shake the feeling that I wasn't ready and that he really wouldn't want me once he got to know me. We walked in a comfortable silence along the beach as the dogs trotted along.

"The beach was a good call," I finally said, breaking the silence.

"The beach is always a good idea," Luke said.

I nodded, agreeing with him. After living in Chicago for my entire life, it was nice experiencing living in a different place.

I looked out at the ocean again and savored the feeling of the mist of the water spraying my face and my hair blowing wildly in the wind. I had to admit this was feeling more and more like home. I wasn't sure if this was where I would stay forever, but I wasn't ready to leave anytime soon.

I bent down to pick up a shell and started sifting through the sand. Adrienne had taught me to always be on the lookout for the ocean's little treasures, so whenever I was at the beach I would find myself subconsciously searching for shells and sea glass.

Luke caught on to what I was doing and crouched down next to me. He dug a purple shell out of the sand and handed it to me. I turned it over, examining the lines and imagining what Adrienne would use it for. I looked back at Luke and sucked in a sharp breath when I realized he was staring at me intensely. We were crouched in the sand, inches apart, and his eyes kept flickering to my lips. I wondered what it would feel like to kiss him and considered finding out. Suddenly, reality struck me, and I stood up abruptly.

"I suppose we should get going," I said, struggling to cover the nervous tone in my voice. I also don't know where I was going with my lame excuse for leaving, since it was barely dinnertime. I looked back at Luke as he was standing and caught a glimpse of the disappointment on his face. Why was he interested in me? He would be better off finding a different girl that wasn't carrying so much emotional baggage. He was such a nice guy, and he deserved better than that. I felt my own disappointment creeping in at the missed opportunity, but I silently convinced myself this was for the best.

Penny and Diesel ran back up to us then, which was a welcome distraction. We turned back, and I felt a little panic at how far we were from Luke's house. I hadn't realized how far we had walked, but I knew it was because I was enjoying the company. Only now we had to walk back with this awkward feeling between us.

After a few minutes, Luke seemed to shake the awkwardness and asked me about living in Chicago. We talked generically about the city, and I was relieved to have a topic that wasn't too personal. Once we got back to the house, we stepped back in to say goodbye to Grant and Cody, who were wrapping up for the day.

"We were thinking of burgers tonight," Grant said. "You in?"

I waited for Luke to respond when I realized Grant was looking at me too.

"Oh! Thanks for the invite, but I think I'm going to spend the night in," I said. I reminded myself how lonely I had been, but then I replayed the look in Luke's eyes when I thought he was going to kiss me. Spending more time with him was not going to help me keep my distance.

"Sure," Luke said, sneaking a glance at me. I wondered if he was disappointed that I'd declined. "Just let me run Quinn and the dogs home and I'll meet you there," he said.

I thanked Luke on the way home for showing me his house and accompanying me to the beach. He was polite and chatted with me, but the lingering disappointment was still there. Maybe he would give up on me after this.

We said goodbye, and Penny and I headed into the house. I looked back sadly at his taillights pulling out of the driveway and sighed. Going out with new friends sounded like so much more fun than spending another evening alone. I wallowed in self-pity as I poured myself a glass of wine and settled in front of the TV.

What was I doing? For the first time in my life, I'd made a rash decision, and I was only starting to question it. I was so devastated by all my loss that I hadn't thought reasonably about any of this. I considered selling my parents' home and running back to the mainland, but what was there? I didn't know what to do, and worse, I couldn't call my mom to ask her opinion. The tears slid down my cheeks as I stared blankly at the TV.

Penny climbed up on the couch and laid her head in my lap. I loved how she sensed my sadness and wanted to comfort me. I stroked her fur, which was comforting, finished my wine, and lay on the couch with Penny beside me. I pulled the blanket from the back of the couch, and somehow it still had a faint, lingering scent reminiscent of my parents.

Most days I fought to be brave and not wallow in grief, but tonight I allowed it and cried myself to sleep.

Chapter 25

Luke

I had really hoped Quinn would accept the dinner invitation, but I blew it when I almost kissed her. I hadn't planned it, but I felt the connection between us and got caught up in the moment. Even though she had initially rejected me, I felt like we had spent enough time together and gotten to know each other more. There was chemistry between us, so I knew that wasn't it. I fought away the feeling of frustration and started to feel convinced that I didn't stand a chance. I wanted to be patient, but I also wanted there to be some sign that my patience would pay off. Instead, I got nothing.

I met the guys at the burger joint and realized our dinner party had grown. Megan and Elicia were there, as well as two other girls I didn't recognize.

"Hey, guys," I said, nodding at everyone as I sat down. I kind of wished it was just me and the guys, but I told myself to get out of my funk. I was just upset about the situation with Quinn and honestly feeling a little stupid for putting myself out there again only to get rejected.

"Hey," Cody said, taking a sip of his beer. "These are Megan and Elicia's friends, Amy and Hailey," he said, pointing at the girls.

Amy was Hawaiian with long dark hair and full lips. I was pretty sure I recognized her from around town, but not Hailey. Hailey had wavy blonde hair and bright green eyes that caught my attention.

We placed our orders, and I got a beer as well. I thought about something stronger, but that could wait until I got home, since I had to drive. Hopefully the beer would take off the edge and help me relax. I'd enjoyed my walk with Quinn and loved being able to show her my house, but the memory of it was tainted with irritation. I knew I was overreacting and scolded myself for feeling that way. Quinn had been through a lot, and I shouldn't push her. But I just couldn't shake this indescribable pull I had toward her, and I guess I just wanted to know I wasn't alone in this.

While we were waiting for our food, Hailey turned her attention to me.

"So, Luke, what are you up to these days?" she asked with a flirtatious smile.

I eyed her curiously, wondering if we had met before. Her eyes were gorgeous, but other than that, she wasn't really my type. But after being rejected again, the attention was a nice distraction.

"Just working and waiting for my house to be renovated," I said, sipping my beer.

"Oh, tell me about your house," she said, resting her chin on her hand and waiting eagerly for my answer. "I heard you live on the beach next to Grant and Cody."

"Sure do," I said. I launched into the story about my house and how I found it. Even after our food came, she seemed completely interested in hearing about the renovations.

"That sounds so awesome," she said. "Can I come by and see it sometime?"

"Um, sure," I answered. For the first time in an hour, I thought of Quinn again. I felt a pang of guilt for thinking about taking another girl to see the house after I had just been so excited to show it to Quinn. I reminded myself that I had nothing to feel guilty for, since Quinn was the one not returning my interest.

"We should go tonight," she said with excitement shining in those green eyes. "All of us!"

"Maybe not tonight," Grant said, joining in on our conversation. "It's already dark, and there aren't any lights. I don't need anybody getting hurt in my construction zone."

"Fun killer," Megan teased.

We all joined in teasing Grant about his professionalism, though I was a little relieved to get out of it tonight. Dinner was great, and I was glad that I'd joined everybody, but I was tired and ready to head home. As we were settling the bill, Hailey slipped a napkin over to me and smiled shyly at me.

"Here's my number," she said. "I'm going to hold you to that tour of your house."

For a moment, I considered inviting her back to my cottage. The way she leaned forward and would occasionally touch my hand made it clear that she was into me. I consider myself a pretty decent guy, but I'm still a guy, and I wasn't immune to the tan glow of her skin or the way she laughed at my jokes. If my house wasn't torn apart I probably would have. I had to draw the line at taking her back to Quinn's, though. That just felt disrespectful, and even though I was disappointed about earlier, I wasn't a total asshole.

"Okay, thanks," I said with a smile yet not promising anything. It wouldn't hurt to hang on to her number because she was sweet and fun, but I wasn't ready to jump into anything until I knew for sure there was zero chance with Quinn.

I drove home and noted the flicker of the TV coming from Quinn's living room as I pulled in the driveway. Diesel thumped his tail as I came in the door but didn't bother to get off his dog bed to greet me. Running at the beach had worn him out. At least I knew what I needed to do on those days where he had an abundance of energy. I looked forward to being able to walk out my back door and having the long stretch of sand right there.

The next day was even busier than the last, and I barely had a break in between lessons. I was hoping to cut out early and just have a quiet night at home with Diesel. I felt bad that I hadn't been around much, and he had been cooped up in that tiny cottage. I was grateful that Quinn was so willing to help, but I hated relying on her as well.

Cody left when things were slowing down, but he wasn't looking at a wild Saturday night. Instead he would be slaving away on my house after a long day in the water. I was considering breaking down the tent when a young couple approached me, looking for a lesson. I wasn't about to turn down the honeymooners, so I put on my energetic surfer dude façade and continued to work.

I took a few minutes to shoot Quinn a text.

Sorry to bother you, but I'm going to be stuck working later than planned. Could you let Diesel out for me?

No bother at all. Got it covered.

Thanks. I owe you.

The couple had a blast, but their inexperience caught up to them, and they were exhausted after forty-five minutes. They posed for pictures with the surfboard afterward and tipped me generously before they were on their way. By the time I made it home, I was beat. Spring break was always a killer. You would think I would be used to it by now, but it still wore me down.

Chapter 26

The next month raced by alarmingly fast, and I could count on one hand how many times I saw Quinn, most of which were her surf lessons. She had canceled on me once but otherwise still seemed to look forward to them. She was improving, and though I wanted to take the credit for that, I knew it was mostly due to her dedication.

It was like our lessons on the water were a completely different version of us. We chatted, though it was mostly small talk, and laughed and had a good time. But then when I saw her at home, it felt more like we were strangers, or at the very least, just neighbors. I knew we would be lucky to have another couple months of surf, and that would be spotty in the least.

Sometimes it was nice to have the break, but I hated not being able to just run out to my backyard and surf whenever I wanted. As the winter swell decreased, the surf lessons tapered off in general. Rather than spending more time at the cottage and around Quinn, I was spending every spare moment at my house, lending a hand with the renovations. I would stop at home long enough to change and grab Diesel, who loved going with me.

The progress was starting to speed up slightly now that the

demolition was complete as well as the wiring and plumbing, which I had updated. The drywall was installed downstairs, but the loft was waiting to be done. Even though I was paying Grant and his crew to complete the work, I enjoyed investing some sweat equity into my home. As the drywall went up, I could envision the contrast the remodel was going to make. Already everything looked brighter and fresher, and that was with drywall dust covering everything.

I wondered if Quinn was still interested in decorating the loft or if she had completely forgotten about it. I hated not seeing her, especially after I thought we were bonding so much. We never seemed to be home at the same time, and if we were, it was only long enough to sleep. I thought maybe the distance was healthy and that I was giving her space to grieve without me hovering and trying to steal kisses. I also thought that it might just make it easier for her to forget about me, as long as I remembered to drop off the rent check at the first of the month.

I was asked to participate in a surf event on Maui in the beginning of April. I hesitated because of Diesel. I hadn't had him for very long and felt guilty at leaving him, not to mention I dreading asking Quinn to help me out again. She had already gone above and beyond with everything she had done, and I felt like I was crossing the line with our landlord-tenant relationship. I decided to beg Cody to help me out.

"Dude, you already owe me so much. First you stole Quinn, even though she doesn't seem to be interested in your sorry ass. Then you got me working on your house and now you want me to dog-sit?"

"I know, man, I'm sorry I've been relying on you for so much," I said sincerely. "But I really need your help."

"Whatever, Luke, you know I got your back. I just giving you a hard time." Cody grinned.

I let out a sigh of relief. Cody meant the world to me, and I never wanted him to feel like I was taking advantage of him.

He had done so much for me since that day he decided we were going to be friends so many years ago.

"I'd say I owe you, but then I'd feel like a broken record," I said dryly.

"No worries. But I not going let you forget," he said, laughing.

The day before I left, I went looking for Quinn, feeling the need to explain to her that Cody would be on the property taking care of Diesel. I didn't think she'd care, but I wanted to be respectful since this was her home. She didn't answer the door when I knocked, so I debated leaving her a note or shooting her a text.

Right then, I heard a burst of laughter coming from nearby. Quinn's laugh still caught my attention, even though I hadn't heard it in the last month. I walked to the property line and could see Quinn and Adrienne sitting on the porch swing while Grandma Malia sat in her rocking chair. I was glad Quinn had Adrienne and Malia to keep her company, since she was virtually alone here in Hawaii. I hesitated about interrupting them when Quinn's gaze met mine.

"Hi, Luke," she said, and a blush crossed her cheeks. She tried to hide it by looking down at the drink in her hand, but not much gets by me.

"Hey, I just needed to talk to you really quick," I said. "But I don't want to interrupt."

"Oh, nonsense," Malia said. "Luke Cole is always welcome at my house. Get up here and I'll pour you a glass of tea," she said, already rising from her rocker.

I protested, but it fell on deaf ears, so I made my way up the steps and sat in the lone empty chair.

"What's up?" Quinn asked curiously. "Is everything okay with the cottage?"

"Oh yeah, that's great," I said. "But I'm leaving for Maui in the morning and won't be back until Tuesday."

"Oh, so you need me to help take care of Diesel?" she asked.

"Actually, Cody is going to take care of him," I said. "His landlord doesn't allow pets, but he's going to come by and take care of him while I'm gone. I just wanted to let you know that he'll be here a bunch, so I didn't want you to wonder what was going on."

"Oh," she said. I didn't miss the disappointment on her face. Was she upset that I was going to be gone, or was it that I hadn't asked her to take care of Diesel? I'd thought I was doing the right thing by asking Cody for help and not bothering her with it. I studied her face for a minute, but it was unreadable.

"Well, I hope you have fun in Maui," she said.

"Doing anything fun there?" Adrienne asked.

I explained the event to them and how I would have the opportunity to catch up with some of my old surf colleagues. In a way it was a harsh reminder of how my career ended, but I was still alive and well, and I tried to focus on that. It would be nice to see everyone, and it wasn't difficult to make an appearance. Even though I was out of the circuit, it sometimes amazed me how many fans I still seemed to have.

"Of course they want you there," Malia said. "You're Luke Cole!"

"You always were one of my biggest fans," I said, laughing.

"Well, of course," she said. "We have to support our own."

I finished my tea and thanked Malia for the hospitality.

"I guess I'll see you when you get back," Quinn said.

I didn't bother to point out we had hardly seen each other in the past month and that I doubted a long weekend would make any difference to her. I still struggled to keep my distance from her, but I had convinced myself this was better than getting rejected a third time.

Besides, I was way too busy for a new relationship.

My time in Maui was awesome, and I was grateful for the opportunity to get away from everything else. Even with being retired, I was treated the same, which meant a lot to me. We did surf lessons with disadvantaged children, which was always one of my favorite things to do. It was a real eye-opener to see what some of these kids dealt with on a daily basis and how a few minutes on a surfboard could change their outlook on life. I participated in these events as much as possible. It always helped keep me grounded.

We also had a dinner for the organization group, and I stayed up too late and drank too much and laughed and caught up with my old friends. There were already a lot of new kids on the championship tour that I hadn't met yet, so it was a chance to make new friends as well. That was one of the things I loved about my profession. You were always part of the family.

On my last night, I was hanging out with some of the guys when a group of female surfers came in. I instantly spotted Nina, my ex-girlfriend. Though things didn't work out between us, there were never any hard feelings, and I still considered her a friend. Her face lit up when she saw me waving at her, and she came over with the rest of the girls. I already knew most of them.

"Hey, Luke." She leaned in for a hug. "So good to see you!"

"You too," I said sincerely. "I see you're still tearing up the circuit," I said, referring to her lead status on the women's championship tour.

"Yep." She smiled proudly. "It's been a lot of work, but I'm finally at the top."

"You've earned it," I said.

She had worked her ass off to improve, even pushing through a shoulder injury. She was one of the first visitors I had when I was in the hospital and a woman I greatly respected.

Looking at her now, I had to wonder why things didn't work out between us, but we just made better friends than a couple. For whatever reason, we never had that spark. Not like what I felt with Quinn. Though it would really help if Quinn felt that spark too.

As if she could read my mind, Nina asked, "So, Luke, are you settling down yet? Met a pretty lady?"

I ducked my head and laughed but knew I didn't have anything to report back on.

"Um, nope, not really," I said, trying to stay cool.

"Oh my God, you totally met someone!" she exclaimed. "Who is she?"

"It doesn't really matter because I don't think she's really interested," I said.

Nina snorted. "Right. Does she know who you are?"

"Yeah, but I don't think that really matters to her," I said honestly. It was true. Quinn was amazed at my beach house, but my former professional surfer status didn't even seem to faze her.

"That's great, though," she said excitedly. "How often have you felt like a girl liked you for you and not for your status? Besides me, of course." She laughed.

"I know," I admitted. "I really like her, and I think she likes me, but she's been burned pretty bad, so I'm just trying to give her space."

"You've been through a lot, too, Luke," she said, putting her hand on my shoulder. "You deserve to be happy. Go for the girl."

"Thanks, Nina," I said, grateful that she wasn't pushing for more information. "How about you? You meet anyone yet?"

The beaming smile on her face gave her away.

"Yep," she said. "I'm actually dating Tim, one of the announcers," she admitted with a blush.

"That's great!" I said. I really was happy for her.

"He's pretty awesome," she said, practically glowing. "I think it's getting serious."

"Good for you, Nina," I said.

"Well, it was really good to see you, Luke," she said, moving to leave. "Hang in there. Be patient. If the girl knows what's good for her, she'll come around."

I replayed her words in my head as I lay awake in bed that night. I had an early flight and really needed some sleep, but I couldn't stop thinking about Quinn and wondering what was going on behind those bright blue eyes.

Chapter 27

Quinn

One of the unexpected benefits from getting a dog was getting into better shape. I had neglected my fitness after my traumatic experience and only after taking Penny on countless hikes did I realize how far I had slid. However, I could feel the muscles in my legs toning up, and my endurance was so much better. Penny would freak out if I even walked near her leash hanging by the door, let alone grabbed it.

I felt guilty not taking Diesel while Luke was gone, even though I knew Cody was taking care of him. I felt a certain responsibility toward Diesel, since we had gotten the dogs together. If I was honest with myself, I was really disappointed that Luke didn't ask me to dog-sit. As soon as he left that night, Adrienne sent a pointed look in my direction.

"Stop reading into it, Quinn," she said firmly.

"What?" I said, attempting to sound clueless.

"He's probably asking Cody because he didn't want to bother you. You *are* his landlord, after all."

"Yeah, but I've been taking care of Diesel so much that there must be more to it," I said, biting my lip.

"I don't think there is," she said. It amazed me how she could be so compassionate but also firm in the same breath.

"Last time I let Diesel out, I saw a napkin on his counter," I admitted. I felt guilty for seeing it, but I wasn't trying to snoop. "It had a girl's number on it. Maybe he's dating someone."

"I doubt it," Adrienne said, shutting me down. "Girls always give Luke their number. He's famous in Hawaii, so it's to be expected."

"I'm sure," I said. I still couldn't get it out of my mind, though. Had "Hailey" gone with him to Maui? Or had he only just met her? I had no reason to be jealous, but I still fought to push the green monster away.

The days Luke was away, I could've sworn a storm cloud hovered above me. I couldn't shake the funk I felt knowing he was gone, which was silly since I hadn't seen him all that much in the past few weeks. I immersed myself in learning new recipes that called for avocado, since I seemed to have an abundance of them on my property. I wasn't even sure what I was supposed to do with them all. I had invited Adrienne to join me, but she was busy taking care of Grandma Malia, who was feeling under the weather. I did take them some avocado brownies and a different guacamole recipe I had concocted.

I could see the stress on Adrienne's face when she answered the door.

"Hey, come in," she said, opening the door wide. The house felt quiet and empty, and I took note of Adrienne's shushed tone as she spoke.

"How is Grandma?" I asked with concern.

"She's having a bad spell right now," Adrienne said, the crease between her brows looking more pronounced.

"Can I do anything to help?" I asked.

"No, but thank you," she said gratefully. "I just have to stick close in case she needs me. Her heart isn't good, and every few months she grows really weak and can't get out of bed for days."

Concern settled over me and I wondered if this was the first spell she had endured since I arrived or if I was just too wrapped up in my own world to notice.

"Here," I said, handing her the containers. Adrienne immediately reached in and grabbed a small brownie.

"Oh my God," she said around a mouthful of brownie.

"You like?" I asked, smiling.

"So good," she said, taking another big bite. I laughed at her enthusiasm and gave her a minute to finish the brownie.

"I won't keep you," I said, "but please make sure to let me know if you need anything."

"Thank you, Quinn," she said, giving me a big hug.

"You do so much for me, Adrienne," I said, swallowing the lump in my throat. "I don't want you to ever feel like I take that for granted."

"I don't. Promise," she said, smiling kindly at me.

I was walking back into my yard as Cody pulled in the driveway. I waved cheerfully at him, and he stopped and rolled his window down.

"Howzit?" he asked with his trademark smile.

"Not bad," I said. "Kind of boring."

"Missing Luke, eh?" he teased.

"Uh, no." I shook my head and felt the instant blush.

"It's okay. I miss him too," he said, continuing to tease me.

"Just kind of quiet without him around," I said.

"Right," he said with a chin-up gesture, appeasing me.

"Is Diesel doing good with him gone?" I asked curiously.

"Yeah, I've been trying to take him out with me once in a while, get him out of the cottage," he said.

"Cool," I said as I stood there awkwardly, not sure what to say next. I liked Cody, and he was a nice guy, but I was never around him without Luke. "I'll catch ya later?"

"Right on," he said and continued down the driveway.

I wondered how much he was just teasing or if the crush I had developed on Luke was that obvious. I really hoped it was just Cody being Cody. As much as I was objecting to my own crush, I had to admit I was failing miserably. The more I saw him, the more I liked him. Even though he was semi-famous, he never seemed to let that get to his head. He was one of the humblest, most patient and kind guys I had ever met. And he was always making me laugh.

Add the fact that he was easy on the eyes, and it was no wonder I had a crush on him. Was that really so bad? Every girl on the North Shore probably had a crush on him. Maybe allowing him in my rental was a mistake. It was bad enough I was getting surf lessons from him, but that was only once a week. Even though I didn't see him all the time, every time I was anywhere near him, my heart started racing just a little bit faster. My mind kept telling me to stay far, far away from the hot surfer, reminding me that I was a hot mess.

Maybe I just needed to get laid. I shook my head at the thought. As much as I would like that, I just wasn't that kind of girl. I would never have the confidence to go out and find somebody simply for a hookup. Not to mention I wasn't really sure that I could separate the physical from the emotional.

I walked back in the house and began cleaning up the disaster I had created in the kitchen. I was hoping the task would distract me, but my mind still wandered dangerously as I imagined sex with Luke. He was generally just sweet and playful toward me, but that moment on the beach when I thought he was going to kiss me... I didn't miss the fire that was in his eyes. And damn, I wanted to touch the flame.

That night was a sleepless night, and for once my tossing and turning wasn't due to my grief. Instead, every time I fell back asleep, Luke was waiting in my dreams, taunting me. Every encounter we had, from the airplane to surf lessons to the missed opportunity to taste him on the beach turned into an erotic scenario that my brain ran wild with.

I woke up in the morning exhausted and hornier than ever. I shuffled to the kitchen and brewed coffee as Penny ate. I was grateful for a slow morning as Penny and I retreated to the lanai so I could shake off the remains of my dreams. I had barely settled into my chair on the lanai when I saw Luke's truck start to pull in the driveway.

My heart did a backflip when I saw his profile in the driver's seat. I scolded my heart for betraying me and sank into my chair, thinking he would drive by without seeing me. Instead, Luke seemed to be looking for me, scanning the lanai with his eyes and breaking into a grin when he spotted me. He lifted his hand in a wave but kept driving. I smiled to myself, glad he seemed so happy to see me but also relived he didn't come talk to me because I wasn't sure I could look him in the eye after last night.

"Oh shit!" I jumped up, spilling hot coffee down my white tank top as Diesel bounded up the steps. His entire body wiggled, and he bounced between Penny and me, greeting us like he had been gone too.

"Diesel," Luke's voice warned.

I froze while attempting to wipe up the coffee staining my top. I was well aware that my nipples were threatening to cut a hole through my top from the friction of trying to wipe it clean. I glanced up in time to see the smirk on Luke's face, which he quickly hid as he respectfully looked away.

I grabbed the throw blanket off the back of the chair and covered myself up.

"I'm sorry," Luke said, but I could still see traces of laughter in his eyes.

"It's okay, we missed him too," I said, reaching down to pet Diesel. Diesel sat happily with his tongue hanging out of his mouth, seemingly content to have us all together.

"I just got back from the airport," Luke said.

"Welcome home," I said, finally meeting his gaze. I could swear he was reading my mind in that moment and knew all the details of my dreams from the night before.

"Yeah, thanks," he said, running his hand through his hair. "Rough night?" he asked with one brow lifted in amusement.

I ran my fingers over my hair, hoping to smooth out my bed head and not die from embarrassment. I hadn't anticipated seeing anybody when I came out here.

"Something like that," I said, blushing. If he only knew how much of this was his fault.

"Did you have a good trip?" I asked, sipping what was left of my coffee.

"Yeah, it was good," he said, nodding. "Busy and a bit tiring, but everything went well."

"Great," I said. I considered offering him some coffee and convincing him to sit and enjoy a lazy morning with me and then maybe making the events from my dreams come true. Instead I said nothing and stared silently into my coffee mug.

"Well, I'll see you around," he said. He hesitated before walking down the steps, like he wanted to say more, but then continued down.

I was disappointed as I watched him walk away. I would've loved to have spent time with him, and I really had missed him while he was gone, but it was better to keep my distance.

"Hey, you want a lesson tomorrow?" he called out from the yard.

"Sure," I said, perking up.

"How's nine o'clock?" he suggested.

"Perfect! See you then!"

At least I had something to look forward to.

Chapter 28

Luke

It was a beautiful evening, and I had nowhere to be, so I decided to take Diesel for a walk through the neighborhood. A few blocks turned into a few miles, but then twilight set in, so I steered us back home. It still felt weird to consider my little cottage as home, but I was pretty content there for the time being. It might have had something to do with that woman who was as petite as she was feisty with bright blue eyes that drew me in every time.

Keeping my distance was proving to be more challenging than any new surfing maneuver I had ever learned. Every night I arrived home, I felt that pull tugging me toward her door instead of mine. I'd give her a friendly wave as she read on her lanai, or I'd see the lights on as she moved around the kitchen cooking dinner.

I spent the past two months catching up on the yardwork per our deal and had restored it to the clean, manicured yard her dad had worked so hard to maintain. Our arrangement was working well, but the proximity was killing me, and I had at least another four months to go while pretending I wasn't crazy about her. I thought by now I would've cracked the wall she had so expertly constructed around her, but it was solid.

Though we had spent a lot of time together in the first month between the dogs and everything else, it seemed she'd been working extra hard to avoid me since I got back from Maui. Our interactions had tapered off but were just consistent enough to keep me entranced by her, something Cody liked to tease me about daily. Quinn's weekly surf lessons became part of our arrangement, and it was the highlight of my week.

"I don't think all the money in the world could wipe that grin off your face," he said after Quinn left from her latest lesson.

I just shrugged and grinned some more. I had no quick, witty comeback for him. I was infatuated. But damn there was something about that girl. Her determination mixed with a little stubbornness was pretty cool to watch, and I admired her willingness to learn how to surf. Not to just be pushed on a wave, but to learn the ins and out of the sport as well as the water safety. I lived to see that smile as she stood up on a wave or paddled back out to me, still beaming from her ride.

"Man, you crack me up," Cody said. "We've all lost money giving surf lessons to pretty girls, but dude, you keep giving 'em to the same girl!"

"It's part of our living arrangement deal," I said, knowing I was wasting my breath.

"Right," he said, seeing right through my bullshit. "Like you wouldn't do whatever it took to spend more time with Quinn."

I just answered him with another grin.

"In all seriousness, though, Luke, I hope you get the girl. She's pretty badass, and I'm glad to see you smile."

Cody wasn't serious all that often, at least not like that, so his sincerity took me aback for a minute.

"Thanks, man," I said with a nod of my head.

"Okay, enough of this sappy shit. You sleep with her yet?"

I busted out laughing at Cody's usual bluntness.

"No, no, I haven't. But it's not like that."

"Sure."

I recalled the conversation as I wandered back down the driveway. The last remnants of pink and orange traced the sky, and the shadows were starting to descend on the property. Like clockwork, Quinn was out on the lanai, with her little lights twinkling and casting a glow on her curled up in her favorite chair. She glanced up, startled, when she heard my footsteps.

"Oh, Luke!" she exclaimed.

"Hey, what's up?" I asked, trying to sound casual.

"Just enjoying the beautiful sky," she said. "Come join me."

She said it so quietly I almost thought I didn't hear her correctly. Diesel had already trotted up the steps and curled up with Penny, worn out from our walk. I walked up the steps and noticed a glass of wine between her fingertips.

"Let me get you a glass." She started to toss her throw blanket aside to get up.

"Let me," I said, motioning for her to sit down. "Is the kitchen to the left or right?" I said from the doorway.

"Left," she said. "Cupboard to the left of the sink."

I walked down the hallway where the room opened up into the kitchen and living room. I was walking past the refrigerator when something caught my eye. I couldn't help but stop when I realized the sole picture on the fridge was one of her and me from her first surf lesson. I grabbed the additional wineglass and headed back out to the lanai.

Quinn uncorked the bottle and poured me a generous portion. I settled into the chair next to her, still surprised at her random invitation. I had been living there for two months, and our recent interactions were brief, other than the surf lessons. I wasn't sure why she had invited me to join her, but I also decided not to question it and enjoy her company instead.

"You're right. The sky is beautiful tonight," I commented.

"So beautiful," she said slowly. I nodded in agreement, but I wasn't looking at the sky.

"Good night for drinking?" I asked.

"Yeah, but don't judge me too much. I'm such a lightweight. This is only my second glass," she said, holding up her half-full wineglass.

I chuckled a little, enjoying seeing her so relaxed.

"I didn't want to read tonight. I just wanted to watch that gorgeous sunset and not care. What were you doing?" She turned to look at me so suddenly that her wine sloshed out of her glass.

"I went for a walk, also to enjoy the beautiful sunset," I told her.

"I'm so sorry," she said. "It's none of my business what you do." She sighed and leaned back into her chair and back to her relaxed state.

"It's okay, we're friends. You can ask," I said, wanting her to feel comfortable.

"We are?" she said, looking at me with those beautiful blue eyes.

"Well, I thought we were," I said, sipping my wine. Beer was usually my preference, but given the company I thought the wine tasted excellent tonight.

"I thought I was your landlord. Or you're my surf instructor, depending on how you want to look at it," she said, staring into her wineglass. "I didn't think you would want to be my friend after I didn't give you my phone number."

The wine was definitely making her bold, and I rather liked talking to her without that forcefield she usually kept intact around her. I looked her over as she chatted along about how most guys would be pissed she didn't give out her digits and would never talk to her again, and how I just kept coming around.

Her hair was in a braid, tucked along the side of her neck. A few random tendrils of hair had escaped, and she kept swatting them away as they tickled her face in the light breeze. Though she had the blanket tucked around her, I could see her bare toes sticking out the bottom and saw she was wearing some cut-off shorts and my favorite pink bikini top.

"It takes a lot more than that to scare me away," I said, looking her dead in the eye.

"I don't want you to go away," she said, biting her lip. Then, "Shit."

"What?" I asked, confused.

"Whenever I drink my filter like, just disappears," she said, gesturing with her hand.

"Feel free to tell me whatever you like," I said, curious how much she would tell me. Part of me felt like I was taking advantage of her honesty under the influence, but at the same time I had been trying so hard to get to know the real Quinn that I felt like I couldn't pass up this opportunity.

"Like do you have any idea, any idea at all, how freakin' hot you are?" she asked, leaning forward.

"I've been told that a time or two before," I said. "But I want to know what *you* think."

"I think it's nearly impossible to sleep every night knowing that you're right next door," she said, jabbing her finger at me.

"Oh?" was all I had for a response.

"I didn't give you my number because I'm nowhere near ready for a serious relationship," she said. "Not because I don't find you attractive."

"It's okay," I said reassuringly. "Besides, I live next to you now. I don't need your number."

"Well, you have it now," she said.

"I much prefer talking straight to your pretty face," I said. I almost missed the light blush on her cheeks in the dim light.

"So why don't you want a relationship?" I asked, bravely digging for information.

"Because that *asshole* broke my heart," she said bitterly. "Three years together, and he just tosses me aside like I never mattered. I thought he was the one. I cried myself to sleep that night. Then I was woken up in the middle of the night with the phone call telling me my parents were dead."

I clenched my jaw when I saw the pain on her face. I'd had no idea she had endured so much heartache. All in the same night. I leaned toward her and covered her hand with mine.

"I'm really sorry you had to go through all of that, Quinn," I said sincerely. I felt infuriated at the pain I saw in her eyes when she looked up at me, and I wanted to make whoever that asshole was pay. What idiot would walk away from her? I set my wineglass down and tucked one of the loose tendrils behind her ear, slightly cupping her face with my hand.

"I'm so tired of hurting," she said, eyes closed as she leaned into my hand.

"I won't hurt you," I said quietly. I ached to touch her more but wasn't sure between the wine and her admissions what I should do. Her eyes snapped open, and she jumped up.

"What?" I asked, thinking I had said something wrong, but I was also slightly distracted now that she was standing in front of me. The blanket had fallen to the floor, those tiny shorts and that damn pink bikini were in full view.

"I just want to feel alive again," she said, her voice slightly shaking. She took a tiny step toward me, and I couldn't stop myself from reaching out for her. I pulled her to me and lightly kissed her stomach. Before I realized what she was doing, she pushed me back and was straddling me on the chair.

"Quinn," I whispered but was cut off as her lips brushed against mine. My brain was telling me all the ways I needed to respect her and make sure she was fully aware of what she was doing. However, my body was only aware of how her hips were grinding against me and how her soft breasts were pushing against me. She had spent so long pushing me away that I almost didn't know how to react. Almost.

Before I could analyze the situation any further, she came in for another kiss, and this time I just reacted. I crushed her body against mine as our kiss deepened, and she continued to grind into me. Her confidence was extremely sexy, and my senses were engulfed by her scent and the sweet taste of wine on her tongue.

I ran my hands along her back until I found the string holding those scraps of bikini together. I untied it, and she tossed it aside along with all her inhibitions. I took her nipple in my mouth and sucked aggressively, which earned me an encouraging moan. I took the other breast in my hand and pulled and kneaded which only made her grind into me more. My board shorts did little to hide my arousal, but that seemed to encourage her more as she reached down and stroked my length through the thin material. I came to my senses long enough to slightly push her back, but she struggled against me to come back for more. Once this woman was awakened, there was nothing stopping her, and I could hardly rein in an ounce of self-control.

"Quinn," I said firmly to get her attention. "You've been drinking, and you're vulnerable. I don't want to take advantage of you."

It was going to require a very long, very cold shower if she told me I was indeed taking advantage of her.

"You aren't," she said, kissing me again. "We both want this." Kiss. "We are both adults." Kiss. "I just need you to fuck me." Her crude language just spurred me on more, and I decided to take her word for it. I stood up, and she wrapped her legs around my waist as I reached for the doorknob.

"Hright ober there." She gestured hastily toward the right to her bedroom door, never breaking her lips from mine. She kicked open her bedroom door with a bang, and I felt the back of my knees hit the bed, and we fell backward in a heap. This only resulted in her amazing breasts in my face, so I was obliged to give them more attention.

At one point she stopped kissing me and pulled back and

looked at me quizzically. "I never asked if you wanted this," she said.

I choked back a laugh as I shook my head.

"You're kidding, right?" I asked incredulously. "I've wanted you since the moment I saw you on that plane."

"Okay, that's all I needed to know." She resumed kissing me. We were a tangle of limbs as we fought to shed clothes, neither of us willing to take our lips off each other long enough to accomplish the task. Every piece of clothing lost only revealed to me what I already knew. This woman was stunning. The last article of clothing was gone when I froze.

"Condom?" I asked.

"Fuck!" she hollered. "No! I don't have anything!" I hesitated for a moment, trying to think when all I could focus on was her naked body beneath me.

"Don't move," I warned, climbing off her and scrambling for my board shorts. I threw them on without tying them and bolted out of the house and across the yard in the dark. I threw open my door and raced into my bedroom to my nightstand table to grab a condom. I started back out the door and then ran back to grab three more. Just in case.

I raced back across the yard, trying to prepare myself for Quinn being dressed and having changed her mind. Instead I walked back in the room to find her in all her naked glory.

"Damn," I said, pausing a moment to appreciate every line and curve on that perfect body.

"Took you long enough," she said with a smirk. I sighed in relief as I settled back over her, this time with a condom in place. I slowly pushed into her and inhaled sharply as her head rolled back with the sexiest groan I had heard in my life.

I wanted to take my time with her and savor every moment, not knowing if this would be my only time with her. Quinn, on the other hand, had other ideas, and it was hard and fast and full of passion. I had never been with a woman who showed such dominance in the bedroom, and I liked it. I saw her determination when she surfed, but never had I seen this level of confidence in her, and it was the biggest turn on. I thought the room was going to catch fire from our chemistry. If I knew anything at all, I knew this: This woman had ruined me.

When she finally rolled off me, we both lay side by side, breathing hard. I was worried regret was starting to sink in for her when she turned on her side and grinned at me and let out the cutest giggle.

"Yes?" I asked, not sure if her giggling was a good thing. Most guys don't want to hear giggling after they have had the best sex of their life.

"Oh my God, that was amazing!" she said with a breathless laugh. "I needed that!"

"Apparently so," I said, reaching out and pulling her close. "It wasn't too bad."

She swatted my chest and laughed.

"I saw your face. You enjoyed it!" she exclaimed.

"That's the understatement of the year," I said wryly.

"I've always wanted to do it like that," she said quietly. I thought the effects of the wine were probably gone by now, but being intimate was keeping her honest.

"Like what?" I had to know what she was referring to.

"My ex. He always had to be in control. And it was more of an obligation. I just wanted passion and, and... *that*! What we just did!"

If she wasn't careful with her enthusiasm and rocking her naked body against mine, *that* was going to happen again. Part of me wasn't sure how to react to being compared to her ex, but the alpha side of me was feeling pretty triumphant at the moment.

She was silent for a few minutes and drew circles on my chest with her fingernail. I didn't want it to end. I thought she was asleep after her hand fell limp on my chest, but then she spoke again.

"I don't want you to think I'm easy," she said quietly.

"Are you kidding me?" I asked, tipping her chin so she was looking up at me. "I don't think that at all." There was nothing easy about waiting these past few months.

"Even if I say I don't want anything serious?" she asked timidly.

My heart stopped for a second. I had really been hoping this was the start of something amazing. To fill the void in my life that I'd felt since I lost my professional surfing dream. I handled being unattached just fine when I was traveling all the time and had something to focus on, but lately I was well aware of how lonely I was, and the day Quinn showed up on the beach for her first surf lesson, I didn't feel quite so lonely. I was really hoping for a relationship. A partner in life.

I swallowed hard and tried to sound reassuring. "Whatever you want, Quinn."

"I just can't handle having my heart broken again after Aaron," she said.

So that was the bastard's name.

"But I felt like if I didn't have human touch again, I was just going to explode!" she said.

"So, what are you saying?" I asked. I didn't want to push, but since I was living here, I kind of wanted to be sure what boundaries were being set.

"I'm not asking for love or anything," she said nervously.

I didn't tell her it was possible that ship had sailed.

"And I don't want you to think poorly of me. But I also wouldn't mind this happening again." She peeked up at me nervously, and I could tell this was a first for her. I hadn't had much beyond casual relationships, but it wasn't for lack of wanting. It was all about timing.

"How about right now?" I wiggled my eyebrows at her and

went in for another kiss. She giggled and kissed me back. Good thing I'd grabbed those extra condoms.

Chapter 29

Quinn

Luke left around midnight, Diesel in tow. We kissed goodbye, but it felt slightly awkward to watch him walk into the darkness back to his cottage. He didn't ask to stay the night, and I didn't invite him.

It seemed silly to send him home, but I wasn't sure how this casual thing worked. Do you stay the night or go home? And how does that work when you live on the same property? I was exhausted yet extremely satisfied after he left. I decided I was too tired to do my normal overanalyzing and went straight to bed. I buried my head in the pillow and inhaled his scent. Pretty sure I fell asleep with a smile on my face.

The next morning, I awoke and stretched out lazily, looking forward to enjoying my Sunday morning. It took me a minute to remember the previous night, but once I did I lay in bed relaying all the details. I had truly never imagined sex could be that good. Aaron and I had enjoyed ourselves, and it wasn't bad by any means, but that was before I had Luke Cole. Aaron wasn't my first, but I felt like my very few, and very awkward, other experiences couldn't remotely compare to how I felt with Luke.

Adrienne and I had plans to go on a hike that morning, and

I had just poured my coffee in my travel mug when I heard the knock at my door. I didn't even realize the goofy grin I had on my face until I answered the door and let her in.

"How are you so cheerful so early in the morning?" she asked with a mock glare.

"What? I'm just normal," I said, trying to play it cool. And failing.

"Um, no. This is not normal," she said, gesturing at me up and down. She stopped when she saw the two wineglasses sitting on the kitchen counter. She spun around so fast and pointed at me.

"You got laid!" she shouted, her mouth agape and her face full of playful shock.

"Holy crap, I think the whole neighborhood knows now," I said, trying to shush her.

"Oh my God! I didn't know you had it in you. Who was it? Wait, was it Luke?"

I just smiled brightly at her and blushed when she said his name. And if the whole neighborhood hadn't heard her scream, they surely heard everything else. Adrienne was bouncing and squealing in the middle of my kitchen with no resemblance of the usual graceful woman she was. Her excitement was contagious, and finally I jumped up and down and squealed a little too. Penny wanted in on the excitement and pranced between us happily. We both laughed, and I glanced around nervously to confirm all the windows were closed. Last thing I needed was Luke hearing us.

"I need details!" Adrienne demanded, tucking her chin down and looking at me sternly.

"I don't kiss and tell," I said coyly.

"You have to at least give me *something*!" she begged. "I'm guessing by the look on your face that it was awesome?"

"It was," I said with a nod.

"So how did you leave it?" she asked. "Are you going to start dating?"

"Not exactly," I said slowly, but I wasn't sure how much detail I wanted to share about our situation.

"Oh, so friends with benefits?" she asked.

"Is that really a thing?" I asked. "Like it really works?"

"For some people," she said with a shrug. "Do you think it will work for you? Wait! This is like a steamy novel. You're his landlord! Kinky!"

I giggled at her reaction and also relaxed, knowing Adrienne wasn't going to judge me. We talked for a few more minutes and then headed out for our hike.

I walked with an extra bounce in my step and flew to the top, Penny by my side. We drank water and soaked up the majestic view of the North Shore skyline, in no hurry to leave. It was surprisingly not busy for a Sunday morning, so we took our time to catch our breath and relax before the hike back down.

"So, when are you going to see him again?" she asked. "With him living there and everything, what are you planning on doing?"

I let out a long sigh. I didn't want to ruin what had happened the night before, but I was really struggling with how not to mess it up going forward. I was well aware of how small the North Shore community was, and I sincerely did like Luke. I didn't want to make an ass of myself and then spend all my energy on avoiding him.

"I really don't know," I said. "This is so new to me, and I don't know how the whole casual thing works. He was obviously fine with it, because what guy wouldn't want no-strings-attached sex?"

"I think you would be surprised," she said. "But he wouldn't agree to it if he wasn't okay with it either."

"So, do we wait a week? Or do I go home and drag him straight to bed?" I started gesturing wildly with my hands. "I feel like this next step is the most awkward part."

"Well," Adrienne said, sipping her water, "try not to overthink it. It will happen naturally, just like last night did." She put the cap on her water and dug her phone out of her pocket. "But in the meantime, we should totally send him a picture of you looking gorgeous, and he won't be able to wait to jump back in your pants!"

"Wait, what? Right now?" I asked in disbelief, running my hand over my ponytail. "I'm all sweaty and muddy! This isn't going to be a good picture!"

"He liked you all sweaty last night!" she said, laughing at her own joke. She brushed a few strands of hair from my face and moved to get the perfect angle, capturing me and the beautiful view in the background. She snapped a few pictures until she was satisfied and then sat, tapping it out in a text to me. "There. No filter needed!"

I opened the text and analyzed the picture. It wasn't bad. I looked more like I was glowing with the sunlight reflecting on my face, and my cheeks were flushed from the workout. And the view around me was absolutely gorgeous.

"What do I say?" I stared blankly at my phone, willing the perfect words to come.

"Just say something like you had fun last night or that you're thinking of him," she suggested.

I wrinkled my nose at her suggestions and tapped out a message and pushed send before I could change my mind.

"Did you tell him you expected him naked in your bed by the time you got home?" she asked.

"God, no!" I laughed at Adrienne's oddly appealing suggestion. "I just said it was a beautiful morning for a hike."

I no sooner said that when my phone dinged with an incoming text. I smiled broadly when I read his reply and then relayed it to Adrienne. "Yes, very beautiful. The view ain't bad either."

I felt my face flush but giggled anyway. It was fun to feel

wanted. We finished our hike, and before we parted ways, I thanked Adrienne for helping me work through my insecurities and for being such a good friend to me. I was fortunate to have her in my life. She was one of the sweetest, most genuine people I had ever met. The way she cared for her grandmother, how she had so warmly welcomed my parents to the neighborhood and then jumped right in to help me when I needed it the most. I didn't understand why bad things had to happen, but I also knew that sometimes good things came out of bad situations. Adrienne was my good thing.

I didn't have any other plans for the afternoon, so I decided to sneak in a nap. My body was definitely not used to staying up late for a romp under the covers. I slept longer than I intended to and was disappointed that it was nearly dark by the time I woke up. I glanced out the window but didn't see any lights on at Luke's.

I tried not to let the disappointment ruin my good mood but failed miserably. I hadn't realized the anticipation of seeing him again was going to be so overwhelming. I should've used letting Diesel out as an excuse to see him, but he didn't mention having a long day. I'd honestly expected to see him at some point, but then remembered our surf lesson was scheduled for the next day. I felt slightly nervous at seeing him under those circumstances. Was it going to be awkward? I had grown to really look forward to my weekly lessons and not just because it was with Luke, but because I was really enjoying surfing.

I didn't sleep well that night, between my long nap and the hope of seeing Luke again after our incredible night. I lay awake until I decided it was an acceptable hour to wake up. I padded quietly around the kitchen and kept myself busy, paying some bills, which reminded me to look through some job listing sites for graphic design jobs. I was going to have to face the music sooner rather than later, but I was rather enjoying my unemployment.

I never imagined I would keep myself so busy since arriving, but there had been so much to do to get settled into my new life, and the time just flew. I did miss my work and knew that getting back into the workforce would be good for me.

I was contemplating whether I could freelance rather than working for a corporation again. I cringed at the thought of working in that environment again and cursed Aaron for ruining that for me along with so many other things. I jotted notes down for a few possible leads and then slammed my laptop shut when I realized how late it was already.

I glanced back as I headed to my car and saw that Luke's truck was already gone. I usually planned it so that I was his first lesson of the day, but he seemed to get there pretty early in order to set things up.

My heart raced as I walked across the sand to Cody and Luke's tent and came up behind them sitting in their normal spots.

"Aloha, Quinn!" Cody said, jumping up to give me a bear hug and peck on the cheek.

Luke stepped in and pulled me in close. I wasn't sure if it was my imagination, but I was pretty sure his embrace was more intimate and less casual. His kiss on my cheek trailed close to the corner of my mouth, confirming I was getting special treatment.

"Good morning," he murmured in my ear. My body instantly warmed, and all my nerves instantly faded away as he held me in his arms.

"Okay, kids," Cody said. "Go get a room or go surf. You can't do both!"

Cody obviously knew we had hooked up. I had told Adrienne, though, so I couldn't let that bother me. We walked over to the boards already laying in the sand. I was surprised when I felt Luke bend down next to me to strap my leash around my ankle. I had been doing it by myself since my first lesson, but I quickly learned the appeal of him doing it for me as he ran his hand up my leg, then around to squeeze my ass and give it a gentle pat.

"Do you do that for all of your clients?" I asked playfully.

"Only the pretty ones," he said with a wink.

If I thought there was sexual tension between us before, it was nearly unbearable now. We paddled out, and I kept focusing on his lean body as I trailed behind him. The swell was smaller than what I was used to, but it still provided for some good surf. I was starting to get better at paddling for the waves on my own, and Luke had begun to catch some waves as well instead of waiting for me to come back around.

We both caught a smaller wave, and I looked over and smiled at him as we rode the wave together. I was startled when he leaped from his board to mine, and I nearly lost my balance, but he reached out and grabbed my waist to steady me. I laughed as we rode out the wave tandem, relishing the feel of his hands on me.

As the wave died out, we leaped from the board into the water. I laughed again after I surfaced but didn't see Luke. He startled me again as he surfaced right in front of me. His body slid up against mine, and he stole a kiss. The cool ocean water did nothing to extinguish the flames between us. He smiled at me and then turned to climb back on his board. I did the same and followed suit to finish my lesson, no longer uneasy about what was to be expected.

This was going to be fun.

Chapter 30

Luke

We finished our lesson, and I knew I had about an hour before my next one. I glanced over at Quinn as she rinsed the salt water out of her hair at the outdoor shower. I had to get her alone, and it couldn't wait. I snuck up behind her as she turned the shower off and wrapped my arms around her waist.

"Your place or mine?" I whispered in her ear. She turned to look at me, eyes wide, and I wondered if I was coming on too strong. Then she giggled at my little joke.

"Definitely my place." She insisted on driving and said that she could bring me back.

"I'm sorry, I have less than an hour," I said as we drove the short distance to her house.

"Isn't that what makes it so much fun?" she asked, giving me that sideways look that drove me crazy.

"I can think of a few other things that make it fun," I replied, getting another giggle out of her.

The car had barely stopped before we were jumping out of the car and racing up the steps. Neither one of us had done a sufficient job of drying off, and we left a trail of water inside the doorway. Needless to say, we never made it to the bedroom.

I had been telling myself that our next time would be slow

and gentle to make her feel special, but this woman was driving me wild. Penny had wandered in and looked at us like we were nuts, and then walked back to her bed like we were disturbing her.

On the way back to the beach park, we kept sneaking smiles at each other. I hesitated before getting out of the car because I knew she wanted to keep it casual. But I decided I would ask for forgiveness instead of permission and stole another kiss from her. Judging by the look on her face, I didn't think I was in too much trouble.

Lessons were few and far between, and the rest of my day dragged, and I kept looking at my watch, waiting for any excuse to leave. My excitement at arriving home quickly deflated when I saw that Quinn's car was gone. I exhaled with disappointment as I trudged into the house. It was too difficult to keep this casual when I felt such a strong connection to her. It had only been forty-eight hours, and I couldn't get enough. It was stupid to expect her to be waiting at home for me to return from work, like we were a married couple or something. I opened the fridge and quickly shut it, completely dissatisfied with the lack of contents.

"Taco truck it is," I muttered, grabbing my keys again.

I drove to the taco truck and placed my order when I heard my name. I turned and saw a couple of the girls who I knew from my touring days. I wouldn't exactly consider them friends, more like acquaintances. Still, I headed their way to say hello as I waited for my food.

"Sit with us, Luke," Sydney said, patting the seat next to her.

I looked around for an escape but came up empty-handed and didn't want to be rude.

"Hey, Emily," I said, nodding to the other girl.

We chatted for about ten minutes and then my food was brought out. I contemplated leaving but decided that some company was better than sitting in my cottage alone. I was right in the middle of an enormous bite of my burrito when I heard a familiar laugh. I looked behind me and spotted Adrienne and Quinn in the corner.

My mood immediately lifted, and I was ready to turn to the girls to excuse myself when I saw three other guys joining Adrienne and Quinn. I tried to stifle the jealousy rippling through me and the desire to go mark my claim on Quinn.

Keeping it casual, I reminded myself. I felt Sydney's hand on my shoulder, trying to turn my attention back to them. I barely registered anything they were saying because all I could think about was what was going on behind me.

Quinn's laughter continued to drift my way, taunting me like a cruel joke. When she told me she wanted to keep it casual, we hadn't specified whether or not we were going to be exclusive in this arrangement. I gritted my teeth at the thought of sharing her with one of the guys currently capturing her attention. That was not going to work for me. I pushed the remainder of my food aside and listening to Sydney and Emily chat for a few more minutes before finally excusing myself.

"Oh, stay longer," Sydney said, grabbing my hand.

"Sorry, it's been a long day," I lied. I couldn't get out of there soon enough, but I purposefully strode by the table that Adrienne and Quinn sat at with their hilarious friends. "Oh, hey." I tried to act surprised that they were there.

"Hi, Luke," Quinn said. "Enjoy your dinner?"

I was puzzled at her aloofness after we'd had such a great morning together, but my mood had gone to shit, and I was just ready to go home.

"Yeah, it was great as always. Enjoy your evening." I nodded at the guys, using all my self-control to not challenge them with a glare. They looked vaguely familiar, and I figured they went to our high school or something.

By the time I got home, I was flat-out pissed. I didn't want to play games. I wanted to be with Quinn, but she was obviously more interested in playing the field. I thought I could handle it, but apparently not. Maybe I needed to pull back and try to put some distance between us. I really needed to stay in the cottage until the renovation on my house was complete. And I didn't want to quit giving her surf lessons, but maybe I could pawn her off on Cody occasionally.

The thought of spending less time with Quinn just pissed me off more, but I wasn't sure what else to do at this point. I had never felt anything like this before. It had been almost three months since I first met her, and it was like fate wanted us to be together.

Why couldn't she see that?

Chapter 31

Quinn

I was so worked up by the time I got home that I decided to skip my usual evening lanai time. I knew I wouldn't be able to relax after watching that girl all over Luke. If this was supposed to be casual, then why did seeing that girl touching Luke every chance she got make me want to go haul her away by her hair? I got so excited when I saw him up at the truck ordering his food. I'd tried hollering out his name, but it was so loud with the crowd that he didn't hear me.

I was just about to get up and go to him and invite him to join us when three guys showed up. Adrienne had graduated high school with them and introduced us. They asked to sit with us and then started telling me stories about Adrienne in high school. It was amusing to hear their tales, and I laughed at all the right places, but I had such a hard time focusing while Luke was there with another girl.

Adrienne kept eyeing me and finally glanced over his shoulder to see what I was glaring at.

"Ahhh," she said quietly so only I could hear. She glanced again right as the one girl was leaning into Luke and laughing and then gave me a sympathetic smile.

After I had dropped Luke back off that afternoon, I had

floated through the kitchen and baked muffins. I felt like I was on cloud nine and kept glancing over to the spot on the floor that we had christened just hours before. Once the muffins came out of the oven, I took a basketful over to Adrienne and her grandma. Adrienne met me at the door and burst out laughing when she saw my face.

"Already?" she asked.

"What?" I asked innocently. "Is it that obvious?"

"Girl, I don't think your feet are even touching the ground!" she said. She reached over and snagged a muffin from the basket as she let me in the house.

"Where is your grandma?" I asked, looking around. I didn't exactly want her grandma hearing us discussing my sexual escapades.

"She's taking a nap. Speak freely," she coaxed me and gestured for me to sit at the kitchen table.

"Adrienne, I don't know if I can do casual," I said, finally admitting what had been swirling around my head since I blurted those stupid words out forty-eight hours before. I had never felt anything like this before. I thought I could have a fun fling. I thought that was what I wanted. Aaron had really done a number on my heart. I just wasn't sure if I could put myself out there like that again. I was probably being presumptuous to think that Luke would even want something more serious. I had asked him if he was okay with being casual, and he had jumped all over it.

"So, tell him!" she exclaimed.

"Do you really think it's that easy?" I asked.

"Isn't it worth finding out?" she asked, finishing off her muffin. "By the way, yum."

"What if he doesn't feel the same way? We haven't known each other that long, and I feel like I just got out of my relationship with Aaron. What if it doesn't work and then it's just awkward?"

"That just sounds like a boatload of empty excuses," she said, leaning back in her chair.

"Maybe I will tell him," I said thoughtfully. "I really like him. Like a lot."

Adrienne snorted at me across the table.

"What?" I asked.

"You don't like him. You have fallen head over heels for him!" she said, laughing at me like it was the most obvious thing in the world.

"Oh, I don't know about that," I said, shaking my head.

But that did get me thinking. Luke and I had spent quite a bit of time together since we first met. I mean, the universe kept throwing us at each other, it was only a matter of time before we started sleeping together! I loved our surf lessons, I found myself looking around the property for him—especially on his yardwork days. Those were my favorite. Sweaty Luke, Salty Luke—it didn't really matter to me. I never saw a version of him that I didn't like.

"I know I haven't seen you together much, but it's obvious you guys enjoy each other, and I think it could be more than that. Don't let being afraid make you miss out on the love of your life."

Adrienne's words echoed through my mind for the remainder of the afternoon, and I kept looking for his truck to pull in the driveway and was growing impatient when I got Adrienne's text asking me to meet her at the taco truck for dinner. I figured that would be better than sitting by the window waiting for Luke. I was trying to work up my nerve to talk to him tonight about possibly making our arrangement more serious. I still struggled with the confidence of approaching him.

I also didn't know if we could make it that far with our clothing intact.

Seeing him at dinner quickly deflated what little confidence I had scrounged up. It was easy to convince myself that he didn't want anything serious and wouldn't want to give up his lifestyle of freedom. When he came by our table, I thought maybe he would join us or ask if I wanted to go home with him. I thought maybe we could drink a glass of wine on the lanai and I could use the liquid courage to help me ask him if he wanted to be my boyfriend. Check yes or no. Then he blew me off like our afternoon had never even happened. I fought tears as he walked away and stared blankly into space, completely tuning out the conversation around me. I finally decided to go home, but Adrienne stopped me before I left.

"Talk to him," she said lowly so only I could hear.

I gave her a noncommittal wave and stalked off to my car. I could see the flicker of the TV in his cottage as I walked up the steps to my house. I decided to do the same and half-heartedly watched *Friends* reruns until I dozed off.

The next morning, I woke up in a foul mood. I wasn't sure whether to be angry with Luke for blowing me off or with myself for suggesting this arrangement in the first place. I was walking around the bed to grab clothes out of my dresser when I stubbed my toe on the corner of the bed.

"Shit!" I hollered as I fell back on the mattress. I muttered cuss words and held my foot until the throbbing in my toe faded. Penny sat by my side, looking concerned.

"That's it," I said aloud. Today was the day. I couldn't keep living in this cramped guest bedroom when there was a perfectly good master suite across the hall. I missed my parents fiercely, but avoiding their bedroom was not going to bring them back. My mom would've slapped me silly had she known I refused to sleep in their room and make it my own. This was going to require coffee. Lots of it.

I contemplated calling Adrienne and asking her for help.

I was sure she would help, but I hesitated to ask her. She was probably the person who would understand the most how difficult this would be for me, but I felt like I needed to do it myself. At least to start with until I could get my bearings.

I carried my coffee down the hall and inhaled deeply before opening the door. It smelled a little musty since I had avoided the room like the plague since I moved in. I quickly opened the windows and turned on the ceiling fan to increase the air flow. I already felt overwhelmed just looking around. Where was I supposed to start? How in depth did I want this to be?

As I looked at the space, I started to feel inspired to redecorate. Besides a few personal touches on the lanai, I hadn't done much to change anything. I thought of the tropical quilt in corals and blues that I had seen in one of the shops in town. I stopped and looked at it every time I was there but didn't feel like I had any reason to buy it, but it would complement the blue on the walls and the white furniture.

I started making mental notes of a few things I could buy or move in there to make it feel like my room. I longingly eyed the walk-in closet and thought how nice the extra space would be. It made sense to start there. It was time to donate my parents' clothes to charity.

Though my mom and I were similar in size, we had different styles, and it felt odd to keep her clothes. I grabbed some garbage bags from the kitchen and started adding items. I set aside a few cardigan sweaters that I thought I might like for the cooler nights on the lanai, but otherwise filled the bags to the brim.

I turned to look at four garbage bags full of clothing, and the reality hit me like a freight train. My parents' clothes, their entire wardrobe bagged up like garbage. Grief violently washed over me, and I crumbled to the floor in a flood of tears. I clutched one of mom's sweaters and inhaled her scent, which only made me cry harder. I still couldn't believe they were gone. I just wanted them to walk in the door and tell me this was a bad dream and that they were still here.

The sobs wracked my body, and then I startled when I felt strong hands wrap around my shoulders. I could barely make out Luke's face through the tears, but he sat on the floor and pulled me into his lap. I dropped Mom's sweater and clung to his shirt as I cried. He kept running his hand over my hair and murmuring sweet, soothing words. Gradually the tears eased, and my body stopped shuddering. Luke kept kissing me lightly on my hair and continued to rub my back. I felt embarrassed that he'd caught me in one of my weakest moments but was more grateful that he had come to my rescue. I finally unfolded myself from his lap and stood up on shaky legs. He stood, and I felt bad knowing that he must be so stiff and uncomfortable after sitting like that for God knows how long.

"Thank you," I said quietly, my voice hoarse. "I just... I just can't do this."

"Quinn, you should've come and gotten me," he said, pulling me back in for a hug. "You shouldn't be doing this alone."

"I didn't want to bother you," I said with a shrug and stared at the floor.

"Hey," he said, tipping my chin up to look him in the eyes. "You aren't a bother. I don't care what it is, what time it is, or how much of a bother you think you are going to be. You call me or run back to the cottage and get me. Okay?"

His eyes were so clear in that moment, and I found myself agreeing to everything he had just said. I was surprised when he bent down and planted a soft kiss on my lips. I stood in his embrace until I felt brave enough to step away. He insisted on loading the bags of clothes in his truck and said he would drop them off at the donation center so that I wouldn't have to do it.

"What's your plan for this space?" he asked me when we went back into the bedroom.

"I haven't been sleeping in here or using it at all, but it's a nice room. I'm going to make it mine, but I just can't get over feeling like I'm in my parents' room," I said, feeling the tears threatening to make an appearance again.

"So, let's make it fun," he suggested. "Do you want to go shopping?"

I raised an eyebrow at him. "You're offering to take me shopping? What kind of guy are you? Besides, don't you have to work?"

"Yes, I am offering, and I'll just give Cody a call. I didn't have anything scheduled for today, and he'll just let me know if it gets crazy."

His eyes appeared hopeful, and I found myself agreeing to his offer. I was still unsure where we stood, but I also didn't have it in me to question his generosity right now. Today needed to be about my grieving and healing, not trying to figure out if I was falling in love with this man. We boxed up most of the items in the bathroom too, as he mentioned the donation center often provided toiletry items to the homeless people in the area.

"You know what will make you feel better?" he asked me as we hopped in his truck to go on our mission.

"What's that?" I asked, thinking that him sitting next to me was making me feel so much better already.

"Pancakes." He looked so serious that I couldn't help but laugh.

He took me to one of the smaller cafes in town that I hadn't been to yet and introduced me to the most mouthwatering plate of macadamia nut pancakes imaginable. I was so stuffed by the time we were ready to leave that I couldn't even move fast enough to snatch the bill from him.

I felt some of the former sadness creep in as we made our way to the donation center, and it was like he could sense it, as he reached out and settled his hand over mine. The sadness didn't go away completely, but it definitely dimmed when his hand touched mine. He insisted I sit in the truck as he unloaded all the bags. Getting rid of my parents' things felt like such a cruel finality, but it was oddly renewing at the same time.

What Luke did for me that day was more than anything I'd ever experienced. The way he took charge when he knew I was at the end of my rope, and not only that, but he managed to get me from sobbing uncontrollably to stuffing my face with pancakes and laughing my ass off at all the eccentric décor items he tried convincing me to buy. We were never far apart from each other, and I often felt his hand on the small of my back, leading me around the stores or reaching out for my hand as we walked.

The back seat of his truck looked like an HGTV show had thrown up in it. I purchased the quilt I had been eyeing, as well as some new towels and a shower curtain covered in tropical flowers. I bought a new throw blanket for the couch and some throw pillows, which Luke gave me a hard time about.

"What is up with girls and throw pillows?" he asked after I threw two more in the cart. Even though he teased me half the time, he also helped me make decisions and was a lot better at coordinating colors and patterns than I ever would've expected.

We were both beat by the time we headed home and opted to grab fast food instead of sitting down for a meal.

"I need to start working again," I said after I finished off my burger.

"What exactly was your job in Chicago?" he asked me. "You mentioned you worked in advertising but never really told me anything about it."

"I actually do graphic design," I said.

"Like websites?" he asked.

"Yeah." I nodded. "But also brochures, magazine ads, and any form of advertising you choose. A lot of it is online nowadays, but some people still like something to hold."

"We need help," he said.

"Who? You and Cody?" This surprised me, since they seemed to have a good thing going.

"We need to step it up," he said. "We keep busy, but neither one of us is good with the advertising. We rely too much on walk-up appointments or the kids we instruct. We should upgrade our website too. We haven't done anything with it since we first started it. And maybe get some brochures to put in some of the gas stations or surf shops where tourists might see them."

"Are you saying this just to help me?" I asked, glancing at him. He always seemed so quick to be my hero, but I never wanted to take advantage of his kindness.

"No, really. You would be helping us," he said excitedly.

"Sure, I can help," I said.

We began discussing ideas, and before I knew it, we were pulling back in the driveway.

"I'll help you carry everything in," he said, parking. After we unloaded the truck, I considered asking him to stay, but between my emotional breakdown and all the shopping, I was really just tired.

"You need to get some rest," he said, reading my mind and pulling me in for a long hug.

"Thank you for everything today," I said, peering up at him.

"Anytime," he said. He bent to kiss me gently, and I nearly begged him to stay. Instead I walked him to the door and watched him head back down the driveway.

I was so in love with this man.

Chapter 32

Luke

Rather than scaling back on the amount of time I was spending with Quinn, I had found a way to spend more time with her. After feeling so frustrated that night at the taco truck, I woke up the next morning in a foul mood. I texted Cody and told him to let me know if he needed me, deciding I needed to tackle some of the yardwork and hopefully work out some of my aggression.

I had just gathered the tools I needed and started walking across the yard when I heard a gut-wrenching cry. I dropped my tools and started running to the house, thinking Quinn was hurt. As I rounded the back of the house, I realized the windows were open, and I could hear her sobbing. I only debated for a moment whether I should give her privacy before ultimately deciding that she shouldn't be alone.

I quietly let myself in the front door and walked down the hallway. Everything clicked the moment I understood she was in her parents' bedroom. I glanced around the room and saw clothes and personal belongings in piles and followed the cries to the closet, where I found Quinn crumpled on the floor, her body wracked with each sob. My heart broke for her right there.

Penny was lying by her side but looked at me helplessly.

Quinn was only startled briefly when I gathered her into my lap, but then she curled up like a small child and clung to me. I wanted to fix it and take away her pain, but all I could do was sit there helplessly, stroking her hair and promising her it was going to be okay.

My back ached, and my knee protested at the odd position we were sitting in, but I didn't dare move until I felt sure Quinn was done. All my anger and frustration toward her the night before melted away, and I considered how fragile she really was. Pushing her for something serious when she wasn't ready and while she was still grieving her parents was not the way to handle this. I needed to give her the space she needed, or she was never going to heal, and I was only going to succeed in pushing her away. She'd had her heart broken and her entire life taken away. She came to Hawaii looking for a new life, and if I wanted to be a part of that life, then I needed to tread lightly.

I wasn't sure if I should give her time alone for the remainder of the day but decided she needed a distraction. Shopping was certainly not my favorite pastime, but how bad could it be if I got to look at this beauty all day? Her mood lightened after pancakes, and I don't know what girl wouldn't be happy with some shopping.

I found myself having more fun than I anticipated and wasn't just doing it to make her feel better. It felt so domesticated, shopping for throw pillows and bathroom towels, and for a minute I pretended we were shopping to decorate our home together. It was so easy to envision being greeted at the door every evening or handing her one of these fluffy towels as she stepped out of the shower. Or better yet, removing the towel from her naked body and tossing the throw pillows to the floor so I could make love to her. I shook my head to clear these visions from my mind and focused on colors and patterns.

While chatting on the drive home, I was thrilled to learn the extent of her work. Cody and I really did need to improve our advertising methods, and our website was in dire need of a facelift. I could use this as an opportunity to spend more time with her, and maybe, just maybe, I could get her to fall in love with me.

I kept glancing over at her as she chatted about all the options we had for our website and fought to focus on the words coming out of her mouth. I kept zeroing in on those sweet lips and had to fight to turn my attention back to the road.

By the time we got home, I just wanted to leave everything in the truck and take her to bed. But as she got out of the truck and I saw her in the porchlight, I realized how exhausted she was and knew she needed the rest. I helped her carry everything inside and settled for a kiss. I wasn't leaving without a kiss.

Thirty-two years old, and I was just now fully understanding what it was like to be in love with someone. I had cared deeply for other girls and respected them and wanted the best for them. But never this. If Quinn was too far away, I couldn't breathe. I ached to tell her how I felt, but I kept reminding myself that if I really loved her, I needed to do what was best for her. I wasn't exactly a martyr implementing our friends with benefits arrangement, but if that's what she needed, I was happy to fulfill her needs.

After she initially rejected me, I didn't think I would ever convince her to give me a chance. The way things had worked out wasn't exactly what I'd had in mind, but I would take her any way I could get her. Hopefully my patience would pay off and she would realize she needed me as much as I needed her. I was still clueless how she'd infiltrated my heart so quickly and dominantly, but she had.

The next morning, Cody and I were setting up our tent, and I was relaying my conversation with Quinn to him.

"I didn't know that's what she did!" he said, eyes lighting up. "I just kinda thought maybe she was rich or something and didn't work."

"Well, I knew she had an advertising job in Chicago, but I didn't know what exactly," I said.

"Let's do it, then," he said. "We could really pick up the business. Think about how much work we could get *really* pushing that Luke Cole brand!"

I glared at him, and he laughed. He knew how much I hated commercializing off my name, especially with how my career ended. But maybe it was worth it to solidify our business and give us room to expand and someday actually have a building and more than just a tent.

"I was thinking maybe we could meet up with her for coffee and outline what we want and see what ideas she has," I said thoughtfully.

"Sure, whatever, man," he said. He plopped down in his chair and then said, "So when are you going to tell her?"

"Tell her what?" I asked confused.

"That you love her," Cody said with a smirk while casually looking out at the ocean.

I groaned and buried my head in my hands which only earned me a snicker from Cody.

"You got nothing? Where's your game, Luke Cole?" he asked, taunting me.

"I don't think she's ready," I said, sighing. "She only wanted it casual. Some asshole broke her heart, and then her parents died like right after. As in, the same day."

"Oh shit," he said, sucking in a breath.

"Exactly," I said. "It's only been six months since all that happened, and I'm afraid if I push too hard, I'll only push her away."

"That's tough," Cody said. "But you get to bang her in the meantime, right?"

That got him a handful of sand chucked at his face.

Chapter 33

Quinn

In the weeks that followed, I focused on working on the advertising for Two Braddahs Surfing. It was invigorating to work again, utilizing my talents and having something to be proud of.

I was so satisfied when I saw how impressed Cody and Luke were with their new website. I added a gallery of surf lesson pictures, an area for customers to leave reviews, a price list, and the option to book online. It was such an improvement from what they had before that they begged me to maintain the site for them for a monthly fee.

Shortly after, the guys brought me more business, referring their friends to me for a tree trimming business, Grant's construction company, and a surf shop. I couldn't believe the business they brought my way, and it was providing me the opportunity to freelance and work under my own terms. The best part was my office was my lanai. No required dress code, gossip around the watercooler, or office politics. I could work in a bikini, enjoy the tropical breeze, and if I was really lucky, I could watch Luke work in the yard shirtless.

The day after my meltdown and switching around the bedrooms, I called Aunt Nancy to check in with her. She was great about texting me to check in on me, but I felt like I owed her a phone call after all the support she had showed me since my parents died. Sometimes I needed to remind myself that she lost her sister too.

"It sounds like you're adjusting to your Hawaii life," she told me after I filled her in on renting out the cottage, becoming friends with Adrienne, adopting Penny, and starting my freelance work. I left out the parts about Luke. She knew I was taking surf lessons, but I didn't give her any details about him. I wasn't sure why exactly I felt the need to hide him, but I felt a little ashamed about our casual-sex arrangement, even though I was an adult. Discussing it with my aunt just seemed a little weird. I wondered if I would've shared it with my mom under different circumstances.

"It's starting to feel more like home," I admitted. I wasn't sure at what point I started feeling that way, but a lot had happened in the last four months. Especially concerning a certain surfer that had wiggled his way into my heart.

"How would you feel about some company?" she asked.

"Really? You're going to visit?" I asked excitedly.

"Well, I wanted to check in with you and see if you were settled. I know you have a lot going on, so if you're too busy, I completely understand."

"Not at all!" I exclaimed. "I would love to have you here!"

Nancy had planned on visiting my parents, but she had also expected to have more time. I knew visiting me wasn't the same, but my mom would have been thrilled.

"I was thinking maybe June, if that would work for you," Nancy said.

"Absolutely," I said. "You pick the time and I will make it work."

She got online, and we discussed flights over the phone until she found a good deal. I was really excited about my first visitor, envisioning taking her to my favorite places as well as my mom's favorites. I felt a pang of sadness that my mom wouldn't be able to show her sister around paradise but took comfort in the fact that she would be pleased that Nancy and I were keeping in touch.

A few weeks later, I was spending the afternoon working on designing some business cards when Luke got home from work. I waved at him from the lanai, silently willing him to come my way. We had only had sex a handful of times, even though I would be okay if it happened more frequently. I felt like he had put some distance between us, and I wasn't sure why. Maybe he thought I was crazy after my emotional breakdown?

But no, we still saw each other a lot between the surfing, working on their website, the dogs, and living on the same property. I always enjoyed his company, but I craved his touch. I felt like he was teasing me when we would work on the website and his hand would brush against mine, and he would always kiss me at the end of my surf lesson.

He retrieved Diesel from the cottage and then jogged up the steps to the lanai and took a seat at the table. I grabbed the tennis ball from the floor and chucked it in the yard, and Penny and Diesel raced each other to reach it first.

"What are you working on?" he asked. I turned my laptop to show him the cards I was designing. "Nice work," he said.

He always seemed interested in my work, which surprised me. In fact, he seemed to take a genuine interest in everything I did. I hadn't realized it at the time, but so much of my life with Aaron had revolved around him. It was his family, his career, and his dreams that took precedence. I was so in love with him that I hadn't really noticed, but it was a welcome change to feel like someone cared about all things concerning me.

"Would you like to have dinner with me?" I asked hopefully. "I have pulled pork in the crockpot, and it should be ready soon."

"That sounds amazing, but I really need a shower first," he

said. "The water was especially salty today, and I feel so sticky."

"You can take one here," I said coyly.

He cocked an eyebrow at me.

"Is that so?"

"I have excellent water pressure," I said. "And the shower is huge. Almost like it was designed for two people."

"Sold!" he said, jumping from his chair and grabbing my hand to drag me in the house. I giggled as he freed me from my bikini, and I returned the favor and rid him of his board shorts. I had missed his body so much. We jumped in the shower, but then we shrieked as the water hadn't had enough time to warm up.

"Is somebody cold?" he asked, poking at my hard nipples. I nodded as my teeth chattered and sidled up against him. I ran my tongue along his pecs and then smacked my lips.

"Hmm, you are salty," I said, gazing up at him. The water warmed up finally and began to steam up the bathroom. I continued to test out which areas of Luke's body were salty and found the lower I got, the more rigid he got. "Something wrong?" I asked him innocently.

"Nope. Everything's good," he said, then let out a groan as I identified the saltiest area of all. I dropped to my knees and sucked as the water ran over my back. I reached around to grab his butt and pull him closer to me. His hands gripped my hair and then ran alongside my jaw as I pleasured him.

Finally, he hauled me up with one fluid movement and turned me around so that my hands were pressed up against the cool tile. I felt him probing me, ready to enter, when he stopped.

"We can't. Unless you want me to go grab a condom," he said, reaching around to fondle my breasts.

"I'm on the pill," I said, glancing over my shoulder. He didn't respond, so I turned around to face him. "Unless you don't want to," I said.

"There's just one thing," he started, trying carefully to choose his words.

"I'm clean," I said. "You are the only one I've been with since Aaron." I hated to bring up Aaron's name in that moment, but I wanted Luke to know.

"It's not just that," he said. He was still holding me close but seemed nervous to look me in the eye. "If we are going to do this, then we need to be exclusive."

"Hell yes!" I said. Then I bit my lip, afraid I'd sounded too eager.

"Still casual, of course," he said quickly.

"Of course," I said. I was curious how well it would go over if I told him right then that I was in love with him and there was nothing casual about it. But I didn't want to push him, and maybe this was the next step.

"So, will you casually fuck me in the shower?" he asked with an adorable smile.

"I thought you'd never ask," I said.

I squealed when he whipped me back around and pushed me against the shower wall. This time there was no holding back. I pressed my face against the tile and braced my hands on the wall as he thrust into me from behind, holding me up slightly by my waist. With no barriers and the intensity between us, there was nothing casual about it.

Chapter 34

Luke

I couldn't wait to get home and show Quinn what I got for her. The weekly surf lessons had done well for her. She was improving tremendously, and we had discussed her moving to something smaller than the twelve-foot beginner board. As luck would have it, one of the guys I knew was moving back to the mainland and wanted to sell his boards. He wanted to know if Cody and I were interested in any of them for our business. We weren't quite ready to expand, but you never wanted to pass up the opportunity for good, cheap boards. He also had a ten-foot board that I thought would be perfect for Quinn. I didn't think twice about it and bought it for her.

"Quinn!" I hollered as I parked and got out of my truck. I didn't see her on the lanai but didn't think she could be far.

She poked her head out the front door with a dish towel in her hands.

"What's wrong?" she asked, looking concerned.

"Nothing! Come here!" I couldn't contain my excitement. I knew she wasn't as passionate about surfing as I was, obviously, but I also vividly remembered how excited I was when I got my very own surfboard. Hopefully she would be excited as well.

She walked down the driveway, and I took a moment to

admire her very short sundress. Her skin had taken on a nice tan glow since moving here, and she looked amazing. I thought she was beautiful the first time I saw her on the plane, but she had also looked broken then. Now she looked happy and healthy, and I wondered how her heart was healing.

She looked very curious and a little apprehensive by the time she made it down to me.

"What's going on?" she asked with a nervous laugh.

"Check it out," I said, pulling the board out of my truck and holding it up for her to see.

"Oh, did you get a new board?" she asked.

I bit back a chuckle since I hadn't surfed on a board that long in ages, besides while giving lessons. She also had no idea the number of boards I had stored back at my place.

"No, but you did," I said with a grin.

"Wait, what? No way! For me?" she asked, stunned. "Where did you get it?"

"A guy I knew was selling his boards. You've progressed enough to move to a smaller board, and I knew this one would be perfect for you."

"Well, you need to let me pay you for it," she said, reaching out to run her fingers along the board. "How much was it?"

"Nope, it's a gift," I said, being stubborn. There was no way she was paying for it. She rarely let me do anything like this for her, and I wasn't taking no for an answer.

"I can't accept this," she said. "It's too much."

"Consider it a bonus for the work you did on our website," I suggested.

She looked at me, contemplating arguing some more, but then she clapped her hands and jumped up and down.

"Oh my gosh! My own board!"

I laid the board down in the grass and barely caught her before she launched into my arms.

"Thank you so much!" She peppered my face with kisses.

That was the only payment I needed. I was thrilled to see her so excited, and knowing I had put that look on her face was worth it.

I kept hugging her as she turned to admire her board.

"So, you think I can surf on something that small?" I laughed because it looked enormous sitting there on the grass.

"You will do great," I said.

"I can't wait to use it. But we aren't doing a lesson for a few more days, right?" she said, trying to remember.

"We can go right now," I said. "The surf is decent today, and it'll be a perfect time for you to try it out."

"Really?" I thought she was going to burst with excitement, and I congratulated myself again for putting that smile on her face.

We loaded her board back in the truck, and she ran in to change into a bikini, and we were on our way.

The beach park was busier than we were used to in the mornings, but there were plenty of waves for everyone. I grabbed a shorter board than I usually used during our lessons because I figured she could do pretty well on her own. We paddled out, and right away she got in position. She started paddling into the wave and jumped to her feet right away. She wobbled a little at first but then crouched down low like I had taught her and gained her balance back. The grin on her face was priceless. She eagerly paddled back to me, grin still intact.

"That was like a whole different experience!" she said, beaming. "I actually felt like I was in control!"

"You'll find you can control it a lot easier. You lose some of the stability, but you'll get used to it. It will be easier for you to paddle, and then you can start to learn how to turn too," I explained to her as we waited for the next set.

We caught the next wave together, and once again, I didn't have to give her a push. Her confidence increased with each wave as she became more comfortable with the new board. We surfed for over an hour, until the sun began to set behind the mountains and presented us with another beautiful sunset. Quinn looked tired but exhilarated at the same time. I was glad my instincts were right with the board and that she received the gift well.

It struck me then that this was the first time we had surfed together that wasn't really a lesson. She was improving enough that as long as she stuck with it, she didn't necessarily need lessons, but I wasn't about to tell her that and risk losing time with her.

After our lesson, we were both starving, and I suggested we stop by one of the local places for a burger. The place was busy, so we opted to sit at the bar and get waited on sooner. We were chatting when I glanced up at the mirror across the counter and saw a few girls in the reflection. They were hovering nearby and whispering with grand smiles. I had been recognized. I wanted to avoid eye contact and enjoy my time with Quinn, since it was the closest thing we had to a date. However, I could see the blonde girl had found the courage to approach me, and she marched over to the bar, running her hand along my arm.

"I can't believe it's you, Luke!" she exclaimed like we were old friends. I wanted to tell her to take a hike, but I swallowed my irritation and plastered on a grin. Most of the time I didn't mind meeting people, and I appreciated my fanbase, but this was not one of those times. Not to mention, how appalling was it that some of these girls thought just because I was somewhat famous that it gave them the right to touch me.

"Hey, what's up?" I said politely, shooting Quinn an apologetic smile. I don't think she saw it because she was pushing around the remaining fries on her plate.

"We just couldn't pass up the opportunity for a selfie," the girl said as her other two friends joined her.

"Sure," I said, hoping it would get them out of there quicker. They pushed in around me, separating Quinn from me and nearly knocking her from her barstool.

"Hey, be careful," I warned, as I reached toward Quinn to steady her. I could tell she was pissed, but she tried smiling politely at the girls and assuring them it was okay.

"Oh, is this your girlfriend?" the blonde asked boldly, still not removing her hand from my arm. I so badly wanted to answer yes to that question but knew that I couldn't. I still had a few more months of residing next to her, and I was determined to honor her request for a casual relationship. Hopefully at the end of our six-month living arrangement and nearly nine months since her life was turned upside down, she would be open to a relationship with me.

"Nope! Just friends!" Quinn responded before I could.

Her quick response felt like a kick to the gut. How long would it take to convince her that we were meant to be together?

"Well, in that case, can I buy you a drink?" Flirty Blonde asked.

"I can find my own way home," Quinn offered quietly. Flirty Blonde looked hopeful at that, but there was no way in hell I was spending another minute with her.

"I'm good, but thanks. You girls enjoy your night." I nodded to them, clearly excusing them as I turned back around in my chair and back to Quinn.

"You didn't have to do that," Quinn said quietly, looking up to the mirror in time to see the girls leaving in a huff.

"Nah, I don't want a drink. Besides, you and I are hanging out tonight," I said.

Once we agreed to be sexually exclusive, I felt completely committed to her, even though I downplayed it for her sake. I didn't really think she was looking for the next best thing, but we didn't really talk about it.

She seemed to keep pretty busy between her work, hanging out with Adrienne, and surf lessons with me, but that didn't mean she wasn't out meeting other people when I wasn't around. I even started utilizing my social media accounts more, just so I could keep an eye on her, thinking that maybe if I was around enough, even digitally, she wouldn't have time to think about meeting someone else.

"Oh, did you have plans for tonight?" she asked, taking a long sip of her drink but looking mischievously at me.

"I was kind of hoping I did," I said slyly.

"Well, I have to pay for that surfboard somehow." Her eyes met mine in the mirror.

"I accept all forms of payment, but especially sexual favors," I said, playing along.

"That will do," she said, quickly signaling for our check.

"In a hurry?" I asked, grinning at her.

"Yep!" she said, grinning back at me.

I struggled to abide by the legal speed limit on the way home. We hurried into her house and darted for the bedroom, where I more than happily tossed the throw pillows to the floor.

Chapter 35

Quinn

I squinted at the bright sunlight coming through my bedroom window and rolled over to avoid it, promptly rolling into a gorgeous naked body. I was a bit startled with the realization that this was the first time Luke had stayed overnight. We had been tired from surfing and eating too much and then coming back for a good romp. We cuddled afterwards, and I didn't anticipate us both falling asleep so heavily as to sleep through the entire night.

He peeked one eye open at me, and I rather enjoyed his ruffled just-woke-up look. He reached a muscular arm out and quickly pulled me close to him. Apparently he wasn't too upset about sleeping over.

"Good morning," I said, trying to subtly test my morning breath.

"Mornin'," he said with a long yawn. "Man, that was the best night of sleep I've had in a long time." He stretched, and I started to move to get up. His arm tightened around me and pulled me closer. "Where do you think you're going?" he asked.

I shrugged in response but relished the feel of his arms around me. He let out a little contented groan that melted my heart. I could really get used to waking up like this.

We lay like that long enough for me to feed that fantasy, when he finally released his hold.

"Okay, as much as I'd love to stay like this all day, I do need to go to work at some point," he said, sitting up.

"What time do you have to be there?" I asked, feeling chilled after losing his body heat. I pulled the sheet up around me, slightly self-conscious about how naked I was. He glanced down at his watch and furrowed his brow.

"I have a little bit of time," he said. He still looked so sleepy, and it was endearing.

"Do you have time for coffee on the lanai?" I suggested.

"Damn straight," he said with a smile.

I rolled out of bed and caught him staring at me.

"Any chance you'll have coffee like that?" The corner of his mouth tipped up as he looked at me hopefully.

I laughed heartily and shook my head. "No, we wouldn't get anything done if we both paraded around naked!"

"And what would be so wrong about that?" he asked, stalking over to me and wrapping his arms around me. I was well aware of his naked body pressed up against mine as he bestowed a soft kiss on my lips.

"Coffee!" I said, reaching around to smack his ass before I hurriedly grabbed some clothes.

He begrudgingly followed me and got dressed as well before we headed to the kitchen to make the coffee. I struggled not to stare at him leaning against my kitchen counters so casually, like it was his house. I wondered if he was imagining the normalcy as I shyly handed him his coffee mug.

His eyes met mine, and I briefly considered telling him I loved him. I had given up on denying my feelings for him like I had done when Adrienne first pointed it out to me. I didn't understand how this man could take the ashes of my life and make me feel so much love again. I had lost everything!

Everything! Yet I felt more light-hearted and happier than I had in a very long time.

We fed the dogs, who didn't seem the least bit bothered to be eating in each other's space. They had been together so much that I didn't think they noticed we weren't normally all together. I wondered how Luke moving back to his house once the renovations were complete would affect the dogs but pushed it out of mind before I could consider how it was going to affect me.

Long after he left for work, I was still reeling from the effects of our night together. I knew I was staying home all day, so I encouraged him to leave Diesel with Penny and me while I worked. I had to admit, I was getting rather attached to Diesel myself, but I used him being a playmate for Penny as an excuse.

They had run and wrestled in the yard most of the morning and were now taking a snooze in the warm sunlight. I sat on the lanai and tried focusing on the website I was developing in front of me but kept feeling distracted as memories from the night before invaded my brain. At this point, it felt like what we were doing was so much more than fooling around. I was desperate to tell Luke how I felt, but I also knew if he rejected me, our living arrangements would be so incredibly awkward. We had over two months until the renovations on his house would be complete, and my gut told me to wait. I dreaded the thought of Luke moving back and not having him near, but even worse would be if he rejected me and I had to see him daily knowing he didn't want me.

Adrienne thought I was nuts.

"How can you even think that, Quinn?" she asked one day while we were soaking up the sun on the beach a few days later.

"I'm not so full of myself to think any guy wants me," I said, avoiding eye contact.

"Luke isn't just *any* guy," she said.

"I thought you said you didn't know him very well," I threw back at her.

"I didn't before, but I have seen you together enough and have seen how you light up when you talk about him. Sure, Luke Cole could probably have any girl he wants, but he's with *you*. That says a lot about you."

"I don't know if that makes me feel any better," I said. I hesitated before saying the next part. "What if he gets bored with me?" The hurt from Aaron's betrayal had faded tremendously, but it was still there and would probably always be a little black blip on my heart.

"Can I say something without offending you?" Adrienne asked cautiously.

Even if I didn't want to hear what she had to say, I was curious.

"Go ahead," I urged.

"If you want to know my opinion, I think you have struggled more with your breakup from Aaron because it happened on the same night your parents died. I think the timing of the loss was worse than the loss itself."

I mulled over Adrienne's words of wisdom as I stared out at the deep blue water.

"I shouldn't have said that. I'm sorry," Adrienne said. I realized she was interpreting my silence as anger.

"No, I'm not mad. Just thinking," I said.

Was she right? I missed my life with Aaron, but did I actually miss *him*? If I was being honest with myself, the moment Aaron looked me in the eye and told me he was bored, I think I instantly fell out of love with him. The shock of losing our relationship and what that meant for my life almost hurt worse than losing him. I missed being a part of his family and having Ashley as my best friend. I missed his company and how that made the workday fun, but losing that sucked the energy out of my job. In the time I had been spending with Luke, I was learning more about myself and what I was capable of. Despite the loss I had experienced, I felt the glimmer of peace starting to break free. A huge part of that was credited to Luke. He was teaching me to be happy again.

"Do you really think it's that easy?" I finally said.

"What?" she asked. She had honored my need for silence like a true friend.

"To trust Luke. To love again."

"Honey," Adrienne said, looking at me with compassion in her eyes, "you already love him. Whether or not you tell him that is not going to change a thing."

"I'm just not there yet," I said. "It's a big, scary leap."

"I just want to make sure you don't miss out on the love of your life because you're scared," Adrienne said.

"I feel like I've heard this before," I said, finally breaking into a rueful smile.

"Because it's true, Quinn." Adrienne smiled back. "You are too close to your own situation to see it. But for someone like me, on the outside looking in, it's obvious. You two are crazy about each other but hiding behind the fear of losing what's right in front of you."

I thought about everything Luke had done for me since the first day I had met him. He had shown me nothing but kindness and patience. He had seen me at my worst but still stuck around. I thought about the plane ride, the surf lessons, and cleaning out my parents' bedroom. He was there for it all.

"I promise I'll think about it more," I said. It was all I was ready to commit to right now.

"At least it's something." Adrienne smiled back at me. I know she was secretly hoping I would run home and declare my love for Luke, but I was glad she didn't pressure me.

I still wasn't ready to tell Luke about my feelings, and I know part of it was our living situation. His renovations were moving along, and I was reminded daily that our time together was limited. I hated the feeling of a deadline looming over us. I wasn't sure if his house being completed and him moving back there ended our arrangement, and I was afraid to find out. Our situation was convenient, and I was always second-guessing myself and whether we were hooking up simply because he lived in my backyard.

How was I going to approach him about making our arrangement permanent when I felt a panic attack creeping in every time I thought about it? Luke had shown me how to love again, but maybe he had no idea the impact he had made on me in such a short amount of time. The love I felt for Luke was so much more powerful than what I ever felt for Aaron. I honestly couldn't believe I ever thought Aaron was the one. I never realized what I was missing out on until I met Luke. But while the feeling of Luke's love was fulfilling to my soul, I was deathly afraid of Luke not wanting anything more than an occasional romp in the covers. I never considered myself the type of girl to need a man in my life to feel fulfilled, but I also never imagined in a million years that I would end up where I was today, orphaned, living in Hawaii and dating a famous surfer. Well, sleeping with him anyway.

I had spent entirely too much time fretting about the predicament I found myself in and barely realized how rapidly Aunt Nancy's trip was approaching. I was looking forward to seeing her under less traumatic circumstances and simply enjoying her company. I tried to get as much work done as I could before her visit so that I could enjoy my time with her. I loved being able to set my own hours and take the liberty of a flexible day whenever I wanted. I went into a cleaning frenzy the last two days before her arrival. I knew Nancy wouldn't care what the house looked like, but I wanted it to be perfect.

The day of Nancy's arrival was finally here, and I was so excited. Every corner of the house was clean and smelled like the mango candles I had recently purchased. The summer season had settled in on the North Shore, and the sun was shining in the windows with a pleasant trade wind keeping the house cool.

I drove to the airport with my windows down, not even caring that my hair would be a tangled mess by the time I got there. My timing was perfect, as Nancy was exiting baggage claim just as I was pulling up. I gasped at first because from a distance, it looked like my mom standing there in a floral sundress and sunglasses. I felt a twinge of sadness and tears prick at my eyes but swallowed hard and considered myself blessed to still have Nancy. It was easy to feel like I had lost everything that awful day, but she had been there for me when I had no one else.

I put my car in park and hopped out, running around to embrace her. I held on to her for what seemed like forever, until I glanced over and realized we were getting stink eye from the airport attendant. I smiled brightly, challenging her to interrupt my reunion with my aunt. She gave me a tight-lipped smile but turned in the opposite direction, and I smiled to myself for convincing her to look the other way.

"Oh, this is for you," I said, reaching into my car to grab the lei I bought for her. I slipped it over her head and noticed how beautiful the flowers looked against her dark hair.

"It's beautiful!" she exclaimed, ducking her head to inhale the sweet scent.

"Let's get out of here," I said, grabbing her suitcase and deciding not to test my luck with the airport attendant.

Nancy looked so youthful as she stared out the windows in awe, reveling in her first trip to the islands. We chatted easily as I navigated through the rush-hour traffic. Traffic could be a bit nuts here, but living my entire life in Chicago seemed to prime me for it.

When we pulled in my driveway, Nancy covered her mouth with her hands and let out a little cry.

"Oh, Quinn, it's so beautiful," she gushed as we parked. My parents' home had certainly become my little piece of paradise. I loved how it was tucked in and surrounded by the towering mango trees and natural foliage. "I cannot believe your yard! How do you keep up with all of this?"

"I can't really take the credit," I admitted. "Luke, my tenant in the cottage out back, maintains it all." I cringed at referring to Luke as my tenant, but what was I supposed to say? My surf instructor? My fuck buddy? The love of my life?

"Well, I'd like to shake his hand," she said, looking around in awe.

"I'm sure you'll see him around," I said.

We carried her luggage inside, and I gave her the grand tour. Even though a lot of my parents' décor was still prominent, I felt like a lot of my personal touches were apparent. Picture frames were tucked into every available space, displaying my new life. Selfies of Adrienne and me on our favorite hike, entirely too many pictures of Penny, and a few pictures of Luke. I'd kept the one on the fridge from my first surf lesson, but I also had one of us that Adrienne took one day on the lanai when we were chilling with the dogs. She was so proud of herself for being so sneaky that day when she came around the house and saw us all sitting there and snapped a picture before we even realized she was standing there. But it was definitely one of my favorites. Along with my new life, I would always display pictures of my parents.

The bright colors I had added complemented the softy beachy tones my mom had decorated the house in. I smiled when I looked at my turquoise throw pillows contrasting against the gray couch, which Luke still loved to tease me about. My mom was never big on burning candles, but it was one of my favorite things—they always soothed me, and that was reflected with the half dozen I had scattered around. Penny jumped up from her dog bed in the corner and came over to greet Nancy.

"Oh, she's so sweet," Nancy said, bending down to pet her.

"She was a lifesaver," I said, smiling.

We rolled the suitcase down the hallway, and I showed Nancy to her room for the next ten days.

"This is so cute!" she said, marveling at the guest room. It was a really cute room, but I was still amazed that I'd utilized it as my room for so long compared to the available room across the hall. I confided to Nancy the struggle I had in taking over my parents' room, and she nodded sympathetically.

"You know, honey, that's just part of the healing process," she said. "It just takes time."

"Here it is," I said, leading her across the hall.

I had to admit, I loved my room. The big window let in a lot of natural light and just so happened to look down to the cottage, where I would sneak glimpses of Luke whenever possible. The furniture was the same, but the new quilt, pictures on the wall, and some artwork Adrienne had created made the room a little more modern and my style.

"Beautiful room," she said, smiling.

"Thank you." I beamed. Even though I wouldn't have the house if it weren't for my parents, I did take a deep pride in it. "Let me show you my happy place," I said, walking back out to the hallway and to the door leading to the lanai.

"Oh my gosh, I could just live out here!" she exclaimed.

"I know, right?" I agreed.

She sank into one of the chairs, and I took the other.

"You've done really well, Quinn," she said.

"It hasn't been easy," I said quietly.

"You seem like a different person than the last time I saw you," she observed. She looked at me closely, and I wondered if she knew what wonders good sex could make. "You actually seem happier than I've ever seen you."

"It's hard to explain," I said. And it was true. I would never completely be whole without my parents, especially losing them the way I did. But losing everything forced me to get outside of my comfort zone and take control of my life. I suppose I didn't think about it that way as I was doing that, but looking back on the last five months or so, I think that's exactly what I did.

Of course, if I hadn't met Luke, I don't know if I would be anywhere near this happy. Still, I loved my job more than ever, Adrienne was the best person I had ever met, and I had Penny. I'd taken on hiking and surfing and had a greater appreciation for my planet and taking care of my environment. I truly was a different person.

"Dear Lord," she said sharply.

"What's wrong?" I was instantly pulled from my self-prophecy.

"You didn't tell me your tenant was hot!"

I searched across the yard to see what she had seen to give her that reaction and broke into a grin when I saw Luke walking down the driveway with Diesel.

"Oh, yeah, that's Luke," I said. I still wasn't sure how to even begin to explain that to Nancy. I mean, it's the twenty-first century and all, and aren't women just as deserving as men to enjoy sex? However, I was still fighting the feeling of being promiscuous and sleeping with someone I wasn't in a relationship with.

"Damn," she said, sitting back in her chair.

I burst out laughing, as I had never seen Nancy be so blunt before. My laughter caught Luke's attention, and his head snapped back and found us on the lanai. He always knew where to look for me. He lifted a hand to wave at me as Diesel pulled him hard down the driveway. Diesel had spotted Nancy and was pulling to get to her. That dog had never met a human he didn't like.

I laughed and looked back at Luke. I could tell he was

curious who I was with. I hadn't mentioned that Nancy was coming. I'm not sure why. I knew he would meet her, and I wanted him to meet her, but I was afraid he would think I was pushing him to meet my only family, and there was nothing casual about that.

Chapter 36

Luke

Iswear I could hear Quinn's laughter a mile away, and my brain had some sort of radar tuned in to it. I had left a while ago to take Diesel for a quick walk and noticed that Quinn was gone.

Okay, fine, I pretty much knew whenever she wasn't home, I just never knew exactly where she was. I *hated* this casual shit. Whenever she was gone, I would always wonder where she was, who she was with, and if she was happy. I couldn't take much more of this. I was at the point in my life where I just wanted to settle down. When we'd set up this casual arrangement, I never expected it to feel like one big mind game. I loved every moment I was with her.

The morning I woke up and realized she was asleep in my arms felt like heaven. I could smell her coconut shampoo, as her hair was fanned out on the pillow beneath her. I watched her sleep for a few minutes and hoped she wouldn't think that was creepy. I just stared at her, willing her to love me and silently promising to protect her. She had been through more hurt than anyone ever deserved to feel, and I had the desire to protect her and to always make her smile. I was desperate to make this arrangement permanent, but I feared my impatience was going to scare her away. It had only been a couple of months since we hooked up the first time, but I had enjoyed my front row seat to her transformation. The sadness faded a little bit more every day, and it seemed like she was smiling more than she was crying. That had to mean something, didn't it?

I was pissed at myself for not being more patient, but I felt the constant tug-of-war of emotions, and it was wearing me out. One day I felt confident that I could wait for her to be ready, but other days I just wanted to shake her and tell her to wake up! This wasn't casual!

I found Quinn on the lanai as Diesel practically dragged me down the driveway and was a bit startled when I realized she wasn't alone. The striking resemblance took me off guard for a minute. If I hadn't known any better, I would have thought the woman seated next to her was Quinn's mother, but I knew that was impossible. However, there was no way this woman wasn't related.

"Hey, Luke, good to see you," she said. She acted so informal, like I was a neighbor she didn't know very well and not the man that had her bent over the bathroom counter two days ago.

"Hi," I said politely, waiting to be introduced.

"This is my aunt Nancy," she explained, gesturing to the woman who was getting kissed by Diesel.

"Diesel, down," I commanded.

"No, it's great!" she said. "I love these dogs!"

Diesel became distracted as soon as he saw Penny, and the two bounded down the steps and started wrestling in the yard.

"I'm Luke," I said, sticking my hand out to shake hers.

"So, you're the tenant in the back cottage Quinn tells me," she said, smiling.

"Yep, that's me," I said, fighting annoyance at being simply reduced to a tenant. I didn't even realize Quinn had any other family, and the fact that she hadn't even told me Nancy was visiting made me wonder if we weren't as close as I had thought.

"Quinn tells me you maintain the yard. I am impressed. It's beautiful," she said, gesturing with her hands.

"Thanks," I said. "I enjoy the work, and it's the least I can do since Quinn cut me a deal."

"The deal which also gets me surf lessons!" Quinn said, smiling.

"Oh, you're the one teaching her to surf!" Nancy said, clearly impressed.

"Yep, she's doing great," I said, smiling at Quinn. My annoyance was fading, as she was clearly excited to have her aunt here, and I liked it when she was happy.

"So, you must be a really good surfer if you teach others," Nancy said. Quinn burst out laughing. Nancy looked between us naively. "What?" she asked, confused.

"Luke was a professional surfer. He's not just good, he's amazing," Quinn explained.

It didn't matter if I was at the top of the surfing world before my injury—hearing Quinn call me amazing was more rewarding.

"Wow, that's so neat!" Nancy said.

We stood there for a few moments, and I decided to let them visit without me hovering.

"Well, you ladies stay out of trouble," I teased.

"Hope to see you around!" Nancy said as I called out to Diesel to follow me.

"He sure is easy on the eyes," I heard Nancy say not so quietly.

"Nancy!" Quinn hissed.

I chuckled to myself as I continued down the driveway. I might just have to get Nancy on my side. Maybe she could help me convince Quinn to date me.

Or marry me. Whatever.

A few days went by, and Quinn and her aunt were scarce. I assumed she was showing her aunt the island and wished I could've joined them. The surf was completely flat on the North Shore, so I spent a few days working on my house with Grant and Cody. There was still a lot of work to be done, but it was much easier to visualize now with the main footprint complete. The walls were done, and the kitchen was nearly complete, minus the new countertops. I was eager to choose my new paint colors and wondered if Quinn would give me her opinion. Maybe she was still willing to help me set up the loft bedroom and I could use it as an excuse to get more time with her.

"How is the timeline looking?" I asked Grant while we worked.

"I don't want to jinx it, but it might be finished earlier than we originally thought," he said as he set the new bathroom vanity in place.

"You think?" I asked. I was a bit surprised to hear that, but it made sense considering the progress we had made.

"We'll see how the next two weeks go, but it's looking promising," he said. "The biggest thing is we won't get the countertops or the flooring for another couple of weeks. I've been keeping an eye on the shipping information, and they are supposed to be at the dock in California by the end of the week and then put on the slow boat."

"Hmmm," I said thoughtfully. "So if we work hard the next two weeks, we'll be ready to finish up when those things are in?"

"That's the plan," he said. I wondered how this would affect things with Quinn. I'd signed the lease for six months, and I would pay her regardless, but I could be leaving the cottage sooner than we expected. It could be a good thing, or it could be a bad thing, but only time would tell.

That evening, I got home late, and my shoulders were sore from the work on the house. I couldn't get comfortable, even though I was exhausted. I was finally drifting off to sleep when Diesel sat up, alert. I thought I heard something, but I wasn't sure if it was just my half-asleep state. I heard a light tapping and then a squeak. I sat up quickly as I realized the squeak was my front door opening. Diesel let out a little bark but then started thumping his tail as Quinn's small frame filled the door to my bedroom.

"Quinn?" I asked, alarmed that something was wrong. She had never shown up like this in the middle of the night.

She walked silently toward the bed as I started to get up. She put her hand on my bare chest and pushed me back on the bed. My alarm quickly turned to arousal as I realized nothing was wrong. In fact, everything was just right as she straddled me and bent down to press her lips to mine. Her hair hung like a curtain around us as our kiss deepened. I gripped her hips, then lowered my hands to cup her ass. She started to move, and every part of me was wide awake. The thin cotton shorts she wore didn't serve as much of a barrier, as did the tight tank top she wore. She broke away from the kiss and leaned her forehead against mine.

"Did you miss me or something?" I whispered, teasing her.

"How can you tell?" she whispered back.

"I thought something was wrong," I said.

"I feel like a rebel, sneaking out of my own house," she admitted with a giggle. "But I didn't feel right having you come over with my aunt in the next room."

"How long is she here for?" I asked.

"Ten days."

"Oh, and somebody couldn't wait that long?" I teased her as I reached up and plucked her breast from her tank top and promptly put it in my mouth.

She answered with a moan and grinded against me.

I couldn't think of anything better than seeing Quinn like this. Her shyness and insecurities were nonexistent, and her passion was alive. I had never seen her more in her element than now. Was she always like this in bed or only with me? I really hoped it was just with me and that I'd brought this out in her. I never wanted it to end.

I tugged at her shorts and wondered how attached she was to them. I decided to take the risk that she wouldn't care and yanked at them until the seams made a loud ripping sound. Instead of scolding me for ruining her clothes, she let out a throaty, sexy laugh as I tossed what was left of her shorts to the floor. She didn't try to rip my underwear but removed them slowly and seductively. Through the shadows in the room I could see enough to make out that incredibly sexy look I'd come to love.

She didn't bother removing her underwear and just pushed it aside and lowered herself onto me. I closed my eyes as I inhaled sharply and was overcome with pleasure. She started out slow but quickened her pace, and I fought to control myself. I didn't want it to be over, and I was afraid to climax before she had the chance to, but she suddenly clenched around me and cried out as she came. Feeling her tighten around my cock was all it took, and I joined her.

She climbed off me and nestled her head on my shoulder. I reached around to pull her close.

"Well," I said breathlessly. "That didn't take long."

She giggled and pressed her face embarrassingly into my chest.

"I'm sorry, I guess I was really horny," she admitted.

"Um, yeah, you never have to apologize for that," I said, running my hand along her hair. "I'm glad to be of service to you."

"So, you don't feel used?" she asked, peeking up at me.

"Nah," I said. Obviously, I was benefitting from this, and there could be worse things than having this gorgeous girl throw herself at me, but I really wished it was more to her than sex.

"This casual thing is working out pretty well for me, then," she said. I sensed she was teasing, but I tensed up slightly at her remark.

"There could be worse things," I remarked, trying to keep the mood light.

"Now I have to sneak back in a tank top and thong," she whispered.

I burst out laughing and felt her shaking in laughter as well. Right then we heard a loud rip and glanced over to see Diesel on the floor tearing her tank top to shreds.

"Make that a thong," I corrected her, laughing harder. "Diesel, no!" I said, reaching and trying to grab it from him.

"Don't worry about it." She grabbed my arm to pull me back on the bed.

"I might be able to give you a T-shirt," I said with a smile.

"Good," she replied, snuggling in closer.

We lay silently for a few minutes cuddling, and I could feel myself fading, especially after my release. I would sleep awesome if she would just do that every night.

"Are you staying?" I asked.

"I better go back," she answered.

"Are you worried you're going to be grounded?" I asked.

"No." She laughed. "I just feel awkward about it. I know I'm an adult and everything, but it's kind of hard to explain to my aunt that I'm fucking the guy out back." Once again, I debated telling her I could be more than her fuck buddy, but I refrained and just continued stroking her hair.

"I get it," I said. I gripped her tighter, hoping she would reconsider. We hadn't slept, *actually* slept together except that one night, and I had been dying to do it again. I could smell her hair, and I loved the feel of her bare breasts pushed up against my chest.

I didn't realize I had fallen back asleep until I felt Quinn straddling me again, attempting to get out of bed. I'm not sure how she thought she was going to accomplish that without waking me and was amused at her slow movements. Without opening my eyes, I reached up with both hands and gripped both her breasts.

She was briefly startled, but then laughed.

"We fell asleep!" she said so seriously.

I peeked one eye open and noted that the sun was barely coming up.

"I know, I slept really good," I said, not removing my hands.

"Luke, I have to go before Nancy wakes up!" she said, alarmed.

"Uh-uh," I said, pulling her back down and plucking her nipple in my mouth. Yeah, I could definitely wake up like this every morning.

She wiggled against me in protest. I stopped sucking long enough to say, "You aren't helping your case if you are trying to leave." She stopped, realizing I was hardening beneath her.

"Luke, you're terrible!" she said.

"This coming from the girl who snuck into my place in the middle of the night to attack me!" I exclaimed. I enjoyed seeing the blush on her face.

"I know," she said. "I still can't believe I did that. But it's not like I got any argument."

I looked up at her and fell in love with her all over again. She leaned over me with her soft hair pulled to the side. Her face was clean and makeup free, and I could see a few of the freckles scattered over her nose that she usually tried so hard to cover. I loved seeing her in this pure, relaxed state, and the fact that she was naked didn't hurt either. I swallowed hard as I reached a hand up and tucked her hair behind her ear. I gripped the back of her neck and pulled her down to kiss her. I thought she would protest more, but instead she responded and kissed me back even harder.

Fortunately, there were no clothes to get out of the way this time.

Chapter 37

Quinn

I gratefully accepted the T-shirt Luke handed me and slipped it on. It wasn't nearly as long as I had hoped, especially considering we couldn't locate my thong. I tiptoed across the lawn, praying the sun would sleep in a little longer, until I was safely in my room.

"Well, good morning."

I shrieked when I looked up and saw Nancy sitting on the lanai, casually sipping coffee.

"Oh my God!" I said, mortified.

She just looked at me and snickered.

"Talk about the walk of shame," she commented.

"Umm." I looked around, trying to come up with an explanation while tugging on the hem of Luke's T-shirt, willing it to be longer.

"Here." She took mercy on me and held up the throw blanket I kept on the lanai.

"I don't know what to say," I said quietly, my face on fire.

"Oh, Quinn, seriously," she scolded me.

I looked up at her curiously.

"You are a grown-ass woman. You have a hot man on your

property. I would think there was something *wrong* with you if you weren't banging him!"

My jaw dropped. Had those words come out of Nancy's mouth?

"Nancy!" I scolded her instead.

"Take a seat." She gestured to the empty chair.

I reluctantly agreed and gratefully took the coffee she handed me.

"So, tell me about him," she said. "And I don't mean the fact that he's your *tenant* or a former professional surfer."

"It's just casual," I said, giving in.

"Does he know that?" she asked, browsed raised.

"What do you mean?" I asked, confused.

"Quinn, nothing about the way that man looks at you is casual," she said.

"Really?"

She snorted in response. "I figured it out the moment I met him!"

"So, you really think he's into me?" I asked.

She looked at me like I had horns sticking out of my head. "Quinn, that man loves you."

I stared at her blankly, not sure how to respond. I had admitted to myself a long time ago that I was in love with him, but I was simply hoping he liked me enough to consider dating me. It had never occurred to me that he might actually love me back.

"What are you waiting for?" she asked me gently. She seemed to know it was a sensitive subject to me.

"I didn't come here looking for love," I said, pulling at a loose thread on the blanket.

"Love comes looking for you," she stated confidently.

"Did you read that on a cross-stitch pillow?" I asked sarcastically.

"Do you know how I met your uncle Don?" she asked me. I

realized I didn't know much about her relationship with Don. They were always just Uncle Don and Aunt Nancy. I knew she'd taken it really hard when he died, but they knew for quite some time that he wasn't going to beat the cancer.

"No, I don't think so," I said.

"I had a boyfriend," she started. "I had just started my job at the newspaper, and I already was dating this boy. He was nice and all, but I didn't feel real serious about him. Then I met Don."

"How did you meet?" I asked, drawn into her story.

"I had to interview him for a story. He was the new head coach for the basketball team at the school. He kept flirting with me the entire interview, but I was trying to keep it professional. Do you know what he did? He asked me on a date on live television!"

I laughed heartily when she told me this. I could totally picture it. Don always had a mischievous twinkle in his eye. He was never the serious uncle. He always had some corny joke to tell me and would slip me money whenever no one was looking.

"I told him I had a boyfriend and that I wasn't interested," she continued. "And he just told me we would see about that."

"So, what happened?" I asked.

"I was meeting my boyfriend for dinner that night, and he had seen the entire interview. I thought he would be mad at me, but he told me to go for it!"

"What? Are you serious?" I asked.

"As a heart attack." She nodded. "I wasn't sure whether to be excited or insulted! My boyfriend told me that he didn't really think we were meant to be together and that everyone who saw that interview was more interested in the chemistry between Don and me than the basketball team!"

"I can't believe I never knew this!" I said. "That's awesome!"

"It was. Don knew what I needed before I did. He took one

look at me and could see we were destined to be together. We were married three months later."

"So soon?" I asked, skeptical.

"I didn't figure there was any point in arguing once he asked," she said. "I knew he wasn't going to take no for an answer. Sometimes you just know."

"And you were happy?" I asked.

"For forty-seven years," she said with a smile. "I miss him terribly, but what if I hadn't interviewed him that day? We were destined to be together. I have no doubt about it."

I couldn't help but think about all the ways Luke and I were repeatedly thrown together. I often thought about the circumstances, and it was difficult to argue that destiny hadn't had a hand in it.

"Wow," I said, sinking deep into my thoughts.

"How did you meet Luke?" she asked, urging me to open up. I told her the entire story, beginning with the plane ride. I thought she was going to fall out of the chair, she was laughing so hard.

"I'm glad you're amused!" I said.

"Do you hear yourself?" she asked. "You can't make this stuff up!"

I nodded, not even attempting to dispute her.

"I'm scared," I said, my voice barely a whisper.

"I know, sweetie," she said, reaching out to touch my hand. "You have been through a lot. It's hard to get back out there and let yourself live again after experiencing something like you did. But you have to."

"I feel like I'm starting to," I said. "I don't feel the sadness suffocating me quite so much anymore."

"You have so much life in front of you," she said. "Give that man a chance to love you. To prove to you that you can be happy."

"What if he hurts me?" I asked, my voice cracking.

"Sometimes the reward outweighs the risk," she said.

"When did you get so wise?" I asked, swallowing hard to fight the tears bubbling beneath the surface.

"It comes with age, my dear." She leaned forward and looked me in my watery eyes. "You are young, beautiful, and one of the sweetest girls I've ever known. You have a lot to offer, and you deserve to be loved. Don't you ever forget that. Your parents would want you to be happy. And I think they would have liked Luke."

A tear escaped and trailed down my cheek.

"I miss them so much," I whispered.

"I do too. Some days I can't even fathom that they or Don are gone. It doesn't seem possible. But look at it this way—we got to experience their love. My sister was my best friend, and I got to see her happy with your dad and even happier when you were born. And Don was the love of my life. I've experienced more love than some people will experience in a lifetime. I want to see you experience the same thing."

"So, you really think I should go for it?" I asked hesitantly. Could I really do this? Put myself out there to Luke?

"I do." She nodded. "It doesn't guarantee you won't get hurt, but I tend to consider myself a pretty good judge of character, and I think he's a keeper."

"Have you and Adrienne been talking?" I cocked my head at her. She laughed at the look on my face.

"No, but I've got to meet this Adrienne you keep talking about. She sounds like a smart girl."

"She's the best friend ever," I said. I missed Ashley so much in the beginning, but Adrienne helped fill that void and then some. I never would've made it through these past months without her help.

"She's been trying to convince me to give it a go with Luke for a while," I explained. "She thinks I struggled more with Aaron's timing than losing Aaron himself."

Nancy wrinkled her nose, causing me to laugh. "I can tell you this now," she said. "But I never really liked Aaron. I always thought he was kind of a putz."

I bent over in laughter. I was seeing a spunkier side of Nancy I had never seen before.

"Wait? Did my mom like him?" I wondered what my mom had told her.

"She was happy if you were happy. That's all that mattered to her. But I do know she was about ready to strangle Aaron if he didn't marry you soon!"

"Ha! Well, I guess he did me a favor, didn't he?" I said. I couldn't even imagine being married to him now and wondered how I had ever seen that as my future.

"Let's just say your parents would've liked Luke much better." She smiled.

"I think I'm starting to feel like I can talk to Luke about this," I said. "But I still might wait another few months, when his renovations are done on his house. I really hate to ask him to make this serious and have him say no and still have him living in my backyard."

"I understand," Nancy said, "but I highly doubt he's going to say no."

I took a deep breath, feeling renewed.

"Can I go put some clothes on now?" I asked.

Nancy laughed hard and waved me on. I headed into the house with a big smile. Life was about to get good.

Chapter 38

Luke

"So, when is the wedding date?" Mia peered into the phone screen during our video call.

I just laughed and shook my head at her.

"You're something else, you know that?" I said.

"That's just what makes me so special!" she said.

"Right!" I snorted in response.

"You're just mad that I'm Mom and Dad's favorite!"

"I can't argue with that. You are their baby girl," I said.

"Whatever. They are so proud of you. But they would love you more if you married Quinn and gave them grandbabies!"

"Shit, Mia. Jumping the gun much?"

"Well, when do I get to meet Quinn?" she asked. "Would you bring her to the wedding?" Her face lit up as the idea occurred to her. "That's perfect! You can bring her to Chicago! Then we all can meet her!"

"That might be too soon," I said. "I'm not even going to talk to her about this for at least another month, but possibly two. Just trying to be patient and see how things go."

"Yeah, but you said your house might be done sooner, right?" she asked.

"Yes, but it's not like there's an exact science to this!" I protested. "I don't even know if she feels the same! I think she's letting her hurt and fear decide what she's doing with her life."

"Don't be stupid, Luke," she said pointedly. "As much as it grosses me out to talk about your sex life, this girl wouldn't be banging you all the time if she wasn't truly interested."

"I can always count on you to give it to me straight," I said.

"Duh," she said. "But my wedding isn't until October. That gives you plenty of time to win her over. Just crank up the ol' Cole charm!"

"We'll see," I said, not committing to anything.

"I want to see a picture of her!" she exclaimed.

"Um, I think I have one," I said. She had texted me one the day after we hooked up for the first time.

"Yeah, send it to me!" she said. "I want to see the girl my brother is head over heels for."

I didn't even argue. I was in deep.

"So, what's new with the wedding plans?" I asked, attempting to change the subject.

"Don't think I don't know you're trying to switcheroo on me," she said. "But I'll use any excuse to talk about my wedding!" She was beaming, and I loved seeing my baby sister so happy. She was going to make a beautiful bride. Everyone probably expected me to get married before Mia, given that I was older, but I was excited for her.

"Do you have everything ready?" I asked. I really was clueless when it came to wedding planning. I was in the wedding of one of my surfer buddies several years ago, but it was a pretty small ceremony on the beach, so I figured it wasn't anything like the huge affair Mia and Derrick were putting on.

"I think so," she said. "Derrick's mom has been really involved, so that helps."

"Are you getting what you want?" I asked. I knew Derrick's mom, Gretchen, could be a bit pushy and tended to grate on Mia's nerves.

"For the most part," she said. "But Derrick's family is very prominent in Chicago, so there are certain expectations."

Derrick was a lawyer working in his father's practice. His father, John, was a well-known power attorney, and apparently they were something like socialites in Chicago. I never really saw Mia being a socialite, but I suppose if Derrick made her happy, that was cool. Mia was always outspoken and opinionated and held her own with the boys. Once she was old enough to figure out how to use a camera, she was never without one. I always admired her confidence, how she never apologized for who she was. I hoped marrying Derrick wouldn't squash the light she projected so boldly.

"So, in other words, it's gonna be super fancy? I can still wear my board shorts, right?" I teased.

"No, no, no," she said. "You have to wear a tux!"

I enjoyed hearing the slight panic in her voice. Like I would really show up to my baby sister's wedding in board shorts.

"I still can't believe you're getting married," I said.

"I know, right?"

"Are Mom and Dad involved much?" I asked. I should call them. I had been so wrapped up in everything here and with Quinn that I hadn't called them in a while. Texting was nice, but it wasn't the same as an actual conversation.

"Somewhat," she said. Her voice had a slightly higher pitch, which usually meant she wasn't completely telling the truth.

"What aren't you telling me, Mia?" I pressed.

She let out a frustrated groan. "Gretchen is fucking driving me insane!" she spat out finally.

"That's not a surprise, right?" I asked.

"Not really, but I really wanted this to be my mom and me planning and maybe running a few ideas with Gretchen. But noooo. Gretchen has highjacked the entire thing and taken the fun out of it for Mom!"

"I'm sorry, Mia. I know you were really excited to plan it.

Maybe you should just tell Gretchen to fuck off?"

"Right," she huffed. "I wish that were an option, but Derrick is rather protective of his mom."

"He should be protective of you," I pointed out. One strike against Derrick. I'd had no reason not to like the guy up until this point, but when my little sister was upset, that didn't help him stay in my good graces.

"I'm just ready to tell him to forget the whole thing and let's just run to Hawaii and get married," she said, sounding dangerously close to tears.

"Maybe you should tell him that," I said.

"Maybe," she said non-committedly, looking away from the phone.

"Is everything else okay?" I pressed.

"Yes." She sniffed. "I'm ready to be his wife. I just want this whole wedding process to be over. I didn't want to let it stress me out. It's not even the planning that has me stressed."

"So, never get married is what you're saying," I teased, trying to make her laugh.

"Nope," she said quickly. "You have to marry Quinn on a beach in Hawaii."

I laughed. "I'll get right on that."

"You better tell me as soon as you tell her you love her," she insisted.

"I don't know if I'm going to go that far," I said. "I don't want to scare her away."

"Whatever," she said, glaring at me through the phone. "Don't wuss out. If you love her, you need to tell her."

"Yes, ma'am," I said. At least bossing me around seemed to keep her tears at bay.

We talked a little longer, but then we disconnected when Derrick got home from work. I had an uneasy feeling about Derrick, but I didn't have enough to go on. Mia and I were fortunate to have a loving mother who only wanted us happy. I couldn't ever imagine a time where my mom would take charge of something and hurt those around her. That thought led to wondering if my mom would help Quinn plan our wedding.

"Damn," I muttered, wondering where that came from. "Way too early for that shit." Diesel walked over then and placed his head in my lap and looked up at me expectantly.

"I know, Bud, I was just kidding. I don't think it's too early either." If Quinn told me today that she would marry me, I would jump in with both feet. The realization was a bit sobering.

I was walking Diesel outside one last time before bed that night and noticed the lights were on and casting a soft glow on Quinn's lanai. I intended on sneaking up there and stealing a kiss and maybe a little over-the-clothes fondling but stopped dead in my tracks when I realized it was Aunt Nancy and not Quinn. Talk about a boner killer. I wanted to retreat into the shadows before I was seen, but it was too late.

"Um, hello," I said, waving awkwardly when she looked up and smiled.

"Hi, Luke, how are you?" She set her book down.

"Great, just taking Diesel out," I answered.

"Were you looking for Quinn?" she asked.

"She's usually up here at night reading, so I just assumed you were her," I said. "Sorry."

"No need to apologize to me," she said. "Quinn's in bed if you wanted to sneak in there." She nodded toward the door.

I gaped at her in shock, and she laughed at my response.

"You kids think you're fooling me?"

"Uh…" I said. I was speechless.

"I caught her sneaking home the other morning, not wearing a whole lot, I might add." Her eyes sparkled with amusement, and I laughed along with her. We were adults, and we weren't doing anything wrong, but it still felt equivalent to being busted by parents.

"You got me." I raised my hands in defeat.

"I think it's great," she said.

"Yeah?" I asked. This entire conversation felt awkward, but I was secretly glad to have a chance to talk to Nancy without Quinn there.

"I don't have to tell you that she's been through a lot," she said. "All I know is the girl who left Chicago and the girl here are two entirely different people. And I think I have you to thank for that."

I ducked my head down, slightly embarrassed.

"She's special," I said quietly.

"She is," Nancy agreed. "I love that girl like she's my own. Please take care of her."

"I want to," I said. "I just don't think she's ready."

"She's getting there," she said. I wanted to ask if they had talked about me, but I didn't know her aunt well enough for that. It just felt weird. Too forward.

"She keeps saying she wants to keep it casual," I said.

"She's just trying to protect herself," Nancy said. "Just give her some more time."

I nodded, wondering how much longer I would have to wait. I felt invested in this, and as crazy as I was about Quinn, I didn't want to keep waiting if she really wasn't interested.

"Well, thanks," I said, not sure what else there was to say.

"It was a pleasure seeing you again," she said, smiling.

Diesel and I walked back to the cottage, where I got lost in my thoughts.

Chapter 39

Quinn

Having Nancy visit was another step in my healing process that I hadn't known I needed until she was here. It was the closest thing to having my mom back, and I was able to confide in her like I used to do with my mom. I enjoyed taking her around the island and visiting waterfalls, my favorite beaches, and taking it upon ourselves to try out every little bakery we could find. We had dinner one night with Adrienne and Malia, and it was almost like having all my favorite people in one room, minus Luke. I wanted Nancy to see more of Luke, but I wasn't exactly sure how that worked in the casual guidelines of our relationship. I had barely seen him except that one incredible night I snuck into his place.

All too soon, I was taking Nancy back to the airport. Even though we'd had such a nice time together, now it felt like a dark storm cloud was hovering over us. I enjoyed her company more than I ever imagined and wished she could stay. When I suggested she move to Hawaii, she just laughed.

"Quinn, you have built yourself a life here. I think it's good in a way that you came here with nothing. The relationships you have built, your career, and everything else were all from your own doing."

"I guess you're right," I said. I'd never really thought of it that way.

"Please consider everything I talked to you about with Luke," she said, getting serious. "I think you will be happier than you could ever fathom if you would just give him your whole heart."

"Okay," I said, promising to think about it. I was so tired of thinking about it. He would be moving out within the next six weeks, and that deadline approaching had me in a bundle of nerves. I was excited about talking to him, but at the same time I hated knowing he wouldn't be in my backyard anymore, and of course the fear of his rejection was still looming large. I pretty much decided that if he wasn't interested, I was moving back to the mainland. I didn't know where or how, but this island was too damn small. I was in way too deep to see him around town and know he wasn't mine.

Before we knew it, we were pulling up at the airport, and it was time for goodbye.

"Please visit again," I whispered in her ear as we hugged.

"I'll wait for my wedding invitation," she replied.

I just laughed and hugged her tighter. I felt sad the entire drive home and couldn't shake the feeling even after I walked in my door. I missed having someone around me. I was the type of person who required alone time, but the endless amounts of alone time I had had for nearly the last year was driving me mad.

I set my purse down and turned, startled to see Luke at the door, hand poised to knock.

"Hey," I said, opening the door.

"Hey, did you just get home?" he asked.

"Yep. Had to take Nancy to the airport," I said. My voice wavered on the last word.

Luke looked at me sympathetically and then held his arms open. I sank into him without hesitation and let the tears flow.

"I don't know why this is so hard," I said through the tears.

"It's hard to live far away from family. I get it," he said, stroking my hair.

"Especially when it's the only family you have left. And she had to get on an *airplane*, of all things!"

Luke was silent for a moment as he took in my words.

"I'm sorry. I never thought about how hard that must be for you," he said. I don't think I even realized how much it was affecting me until I said the words aloud. I only had Nancy left, and putting her on a plane was almost harder than getting on a plane myself.

"Know what would make you feel better?" he asked.

"Pancakes?" I asked.

He laughed heartily. "I don't think we'll find anyone serving pancakes right now, but I can make some for you if you really want," he said.

"No, it's okay, I'm not really hungry," I said, in no hurry to move from his arms.

"I thought maybe you could go check out the house with me," he said. "I grabbed some paint samples, and I wanted to take them to the house and try to figure out which colors to pick."

I nodded slowly. That sounded like a welcome distraction.

"Unless you're too tired. No pressure," he said.

I finally pulled back from him, slightly embarrassed that I'd cried all over him again.

"No, that sounds fun," I said, wiping my eyes.

We grabbed the dogs to go along with us and headed the ten minutes to Luke's house. When we walked inside, I was taken back by the transformation.

"It's almost done," I said quietly. The reality of him leaving my property was sinking in.

"It's probably going to be done early," he said.

"So, you're moving out sooner?" I asked, dread apparent in my tone.

"I'll still pay you for the whole six months," he said.

That wasn't even what I was worried about. I felt even more depressed now, knowing that we didn't have six weeks like I'd thought.

"That's fine. Whatever," I said stiffly.

"We're waiting for the floors and the countertops to arrive. Everything else is close to being done," he explained.

"Okay," I said. It looked beautiful, even in the unfinished state. "So, let's see the colors you picked," I said, trying to shake my bad mood.

He pulled out a stack of samples, and I admired the earthy tones he'd picked, along with some neutral colors that would complement the beach house.

"Do you have any colors in mind for any particular rooms?" I asked him.

"Not really," he said. "I just started grabbing colors I liked. Anything is better than the dark wood paneling that was in here. I'm not real good with this decorating stuff."

"I'm not an expert by any means," I said, walking around as I shuffled through the colors. "What do the floors look like?" I asked, trying to envision the house completed.

"They are lighter bamboo floors with a bit of a gray tone," he said, pulling out his phone. He located the picture he wanted and held it up to show me.

"Okay." I nodded. The new cabinets in the kitchen were blue, which wasn't something I would've ever pictured Luke picking out, but I was practically drooling over them. The color was beautiful and set the beach tone for the entire main floor. "What about this one?" I said, holding up a sample titled "Sand." It was a light tan color, suited to its name, and would be a nice contrast with the blue cupboards, and I hoped it would bring out some of the colors of the floor.

"Yeah, great. Whatever you think," Luke said.

I was a little nervous that he was relying on me to pick out the colors and hoped that it would turn out how he wanted.

"Do you want different colors on the main floor?" I asked, looking around. With the open concept, it would be somewhat difficult to break up the colors, other than the bedrooms or bathroom.

"I thought about doing it all the same," he said. "But I think that one is neutral enough that it will work and not get annoying."

"Well, then that's decided," I said.

We walked into the master, and I took in the French doors leading out to the lanai and that gorgeous ocean view.

"I prefer blue for a bedroom," I said. "It's soothing."

He nodded quickly. "Blue it is."

"You're easy," I said, smiling at him.

"Don't you know it?" he said mischievously. I grinned at him as we moved to the guest bedroom.

"Is yellow too girly for you?" I asked. He had a cream color picked out, but I thought yellow would be nice for a guest bedroom.

"I don't think so," he said. "I didn't grab any yellow, though, did I?"

"No, but that's simple to pick out," I said. "Just don't go too bright or it will look like Big Bird threw up in there."

He laughed at my analogy, and we moved to the bathroom, where we picked out a light gray color.

"Thanks a lot for helping me with this," he said as we walked upstairs to the loft.

"No problem," I said. "I actually really enjoy this." The loft still took my breath away. I absolutely loved the large A-frame windows that looked over the beach. I fantasized about having a desk pressed up against the glass where I could work from. I momentarily forgot about picking out colors and walked over to stare out the windows.

I felt Luke approach me from behind and stilled when his hand caressed my hip.

"You like what you see?" he asked lowly in my ear. His breath tickled my neck, and I shivered.

"I do," I said. "You like what you see?"

"I do," he said, trailing his tongue down the side of my neck.

I was well aware we were up against the large windows and that there were people on the beach. These were the days when everyone had a camera at their fingertips, and I wasn't really digging the risk of being caught on camera.

"There are people down there," I whispered, barely able to form the words with his tongue on me.

"Don't move," he said. He disappeared for a moment, and suddenly the room went dark. I could still see the people on the beach, but nobody would be able to see us. I didn't say a word as he picked up right where he left off. He reached around and tugged lightly on the top of my dress. It was strapless, and he easily pulled it down, revealing that I wasn't wearing a bra.

"Nice," he whispered in approval. He couldn't see me, but he could feel me, as his hands were all over me. He continued to press against me and pushed me up against the glass. I liked the feel of the cold glass, and instead of feeling nervous or embarrassed, being so exposed was so exhilarating. I relished how Luke made me feel. I never felt more alive than when he was touching me.

I slightly arched my back so that my ass pressed up against his length. I smiled when I felt how hard he was and felt so empowered knowing I did that. I reached a hand behind me and seamlessly untied his board shorts.

"Easy access," I commented with approval as I freed him.

"Likewise," he said as he hiked up the skirt of my dress.

When I was with Luke, I never thought about being sad or

the loss I had endured. He made all the bad in the world melt away, and only the good of him existed. And right now, he was making me feel really good.

When we finished, I glanced shyly over my shoulder at him to find him grinning back at me.

"Well, at least the house is officially christened," he joked.

"You don't happen to have any tissue on you?" I asked, biting back my laughter because I already knew the answer.

"Guess we have a problem," he said. We laughed the entire time we attempted to figure out our predicament.

"Why does sex with you always end in laughter?" I asked.

"I'm not sure how to take that!" he exclaimed in shock.

"Don't worry, it's good," I said.

"It's official," he stated.

"What's that?" I asked.

"This is now my favorite room in the entire house," he said. "I never knew what to use it for, but I have found its purpose!" he declared.

I laughed harder, but inwardly wondered if it would happen again. Here we were, picking out paint colors and me helping him decorate. It was almost like he was setting it up to be my house too. I glanced at him curiously.

"What?" he asked when he noticed the expression on my face.

"Nothing," I said, chickening out. I was two seconds from telling him I was madly in love with him and begging him to let me live with him. "Was this what you had in mind when you invited me here?" I asked, steering the conversation from my real thoughts.

"I'd be lying if I said no, but I honestly didn't expect it to be like this," he said.

"So, do you think about sex with me often?" I asked. Part of me was teasing him, but I really wanted to know the answer to that.

"Do you really have to ask that question?" he asked. "Why would I have agreed to this arrangement with you if I didn't enjoy sex with you?"

I cringed inwardly when he referred to our arrangement. That damn arrangement was always a quick reminder of what the reality of our situation was.

"You really have no idea how beautiful you are, do you?" he said.

I turned to him, stunned by his comment.

"What?" I asked, figuring I heard him wrong.

"You are very beautiful, Quinn," he said, all joking aside.

"Thanks," I mumbled, looking down. Aaron was never overly sentimental, so it wasn't something I was really used to hearing.

"Look at me," Luke said, tipping my chin up to meet his eyes again. "I don't know who ever convinced you this wasn't true, but it is. You are beautiful, inside and out."

"Thank you," I repeated, meeting his gaze.

"And I'm not just saying that to get in your pants," he teased, lightening the mood.

"You don't have to when I'm wearing a dress," I teased back.

He pulled me close and hugged me tight, just briefly.

"You're something else, Quinn," he said affectionately.

"You aren't so bad yourself, surfer boy," I replied.

Later that week, I convinced Adrienne to take a break and go with me to the beach. I felt like she had been spending so much time caring for her grandmother or working that she had little time for anything else. I admired her and the burden of responsibility she bore and how she handled it with such grace. I also had been doing a lot of thinking and realized how much Adrienne had been there for me this past year and how she never asked for anything in return. I hoped I was a good friend to her and that she didn't feel like I was taking advantage of her friendship.

"How are you doing?" I asked her. I couldn't see her eyes through her sunglasses, and her face was blank as she lay on her beach towel, soaking up the sunshine.

"Great!"

Her reply was so automatic that I instantly questioned it.

"Are you really?" I asked, my gaze not wandering from her face.

She turned slowly to look at me. I struggled to read her expression without being able to see her eyes. Then she finally removed her glasses, and I could see the tears threatening to spill over.

"Oh no, what's wrong?" I asked, scooting over to be closer to her.

"I'm just really tired, and I'm sick of all my family drama," she said in a wobbly voice.

I had never seen Adrienne be anything but strong before, and she had never mentioned family drama.

"I'm so sorry," I said, reaching out to touch her arm.

"Why are you sorry?" She turned to me in confusion.

"I've been a really shitty friend," I said. "I've been so wrapped up in my own problems that I never even considered what you might be dealing with. I never meant to take you for granted, and I promise I'll be better."

"Quinn!" she scolded me. "Shut up! You've been through so much this year. I'm glad I could help. And having you here has been such a blessing. I've never felt like you were taking me for granted."

"Truth?" I asked.

"Truth," she promised.

"Okay, so tell me what's going on," I urged her.

"Sometimes I feel like all I do is take care of everyone

else, and there's no one to take care of me," she said, exhaling loudly. "I grew up in the middle of Honolulu with my parents and my two older brothers. Being the only girl, I had a lot of expectations put on me to take care of the home with my mom. I never really minded helping my mom out, but I was never given the opportunities that my brothers were."

"They treated you differently for being a girl?" I asked.

"Pretty much," she replied. "So anyway, I was always really close to my grandma, and I spent most every weekend with her on the North Shore. She always treated me like I was special and capable of doing great things. I wanted to go to college to get my business degree, but my parents always discouraged me. They thought I should settle down with a nice Hawaiian husband and be a good little wife."

"That is so old-fashioned!" I exclaimed in horror. My parents never had specific expectations for me. They always encouraged me to follow my own path. They could've pressured me to take over the diner for them, but they never once did. I couldn't imagine being born with expectations already in place for my future.

"I know, but it's how they were raised and how they raised us. Grandma encouraged me to go to college and even insisted on helping me pay for it, because I sure as hell wasn't going to get help from my parents. My parents were furious, and my dad and Grandma, who is his mother, had a huge falling out. They didn't talk for a few years, which made it awkward for me still living at home and going to college. Grandma started having more and more health issues, and it's like the rest of my family didn't care. They let something so stupid and petty ruin their relationship!"

"So, what did you do?" I asked.

"I moved in with my grandma to help take care of her."

"Did you finish college?" I asked.

"Nope," she said, disappointment clear on her face. "I was

only about twelve credit hours short, but the pressure was too much. My grandma needs my help more than she will ever let on, and I couldn't keep doing it all. I had a full load of classes and was cleaning houses full-time."

"And you never got to enjoy being a young college girl?" I asked.

She shook her head.

"So, no college parties, no dating or just being young?"

She snorted when I mentioned dating.

"Is this where you tell me who broke your heart?" I pressed on. I hadn't pushed her to tell me before, but I sensed she needed to talk to someone about her problems for once instead of trying to fix everyone else.

"Grant and I kind of had a thing," she said quietly, flipping her long braid over her shoulder.

"Like Luke's Grant?" I asked in shock. I never would've pictured that pairing.

"Yep, the one and only," she said wryly.

"What happened there?" I was really curious now.

"I was a freshman when he was in high school. I knew him but didn't know him all that well," she said. "When I started coming up to my grandma's on the weekends, I would see him and Cody and their group of friends. Not Luke, though—he was usually on tour. Anyway, I started hanging out with them, and Grant seemed to take a special interest in me. I was interested, obviously. I mean, look at him." She laughed.

Grant was a good-looking guy, but he definitely wasn't Hawaiian like her parents wanted. He was white as could be, but he definitely had the tall, dark, and handsome thing going for him. I had only been around him a few times, but he seemed really nice, was funny, and obviously had a good work ethic.

"Anyway, I just didn't have time to get into a relationship at that point, or at least I thought. I was enrolled in classes, helping Grandma, and working as much as I could. I didn't mind the responsibility, but I was afraid committing to a relationship would be too hard. Grant kept trying to convince me otherwise, and he was slowly earning my trust, and I was really falling for him."

"Then why aren't you together?" I asked.

"Well," she said bitterly, "I got invited to a bonfire on the beach one night, and Grandma insisted I go and have fun. I couldn't wait to see him and felt ready to commit to the relationship he wanted so much. I get to the bonfire, and I can't find him. Someone pointed toward the direction he was in, and I went looking for him. I was about ready to give up when I heard a giggle coming from the shadows. There was a hammock hung between two trees, and Grant was in there with another girl. I turned around, instantly heartbroken, and he realized I was there. He tried stopping me, and then the girl fell out of the hammock, completely naked."

"Oh, hell no!" I said.

"He broke my heart," she said. "He'd spent all that time convincing me to trust him and give him a chance and then he didn't even care enough about me to see it through."

"Did you ever talk to him about it?"

"No, not really. There was nothing else to say. Besides, I got even busier once I moved in with Grandma and had to drop out of school, and after that I just had no interest."

"Don't you think he's changed?" I asked. I didn't know him well enough to make that judgement, but he seemed to have his shit together now. Maybe he had regrets too.

"I highly doubt it," she said. "And I don't have time for games. So, I just stay away from men."

"Then why have you been encouraging me to go for Luke?" I wondered.

"Because Luke is in love with you, and you need to go for it before he changes his mind," she said. Everything made sense now, why she had been pushing me so hard. She blamed herself for not giving Grant a chance sooner.

"It's not your fault, you know," I said gently.

"It was hard to convince myself of that when I saw him naked with another girl," she said. The hurt was still there. "I liked him so much, and I didn't even realize my stubbornness was pushing him away."

"Well, aren't we a pair," I said, reaching over to hug her. She laughed and put her sunglasses back on.

"I needed this. Thanks for making me get out of the house," she said, now smiling.

This conversation had made up my mind. The next time I saw Luke, I was going to talk to him. I was done doing this casual bullshit. If everyone was right, he might really love me. And I knew I loved him. I was done letting my grief control me.

It was time to take control back of my life.

Chapter 40

Luke

Over the next week, we worked on finishing up the final touches of my house while we waited for the arrival of my floors and countertop. I bought all the paint Quinn recommended, admiring her choices. I didn't give two shits what color my house was, as long as she liked it. I wondered if she sensed I wanted her to pick everything else in the hopes that it would be her house someday too.

"You have a lot of painting to do," Cody said, helping me carry in all the paint cans. I had to admit I was overwhelmed looking at everything. Painting wasn't a part of the quote that Grant had provided to me, and I felt I was capable enough to do it myself.

However, that was before I looked at the dozen paint cans stacked up around me. Grant said it would be easier if I painted before he put the floors down, and then the trim and baseboards could go up last. I suddenly felt pressured to get it all done.

"I know," I said, rubbing my hand over my face. Instead of digging in and getting to work, I simply stood there staring at the paint, willing it to cover the walls itself.

"Come on, dude, don't stress about it. We'll help you," Cody said, smacking my back.

"We'll help with what?" Grant asked, coming in the room.

"Paint the house for him," Cody said.

"That wasn't in the quote," Grant said, clearly puzzled.

"Take off your contractor hat for a minute," Cody teased him. "Help him because he's your friend."

Grant looked like he wanted to make some smart-ass remark, but then he just nodded his head and laughed.

"Fine, I'll help. I don't know how you rope me into this shit," he said.

"We can make it fun," Cody suggested.

"I'll supply the pizza and the beer," I offered.

"We can recruit more help," Cody said.

"Like Quinn?" Cody waggled his eyebrows at me. He was never going to let me forget that I stole her from him.

"And Adrienne?" Grant asked hopefully.

"Yeah, we can ask the other girls too," Cody said. "Eh, it can be a *naked* painting party!"

"Um, no, I don't think so," I said, laughing.

"Fine," Cody said grudgingly.

"I'll ask Quinn and Adrienne if you want to ask the others," I said. "How about tomorrow? It's short notice, but it's Saturday, so maybe everyone is available. If they want to start early, I'll even supply coffee and donuts."

"Sounds like you two have it all figured out," Grant said. "Just make sure Adrienne comes."

"Right." I nodded at him. He was still so hung up on her, even after all these years.

I went back home in the afternoon, but Quinn was gone, so I opted to text her instead. I hoped she wouldn't feel used for manual labor. I actually didn't care if she came and sat there and just watched me paint. I just wanted her there.

Hey, painting party at my house tomorrow morning. I'll feed you well. Let me know if you and Adrienne are interested.

Awesome! Yeah, we'll be there. I was surprised at how quick her reply was. And she must have been with Adrienne since she answered for her too.

Okay, see you at 9?

I got a thumbs up emoticon in response. I wondered what they were doing since her responses were so brief.

I was excited. I wondered if I could somehow pair Adrienne and Grant up without it being obvious. I didn't care how blunt I was about Quinn. She was working with me. Even though I wasn't as into decorating, I had to admit I was eager to get some color on the walls and have it look homey. I had grown accustomed to Quinn's cozy cottage, and the sweet and simple décor was definitely growing on me. I wanted as much of Quinn's influence on my house as possible. Hopefully that wouldn't bite me in the ass.

Cody and I spent the rest of the afternoon working on an order for supplies for our business. After Quinn's help with our website overhaul, we were going through surfboard wax and leashes like crazy. We were trying to take the business more serious and doing periodic inventory rather than flying by the seat of our pants. It was important to use down times like this to take care of the details.

We were both participating in some surf clinics and other fundraiser events on the south side of the island for the remainder of the summer. The North Shore was known for big winter waves and the South Shore supplied the summer waves, and everything else was a little in between. Otherwise, we were still knocking out a dozen yards a week for lawn care and working on my house. We certainly knew how to keep busy.

The next morning, I woke early to give me plenty of time to get the donuts and coffee. The house was empty when I arrived, and I took a few minutes to enjoy the silence as I sipped my coffee and took it all in. As much as I didn't want to leave Quinn's property, I was eager to be back home. There was a reason I had fallen in love with this house, and seeing it now was a dream fulfilled.

Cody shuffled in half asleep. "Morning, Dickweed."

"What's up, Numb Nuts?" I replied without hesitation. Cody gratefully accepted the coffee I handed to him, and we settled on the lanai for a few minutes, waiting for rest of the crew to arrive.

"Where's Grant?" I asked, looking around.

"He'll be here," Cody said. "I've never seen a guy spend so much time looking in the mirror before going to paint."

"Oh my God, that's awesome," I said, laughing. "I'm definitely going to tease him about that."

"He's really hoping to win Adrienne over. Again."

"He messed up pretty bad," I said.

"Didn't we all?" Cody said. I figured he was thinking about his ex-girlfriend, Carrie, and how ugly that relationship got at the end. "But before we know it, you and Quinn will be married and spitting out babies," he said, perking up.

"You ready to be an uncle or something?" I asked. "You seem to really want us to have babies."

"Nah," Cody said. "Not that I wouldn't be cool with some little rugrats running around, but I don't want to help you babyproof this place yet. Just want to see you happy, man."

"Thanks," I said, looking over to where the grass met the sand. Shit, babyproofing. That would be a lot of work in this house. One thing at a time, though.

I was really considering talking to Quinn this weekend. The renovations were so close to being done, and we were looking at only a matter of weeks before I was moved back in here. Our situation had come to a head. I knew I couldn't keep going with casual. I may be a guy, but I also knew when my heart was at risk, and Quinn had the power to crush it. Until her, surfing was pretty much the most important thing to me. I loved my family and my friends and was proud of the business Cody and I were building, but I wanted someone to share it with. I wasn't getting any younger. I just didn't know what I would do if Quinn wasn't ready. I had already decided if she didn't want to make it serious, our casual arrangement was done. Making love to her was my new favorite hobby, but I couldn't keep doing it if she wasn't all in. Every time she was in my arms, I never wanted to let go. I was the happiest when I woke up with her beside me, and I couldn't wait to get home every night with the possibility of seeing her.

We both turned around when we heard loud female laughter at the door. Elicia, Megan, and Hailey filed in alongside Grant. I cringed when I saw Hailey. She was a nice girl and all, but I had managed to avoid her after our initial introduction. In a different world, I probably would've utilized the phone number she gave me and taken her out to a nice dinner and probably taken her back to my place.

But Quinn had ruined girls for me. I didn't think any other girl would ever hold a light compared to Quinn. I felt slightly nervous about how Hailey being here today was going to impact things. I wish I would've clarified who I wanted to come help out today. I kept looking at the door, waiting for Quinn to arrive, but they weren't there yet. We went ahead and put the paint cans in each room they were selected for and divided into teams. I was ready to speak up when Cody asked Megan and Elicia to help him with the loft. I knew Cody was trying to give Grant a shot at having Adrienne work with him, but he screwed me in the process.

"How about you and I work on the kitchen and dining room?" Hailey suggested.

Fuck. I didn't want to look like a total asshole, since everyone had showed up to help for free.

"Sure," I said, glancing at the door again.

"I'll start the master bedroom," Grant said. "Feel free to send Adrienne in when she gets here."

"We'll take Quinn since this is a big area," I said, darting a glance at Hailey.

It didn't take long between the two of us to get everything taped off, paying special attention to the new cabinets in the kitchen. Between the open floor plan and all the doors and windows, there wasn't a lot of space to actually paint in this area, but the living room would take several people to knock it out. I wasn't expecting to get everything done today, but the more we could accomplish then maybe I could finish up on my own tomorrow.

"You never called me," Hailey said casually as she started painting around the French doors leading to the lanai.

"Yeah, sorry, I've had a lot going on," I said. I was on the ladder painting around the ceiling, so it was easy to avoid looking at her. It didn't go unnoticed that she was wearing tiny cut-off shorts and a white T-shirt tied in a knot and revealing her midriff.

"Maybe you can have a housewarming party," she suggested.

"That would be fun," I said. I glanced at my watch a few times and noticed it was nearly ten a.m. I considered calling Quinn to make sure everything was okay. I finished around the ceiling and then stepped off the ladder to take a break. Hailey offered me a bottle of water, which I happily accepted.

"Oh, here," she said, giggling. "You have paint on your cheek."

She reached out to rub her thumb along my cheek, and her hand lingered there as she looked at me with those green eyes.

Suddenly, the front door open, and Quinn walked in just in time to see Hailey and I standing in a position that would clearly look intimate.

Fuck.

Chapter 41

Quinn

I was surprised when Adrienne called me in a panic at 8:30 Saturday morning. I was pretty much ready to go and lazily sipped my coffee.

"Quinn!" Panic laced her voice. "Grandma fell, and I need your help."

"Be right there!" I said and tore out of the house.

"In here!" Adrienne called out from Grandma's bedroom as I entered her front door.

I ran in there and found that Grandma Malia had fallen off the bed and was stuck between the bed and the wall. Adrienne had pulled the bed away from the wall slightly but was having trouble lifting Grandma by herself. I scrambled over the bed and wedged myself between the bed and the wall and lightly gripped Grandma's arm.

"Oh, this is ridiculous," Malia said. "All this fuss, and it's not a big deal. I just can't seem to get up."

"It's okay, Grandma," Adrienne said. "We got you." Together, we were able to lift her up and get her back on the bed.

"Are you okay?" I asked.

"Yes," Malia answered, slightly breathless. "I just wanted to go the bathroom and my mind got a little fuzzy, and I rolled in the wrong direction."

"Are you sure you aren't hurt?" Adrienne asked again. I rested my hand on the bed beside Malia and realized the sheets were wet.

"Maybe Adrienne could help you take a bath?" I suggested, trying not to embarrass Malia any further.

"I suppose I need one. Nothing like pissin' yourself," she said bluntly.

I fought back a laugh and helped Adrienne get her into the bathroom.

"Sheets are in the hall closet," Adrienne whispered before she shut the door. I located the sheets and cleaned up the mess in the bedroom. It didn't take me long, but Adrienne and Malia were in the bathroom for a while. I knew we would be late to Luke's, but I figured Adrienne wouldn't be going with me at that point. I ventured into the kitchen and worked on washing the few dishes in the sink.

Finally, they came out, and I could hear Adrienne and Malia arguing.

"I don't need you to babysit me!" Malia insisted.

"I worry about you, Grandma!" Adrienne exclaimed.

"Your friends are waiting for you, so go help them like you committed to!"

"Grandma!"

"Go! It's okay, Adrienne." Malia assured her. "I'm just going to nap and watch my shows," she said.

Adrienne hesitated, clearly torn.

"We can come back and check on her in a little bit," I suggested.

Finally, Adrienne relented.

"But only if you keep your phone right by the bed and call me if you need anything at all," Adrienne demanded.

"Of course, sweetheart," Malia said, softening a bit. "I'll be fine."

Adrienne had to change her clothes again after helping Malia change, but then we were on our way.

"You don't have to do this," I said after driving the first few minutes in silence.

"I hate leaving her like this," she said quietly.

I glanced quickly at her and noted the tears threatening to spill over.

"I know," I said sympathetically. "But we aren't far, so we'll check on her in a few hours, okay?"

"Thank you for your help," she said, glancing over at me.

"You don't need to thank me," I said. And I meant it. I was glad to help.

We reached Luke's over an hour late. I felt bad that I never texted him to let him know, but from the sounds of laughter coming from the open windows, they had plenty of help. What I didn't expect was to walk in and see Luke standing with some gorgeous blonde touching his face.

I stood in stunned silence at first, taking in the scene. I reminded myself that I had no official claim on him and that was all my doing. I quickly recalled what happened between Adrienne and Grant and thought it was ironically similar.

Luke turned to me, and I saw fear in his eyes. He quickly pulled away from the girl and started to walk toward me. I contemplated turning around and walking out the door, but I refused to let my petty jealousy win. Then, as if my feet had a mind of their own, I walked toward Luke. He looked hesitant, and I could tell he was nervous about how I was going to react. I didn't even know how I was going to react until I reached him, my eyes searching his the entire time.

Then, I stopped thinking, I stopped fearing, and I began living. I reached up and gripped Luke's neck and pulled his face down to mine and kissed him. There was nothing subtle or casual about the kiss as I staked my claim on him. He hesitated only for a second until he encircled his arms around me and pulled me close. Our kiss deepened, and I didn't care that we were making out in front of everybody like high school kids.

"Eh, go find a room!" Cody hollered from the top of the stairs. Luke took one arm off me long enough to flip Cody his middle finger but continued to kiss me. There was so much meaning behind that kiss. At least, I hoped I was conveying that to him.

We broke away, and he looked at me, his gaze never wavering from mine.

"Can we talk?" I asked.

"Yeah, sure," he said.

My confidence slipped momentarily as I realized everyone was watching us. Not only was I late to his painting party, but I'd chosen to have my impending life-changing conversation with Luke right now, while everyone was here to work.

"Maybe we should wait," I said, tugging on his arm.

"No, go," Adrienne urged. "We got this."

"Hey guys, how about you take a break for some donuts?" Luke suggested.

"Yeah, you lovebirds go cuddle while we just keep working for free!" Grant quipped.

Adrienne glared at him, and I hesitated about leaving her alone with him since I knew she still had those lingering bitter feelings.

"Do you want me to stay so you aren't alone with him?" I asked quietly so only she could hear.

"I appreciate you offering, Quinn, but I can handle Grant. You need to go with Luke." She smiled brightly and nudged me toward Luke to encourage me to go.

We walked outside and automatically headed down to the beach. I became more nervous with each step, but I was too invested now to pull back. I had to talk to Luke or I was going to go crazy.

He found a quiet area, mostly free of people, and we settled in the sand.

"Well?" he prompted me.

All the words I had practiced in my head escaped me in that very moment, and I just looked at him, speechless.

"Uhhh," I stammered, darting my eyes around nervously. I stared down at my hands, which were trembling.

"What did that kiss mean?" Luke asked, giving me mercy.

"Luke, I can't do casual," I finally said. "I'm not good at it, and it's not what I want."

"What are you saying?" he asked me. The look on his face gave me zero insight.

"I want it to be more," I whispered.

He stared at me a moment, and when he didn't respond, panic washed over me. I knew it. He didn't really feel the same way as me, and everyone had convinced me he did, and now I was sitting there like a fool with my heart in my hands.

"I'm sorry," I said, starting to push up in the sand to get up.

"Quinn," he said, grabbing my arm and pulling me back. I sat on my knees before him and once again met his gaze. "You really don't know, do you?"

"Know what?" I asked, fearful of the answer.

He hesitated a moment and glanced down quickly before looking back up at me. His clear blue eyes shone with emotion, and he swallowed hard before continuing.

"How much I love you," he said.

I blinked several times at him, convinced he hadn't actually said it.

"You do?" I asked.

"Yes," he said firmly. "I think I fell in love with you the moment I saw you on that airplane."

I sucked in a breath at his confession. I had been hoping he would be willing to give us a chance. Never in a million years did I imagine that he loved me already. That he had loved me all this time. I blinked back tears as I struggled to find the words.

"It's okay if you don't feel the same way yet," he said. "You need time to heal, and I get that, but I really want more too. I want us to be together."

I shook my head furiously as the tears blinded me.

"I love you too," I said softly. His eyes got big, and then an amazing smile covered his face.

"For reals?" he asked.

"For reals." I nodded.

I leaned forward to place a kiss on his lips, but he grabbed me, and I toppled on him as we fell backward into the sand.

"You really love me?" I asked, needing to hear those words again.

"I love you," he replied without hesitation.

"I can't believe this," I said, my lips pressing lightly against his as we whispered our words of affirmation.

"So, no more casual," he stated once again. "I'm all in."

"Me too," I said. "How do we do this? We haven't even dated, but we already love each other."

"We do it however we want," he said, tightening his arms around me. "We can take it slow if you want. Whatever you want, as long as you tell me you aren't going anywhere."

"I don't want to go anywhere," I said. "You feel like coming home." I grinned at my own cheesy line. Cheesy or not, though, it was true. I left Chicago behind with some luggage, cradling my broken heart, but moving to Hawaii was the best decision I'd ever made. I never once imagined my heart would be pieced back together by the gentle ways of Luke Cole.

"So, how much trouble do you think we'd get in if we had sex right now?" I asked, glancing around. A couple walked along, holding hands and smiling knowingly at us. Children shrieked with laughter in the distance as they played tag with the waves.

He his chest rumbled with laughter as he held me close. "I think you might have to wait a bit," he said. "Though I like where your mind is." He wiggled around, reaching his hand to pull his phone out of his pocket. "Don't judge me for being girly right now," he said, positioning his phone to take a selfie of us. I didn't even have to pose, as I felt like the grin on my face was permanent.

"What did you want that for?" I asked curiously.

"Well, for one, to mark the moment," he said, tapping out a text. "But two, I have to send it to my sister, Mia. She's been waiting for this."

"Really?" I asked. "She knows about me?"

He gave me a "duh" look and smirked at me. "Of course she does. My whole family does."

I felt a little self-conscious knowing he had an entire family out there that I hadn't met yet.

"Well, you met my aunt Nancy already, so she knows you," I said.

"Good ol' Aunt Nancy," he said.

"What?" I asked curiously.

"Nancy and I had a chat while she was here," he said. "She said some things to encourage me to keep waiting and that you would come around."

"She did? When? I didn't know you guys were ever alone!" I said, surprised.

"Just late one evening when you were already in bed," he answered.

"It's like everyone was conspiring against us," I said.

"Or for us," he said. "So, I have to know. How long have you loved me?"

I smiled, easily knowing the answer to that.

"The day you helped me clean my parents' room out."

"Hmm," he said thoughtfully.

"I knew I was developing feelings for you, and our connection was undeniable, but that day sealed the deal," I explained.

"You know, we would've made these past few months a whole lot easier on ourselves if we would've just talked sooner," he said.

I groaned loudly.

"I had to propose that stupid casual arrangement," I mumbled. "I don't even know where that came from."

"I was glad you pursued me that night," he answered honestly. "But I thought we were starting something until you told me you wanted to keep it casual."

"Only because I didn't think you would want me," I admitted quietly. "I was a huge mess. Still am in a way."

"It's okay. You're my mess now," he said, smiling and stealing another kiss as I swatted at him.

"We should go back in," I said, not wanting to leave his arms. I felt so light and carefree and better than I had in the last year. Or possibly forever.

"Yeah, we should," he said, not attempting to move.

We finally rolled in the sand and stood up. We began walking back to his house hand in hand, and as we were approaching the house, we glanced up and saw the entire painting crew watching us from the loft. The sounds were muffled, but they were grinning and hooting at us, and Cody was making some vulgar motions. We looked at each other and laughed.

"So, did I piss off your new girlfriend?" I asked. I still didn't know that girl's name. I felt a little bad for her since I reacted so quickly and strongly.

"Ah, Hailey, no, she'll be fine. We only met one other time, and she was nice, but I was holding out for some *other* girl."

Ah, the infamous *"Hailey."*

"Some other girl, huh?"

"The one and only," he said, winking at me.

We walked back in the house and endured endless teasing and remarks.

"You two better have made this official. I didn't show up just so you could make out in the sand!" Cody hollered.

"Are we right?" Adrienne asked expectedly.

I beamed at Luke, and we both nodded.

"I won," Luke said to Cody.

"Wait, what?" I asked, looking between the two of them.

"I'll tell you later." Luke laughed.

Hailey walked over and looked at me sheepishly. "I'm sorry, Quinn. I didn't know you guys were involved. I never would've tried had I known," she said, her face beet red.

My preexisting thoughts about her melted. That had to be hard for her to say.

"Hailey, right?" I asked. "You have nothing to be sorry for. We didn't have our shit together until now, so you couldn't have known."

"Okay, thanks," she said. "I'm just not like that. To other girls, I mean," she said.

"No worries," I replied easily. "We girls gotta stick together." I reached out to hug her, respecting her good-natured attitude.

"Now are we going to work or what?" Grant asked with his hands on his hips.

"Yeah, yeah," Luke said, all smiles.

We spent the remainder of the day painting, but it was hard to make progress when Luke and I couldn't keep our hands off each other. The work we did accomplish resulted in an amazing transformation, and I was relieved that the colors I chose complemented the house.

Adrienne left around lunchtime to check on her grandma, and it didn't go unnoticed that Grant invited himself along. She gave me a knowing look, and I was surprised when she finally relented, and they left together. They arrived back at the house in time to finish up for the day, and Luke fulfilled his promise of beer. We sat on lawn chairs in a circle and ate off paper plates, admiring our work.

Luke looked over at me and grinned, which I'm sure I mirrored.

"What did Mia say?" I asked curiously.

He pulled out his phone and furrowed his brow as he looked at it.

"No answer," he said, clearly concerned.

"Maybe she's just busy," I suggested to ease his mind.

"Mia always has her phone," he said. "I swear she had it surgically implanted in her hand."

"I'm sure you'll hear from her in a bit," I assured him.

I saw Adrienne get up and walk out to the lanai to make a phone call. I assumed she was going to check on her grandma again, so I followed her out there to see how she was doing.

The phone call was brief, and Adrienne sank onto the outdoor couch, clearly exhausted.

"You okay?" I asked.

"Yeah, days like this just scare me," she said. "I feel like I'm on borrowed time with my grandma."

"I don't know how you do it," I admitted. "My grandparents all died when I was young, so it really was just my parents and me. You are doing a really good thing for your grandma."

"I wouldn't want it any other way," Adrienne said. "Grandma is the only one that's been there for me every step of the way."

"Hang in there," I said, rubbing her shoulder. "And promise you'll tell me if you need any help."

"I will," she said.

"Sooo…" I said, looking at her with a smile. "How was your time with Grant?"

Adrienne blushed but tried dismissing me with a wave of her hand.

"I'm not even sure why he wanted to go with me. We barely even talked," she said.

"Maybe he just wanted to be around you," I said.

"I doubt that," she said.

"Why?" I asked. "He probably realizes he screwed up big time and wants to make it right. You are one of the sweetest people I've ever met," I said. "And I'm not the only one who sees that."

"I don't know about all that," she said.

"Think about it," I pointed out. "You can't tell me it was a coincidence that you got paired with him all day."

"We worked, but we didn't really talk much," she said, though I could tell she was thinking about it.

I smiled at her but didn't say anything else.

"Enough about me," she said.

I could tell talking about her own problems made her uncomfortable. I admired Adrienne for her strength and how she took care of everyone around her, but I worried about how long she could keep it up.

"Well?" she said. "I'm dying to hear how it went with Luke!"

"It was so simple!" I exclaimed. "I don't know why I didn't talk to him sooner!" Adrienne laughed hard, and I smiled at her. "I know, I know, you've been trying to tell me for months."

"I'm really happy for you, Quinn. You deserve to be happy."

"I just can't believe it," I said. "I'm excited, but I'm also a little nervous. Everything in my life has changed, and I feel like a different person. I don't want to mess this up."

"You won't," Adrienne said confidently. "Just enjoy this time. Live in the moment."

"I'm dying to get him back home," I admitted with a grin.

"Ha! I bet you are!"

"I want to make it *completely* official, you know," I said, laughing.

"Well, then get your ass back in there," she said, swatting me.

We walked back in the house to find everyone cleaning up

the pizza boxes and garbage. Before we left the house, I took one last long look at our work and smiled. I could totally picture living here.

Chapter 42

Luke

When Quinn walked in that door, I was convinced we were done. Hailey and I weren't doing anything wrong, but I know it didn't look that innocent, and Quinn's heart was still fragile. I didn't spend all this time trying to win Quinn's trust only to lose it over something meaningless.

Hearing Quinn tell me she loved me back was probably the single most exciting moment of my life. Winning a surf competition paled in comparison. I felt like my entire life had prepared me for this moment. I couldn't wait to get her home alone and show her how much I loved her, holding nothing back this time. And I was sure as hell going to wake up next to her in the morning. I loved having her in my house and watching how excited she was as we covered the walls with the colors she'd picked out. She had an awesome eye for it, and the paint gave the place such a homey feel. I loved knowing her touch was going to be on my home. It made me even more eager to get the floors and rest of the work done so I could move in. I didn't have that sense of dread hovering over me anymore, fearing that moving out of the cottage would cause Quinn and me to drift apart and ruin any chance I had with her.

Here, it was easy to envision Quinn and I enjoying our

coffee on the lanai, moving around in the kitchen as we cooked dinner and making love on every surface. I wondered what Quinn would choose to do with the room upstairs and whether she wanted it to be her office. She could do whatever she wanted with the house, just as long as she was here.

I shook my head. I was getting ahead of myself. We'd only just professed our love to each other, and I wasn't sure what the next step was. I wanted to just enjoy some time with her and not worry about what the future held.

I couldn't wait to tell Mia everything, and it was driving me nuts that she hadn't replied yet. I sent her another text and asked if she was ignoring me, but still no response. I wasn't sure if I should be worried or not, but it was probably too late in Chicago to call. If I didn't hear from her by morning, I was definitely calling her.

I took the garbage out, and Cody met me at the door.

"Hey man, just wanted to tell you I'm happy for you," he said.

"Thanks," I said. "I'm pretty stoked."

"I think it's awesome. I know it's been killing you, but I think she was worth the wait."

"Me too," I replied. "And yes, I know, I still owe you."

"Damn straight," He grinned. "Well, I'm beat, so I'm going head home."

"Don't get lost," I said as he walked out of my yard and into his own, Grant trailing behind. Elicia, Megan, and Hailey left then too, and I thanked them for their help. I didn't even know them that well, so it was really awesome of them to dedicate their entire Saturday helping me. I was considering throwing a housewarming party to thank everyone for their help and show off the house. Maybe I would do it in conjunction with my birthday at the end of July. I bet Quinn would be excited to coordinate that. I also needed to see if she would go shopping with me to get some stuff for the house. I might even let her pick out some throw pillows.

"You ready to head home?" I asked her quietly and made sure to grip her hip to ensure my meaning was correctly conveyed.

"I thought you'd never ask," she said, giving me the sexiest look I'd ever seen in my life.

"You riding with Luke?" Adrienne asked Quinn, waiting at the door.

Quinn hesitated, not wanting to offend Adrienne since they'd come together.

"Just go." She laughed and walked out the door.

We were finally alone. I reached for her, and she stepped in my arms, and we just hugged silently for a few minutes. Damn, it felt good.

"Let's go," she said, placing her small hand within mine. The anticipation was building between us, and I wondered if she felt the same as me. Even though we had been sleeping together for the past couple of months, this almost felt like the first time.

We climbed into my truck and was thrilled when she scooted over and sat in the middle of the bench seat, right next to me. The ten-minute drive felt like an eternity, and I kept glancing over at her to gauge her mood. She remained silent and kept smiling shyly at me. I rested my hand on her thigh, totally digging her sitting so close to me. I could get used to this.

"Your place or mine?" I asked teasingly as we pulled in the driveway.

"I have a bigger bed and I plan on utilizing it tonight," Quinn said, no longer shy.

Yes.

"I'm going to run down and let Diesel out real quick, and then I'll be back up," I said. "Don't take a shower until I'm back up here." I was going to enjoy every moment of this evening with her.

She blushed at my instruction and nodded.

I let Diesel out and apologized to him for leaving him alone all day. I had considered bringing him to the house but figured he would end up with various colors on his fur if I did. I decided to take him up to Quinn's with me, figuring he and Penny could cuddle while their masters did unspeakable things.

"Oh, good, I was hoping you would bring him," Quinn said as she opened the door. The dogs instantly started wrestling, so we left them alone to terrorize the living room as we retreated to the bathroom.

"You have paint everywhere." I grinned at Quinn, picking up a strand of her hair streaked with tan.

"So do you!" She laughed, rubbing her fingers across my ear. She started the shower, and I bent down to kiss her as the bathroom filled with steam. Just as I reached to lift her shirt up, my butt began vibrating.

"Dammit," I muttered, wondering who the hell was calling me right now. I reached in my pocket and pulled out my phone, surprised to see Mia calling. It was well past midnight in Chicago, so I wouldn't have expected her to still be awake.

"Answer it," Quinn said, seeing that it was Mia.

"Sorry," I whispered as I answered. "Hey, sis."

I was met with silence on the other line, and I prayed my sister didn't butt dial me in the middle of doing the dirty deed with her fiancé.

"You there?" I asked. Quinn reached over to turn off the shower, and I stepped back into her bedroom to escape the steam.

"Luke?" My senses were instantly on high alert when I heard the tears in Mia's voice.

"What's wrong?" I asked. "Are you okay? Are Mom and Dad okay?" Quinn looked at me with concern, and I wondered if this is how she felt when she got the call about her parents.

"Luke," she repeated again, "I need you to come get me."

"In Chicago?" I asked, puzzled.

"No. I'm at the airport. In Honolulu."

My jaw dropped open. "What the hell is going on, Mia?" I asked. I looked at Quinn with alarm, wondering why the hell my sister was in Hawaii without telling me.

"I caught Derrick cheating on me."

"What. The. Fuck." I was going to kill that motherfucker.

"With Sarah," she said with a sob.

"Your best friend? You've got to be kidding me."

"I didn't know what else to do. I just grabbed a few things and left."

"Okay, listen, I'll be there as fast as I can," I said. "I'll pick you up at baggage claim. Just wait inside, and I'll call you when I'm close."

"Okay. Thanks, Luke," she said, sniffing. I disconnected the call and looked at Quinn, not even beginning to know how to apologize to her.

"Go," she said, softly touching my arm. "She's here? In Hawaii?"

"She walked in on her fiancé cheating on her with her best friend."

"Oh my God," Quinn said, disgusted. "That is so awful!"

"That's all I know," I said. I looked down at myself covered in paint, but there was no time to change.

"I'm so sorry," I said.

"It's okay." She smiled sweetly. "I love you."

"I will never get tired of hearing that," I replied, bending down to kiss her. "I love you too."

And then I was off, pushing the speed limit on my way to the airport. My mind raced, wondering what the hell happened. I didn't know Derrick well, but that would make killing him easier. Mia was one of the coolest chicks I knew, and that wasn't just because she was my sister. She was fun and lovable and full of life. Just knowing she was hurting and obviously devastated broke my heart, but I was more infuriated than anything. I debated calling my parents but figured I should wait until after I talked to Mia.

Quinn couldn't have been cooler about the whole situation. The timing couldn't have been worse—actually, on second thought, it could've been—but she didn't even hesitate. I had considered asking her to come with me, but I didn't really want them to meet for the first time under these circumstances. Shit, I didn't even know where Mia was going to stay. My house wouldn't even be ready for another two weeks at the earliest. I wondered if Quinn would let Mia stay in her guest bedroom. I wasn't even sure how to go about asking something like that literally in the first day of our relationship. I guess we'd figure it out when I got home.

Traffic was light that late on a Saturday, and I made it to the airport in record time. I called Mia, and she picked up right away.

"Go ahead and come outside," I said, slowly making a pass through baggage claim.

I was taken aback at how tiny and fragile she looked, standing at the curb clutching her purse and a small duffel bag at her feet. I pulled up beside her and jumped out. She looked at me and attempted to smile, but it was clouded by her tears.

"Mia," I said, engulfing her in a hug. Her body shuddered as she cried, and I once again battled the urge to hop on a plane and hunt Derrick down and beat him to a bloody pulp. I wasn't a violent person, but this asshole was bringing out a new side in me. While I was at it, I should hunt down Quinn's ex-boyfriend, since they lived in the same city. That could be convenient.

"Okay, let's go," I said, reaching down to grab her bag. "Is this all you brought?" Mia was never known to pack light.

"I don't really even know what's in there," she said, gesturing wildly. "I just grabbed some shit and my camera and got the hell out of there."

"I can't believe you're here," I said. I buckled her in the front seat, not entirely sure she could do it herself in her state of distress.

"Me, either," she replied. "Uh, I just got your text after I landed," she said. "I'm so sorry that I ruined your night with Quinn. So, you guys are dating now?"

"Yep," I replied. "Don't sweat it. She knows how important family is. She's worried about you too."

"She doesn't even know me," Mia mumbled.

"Well, she loves me, and I love you, so it is kind of a package deal."

"Wait! Did you say she loves you?"

I couldn't keep the smile from my face.

"Yeah, our talk went pretty well," I said.

"Wow, Luke, that's awesome. I'm really happy for you," she said.

"Thank you," I said, feeling a little guilty that I found love at the same time she was enduring such betrayal. "So, do you want to talk about it?"

"Not really," she said, fumbling with her purse strap in her hands. "But considering I showed up unannounced, I guess I should." She paused, trying to compose herself.

"The stress of the wedding has been going on for a while," she started. "I already told you how difficult his mother was making everything. I tried talking to Derrick about it and he just brushed me off. I've been trying to just shrug everything off because I didn't want to be a bridezilla, but I just kept feeling like this should be fun, and my gut was telling me something was wrong.

"I had another planning session with his mom, and she was being so rude and pushy and demanding that things be handled a certain way, and she just vetoed everything I wanted! I was seriously pissed off when I left, and I didn't want to go home because I knew Derrick would just take her side. I decided to go to Sarah's because I knew she was going to be home. She told me she was just staying in for a quiet evening. Well, let me tell you, it wasn't quiet when I opened that door. I was so embarrassed that I'd walked in on her until I heard his voice. I thought there was no fucking way that was Derrick's voice. So, I tiptoed over to the bedroom door, and sure enough."

Mia gasped for breath as she cried, and I reached over and held her hand.

"Did they try to make any excuses?" I asked.

"Nope," she said. "But I didn't even give them a chance. I punched Derrick in the face and then bitch-slapped Sarah. Then on the way out the door, I grabbed her purse and gave it to a homeless man outside her building."

"Oh my God, Mia." I shook my head and failed miserably at not laughing. My sister sure could take care of herself. "How is your hand?" I glanced over and noticed she was cradling it.

"It hurts," she cried.

"Maybe I should take you to the hospital first," I suggested gently.

"No, not right now." She shook her head.

"What I am going to do with you, sis?" I asked.

"I don't know what to do," she wailed. "I have to call off the wedding, and I don't even want to deal with it!"

"Make them deal with it," I said. "He's the one that cheated."

"Oh yeah, that's the best part," she said. "He must've called his mom right away, and she had the audacity to call me and tell me this was just a little hiccup. A fucking hiccup! Like, oh yeah, he just accidentally stuck his dick in my best friend!"

I gripped the steering wheel tightly, fighting a really strong urge to get on a plane and kill this bastard.

"Did you fly out this morning, then?" I asked.

"Yeah," she answered. "I couldn't get a direct flight on such short notice, so I had a layover in Los Angeles for three hours."

"Why didn't you call me then?" I asked.

"I didn't want to talk to anybody. I feel so stupid."

"Why would you feel stupid?" I asked angrily. "You have nothing to feel stupid for! You were planning a wedding, for fuck's sake! He's the one that is going to come out of this looking like a fool!"

"I know, but it's still so embarrassing. This wedding was supposed to be such a big deal, and they have the nerve to think I'll still go on with it?"

"Yeah, that's bullshit," I agreed. "Have you told Mom and Dad yet?"

"No, but I need to call them tomorrow. I drove straight back home and just packed a few things and then drove around Chicago all night and then decided I was coming here."

"Okay," I said, nodding slowly. "Well, we have a few things to consider. For one, my house isn't going to be ready for a couple of weeks."

"I can just get a hotel," she said.

"No, that's not necessary. Quinn has a spare bedroom, and I'm sure she won't mind."

"What about your cottage?" she asked.

"It's too small for both of us," I said.

"No, I mean, you could stay with Quinn and I could stay in your cottage," she suggested.

I didn't mind that idea, but I didn't want Quinn to feel like I was pushing her too fast. We had literally made our relationship official less than eight hours ago, and I didn't want her to feel like we had to move in together. Though it would be temporary until my house was completed, and then Mia could just stay with me. I wasn't even sure if Mia had a long-term plan or how long she would be here.

"We can do that for tonight, if you want," I said. "But should you be alone?"

"Honestly, I just want to sleep for a really long time," Mia admitted. "I'm so tired, and I barely slept on the flight. I'm just exhausted."

"Okay, that's fine," I said. I had been planning on painting all day Sunday, but I needed to push that aside for Mia.

"Do you have a long-term plan?" I asked her. "What about work?" She photographed a lot of weddings and family photos.

"I'm really shooting myself in the foot with my career," she said. "But I think I could get one of my colleagues to take over for now. I just have to figure out what to do for money."

"I'm sure you could find photography work here," I said. "Maybe give it a little bit of time?"

"Okay," she agreed.

"Sleep on it. On everything. You don't have to decide anything right now. We'll figure it out together," I said.

We drove the rest of the way in silence as she dozed off in the seat next to me. I had never seen my little sister so distraught before, and I hated feeling so helpless.

Chapter 43

Quinn

I tried staying awake until Luke got back home, but my eyelids grew heavy, and the day of work along with the emotional rollercoaster we went on caught up to me. I wasn't sure if I would see him when he got home, and I was worried for his sister. I knew what it was like to get your heart broken, though I didn't know what it felt like to be cheated on. And obviously she lost her best friend at the same time, and I could certainly relate to that.

"Quinn," Luke whispered as he shook my shoulder. I glanced around groggily and realized I'd fallen asleep on the couch.

"Where is Mia? Is she okay?" I asked, fighting to wake up.

"She's in my bed. She's exhausted. Is it okay if I stay here tonight?"

"Of course it is," I said. I had hoped he would even before Mia called.

Luke gave me the quick rundown of what happened, and I gasped when he told me she punched Derrick.

"Oh, good for her," I said. "I kind of wish I would've punched Aaron."

"You women are so violent!" Luke exclaimed. "But I suppose I want to punch him right now too."

I giggled, which was quickly followed by a yawn.

"Let's go to bed," he suggested, pulling me off the couch. We went to the bedroom, and I stood for a moment, staring at the bed. This night was supposed to go a lot differently, and now I felt guilty for just going to bed.

"Don't worry about it," Luke said, reading my mind. "We have all the time in the world. Honestly, I would really just like to hold you tonight."

My heart melted.

"That does sound pretty great," I said, smiling. We climbed in, and I quickly fell asleep in his arms, feeling the happiest I've ever felt.

Despite being up too late, I stirred early the next morning. Luke lay beside me with his arms folded behind his head, staring at the ceiling.

"Hey, are you okay?" I rolled over toward him.

"Yeah," he replied with a deep sigh.

"That wasn't real convincing," I said.

"I'm just worried about Mia. I want to talk to her more, but I don't want to wake her if she's still sleeping. And I need to take her to Urgent Care to have her hand looked at."

"Did you have anyone coming to paint today?" I asked.

"No." He shook his head. "I was hoping to get more done. The floors arrive in a few days, and I wanted it to be done before then, but I guess I'll just figure it out."

"I can do it," I offered. He looked at me, surprised. "You need to spend the day with Mia."

"I can't ask you to do that," he said. "Especially after you did it all day yesterday."

"I have nothing going on," I said. "I don't mind. Really. And you aren't asking, I'm offering."

He hesitated but finally relented. I knew he was stressed about completing it, and it was something I could do.

"Okay, but if I get a chance, I'll come over and help," he said.

"No," I said firmly. "Just be there for Mia. I can handle this. I want to help, and this is something I can do."

"Have I told you how much I love you?" he asked.

"Not today, but you can start now." I grinned as he kissed the tip of my nose.

"Do you think pancakes will make Mia feel better?" he asked.

I laughed. He thought pancakes would fix everything.

"We can try," I said. "Well, if it's okay if I go. I'd like to meet her," I said hopefully.

"I'll try her," he said, sitting up in bed. Then he turned and flopped back down on the bed, rolling over to grab me. "I love you." He kissed me long and slow, and I almost didn't allow him out of the bed. He pulled on the clean clothes he had grabbed last night and headed down to the cottage. I stretched lazily in bed and waited for him to come back. Despite the lack of sleep, I felt renewed.

"She's game," he said, walking back in the room ten minutes later. His eyes raked over me in my booty shorts and tank top. "Maybe I need to tell her to give us an hour."

I blushed and rolled out of bed.

"As appealing as that sounds, it's going to have to wait," I said. "We need to focus on your sister."

I was slightly nervous about meeting her, with thoughts of Aaron and Ashley lingering in my mind. I wasn't sure if I wanted to allow myself to get close to her, but as soon as the thought formed in my mind, I dismissed it. It took Luke a long time to convince me he wasn't going to break my heart like Aaron did, and I couldn't continue having lasting negative thoughts about people in general if I wanted to move on and feel completely healed.

Mia was walking up the driveway in leggings and a thin off-the-shoulder sweater as we walked out the door. She was looking around the property, taking everything in now that she could see it in daylight. Her dark hair was close to the same color as mine and tied in a messy knot at the top of her head. Her eyes were red and puffy, and I imagined she'd spent more time crying than sleeping last night.

She looked up when she saw us approaching and waved timidly. I didn't hesitate and walked up to her and engulfed her in a hug. I could tell she was taken aback for a moment, but then she sank into my embrace.

"I'm so glad to meet you," I whispered.

"Me too," she replied. "I'm really sorry about crashing in on you guys."

"No," I said firmly. "I'm glad you came. You came to the right place if you need some healing. I would know."

She smiled gratefully at me, and we all climbed into Luke's truck and drove to the cafe.

"Nothing has changed in two years," she said, looking out the window.

"Well, some, but not much," Luke said.

We got to the cafe early enough to dodge the Sunday morning rush. We placed our orders, and Mia clutched her cup of coffee like it was her lifeline. My heart went out to her and the hurt that was obviously consuming her right now.

"I want to take you to Urgent Care today," he said. "We need to have your hand checked out," he said, nodding toward the black and blue bruises forming.

"Okay," she said, not arguing.

"And I think you need to call Mom and Dad. Or at the very least let me call them."

"I think I'm ready to talk to Mom," she said. "Dad is going to be pissed."

"Dad is going to want to kill him as much as I want to," Luke said through gritted teeth.

"Has Derrick tried calling you?" I asked curiously.

"Yeah," she muttered. "I finally had to shut my phone off last night. He and Sarah wouldn't stop calling. Then Derrick texted me and said he knew I was in Hawaii and that I needed to stop being ridiculous and come home."

"How did he know you were here?" I asked.

"Because I charged my flight on his credit card," she said, smirking.

I liked her. She was a fighter.

Our food came, and we refrained from talking while we ate. Mia choked down a few bites of her pancakes, but otherwise just shuffled her food around her plate. I didn't blame her. I didn't eat for days after my world was turned upside down.

After we were done, Luke tried to argue with me again about painting his house, but I silenced him with a kiss and stole his key. I changed into work clothes and headed back to his house. I sat in the driveway for a few minutes and stared at the adorable beach house. He had shown me some pictures from when he first bought it, and it was hard to believe it was the same house. Once these renovations were complete, he was going to have a hard time dragging me out of there.

I got out of my car and was walking up to the house when I heard my name.

I turned and saw Cody and Grant sitting on their lanai, polishing off some breakfast burritos.

"What's up?" Cody asked around a mouthful of burrito.

"Yeah, where's Lover Boy?" Grant asked.

"Um," I hesitated, not sure how much I should say. "He's with his sister." This caught Cody's attention, and he sat up straight in his seat.

"Wait, what?" he asked. "Mia's here?"

"Yes," I answered, not offering any other information.

"Is she okay?" he asked, obvious concern in his eyes. I hesitated a moment longer, but then remembered that these were Luke's best friends.

"She caught her fiancé cheating on her. With her best friend," I added.

"Are you fucking kidding?" Cody bolted from his chair, knocking it backward.

"What a dick move," Grant said. He wasn't as upset as Cody, but I figured Mia was probably like a sister to him, and he was protective of her like Luke was.

"Yes, it's pretty bad," I agreed. "So, I'm going to try to get more painting done while Luke takes her to Urgent Care."

"Why?" Cody demanded. "What's wrong with her?"

"She hurt her hand punching him in the face," I said, smirking.

"That's my girl," Cody said quietly.

"She's a feisty one," Grant added.

"You know how long she's staying?" Cody asked.

"No, not yet," I said. "I was going to offer her my guest room until the house is finished, but I haven't had a chance to talk to her about it yet."

"Well, we can help with the painting," Grant said, finishing off his burrito.

"Yeah, for sure," Cody said without hesitating.

Luke really did have the best friends.

"I'd say you don't have to, but I could really use the help!" I cringed a little. I really wanted to finish it for Luke today, but I wasn't sure how I was going to do it myself.

"We will be over in a few minutes," Grant said.

I let myself in the house and got to work right away. The living room was already taped off, so I didn't have to do any prep work, which was awesome. I didn't make it very far before the guys got there.

"I go prep the bathroom, and then I can trade places with Quinn," Grant said. "That bathroom isn't real big, so if you like you can do that since you are fun size."

"Ha-ha," I said sarcastically to him. He wasn't the first person to tease me for my petite nature.

By the time my pancakes wore off and I was ready for lunch, we were done.

"Thank you, guys, so much!" I exclaimed. I was really proud of us for getting it knocked out so quickly, and now it was done.

"This is awesome," Grant said. "It's almost done. Everything is being delivered on Tuesday, and we can finish up. It looks totally different."

"You do really good work," I said.

"Thanks," he said. "My dad has taught me well."

We turned when we heard the front door open, and Luke and Mia entered.

"Oh, wow," Luke said when he realized the guys were there and that the painting was done. "I can't believe you guys finished."

"We couldn't let your girl do all the work herself," Grant said.

Cody said nothing as he stared intently at Mia. She was pulling at the sleeves of her sweater, avoiding eye contact with Cody. Finally, she ran over to him and fell in his arms. He wrapped an arm around her and led her out to the lanai for privacy.

"What's that about?" Grant eyed Luke.

"I have no clue," he said, staring at them.

"She's like a sister to him, right?" I said.

"I... thought so," Luke said. "I always suspected there was more, but she was so much younger than us."

"I wanted to talk to you about all this," I said to Luke.

"I'm going to head out," Grant dismissed himself.

"Thanks again, man," Luke said gratefully.

"What did you want to talk about?" Luke asked after Grant left.

"I was going to offer Mia my guest room," I said.

"Wow, that's really generous of you," Luke said. "She actually suggested she sleep in the cottage and I stay with you. But..." He trailed off, not finishing his sentence.

"But what?" I wanted to know.

"I don't want you to feel pressured," he said warily.

"Luke, I'm fine," I said, reaching out for his hand. "I know I pushed you away for a long time, but I'm done with that. I'm all in."

"Okay," he said, relieved.

"I would love if you stayed with me," I said. "Mia is welcome to stay in the cottage. Even after you move into your house, she can still stay. Do you know how long she's staying yet?"

"She thinks she wants to stay for a while," he answered. "She talked to my parents, and they're going to drive to Chicago and pack up her belongings and ship what she needs now and then hang on to everything else. They're also going to ship her car."

"Wow, that's really awesome of them," I said. I knew how hard it would be for Mia to face Derrick again. I used to feel sick at the thought of seeing Aaron again, but I think now I would just walk up and shake his hand and thank him for doing me a favor. I didn't even feel anger toward him anymore. I felt nothing.

"Wait, what did she find out about her hand?"

"It's just bruised, so she should be fine in a few days. It's just sore right now," he said.

"Okay, so it's decided," I said. "You can stay with me until your house is done. If you can handle being around me that much, that is." I grinned up at him.

"I think I might spend more time *in* you," he said, leaning down to kiss me.

"I suppose that's okay too," I said, faking indifference.

Cody and Mia walked back in then, and she actually looked a little less distraught.

"Ready to leave?" Luke asked her.

"Yeah," she said. "Let's go."

We went back to my house, and I offered to make them dinner, but Mia opted out, insisting she was too tired.

"That's okay," I told her. "Just don't hesitate to come up here if you change your mind."

"Thanks for being so kind, Quinn," she said. "My brother has good taste."

I smiled at her compliment and watched as she bent to pet the dogs before she walked out the door. I had just started to prepare dinner when Luke came up behind me and wrapped his arms around my waist. He started to nibble my ear and along my neck, which was making it very difficult to focus.

"Hmm, I do have good taste," he said slyly.

"Don't you forget it," I shot back.

"Are you really that hungry?" he asked me.

"I'm famished, actually," I said, turning in his arms. "But I don't have to eat food."

He laughed before bending down and grabbing me and tossing me over his shoulder. I shrieked at his caveman technique, and the dogs jumped around excitedly as he ran me down the hallway.

"Sorry, guys, you aren't invited." He shut the door in the faces of two bewildered dogs. He set me on the floor and eyed me appreciatively.

"Finally," I whispered. I didn't waste any time before untying his board shorts. "I'm really digging this no underwear thing," I remarked.

"You should try it," he suggested.

"I'm kind of a mess," I said. I would've liked to have taken time to clean up and look good for him.

"You're beautiful just as you are," he said, bending down to kiss me, and I knew he wasn't fooling around. His kiss conveyed all the love and passion that simmered between us.

I scolded myself again for resisting this for so long when it was obvious we were meant to be together. Yet that struggle was a part of our story. During that time, I had evolved into a different person. I was stronger and more independent, but I also knew my own self-worth. I couldn't give my heart to Luke until I healed. The pain still lingered below the surface, and I knew it would always be there, but I wasn't drowning anymore. Now I could love this man with all that I was.

And that was exactly what I was going to do.

Chapter 44

Luke

In the first few weeks that Mia was in Hawaii, I watched her work through Derrick's betrayal. She was in shock when she arrived, not yet knowing how to process what had happened. She hit denial right away, the day I took her to Urgent Care. She kept replaying everything that had happened and started to question her own sanity and whether Derrick and her family were right about her being ridiculous, saying that maybe she should just forgive him and go home.

Anger was the most fascinating to watch, because that little woman could make a lot of noise when she was pissed. I finally had to ban her from her social media for a bit until she could calm down after she posted a status that said, "Changing my relationship status to single since my fiancé couldn't keep his dick out of my best friend. I'm in Hawaii now, you fuckers can have each other."

I secretly laughed when I saw it, but I knew airing her dirty laundry online wouldn't make her feel any better and convinced her to delete it. She slipped momentarily into depression for a few days, and Quinn found her curled in the fetal position with an empty package of Oreos.

Finally, she reached acceptance, and I could see the glimmer of hope in her eyes. She was still sad and still very angry, but she began to function better and consider what she was going to do with her future. Quinn convinced her to go on some hikes with her, promising her that the physical exertion was oddly healing. I was impressed and even more in love with Quinn when she made it her mission to help Mia heal. I also learned a little bit more about Quinn in that process.

It was during Mia's anger phase that she lashed out at Quinn. We were all having dinner together, and Mia was fuming over the things she was seeing on social media from mutual friends of hers and Sarah's.

"I can't believe they all took her side," Mia spit.

"Do they know what actually happened?" Quinn asked innocently.

"Don't you take her side too!" Mia roared. "You don't know what it's like to lose your best friend the same day as your fiancé!"

Quinn sat there staring at her for a few seconds. I wasn't sure what to do. I knew Mia was hurting, but it didn't give her a right to treat Quinn that way, and I wasn't going to tolerate that. But before I had a chance to intervene, Quinn spoke up.

"Actually, I do," she said calmly.

I turned to look at her curiously.

"Aaron wasn't my fiancé, but he was my boyfriend, and his sister was my best friend. And the day he broke my heart, they both abandoned me. So don't try to tell me what I do or do not know."

Quinn had never told me that, and I stared at her in stunned silence. In Mia's emotional state, I expected her to make some rude remark, but she was as stunned as me.

"I'm sorry," she whispered, looking down at her plate. "I'm such a bitch."

"No, you aren't," Quinn said. I was impressed at how gracious she was. "I understand you're hurting, but I'm trying to help. This isn't easy for me either. I'm an only child, and I keep getting involved with these inseparable brother-sister teams who have a bond I can never begin to understand."

"Thank you, Quinn," Mia said quietly. "I'll try to do better."

And that was that.

They never had any issues after that day, at least that I was aware of. Quinn went above and beyond to help distract Mia while I was at work. They hiked some, but they also did a lot of shopping. They kept claiming they were buying stuff for my house, which I insisted was not necessary. I didn't need a bunch of decorations or knickknacks sitting around.

"You didn't just spend all this money to make your house look nice to keep it like a bachelor pad," Quinn teased me one day after returning home with shopping bags.

"Yeah, trust your girlfriend," Mia said, backing her up. "She's got great taste."

I was outnumbered.

The summer season was in full swing, and the ocean was completely flat with hardly a ripple. Cody and I booked a few stand-up paddle boarding tours during the final week of my renovations. I had hardly seen him since Mia arrived.

"You've been scarce," I commented one day after finishing up a tour group.

"Working on your house!" he shot back.

"Hey, you're getting paid!" I said.

"I know," he said, laughing. "After putting everything I had into our business, I wanted to start saving up again. Maybe buy a house someday."

"Oh, are you thinking about settling down?" I teased him.

"I don't know, maybe," he replied.

I looked at him. He was serious.

"Since when?" I asked.

He shrugged. "Being single gets kind of old after a while," he said.

"Never thought I'd hear you say that," I said. I quickly

realized my mistake and apologized. "I'm sorry, man. I know you got burnt badly." Sometimes it was easy to forget through Cody's jokester persona that he'd had plans to marry Carrie and settle down, start a family.

"It's cool," he said, shrugging it off. "It's just, we not getting any younger, and now seeing you and Quinn together makes me think it could be all right."

"Good, I'm glad," I said. I felt a little bad that I hadn't been more considerate of what seeing Quinn and I together would make him feel. I was also curious if his change of heart had anything to do with my sister being back in town. I almost asked him about it but decided I didn't want to open that can of worms. Mia still had the tan line around her ring finger. She wasn't in any shape for a new relationship, and I hoped Cody realized that.

"So, I think we're having a little party next weekend for my birthday and to officially christen the house," I told him changing the subject.

"Sweet," he said. "Can't believe it's the end of July already."

"I know," I replied. "The past year has been kind of crazy."

It was only a year ago that I began to feel restless, mourning my surfing career and feeling no passion about my life. Cody and I started a great business, but at the end of the day it was just work. I thought about the irony that I'd met Quinn on the plane ride home from Mia's engagement party.

"Your house is gonna look pretty sweet," he commented.

"Mia and Quinn have been shopping like crazy," I said. "I'm kind of afraid of what it's going to look like."

We laughed, but we both knew it would look awesome. Quinn had a knack for making houses homey, and I couldn't wait to see what she came up with.

Later that evening, I told Mia I needed to steal Quinn for a little bit.

"What's going on?" Quinn asked suspiciously.

"I have a surprise for you," I said with a grin.

"Last time you said that you bought me a surfboard!" she said.

We got to my house, and she eyed me nervously. "What would you have gotten me that is at your house?"

"You'll see," I said, practically dragging her by her hand into the house. The floors were completely installed and looked amazing. The countertops were done as well, and all that was left was the trim, which would be done already if I hadn't pulled Grant aside for a side project.

I led her up to the loft and waited for her reaction. She gasped and covered her mouth in awe. At the center of the large window overlooking the ocean was a large desk I'd had built out of koa wood. On each side of the A-frame window were built-in bookcases for her to display office supplies, pictures, or whatever she wanted.

"Is this for me?" she asked, turning to me with tears in her eyes.

"Yep," I said proudly. "I thought if I had a place for you to work that I could get you here as much as possible."

"This is incredible," she said as she ran her fingers along the smooth surface of the desk. "Where did you get this?"

"Grant and I made it," I said.

"No way!" She turned to me, eyes wide with excitement. "I can't believe this!"

"I want you to feel at home here," I said. "And I know how much you love this loft, so I wanted it to be special for you."

"Oh, Luke, it's perfect," she said. "Look at all this shelf space!" The space was large enough that she could have her office nook, and it didn't even cut into the space she had designed as a guest room area.

I had to admit it looked pretty perfect. The dark grains of the koa wood contrasted against the gray floors and the slate blue we had covered the walls in.

"So, how sturdy is this desk?" She turned and looked at me suggestively.

"Damn, woman, there is no satisfying you, is there?"

She paused for a moment. "Does that bother you? Do you think we have sex too much?"

We'd had sex a lot in the past few weeks. The convenience of sleeping in the same bed made it too easy to pass up.

"Are you seriously asking me that?" I asked, quirking a brow at her.

She giggled a little but still looked at me expectedly for an answer.

"I think if you're happy and I'm happy, that is all that matters," I said. Apparently, that was the answer she needed, because she hopped up on the desk and pulled me between her legs.

"Good thing I'm wearing a dress." She smiled.

How did ever I get so lucky?

Chapter 45

Quinn

Moving day for Luke had arrived, but it wasn't nearly as daunting as it once was for me. I had no doubt that we would be back and forth to each other's houses. After sleeping in the same bed every night for the past two weeks, I didn't know how I was going to sleep alone. I loved falling asleep in his arms—that is, until we both grew too hot and had to roll over to our separate sides. Some mornings he would slip out of bed to make my coffee, but some mornings he would pull me against him so I could feel how happy he was to wake up next to me.

Under normal circumstances, our relationship would've changed things enough, but Mia's presence and his home renovations being complete definitely contributed to the whirlwind. I felt bad that I hadn't spent more time with Adrienne and snuck over to see her briefly before we started loading Luke's truck up.

"Good morning," I said quietly when I saw Malia dozing on the couch.

"Hi," she said cheerfully and gestured for me to sit on the lanai. "What's up?" she asked.

"I just wanted to check in on you," I said. "I feel like we haven't talked in a while."

"I know, I'm sorry, I've been so busy!" she said.

"I was the one who wanted to apologize," I said. "It's just been a bit crazier with Mia here and everything."

"How is she doing?" Count on Adrienne to be concerned for someone she barely knew.

"She's hanging in there," I said. "I think she's going to stay in the cottage, though."

"Oh, really? That's great," Adrienne said. "At least you don't have to look for another tenant for now."

"Yeah," I agreed. "Makes it easier."

"Then she can just move into your house after you move in with Luke." She winked at me.

"What? We aren't moving in together."

"Sure," she said, smirking. "You have been together every night for the past two weeks, and he's been in close proximity for nearly six months. How long you think you guys will last apart?"

I bit my lip as I considered her words. It had crossed my mind a few times, but I wasn't sure if it was too soon. I voiced my concerns to Adrienne.

"Do what you want," Adrienne said. "Who do you have to answer to?"

"I know you're right, but I don't want Luke to feel pressured."

"Are we seriously going to do this shit again?" She gave me a pointed look.

I didn't even realize I was falling into the same patterns, but she was right.

"You can rent out your house. It's not like you have to sell it right now," she said. I wasn't sure if I could ever sell my parents' house. It seemed wrong, but she was right. I could hang on to it regardless of where I lived.

"I think you're right," I said, nodding slowly.

"Of course I am!" she said.

I laughed and reached over to hug her.

"You're coming to Luke's next Saturday, right?" I asked.

"Yeah, I'll be there, as long as Grandma is feeling okay." She glanced in the house as worry furrowed her brow.

"We need a day together soon," I said. "Let me know when you have time and we can do whatever you want."

"Sounds good," Adrienne said.

It didn't take long to get everything moved into Luke's house, especially since some of his belongings were still in the garage at Cody and Grant's. He left the sofa in the cottage, since he had bought a large sectional to go in the new house as well as upgraded to a king-sized bed. He informed me he planned on utilizing the new larger space. I was giddy as I flitted around his house, making beds, hanging pictures, and playing house.

"You know, it doesn't all have to be done today," Grant said, eyeing Mia and me as we divided and conquered.

Cody looked around, bewildered. "I never seen so many throw pillows in my life."

"Don't fight the throw pillows," Luke warned Cody. "Girls mean business with their throw pillows."

"How can you guys not enjoy this?" Mia asked as she meticulously hung a mirror over a table in the entryway.

The guys just looked at each other and groaned.

"How did you learn to do this shit?" Grant asked.

"It just comes naturally," Cody remarked. "Girls are born with it."

It was late once we finished, but I couldn't stop once I got started. I really enjoyed doing this type of thing, but I never got much opportunity to do it. Aaron and I always clashed on décor styles, so even when we did decorate, I didn't get to pick anything out. Luke didn't seem to care, as long as it made me happy. Mia and I walked around, admiring our work. Even though the guys had finished the heavy lifting hours ago, they all stuck around. I think they were secretly impressed with our decorating abilities.

"It's like a totally different place," Cody marveled.

"It is," Luke agreed, standing there with his arms crossed and bestowing his approval on our work.

"I'll take all the credit," Grant said, mocking seriousness. Everyone laughed.

"It really does look amazing, Grant," I said.

"Thank you." He nodded and smiled at me. He could pretend the compliments didn't mean a lot to him, but I could see he took intense pride in his work.

"Well, my work is done," Mia said, yawning.

"Can you hang on a little bit longer?" Luke asked. "I wanted to show Quinn something."

"Oh, gross." Mia grimaced. "Hasn't she already seen it?"

Cody and Grant roared with laughter, and even I cracked a smile.

"Shut up," Luke maturely responded.

"I can take Mia home," Cody offered.

I smiled, quickly catching on that there was something going on between those two. I knew they would both deny it given the circumstances, but I wasn't blind. I glanced over at Luke. He hadn't missed it either.

"And that's my cue to leave. Catch you guys later," Grant said, stepping out.

"All right, let's see it." I gestured toward Luke's lower half once everyone left.

"Real funny," he said, smirking at me. "Follow me."

He walked into the master bedroom, which had been transformed into a haven of sorts. The new king-sized bed was positioned in the center of the room, facing the French doors. I couldn't wait to wake up to that ocean view. I laughed to myself because he had purchased the entire bedroom set, complete with nightstands and two large dressers, and I knew for a fact that he didn't own enough clothes to fill those dressers. Board shorts and T-shirts didn't take up that much room. The blue walls looked amazing against the antique white furniture, and I hoped he liked the gray and blue quilt I'd picked out for the bed.

He went into the walk-in closet and flipped on the light.

"Is your closet big enough?" I asked then stopped and looked at it in awe.

"I asked Grant to make it bigger," he replied smugly.

"You won't even remotely fill it," I said, eyeing the enormous space.

"Good, because I'm not going to," he said.

I looked at him, trying to gauge the direction he was going with this.

"Will all your clothes fit in here?"

"Um, yeah," I replied sarcastically, knowing I would probably only fill a third of it.

"Good," he said.

"That's it?" I asked. He just stood there smiling at me.

"What do you think?" he asked.

"About my clothes fitting in here?" I asked, confused. He nodded, still smiling. Suddenly, realization washed over me as I finally understood what he was asking.

"You want me to move in with you?" I asked excitedly.

"I don't want you to feel pressured," he said. "But it's an open invitation. I'd really like to live together."

"And you don't think it's too soon?" I asked.

"Maybe," he admitted. "But honestly, I don't really care. I just know I want to be with you, not only in every waking moment, but every sleeping moment as well. Since the moment I met you, I have thought about you in every decision I have made for this house."

"I feel like I should say no," I said, watching the disappointment on his face with a twinge of amusement. "But I don't want to!" I shrieked and jumped in his arms.

He laughed along with me and held me close. I finally stepped back and admired the closet space. "This is like every girl's dream!" I exclaimed.

"Knock yourself out," he said, amused. "And feel free to stock it up with hot pink bikinis."

I laughed, remembering the bikini I was wearing the day he came to look at the cottage. I knew there was a reason that was my favorite bikini!

We walked back into the bedroom, where I once again admired the finished room.

"It would be a real shame to mess up that nicely made bed," Luke said, eyeing it.

"Such a shame," I agreed.

Instead of respecting the well-made bed, he picked me up and tossed me on it, rumpling the covers.

"There's probably no point in ever making this bed," he murmured before lowering himself over me.

"We'll just stay in it," I said, nipping at his lips.

"Sounds good to me," he agreed.

Chapter 46

Luke

As an adult, I didn't get real excited about my birthday. It didn't seem like a very big deal after I passed twenty-one. However, when you are woken up very abruptly by your gorgeous girlfriend sneaking under the covers to pleasure you... Well, let's just say nothing beats that.

"Happy birthday." She smiled shyly at me when she reappeared.

"You didn't have to do that," I said, holding her close as I drifted back down to Earth.

"Sure I did," she said. "It's your birthday!"

"And it's started as the best birthday ever," I replied.

"Thirty-three," she said slowly. "Damn, you're old!"

"Watch it now," I warned her.

"Robbing the cradle," she continued teasing me.

"Six years isn't that bad!" I said.

"Says the old man," she remarked.

"That's it!" I flipped over and started mercilessly tickling her.

"No!" she shrieked. She had a special giggle that I only heard when I was tickling her, and I wouldn't stop until it slipped out. Her body wiggled and thrashed against me when finally, that giggle slipped out, bring me back to full arousal again.

"Well, then," she said, quickly noticing. "Is that how thirty-three is treating you?" She raised her eyebrows expectedly.

"It is my birthday," I said, looking at her expectantly.

"Well, in that case, I'll do all the work," she said, climbing on top of me. I paused for a moment, taking it all in. Her dark hair was cascading over her shoulders, shining from the bright light sneaking in the windows. She had that fresh, just-woken-up look on her face, and her skin glowed from the happiness within. Words couldn't even describe how much I loved this girl. My mind trailed to the shoe box under my bed, where a ring box was hiding. I wasn't going to rush into things quite yet, but I was prepared. There wasn't a doubt in my mind that I wanted to spend the rest of my life waking up to this incredible woman.

I reached up and gently tugged on her hair, which I knew she loved, and pulled her close to me so I could claim her lips with my own.

Best birthday ever.

That evening, I walked around the house, mingling with all my guests. Quinn and Mia succeeded in throwing me an awesome birthday bash/housewarming party. I never would've gone to the lengths to turn it into such a big ordeal, but I was pleased as I wandered around and chatted with my friends and colleagues. The dogs were having the time of their lives, putting their puppy eyes on full display in exchange for bits of food.

"The house looks amazing," Megan told me as she arrived with Elicia and Hailey. Hailey still seemed to be embarrassed around me, but after she walked away, I saw Quinn dart over to her for a big welcome hug. My girl was awesome.

"Hey," Mia said, sliding up beside me. "I heard Hailey was

looking for a place. Do you think it would okay to tell her about the cottage?"

Mia's plans to take over the cottage had quickly evolved into taking over Quinn's house once she moved in with me. It was basically furnished, and Quinn seemed to feel comfortable with that arrangement. I never wanted her to feel like she had to sell it, but it was perfect for Mia. Quinn also promised her that the house came with built-in healing.

"Ask Quinn first, but I don't think she would care," I said, shrugging.

"Okay, cool," she said, bouncing away. It was nice to see some of that energy coming back to my sister. It was times like these, when she was surrounded by people, that she seemed to forget what happened to her. She even met a couple looking for a wedding photographer and got her first job since arriving on the island. I knew my parents had sent her some money, but Mia wasn't one to take handouts, so I knew she was eager to get back to work.

I jumped when I felt a hand settle on my backside and turned to see Quinn.

"Who else were you expecting?" she teased.

"Oh, you know, the dozens of other women coming to wish me a happy birthday," I teased back.

"Nice," she replied.

"Thanks for doing all this," I said, sipping my beer but holding her close with my free hand.

"Of course," she said. "I loved doing it. Are you ready for your present?"

"You didn't have to get me anything," I said, protesting. "You already did so much with the house and this party."

"Well, I hope you like it, because I can't return it," she said, suddenly appearing nervous.

"What?" I asked. I still couldn't figure out what she could've gotten me.

"Come here." She tugged me toward the bathroom. I wondered if I was getting another birthday present like I had that morning, but I wasn't entirely sure I had it in me. It was hard to keep up with this woman!

We closed the door, and she spun around, lifting the hem of her dress. I instantly spotted the fresh ink on her hip. There was a large wave that looked incredibly real. The crest of the wave curled up, and if you looked closely enough, it looked like a heart. The colors were so vivid, and the way it wrapped around her hip was amazingly sexy.

"I love it," I said, reaching out to grip her hip but careful to not touch the tattoo.

"Really?" She beamed. "I was kind of nervous about getting it, but I wanted to surprise you."

"I love it," I repeated. "And I love that you got it right there."

"I know." She giggled. "You always grab me right there, so that's why I chose it."

"Thank you," I said, kissing her.

We walked out in time to see Cody and Mia heading out to the lanai.

"Are they hooking up?" she asked, looking up at me.

"I don't know, but they need to wait," I said. "She's too messed up right now."

"Don't be too quick to judge," she gently reminded me. "I fell in love with you when I was at my worst."

I looked down at her and let her words sink in. She was right, but I still felt like I needed to protect my sister. Cody was my best friend. Hell, he was more than that, but he had also spent the last several years bouncing from girl to girl, trying to erase his broken heart. I wanted to be sure that he was ready to leave that lifestyle behind before he became involved with my sister.

"You're right," I said, agreeing with her. "I just want her to be safe and happy."

"Do you think Cody could provide that for her?" Quinn asked.

"I think so," I said. "They've always had a bond of their own, but I always thought was a brother-sister thing up until a few years ago. I'm not one of those guys who warns my friends away from my sister, but I just want to make sure he doesn't screw her up worse than she already is."

"She's resilient," Quinn quietly commented.

"Kind of like another girl I know." I smiled down at her.

She smiled in response and asked, "So, have you had a good birthday?"

I kissed her lightly and smiled. "Of course. I have everything I need."

Acknowledgments

This book would not have been possible if my husband, Nick, hadn't been nudging me for years to follow my dreams. He believed in me more than I believed in myself and gave me the confidence to accomplish this. He entertained the kids, put up with a messy house, and listened to me constantly talk about my characters like they were real people. He's been my biggest cheerleader, and I couldn't have done it without him.

My children, Cole and Cody, who talk about their mom being a famous author because they believe in me. You boys have supported me and not only kept yourselves busy so I could write, but you also helped around the house more so that I could focus on my work. The faith you have in me has inspired me to fulfill this dream because I want you to be proud of me.

To my mom, who read every little story I've written since I was a child. When I said I wanted to be a writer, she always encouraged me to do it. Sorry, Mom, it just took me a little longer to do it. Thanks for always being there for me.

To my sister, Beth, who knew that this book would be what brought us closer together, despite the distance between us. Since the day I shared my story with you, you've done everything in your power to help me make it happen. I appreciate the energy you've poured into my project.

To my bestie, Nikki, you also convinced me that I could do this and that I had it in me. You never made me feel anything but capable and talented and have listened to me go on and on about this book for over a year. Thank you so much for your help with this book and the cover and everything in between.

Lastly, to anyone that has purchased this book to support me, thank you. It's difficult to take the words swirling around in your head and put them to paper and to believe that it's worthy of somebody's money. I hope you enjoyed reading it as much as I loved writing it.